THE LORDS OF THE WIND

C.J. ADRIEN

First Edition

Originally published in the United States in 2019 by Runestone Books

ISBN: 9781078386166

For more information, visit www.cjadrien.com

Pour mon petit Viking, Leif.

TABLE OF CONTENTS

"For indeed the Frankish nation, which was crushed by the avenger Hasting, was very full of filthy uncleanness. Treasonous and oath-breaking, they were deservedly condemned; unbelievers and faithless, they were justly punished."

DUDO OF ST. QUENTIN

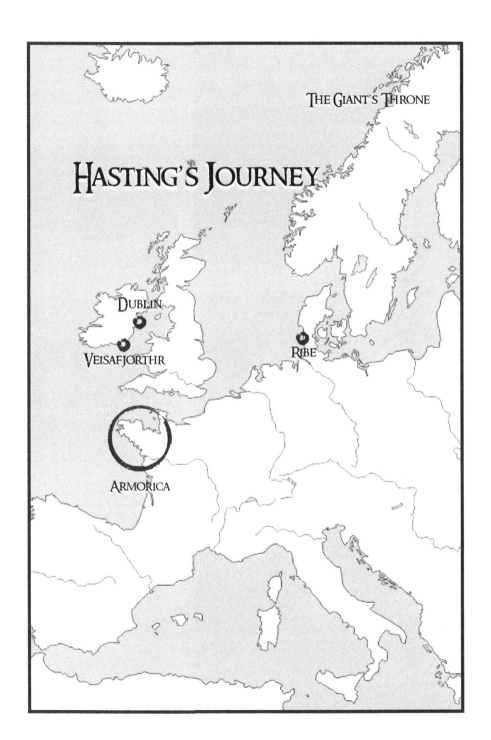

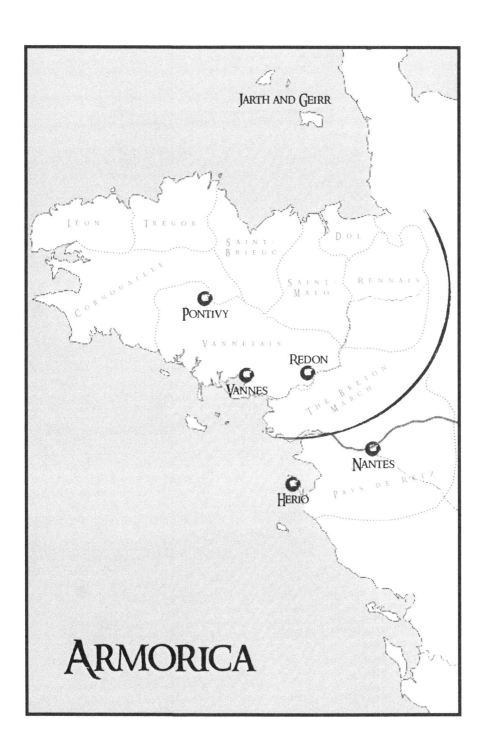

JARTH AND GEIRR

LÉON   TREGOR

SAINT-
BRIEUC   DOL

SAINT-
MALO   RENNAIS

CORNOUAILLE

PONTIVY

VANNETAIS

REDON

VANNES

THE BRETON
MARCH

NANTES

HERIO

PAYS DE RETZ

ARMORICA

I

Reputation is Everything

They call me the Scourge of the Somme and Loire. I like the name. Christian priests gave it to me—those who believe the Devil sent me to punish them for their sins. The name implies I am fearsome, and fear compels respect. It is essential for a man such as I to command fear from my enemies; it weakens their resolve. Much of a Viking's life is an illusion, and a Viking's illusion is his reputation. There is truth to my name—that I am a scourge, a bane, an affliction on the lands I rove—but a name is given. A reputation is earned. I have spent a lifetime crafting my reputation, as blacksmiths labor to forge the perfect blade. As the gods have us know them through their deeds, so shall I be known and remembered for mine, forever.

I am Hasting. I was born a Dane, but I have spent little time in the land of my birth. My father, as I remember him, was a wealthy chieftain named Ragnar. We lived in a great hall made of stone and earth, with pillars that reached for the sky and totems of the gods Freyr and Freyja that stood at the door to watch over our family. The hall looked over our land to the ocean in the East and the plains of Jutland in the West, and we watched many sunsets there. My father spent a great deal of time with me, to teach me the ways of my people and the lessons a boy needs to grow into an honorable man. I wanted to be like my father. He was a force of nature. Most of his lessons I have forgotten now, except one. It burned into my memory the moment he said it, and I remember the words clearly.

"One day, I will die, and your mother will die, and your brothers and sisters will die, and you, my son, will die," he said to me. "What does not die is the reputation a man leaves behind at his death."

I wish I remembered more of my father, but he was slain by another Dane for his wealth when I was at an age few men remember. It is a strange thing, memory, and fickle, especially for a boy as young as I was that day. My mother and sisters and brothers were sold into slavery, split apart as a family, never to see one another again. I cannot say where they sent my family, but I boarded a longship whose destination determined the rest of my life. As a slave, I was stuffed into a corner of the ship, bound and gagged, and given drink to force me to sleep; this is all I remember, mere glimpses of a harrowing voyage. I believe my mind has forced me to forget this time as a means to heal. All this because another man coveted my father's wealth. It was then I learned the wickedness of men—all men—and the savagery that dwells in the hearts of our race.

Mine is not a story of revenge. No, the man who killed my father was himself slain before I grew my first beard, or so I heard in my travels. Such is the lot of a Dane. Blood feuds fuel constant fighting that robs families of their kin, of their wealth. And, in my view, this has prevented the Danes from rising as rivals to the Franks. Knowing this, I decided early on to avoid entangling myself in the fray of the politics of the North.

Mine is a story of a boy who was a slave, who became a warlord, and who helped topple an empire. This is the story of how I betook myself a-Viking, took what I desired by my own two hands, and how I came to earn the reputation of Scourge of the Somme and Loire.

My story begins when my captors sold me to a man named Hagar. He lived on a far-away island called Ireland, where the trees and grass and shrubs are the greenest of any green any man has ever seen. Rain pours over the countryside in near perpetuity. At first, I believed the rain would pass, which it did once or twice in the summer when I lived there, but never for long. It is how I remember it, at least, and I have since met an Irishman or two who have laughed with me for describing their homeland in such a manner.

The ship that carried me arrived at Hagar's longphort on a grey afternoon. A small party of warriors interrogated the captain before allowing the vessel to tie off. The longphort was a lengthy, open pier extending out from a thatch-roofed dock that housed Hagar's ships. The poles holding the dock together had barnacles and mussels growing on them up to where the water reached high tide. We had arrived at low tide, so the crew moored the ship as close to the dock as they could, roped it to the poles, and jumped into the shallows below. They sloshed their way through the knee-deep muddy water, one of them with me thrown over his shoulder, all the way to the rocky shoreline.

Hagar's village was also a fort. He had erected a wooden wall the height of three men that surrounded the longhouses, with two open-air towers to keep watch over the surrounding land. To the east, the towers looked over the coast, the ocean, and the horizon, and in the west, they overlooked a thick, lush, untouched wilderness of oak, aspen, and ash. Farmland surrounded the walls of the fort, split into uneven plots by loose wattle fencing. Slaves labored from dawn until dusk during the harvest. Within the fort, there were five longhouses, each built in a different direction to form a semi-circle that faced north. The longhouse walls were made of turf cut into thick, sturdy pieces, stacked at breast height beneath a low thatched roof. The largest of these, Hagar's hall, is where my captors took me on the first day. I cannot remember what was said, nor the names of the men who brought me to that place, but I remember what they sold to Hagar. They had not merely carried slaves across the sea, but also many of my family's belongings, including my father's sword. When Hagar girded it, I vowed that I would one day take it back from him.

For the first few years I lived in Ireland, I saw little of the outdoors. All of Hagar's slaves lived in the same longhouse on the easternmost edge of the village. Most of them ate and slept there, and not much else. During the day, the older slaves left the longhouse to toil wherever their masters bade them. Many children lived in the slave house, and many of them were even younger than I. While the grownups worked, the children remained confined to a room on the far side of the chamber, watched over by an Irish woman named Eanáir with long black hair and deep green eyes. She was a wretched soul who, in the presence of others, appeared loving and nurturing, but in their absence abused and neglected the children. She spent her days away from the longhouse and left the children to cry in our cribs.

My crib, worn by years of use and full of splinters, and which felt more akin to a cage, sat in a dark corner where the only light shone through a vent in the roof where smoke from the fire could escape. In one of my earliest dreams, Odin appeared to me in that crib and granted me the power to make myself as light as a feather. I escaped my prison and jumped into the fire, and the smoke carried me up through the hole in the roof to freedom. The dream gave me hope that someday, perhaps, the gods might spare me this suffering. It was this hope, I believe, that allowed me to endure my early captivity.

For how long I lived like an animal in a cage, I cannot say. I remember little of what happened under

Eanáir's supervision. The lost memories I blame on a potion she gave us that made us sleep for most of the day. She mixed it into our food, and so the choice was to eat and sleep or starve. At times, she screamed at some of the older children, myself included, for no apparent reason, but mostly she left us alone, with little food during the day, and with nothing to clean the infants who soiled themselves.

The children and babies wallowed in their excrement for days at a time. One boy fell ill from the filth and died, but Eanáir did not notice when she returned to check on us. His body rotted for most of the afternoon before another slave returning from the fields smelled him and found him in his crib. No one so much as raised an eyebrow, for the boy did not belong to anyone. He was like me, a child bought by Hagar from the slave trade, an exile with no loved ones to care for or about him. When I saw them carry his body from the longhouse, I feared I might soon meet a similar fate.

Eanáir made sure to take proper care of the other slaves' children to avoid problems with them. She did the minimum to keep them clean for when their parents returned from their day's labor. Those children spent time in the main chamber in the evening and at night, a social environment crucial to the upbringing of a child. The children with no parents remained in the room, alone, occasionally visited by Eanáir who gave us enough nourishment to survive, mixed with the sleeping potion, and not much more.

To muffle our cries to the outside world, she padded the walls of the room with thick blankets sewn together and filled with straw. To prevent the older children from escaping, which I attempted once or twice when I had my wits about me, she locked the door to the room from the outside—and she never forgot to lock that damned door. Nights in the room were quiet and dark. If I woke, I saw nothing but blackness and heard the sound of wind or rain falling against the thatch. I experienced my first terrors in that darkness. Eventually, I stopped crying. I understood its futility and accepted that no one would ever come to save me.

One day, it all changed. Eanáir entered the room with Hagar behind her and pointed to me in my corner. It was the first time I had seen him enter the slaves' longhouse. He approached my crib and looked at me with sunken, tired eyes. He reached down, grabbed me by the nape, and lifted me from the ground. His face scrunched at the smell of me, so much so that he pinched his nose with his other hand and turned his head away.

"He's filthy... and sickly," Hagar said, his voice muffled by his hand.

"It is his constitution, my lord," Eanáir said. "I have cared well for him."

"I've heard rumors," Hagar said. He released my neck from his grip. "It seems they are true."

Eanáir gulped. "Rumors?"

He turned to face her, his eyes focused and menacing. "The others say you do not care for these children as you should. Two have died this year alone from illness. That is two too many."

"Children die, my lord, you know this," Eanáir pleaded. "Few will live through their childhood."

Hagar's brow sunk low over his eyes in anger. "Lies," he said. "I have heard them too often. And shame on me for believing them for so long! I did not buy these children to have them die in their cribs. I need them to grow strong to work in the fields."

"And several will," Eanáir said as she passed trembling fingers through her long black hair.

Hagar looked around at the other children who were all in a similar or worse condition than I. "I trusted you to care for these children. You have betrayed my trust." He rolled up the sleeves of his tunic to reveal his thick, powerful forearms. "Ingrid!" he shouted.

A young woman with fiery red hair who wore a simple farm dress covered by a stained brown work apron scurried through the doorway. "Yes, my lord?" she said with her head lowered.

"Have these children fed and cleaned. And have Orm tear down this wall. There is no place for such a thing in a longhouse. Why was it built?"

"It was Eanáir who suggested we build it, so the children's crying would not disturb the others at night," Ingrid said.

"Who approved the construction?" Hagar asked.

Ingrid shrunk a little and said, "Orm."

"That fool." Hagar raised his voice to a near shout. "From today forward, if a child cries at night, one of the other slaves will have to care for it. As it is supposed to be!"

Hagar turned his gaze to me and said, "That one is old enough to start working. Take him to my hall and give him over to Gyda. Tell her what has happened here." Hagar reached for the back of Eanáir's head, clenched her hair at its thickest, and tugged on it with brute force. She screamed louder than I had ever heard a person scream. He dragged her by the scalp out the door and through the hall. "You are lucky I travel so much, or else I would have caught this a long time ago," I heard him say.

We were saved. What I did not know then, but I soon learned, was that I had traded one egregious caretaker for another. I did not understand at that moment that the real monster was not Eanáir, but Hagar, even though Hagar had shown himself to care at least a little for the children he owned.

Ingrid called for other slave women to help her with the youngest children while she walked with me to Hagar's hall. There, we were greeted by a tall woman with wide hips, broad shoulders, and black hair cut short above the ear.

"I am Gyda," she said. "Who are you?"

"Hasting," I stammered.

"How old are you, Hasting?" she asked with a firm tone and a piercing gaze.

"I... do not know." I struggled to find the words to speak, for I had not spoken in a long time.

Gyda knelt to look me in the eye. "Where are you from?"

"I am a Dane," I said.

"You're the jarl's son," she said. "I remember when Hagar bought you."

"I'm hungry." I spoke the truth; I had not eaten for at least a day. The weather had turned foul, and a light drizzle and cold ocean breeze swept over the village. My legs trembled like a leaf in the wind.

"Take him to the washroom," Gyda said to Ingrid. "You will eat when you are clean. From now on you are mine, and you will do as I say. That is your job, do you understand?"

I nodded. Ingrid took my hand, and we walked across the village to a small shack built against the wooden wall. It had a sloped roof made of wooden planks coated in tar and a short chimney that spewed white smoke. She helped me undress and stood me in front of the door. When she unlatched it, a thick billow of steam broke free and floated toward the clouds. I entered the shack to find two other women naked and scrubbing themselves with damp cloths.

In the center of the room was a large iron bowl filled with glowing rocks. The women paused as I entered the room with Ingrid who, when I looked back at her, had undressed without my noticing. I had never seen a woman without her clothes, and her nakedness stirred feelings within me. If I had to name those feelings today, I would have to describe them as akin to lust. Boys of that age do not feel the same passions as grown men, but they are not immune to arousal.

Ingrid nudged me forward and sat me on a bench along the side of the steam house. She reached for a bucket of water below the iron bowl and poured it over the rocks. They sizzled and filled the room with more dense steam. Droplets of water beaded on my skin, and Ingrid took a cloth and scrubbed me down with repeated, aggressive strokes. By the time she had finished, my skin had turned bright red like a freshly cut beet.

With clean clothes on my back, Ingrid returned me to Gyda who took me under her charge and led me into Hagar's hall where she sat me on one of the mead-benches. The main chamber was much larger than the slaves' longhouse—its roof stood higher above the ground, it was longer, and it had a grand entrance with a massive double door that opened to reveal an enormous central fire pit.

From the fire pit, which had a large pot flanked by two thick iron rods hanging above it, Gyda poured me a bowl of pottage. I stirred it around for a moment and slurped down a few mouthfuls when I felt it was not too hot. I remember how good it tasted, though I knew it was not good pottage; it had a bland mixture of cabbage, ham, onions and leeks, and some herbs for flavor. Most would not consider it a feast, but compared with what Eanáir had fed me until that day, it was delicious.

As I sat eating my first real meal in far too long, Hagar and his men entered the hall with Eanáir in tow. Some freedmen and women also gathered in the chamber and sat beside me at the mead-benches. To my surprise, they said nothing about my presence, nor did any of them acknowledge my existence. Hagar made Eanáir kneel before his high chair, and he stood over her in an odd display of dominance. With his hands on his hips, he strutted side to side and cleared his throat.

"Thank you for convening on such short notice," he said to the men and women in his hall. "I have called for a meeting to accuse this woman. She has mistreated my property, a grievous crime by our laws. She is Sven's slave, so I ask permission from Sven to punish her. Sven, you will be compensated for the loss."

A slender man with a narrow face, a braided black beard, and long, matted hair stood up and said, "You have my permission, lord. The slave has been trouble to my house for some time."

Hagar shot his audience a malicious smile. "The abuse of children is among the worst of all misdeeds in the eyes of the gods." He tugged hard on Eanáir's hair to pull back her head and face her eyes to the ceiling. He drew a long hunting knife from his belt and pressed it against her exposed throat. "Hake, what do the gods say about punishments befitting a slave such as this?"

Gyda leaned close and whispered in my ear. "Hake is our skald. He knows the deeds of the gods, and from them he interprets their will."

Across the hall, at the opposite mead-bench, another man stood. Built like an ox, he had a barrel chest, thick arms, and sturdy legs. He wore his hair short and his beard in a forked braid. He placed his hands on his hips and said, "Odin once brought the wolf Fenrir to Asgard, in the hopes that they might tame him. No matter what the Aesir did, the wolf grew more dangerous. They could not change his nature. So, too, will we not change this Irish slave's nature."

"Remind me what the gods did to the wolf?" Hagar said.

"They tied him to a stone slab with chains that grew tighter the more he struggled," Hake said.

Hagar lifted his blade from Eanáir's throat. "Fetch me chains," he said.

He picked Eanáir up off the floor and threw her at some of his followers who caught her and bound her with rope. They left the hall through the double doors, and as all the townspeople present stood and followed, Gyda placed her hand on my chest to prevent me from moving. She looked down at me with troubled eyes. "Do you wish to see her punishment? It will not be pleasant. It will frighten you."

Without a hint of hesitation, I said, "Yes."

Gyda took my bowl and placed it behind her on the mead-bench. With my hand in hers, she led me through the doors to the village's central courtyard. I had a sinking feeling I could not shake, even though I had not understood what Hake had meant by his story. I knew Eanáir would suffer, and I believed she deserved it, yet I felt hesitant to see the outcome, almost frightened, as if the possibility still existed that she might be released and allowed to harm others.

This same feeling of dread, of the unknown, of knowing that events more often than not did not unfold in my favor, has haunted me at pivotal moments in my life. Here I walked for the first time with this lurking feeling in the pit of my stomach, as though I had done wrong. I suppose this is something many victims feel—individual powerlessness in the face of evil, a feeling of guilt and shame as if I had let it all happen, that it was I who should have prevented myself from falling victim to another.

Gyda and I walked from the village to the longphort where Hagar examined large rocks along the coastline toward the south. Hagar's hair swayed in a blustering wind that had picked up from the south, and it blew into his eyes and his mouth; none of it appeared to bother him. I had not seen the coastline since my arrival, and I marveled at its majesty in the face of thundering waves that broke white along jagged rocks.

At high tide, the ocean's grandeur and power expressed itself in a terrible struggle between land and sea, spurred by a fierce, unrelenting wind whose deafening whoosh broke at the crashing of waves against rock. Seabirds floated against the current of the wind and surveyed the ocean's bounty below. They dove like spears into the water and reemerged with fish squirming in their beaks. The marvelous creatures had mastered the wind in all its fury to make themselves untouchable predators. Their sudden dives, I imagined, must have inflicted unspeakable terror on their prey. How powerful might men be if they could harness this power and leap on their enemy with such precision, lethality, and surprise?

My imagination ran wild but broke at the sound of clanking chains nearby. Hagar clamped Eanáir's wrists in irons and tied her to a waist-high rock with three tight loops. The men laughed into the wind as they left her there to suffer in the cold rain. To my utter relief, this was the extent of her punishment. They drew no blood, nor abused her in any fashion.

Hagar and his men left her there to linger where none would give her the honor of witnessing her death. A fortnight later, while on an errand for Gyda, I returned to see what had become of that woman. I do not have the words to describe what I saw. It was so terrible that I have put it out of my mind, and I have told no one since about what lay chained to that rock.

For two years I lived under Hagar's roof. Not once did he bother to learn my name; he called me *boy*. I hated him. I loathed him. At night I dreamt of all the ways I could kill him. He was a drunk, and a violent one too. Each day, he sat on a large oaken chair mounted on a raised dais on the far end of his hall so that he could sit above his subjects. He thought of himself as a king, and few ever challenged him. We were in a land far removed from the society whence we all came. In Jutland, at least, the law reigned supreme, and all had to obey it or else face exile or death.

In my heart I knew, at least, that the man who killed my father should have—must have—answered to the law of the Danes. In Ireland, there was no law except Hagar's. He took slave girls at his pleasure and beat those who dared challenge him until their blood soaked the ash-covered ground.

Hagar was a complicated man. Although he often acted with arrant depravity, particularly when he drank, he also abided by a strict code of honor that weighed on his decisions and actions with the other free men. He never refused a challenge, and he never allowed himself a distinct advantage over an opponent in a fight. His legitimacy as king hinged on his ability to strike down any man who wished to take his place. He also respected the village elders and showered them in gifts and praise. They had a say in the village assembly called the *thing*, where many of the crucial decisions about our community were made. With their support, he could sway the free men's conclusions in his favor at every *thing*.

Hagar was not a Dane, but a Vestfaldingi, a Northman from the Oslo Fjord. His hair ran long below his shoulders and glimmered red in the firelight of his hall, and his beard twisted and turned in knots from his chin to his chest. Slave girls washed, groomed, and braided his beard each and every day. He reminded us all of his heritage often and expressed his hatred for the Danes, in particular those he claimed had expelled him from his homeland.

Some days he beat me for all to see, just to show them how much he hated the Danes. Each time, Gyda helped wash the blood from my nose and lips, then cleaned and dressed me so that I might continue my chores, lest I face Hagar's wrath again. She scolded Hagar more than once about hitting me, but Hagar always had an answer. "It builds character... makes him stronger," he said, more times than I could count.

Hagar often hosted visitors from other lands. They visited him to trade and, through his trade, he earned much wealth. He did not need to raid or fight for this wealth. The longphort's location and its reputation attracted rovers from all over the world. His longphort repaired their ships for a price, and his men were, as he explained to his patrons, the best craftsmen and woodworkers in Midgard. Northmen were not alone in their trade with Hagar, either. The Irish bought many of the goods the Northmen brought to the longphort in exchange for Irish slaves. In this way, Hagar profited from every side and every kind of visitor, and his wealth grew.

Hagar had no sons or daughters. Many of us often wondered about this, since his appetite for young women seemed insatiable. He should have fathered many children over the years, and his lack of progeny, as he said himself once or twice during my time in his hall, made him vulnerable to challenges from his warriors.

To keep them happy, he had to prove that he could make them wealthy, or else lose his self-given title of king to another who could provide. Such was the life of a chieftain in Hagar's position. He had one duty: to make and distribute wealth to his warriors.

It was this warrior culture, I later learned, that spurred much of the raiding and conquering that defined the lives of men who roved and fought, who left their home in search of wealth and fame and were called Vikings. Hagar had seen great success as a young man, and his village stood as a testament to his triumphs and how a man could make a life for himself if he dared to take it. I may have hated Hagar, but from a Viking's perspective, he was exemplary.

There were other children in Hagar's village apart from the slaves. They were the sons and daughters of the freemen. So long as I finished my chores, Hagar's husmän Karl, a slender man with a long black braid on his chin and a thick scar across his face from his hairline to his nose bridge, let me play with the others.

A husmän was the chieftain's deadliest warrior and closest confidant. Karl's sons, Ole and Sven, visited Hagar's hall every day, and we became close friends. They were wild boys and always up to trouble, and I loved them for it. It was they who earned me the scar on my face, although not on purpose. As I recall it, Ole had collected droppings from the pigpen, and he and his brother hatched a plan to have them drop on their older cousin, Inge, from a bucket tied above the doorway of their father's longhouse. They loved to torment Inge; he was a cruel and wretched boy who harassed smaller children and beat them up for fun. In a scuffle between cousins, Inge nearly broke Sven's arm and then convinced the parents that Ole had started the fight. Karl's sons wanted revenge.

They prepared their trap and set a lure for Inge outside. Inge gravitated toward anything involving food— his favorite in particular: fresh rye bread. Karl's wife had baked a large batch, and the smell of it filled their longhouse. Ole barely said the words and Inge darted across the village with his nose out in front of him. When the door opened, Sven tugged the rope that tipped the bucket of droppings and released its contents. It was not Inge who had opened the door for a taste of bread. It was Hagar.

I took the fall for the incident at Ole and Sven's pleading. I did so because I knew Hagar, and I knew he would not let Karl's boys off. It would have proven disastrous for the whole village to have the king and his husmän fighting over something as trivial as children's mischief. As my punishment, Hagar struck me with the back of his hand, and the gem-encrusted gold ring on his middle finger, whether a gift from a trading partner or loot from a faraway monastery, cut into my cheek from nose to ear.

During my time as Hagar's slave, I felt the burning desire in my heart to act, to escape, and to kill. I grew resentful, bitter, angry, and with every mistake, every small misstep, I faced even more biting wrath from my captor. These were the years I earned my deepest, most enduring scars, the ones we wear that none can see but ourselves. I wear the scar across my right cheek with pride today, for it is a symbol of my struggle, my survival, my indomitable hunger to make something of myself, to earn a name, and to be remembered.

My salvation was Gyda. She cared for me and helped me on many occasions to avoid facing Hagar's bouts of rage. She made a place for me to sleep near her in the slaves' quarter of Hagar's longhouse, and she watched over me when I fell ill. Over time, we grew inseparable. Wherever she went, I followed, and she always arranged for my chores to coincide with hers in some way. She taught me what it meant to give and receive love and to feel the warm embrace of another human being, something I had missed during my captivity. I knew she felt guilty for what had happened to me under Eanáir's supervision and for not discovering what was happening right under her nose.

After many long years of serving Hagar, the gods sent me my salvation. Whether indeed by the hands of the gods, or by pure luck, a ship arrived at the longphort, as so many others had done, carrying a man who changed the course of my life. On the night this particular ship arrived, Hagar had tasked me with serving mead. My responsibility was to ensure that the goblets of Hagar's men and his guests remained full at all times. For each empty cup, Hagar promised, I would receive a strike from the back of his hand at night's end.

The guests arrived, and from the clothes they wore I knew they were Vikings. They wore dark, thickly woven tunics with decorative trim, and their hair was short, as warriors often wore it, and their beards were well-groomed. Each man carried a heavy cloth sack over his shoulder, filled with what seemed at first to be water. They approached Hagar on his throne and threw their wares at his feet. One of the bags burst open as it hit the ground, and it covered Hagar's dais in salt.

"Taste it," one of the Vikings said.

Hagar leaned forward, swiped some salt from his foot, and pressed it against his tongue. He sat back in his chair with a smirk. With a click of his fingers, he summoned his servants to tend to his guests, seat them, feed them, and offer them drink. I scurried from my corner with a carafe and set about filling all the goblets with mead.

As I passed the leader of the Vikings, he looked at me with keen interest. He had blue eyes the color of a clear summer sky, sand-colored hair, and a bright red beard. At first, he gave me pause. I thought he was yet another one of those depraved men who preferred the company of boys to women. To my relief, he had no such intention. His nearest companion, a far rougher-looking man with thick, dark circles under his eyes, also examined me and whispered something in his ear.

"Where did you get it, Eilif?" Hagar asked of the salt.

The man who stared at me replied, "Frankland."

"Imagine the wealth you could make with this," Hagar said. "Men will pay a high price for salt of this quality."

"I know," Eilif said as he took a hearty gulp from his goblet. His voice was clear and confident. He wiped his beard and mustache with his sleeve and said, "In Jutland, it is worth its weight in silver. These three sacks are my gift to you for your hospitality and for repairing my ships in your longphort."

Hagar raised his goblet to acknowledge his guests' offering and drank his fill. As soon as I saw the bottom of his goblet rise above his chin, I knew he had begun his descent into a drunken stupor. For hours the men talked, sang, and drank, and I rushed from empty goblet to empty goblet until the firelight dwindled to a dull glimmer.

As the night drew to its conclusion, Hagar's skald Hake took to the ashen floor and told a story. It was not a story about Hagar, which he had told throughout the night, but a tale of Odin, the king of the Aesir, our gods. I had heard many tales of the gods from Hake over the years, and his stories always made me think.

This story I had heard once before; he told of the wolf named Fenrir, a child of Loki and a menace to all of creation. Odin foresaw that the beast would grow so large that he would one day devour Yggdrasil itself, so the gods moved to capture him. The god Tyr sacrificed his arm to distract the wolf so his allies could defeat him and bind him for eternity. They tied the wolf in chains that tightened the more he grew, and he stopped growing. Odin knew the shackles that bound Fenrir would not last forever. A völva, or seeress, foresaw that the wolf would devour Odin at Ragnarok, the end times.

"And so," Hake said, "the world of men will see the wolf again." As I listened to his tale, my imagination took hold of me. Thoughts of the wolf filled my mind, and I feared him. Above all, I feared to one day see him.

Eilif's men gathered along the walls of the hall with cots and blankets to settle in for the night, while Hagar slumped in his throne with a half-filled goblet hanging from his hand. His snores shook the floor like Thor's thunder, yet no one seemed to mind.

As the men fell asleep, the other slaves entered the hall to help clean the tables. Gyda volunteered to clear the salt from Hagar's feet. She swept the floor with the lightest touch and was careful not to bump her master for fear of awakening him. All seemed well until Hagar, for no reason at all, woke himself from his slumber with a loud snort and saw Gyda below him. He reached down, grasped her arm, and pulled her toward him. She knew what he wanted. Hagar was a voracious and lustful hound, and he leaned in and sniffed at her neck. He pulled her hair and groped her breasts through her dress. I had never seen him lust after a woman of Gyda's age, and the sight of him assaulting a woman I had grown to love, the closest figure to a mother I had ever had in that wretched place, incited a deep, burning rage within me.

Without thinking, I charged the throne empty-handed and leaped toward Hagar and Gyda. She did not see me, for she had closed her eyes while tears streamed down her face. In the dim lighting, even Hagar did not see me at first, though he saw me soon enough.

I grasped the hilt of his sword, drew it with a mighty heave, and drove it toward his chest. It all happened so quickly, I thought I had done it. I thought I had succeeded in killing Hagar. But before the blade cut into his flesh, Hagar snatched the sword from my hands and kicked me back with great force. I flew from the throne onto my back in the dirt and ash below.

"I'll kill you, boy!" Hagar screamed.

Gyda pulled at his beard and clothes to stop him, but the man was strong, and he pushed her aside with ease. He raised his sword and aimed it at me. Still dazed from my fall and with the wind knocked out of me, I lay motionless, a perfect target for a drunken warrior.

"Stop!" I heard a voice call out.

"Stay out of this, Eilif," Hagar said with spittle spewing from his mouth. "What I do with my slaves is my business."

"I will buy him." Eilif emerged from the dark. "How much for the boy?"

"He's not for sale," Hagar said.

"Everything is for sale, old friend," Eilif said.

"Why? Why buy the boy?" Hagar asked. "He's worthless! Just now he tried to kill me with my own sword. A rebellious slave is better dead."

"Name your price," Eilif said.

Hagar lowered his sword. "You want him? He's yours. I meant to rid myself of this little devil for months. He's been nothing but trouble from the start. I should never have agreed to take him in the first place. He has too much of his father's heart in him!"

In a fit of anger, Hagar stormed off behind his throne to his bedchamber. I recovered, and Eilif reached a hand out to help me to my feet. I gazed at him, in awe that he had dared to stand up to Hagar. He looked down at me with a kind smile no man had ever given me.

"Why did you save me?" I asked him.

He knelt and spoke with me eye to eye. "You see that man over there?" He pointed to the man who had sat beside him at the feast. "His name is Egill. He has a unique gift: he can commune with the realms beyond ours. And do you know what he said to me?"

"No," I said. My eyes remained fixed on Egill.

"He says you have an extraordinary destiny."

2

To Become a Viking

Only the bravest men betake themselves a-Viking. It is a dangerous profession, but a lucrative one for those who are successful. When Eilif bought my freedom, he recruited me as ship's boy. He first taught me how to tie knots. I thought a Viking should first learn how to wield a sword or throw a spear. But a Viking, Eilif said, is nothing without the skill to sail his ship, and to sail his ship, he must know his knots.

Ours was a warship named *Sail Horse of the Mountains of the Swans*, or Sail Horse for short, and it was one of many kinds of boats sailed by those who roved. Sail Horse contained all manner of ropes, and each use required a different knot. I thought to find a life of excitement at sea, perhaps filled with unbridled adventure. That was how it was always described in Hagar's hall. Instead, I found myself spending my first days aboard the longship fiddling with ropes to make one knot or another.

"A true Viking is a seafarer first and a warrior second," Eilif said. "His strength is his ship, not his sword or his ax."

I admired Eilif. He was strong-minded, intelligent, and he had exceptional skill in navigation. What I admired most about him was his ability to command the respect of his men. They obeyed him without question. When a new recruit stood against him in protest or defiance, it always ended badly for him. Eilif hardly had to lift a finger before his loyal followers put the challenger in his place. Seldom did he have to raise his voice. He could cut through men's courage in a single glance. The men feared his wrath, but he did not have to threaten them with any violence to earn their loyalty. It was Eilif who taught me the power of respect in commanding fealty.

As ship's boy, it was my duty to learn the craft of sailing, roping, and cleaning, and also cooking. My first night aboard Eilif's longship, the second-in-command, Egill, taught me and the other ship's boy how to make the foods needed for a long sea voyage.

For most of the day the men ate dried, salted fish, but at night they preferred fresh cuts of herring or mackerel with bread if we had any in the hold. On some days, when a favorable wind blew, we made a fire in a large iron pot suspended from a tripod that was bolted to the deck. The pot swayed with the ocean's waves, so the coals did not spill out. From the same stand, we hung a smaller iron pot and dipped it into the flames. This was how we made our stews. As our days in open water passed, the ingredients to make the stews dwindled, leaving us with nothing but raw fish to eat until we reached land.

Egill was no ordinary Northman. His father lived in the Far North, beyond the edges of what Danes considered to be the known world, and he traded with a mysterious people called the Sami. It is believed by the Northmen that the Sami possess magical powers—powers that have allowed them to survive in the harsh Northern wastes since the creation of Midgard. They gave him rich white furs, and in return, he gave them grains, iron tools, and mead.

To forge trade relations with the Sami, Egill's father married one of their chieftain's daughters. Eilif believed Egill had inherited his mother's ability to see into the other realms and to interpret the will of the gods. At first, I did not believe Eilif, but I later learned to respect Egill's abilities and magical powers. Although he shared half his blood with the Sami, he had the look of a Northman. He had long, curly brown hair and a coarse beard that he boasted could stop an arrow from piercing his chest. So proud of his beard was he that he drunkenly dared me once to throw a dagger at it to prove to me it could stop the blade. Years of braiding and exposure to the sea had made the beard hard as wood.

My first few weeks at sea were uneventful. We encountered no storms, held a favorable wind to our back, and praised the gods we did not encounter any beasts beneath the waves. As a child, I feared the monsters of myth, as most children do, and it did not help that the men told stories of ships devoured whole in the open ocean by giant serpents.

I cannot say if the men believed the stories or if they intended to frighten the ship boys as a cruel amusement. The other ship boy, Bjorn, also feared the monsters. To him, the myths were real. I saw him one night, peering over the gunwale into the ocean's dark waters, illuminated by a bright crescent moon under a clear night sky. When I joined him, I heard a muffled knocking against the hull, and we saw the dark silhouette of a shark that rammed itself repeatedly into the ship's strakes. Bjorn said the shark's behavior was an ill portent of things to come. I was not so quick to believe the shark acted with the will of the gods. I searched for a cause and found a bucket of fish guts tied to an oar-port that was leaking blood down the hull and into the water. Bjorn sighed in relief at the revelation.

"Monsters be damned," I said to him.

Once we arrived at our destination, our good fortune turned against us. No sooner had Egill screamed from the prow that he had spotted land, a fierce wind overtook us from the south. The men reefed the sail, and they set their oars to the water to take the ship to shore, hoping to avoid the approaching tempest. The gods had something else in mind for us. Dark clouds filled the sky and unleashed rain, thunder, and wind that swelled the waves as tall as the ship's mast. I saw fear in Eilif's eyes for the first time. His knuckles were white as he gripped the steering paddle and worked with all his strength to keep the ship on course.

Bjorn came to me in fear as I held onto the gunwale to steady myself in the waves. I took his arm to pull him toward me and place his hands by mine. The waves rocked us with relentless force, the likes of which I had never witnessed. In my fear, I had not noticed that Bjorn and I stood in the path of a loose crate of supplies. A violent gust of wind swept across the ship and, with the help of a towering wave, tilted Sail Horse until we nearly capsized. The crate slipped and slammed against the gunwale and hurled the two of us into open water.

I should have drowned that day. My body sank beneath the waves, and I felt the cold embrace of the ocean's water all around me. As I drifted deeper and deeper, I watched helplessly as the light from the living world dimmed to near blackness.

The ocean claimed me for herself and swallowed me whole until my final breath escaped from my chest. I should have sunk and perished, but I remained suspended in place at the precipice of where the light from the surface met the darkness of the deep.

There I saw the silhouette of a monstrous wolf with deep red eyes running through the water as if through a field of grass. The wolf opened his jowls, which stretched from the surface to the deep, as if to devour me, but it passed me by and swirled around my body. It turned back and ran at me again, but then I saw it charge at something below me. It was Bjorn. I reached for Bjorn's lifeless hand and grasped it with all my strength. At that moment, I felt two powerful hands clasp around my shoulders and pull me from my watery tomb.

I awoke after the storm had given way to a calm sky, with the rhythmic lap and splash of oars cutting through the water. Although my lungs had taken in seawater, the men had managed to pull me back aboard and save me from death. They had set me to rest at the aft of the ship with a fur blanket to keep me warm. When my eyes opened, Eilif knelt at my side.

"The gods have spared you, boy," he said with relief. "How do you feel?"

I had to think hard about this question. My head still swirled, and my eyes itched as though filled with sand. "My head hurts," I said with a raspy voice. "What about Bjorn?"

Eilif pointed midship where I saw Bjorn resting under a wool blanket. He said, "When we pulled you from the water, you would not let go of him. If not for you, he would have drowned." He stood again and resumed his station at the steering paddle with a solemn frown. Egill took his place at my side with a goblet of watered-down wine.

"For your head," Egill said. His voice was deep and soothing. As I drank from the goblet, he touched my forehead with his fingers. "Still no fever. You are lucky. One of the gods watches over you."

"I saw a wolf," I stated.

Egill raised his eyebrows. "A wolf?"

"In the water," I said as I took a sip from the goblet. "He tried to take Bjorn."

Egill sat back and stared at me. He rubbed his wooden pendant of Mjolnir between his fingers and said, "Did this wolf speak to you?"

I shook my head.

"How big?" he asked with a tremble in his voice and a furrowed brow.

I looked up at the bronze weathervane atop the mast and said, "Big enough to swallow the ship whole."

Egill stood and approached Eilif. They spoke a moment, and Eilif called for one of his men to take his place at the steering paddle. They both knelt at my side.

"Egill tells me you had a vision in the water?" Eilif asked.

I nodded.

"A wolf? You are certain?"

I nodded again.

"He saw you?" he asked with a slight crack in his voice.

"I… he…" I said in shock. "He passed me by."

"It was the wolf Fenrir," Egill muttered. The name sent a chill through my bones. "He has escaped his chains in Asgard and has come to Midgard to feed on the souls of the living. It was Thor who brought the storm upon us, in chase of the beast. The Aesir will seek to bind him. I have seen it in the runes."

"Show me," Eilif insisted.

Egill pulled out a leather satchel that contained several dozen small bones with runic symbols carved into them. He tossed them onto the deck and sorted through the pile with his fingers. Those in the center he arranged into a line and read them. "The first rune is the fox," he said. "The fox is cunning and good at escaping. Next is the wolf, which the boy saw in his vision. Last, I see the runes for Thor and Odin's ravens, Huginn and Muninn. They are looking for Fenrir, who has hidden himself in our realm."

Had I encountered the most dangerous being of all time, known to have the ability to feast on the gods themselves? I shuddered at the thought, and so did Eilif and Egill. Eilif took a deep breath and clenched his hands. He turned to look into Egill's eyes.

"He is with us, even now?" he asked.

"I cannot say," Egill replied. "To know, I would need to cross into the spirit world. I do not possess this gift."

Eilif stroked his beard and stared off into the distance. He whispered, "Let us hope Thor caught him."

"This boy stood before the beast and lived, as no man has done before him," Egill said. "The gods watch over him, and we would do well to honor them." He reached out his hand and placed it on Eilif's shoulder. "It is a sign. And a good one... I think."

Eilif laughed. Both he and Egill stood again, and I sat up to regain my strength. None of the other men aboard the ship made a sound; they rowed rhythmically in silence. Their time together had taught them to row in unison without the need for a drum. Drums made too much sound and risked attracting too much attention. As I sat, I took in the sight of the surrounding lands. We had traveled far since the storm and glided up a wide river with a calm flow, flanked on both banks by dense brush and wild, thickly leafed trees.

"Where are we?" I asked.

"They call this Frankland, and this river the Loire. We are half a day's journey from a city called Nantes," Eilif said.

"We are here to raid?" I asked.

"No, boy. We are here to trade," Eilif replied.

"What do we have to trade?" I asked.

Eilif tapped his foot on the deck and said, "We have white furs and ivory in the hold. One hundred pounds of silver's worth at least. Perhaps more."

"What will one hundred pounds of silver buy us?" I asked.

Eilif smiled. "You ask many questions, boy. It is a good thing; it means you are not dimwitted. But you must also learn when to be silent."

We rowed the remainder of the day along the river with no chatter between us. The men seemed unnerved, although I did not know at the time why. As we moved upriver, local barges passed us in the opposite direction. Their occupants stared at us with keen interest. As far as I could tell, they did not fear us.

The barges increased in number the farther we traveled, and we even passed a few headed in our direction. Not until we reached a fork in the river did we see any visible signs of a settlement. What I saw there caused my jaw to drop, much to the amusement of my shipmates.

Before us stood a massive, towering wall that enclosed an entire island on the river. Each branch of the river led to a low stone bridge that connected the island to the mainland, flanked on each side by fortified stone towers. The wall itself was spaced apart by soaring, squared towers capped with conical wooden battlements. Compared with Hagar's watchtowers, these stood three times as high and three times as thick.

"Welcome to Nantes," Eilif said.

Our ship maneuvered along the southern branch of the river and docked at the wharf under the bridge. A Frankish man walked the dock to our boat and addressed Eilif in the Frankish language. He had long black hair and a shaved face. To my amazement, Eilif spoke back to him in the foreign tongue and gave him a handful of silver coins. The Frankish man wrote in a leather-bound ledger and walked back up the dock to the city.

"Do you feel strong enough for a walk?" Egill asked.

I nodded.

"Good. Wear this." He placed in my hand a wooden pendant in the shape of a cross. I stared at it a moment. "Go on, put it on," he said. "The Franks only allow Christians in the city. If we want to trade, we must look the part."

I slipped the pendant over my head and around my neck, and I followed Egill off the ship and up a small stone staircase to the bridge where we caught up with Eilif and a few others. Most of the men stayed with Sail Horse where they set about cleaning the deck and inspecting the hull for damage from the storm. Bjorn stayed with them under his blanket, still too weak to join us.

Among the group who ventured into the city, several carried large sacks filled with wares—I assumed the white pelts Eilif had told me about. They also brought some amber and honey, although these were not as valuable as the furs and ivory from the wild North. As we walked, Eilif called me forward to join him at the front of the group. I marveled at the stone archway through which we passed to enter the city, and Eilif took my arm and pulled me in to whisper.

"I want you to keep an eye on everyone who passes us," he said.

"What?" I did not understand what he had asked of me.

"Do as I say, boy. The city is full of pickpockets. Their hands steal quicker than eyes can catch. Watch my back, and I will watch yours."

As we walked through the gateway into the city, the air turned putrid and smelled of a mixture of rotten flesh and pig droppings. The stench took me by surprise. Eilif and the others appeared unaffected, while I had to cover my nose and mouth with my tunic.

"Stone walls keep out enemies… and fresh air," Egill said to me with a chuckle.

The farther we ventured into the city, the more the streets narrowed. Flocks of people filled the space between the buildings, which all stood at least two stories in height and cast the streets in shadow. We bumped and pushed our way through the crowd, and at times it was a battle to keep pace with Eilif. The people there all seemed in a terrible hurry, and none appeared to notice us or consider us of any significance. In fact, many of the people we saw walking the streets of Nantes were not Franks, either. One man had the darkest skin I had ever seen and wore long and colorful robes. Another man I saw wore less lavish clothing but also had darker skin and wore a strange cloth on his head.

Eilif led us through the crowd to a bustling market filled with thin-roofed, open-air stands packed with exotic goods. The market was a sizable open place overshadowed by the most massive stone structure I had ever seen. We had arrived in the evening, and the setting sun's rays engulfed the building in a majestic golden glow.

"What is that?" I asked.

"It's a small church," Egill said.

"Small?" I said in disbelief. For me, at the time, it was the tallest structure I had ever seen. The most impressive building I had seen before then was my father's great hall, and even the memory of it had mostly faded.

"There's another one on the other side of the city, twice as big at least," Egill said.

Eilif marched his way toward a stand filled to the brim with fur pelts. The man in charge wore a simple grey tunic with an auburn hem that covered him to the knees. His hair was a greying blond, brushed straight and held behind his ears by an auburn cap.

As we approached, he was in the middle of bartering with a local on the price of one of his furs. They argued in the Frankish language back and forth until Eilif imposed himself on the two. The Frankish man cowered a little, handed over a sum of coins to the stand's keeper, and darted into the bustling crowd with a new fur pelt in hand.

"What have I told you about scaring my customers?" the stand's keeper said. I could not tell if he smiled or frowned through the curls of his beard.

"Save me the lecture, Váli," Eilif said. He held his arm out to grasp Váli's and patted him on the shoulder. "I have thirty pelts for you."

"Not wolves, I hope. Frankland is full of wolves," Váli said.

"No, white furs from the North," Eilif said.

Váli clasped his hands in delight. "White fur is what the demoiselles want!" He welcomed us to the back of his stand and had the men unload the pelts behind a stack of other wares. I stood by Eilif with watchful eyes.

"Who's the boy?" Váli asked.

"A slave I freed from Hagar," Eilif said.

"Still not trading in slaves?" Váli asked. His smile reminded me of Karl's sons when they took to mischief.

"No," Eilif stated. He shot a glance in my direction to see if I was listening. He looked bothered by Váli's question, as if it aroused memories he would have preferred not to remember.

"You should. There's money to be made. My cousin Thráinn made three hundred pounds of silver last summer trading slaves."

"I know," Eilif said. His eyes wandered as he spoke. After a deep sigh of exasperation, he looked Váli in the eye and said, "I want fifty pounds of silver for the furs and thirty more for the ivory."

"Should I bother bartering with you?" Váli asked with a smirk.

Eilif chuckled. They grasped each other at the wrist to shake on the exchange. Váli disappeared behind his stand for a short while to count his silver and returned with ten leather satchels, all packed into two wooden holders. Egill ordered two of the men to carry the silver back to the ship while Eilif and I stayed behind to speak with the shopkeeper.

"Have you seen any other Northmen or Danes in these parts of late?" Eilif asked.

"No," Váli said. "The Franks do not allow new trade with them, not since the raids on Herio and Bouin."

"Them?" Eilif said with a raised eyebrow.

"I have lived here so long, I forget my place," Váli said with an embarrassed smile. He reached for an antler comb sitting on the table behind him and ran it through his beard with a few quick strokes. "How did you pass the Frankish defenses on the river? I hear they've been sinking Northman ships on sight."

"They'll only sink you if you have no silver. For the right price, any ship may pass," Eilif said. "These Franks are more interested in drowning themselves in their wine than sinking ships. And it's getting worse."

"It is true. The best soldiers are fighting in the princes' rebellion. Thankfully, Nantes has been spared the worst of it, though the count has ridden off for war and left behind an imbecile to govern in his stead. He's raised merchant taxes three times in the past year!"

"And the Celts? Any news of them?" As Eilif reached for his coin purse, a young girl about my age, dressed in dark unwashed rags, bumped into him. She apologized, then darted off. Eilif felt his belt where his purse should have been, then turned to me and shouted, "Thief!"

On pure instinct, I bolted after her. I dodged, leaped, and lunged through the sea of bodies amassed at the market until I emerged at the far end of the church where I caught a glimpse of the girl's feet as she ran ahead into a deserted alleyway. Keeping in close pursuit, I saw her turn sharply to the left down another alley. I followed, and this took me to a narrow corridor that led to a dead end against the city wall.

There, I could find no sign of the girl. But I was not fooled. She had nowhere to run, so I knew she had hidden somewhere close. Standing still, I listened for any sound of movement. In the far corner, tucked behind a stack of barrels and tarps, I heard the faint sound of the girl's breathing.

"I know you are there," I said. The girl remained silent. "Either come out and face me, or I will come and fetch you!"

"Try," she said.

Her response surprised me. She spoke my language, which at that moment I realized was unusual.

"You speak the language of the Danes?" I asked.

The girl drummed up the courage to step out from behind a stack of crates pushed up against the wall. She was wild—her hair was a tangled blond mass, and her arms were covered in dirt and scratches.

"My father was a Dane," she said.

I took a good look at her and saw the marks of shackles on her wrists and ankles. "You are a slave," I said.

"Was," she said.

"You were freed?"

"I escaped."

I laughed. "You escaped from a slaver?"

"I did."

"Where are your parents, girl?" I asked.

"I do not know, boy," she growled.

The girl suddenly shuffled back with a look of fear in her eye. She had seen something behind me that had frightened her. I glimpsed again and saw Eilif approaching.

"You have the thief cornered," he said, smiling.

"She is one of us," I said to him.

Eilif paused. "In Nantes?" he said, astounded. He laughed. "Stop wasting time and get my silver back."

I approached the girl and reached out my hand. I motioned with my fingers for her to hand over the purse. She took another step back.

"If you want it, you will have to take it from me," she said.

As the last word flew from her tongue, I clenched my fist and struck her square in the jaw. She fell back and dropped the purse. Curiously, she did not cry. I reached down for the silver, and she leaped forward to attack me. She threw her body on mine and began to hit me wherever she could. As we fought, I heard the yells of more men behind Eilif. When I looked back, I saw Frankish soldiers with spears and shields jogging toward us.

"Stop!" I said to the girl. "Look!"

She ceased her attack and stood behind me. We watched nervously as Eilif spoke with the soldiers. He motioned with his hands as if to negotiate a fairer price for goods, but I could not hear what he said. The soldiers argued back at him with angry shouts. Their language sounded barbaric to my ears. When Eilif looked back at me he said, "The silver, bring it to me."

I hurried over to Eilif and handed him his purse. He dumped its contents into his hand, split the sum of the silver into two parts, and gave each soldier a share. They, in turn, took the silver, smiled, and walked away. When they turned their backs on us, I felt relieved.

"What did they want?" I asked.

"The same as what the girl wanted: my silver," Eilif replied.

"They robbed us?" I exclaimed.

"The guards are corrupt. Come, the city is not as safe as it once was," Eilif said. He paused again, looked back at the girl, and said, "Come with us, girl. You owe me a debt, and I expect to be repaid."

"I owe you nothing!" she barked.

"Stay, and those men will rape you," Eilif said bluntly.

"Why should I believe you will not do the same?" the girl asked.

"You have two choices: stay and be raped, maybe killed, or follow the man who paid silver to save your neck," he said.

"You spent the silver to save your own neck," the girl snarled.

Eilif rolled his eyes. "She has quite the tongue on her, doesn't she?" The girl seemed at a loss for words. She bolted back to her hideout in the far corner of the alleyway and disappeared. Eilif shrugged and walked back toward the market. I followed while keeping one eye on the alley behind us. We reached the fringes of the marketplace when I felt a tug on my tunic. I looked back and saw her standing before me with a knapsack thrown over her shoulder.

"I am Asa," she said.

She pulled back her hair and revealed the face of a beauty unlike any I had ever seen. Her eyes were brilliant emeralds suspended above high cheekbones and contoured by light blond eyebrows. When she looked at me, her gaze was focused and piercing, yet I saw longing and pain in it too.

"I am Hasting," I said. "And he is Eilif."

Eilif led us through the market to the entrance of the city where we passed again under the stone archway and down the path to the wharf. The men had prepared the ship to sail, and Egill waited for us on the dock. He stroked his beard in thought as we approached, and he appeared intrigued by our new friend. He gave a quick wave to the men which signaled to them to prepare to launch Sail Horse.

"Another one?" he joked.

THE LORDS OF THE WIND

"I will explain later," Eilif said. "We should leave. This place has changed since the war began. It is not a place for us to trade any longer."

As Eilif boarded the ship, Egill reached out and caught him by the arm. "Do you think it wise to bring a girl onto our ship? The men have not known a woman for many weeks."

"She is under my protection," Eilif said. "And she'll work."

The men set their oars to water, and we began our journey back downriver toward the ocean.

3

Armorica

For two days we rowed hard along the coast of Frankland. The gods had robbed the ocean of wind, which made the men uneasy. Superstitions about the weather varied from man to man, but they all agreed that a weak wind, or none at all, did not bode well for us. At night, Egill, whose mystical powers I no longer doubted, stripped naked and chanted at the night sky to beg the gods for their favor. He took mead and meat and threw it into the ocean as an offering to Odin, but by the second night he threw out less of the meat and drank more of the mead.

I continued my duties of cooking, cleaning, and learning all the knots required for the ship's rigging. Asa helped with some of these tasks, but most of the time she sat at the stern, idle and out of sight of the crew.

At night we slept together in a huddle under the ship's tarp to keep warm. Eilif had made it my duty to ensure Asa remained out of reach of the others while we slept. Though none had shown an interest in her, men are men, and we did not wish to give any the opportunity to cause trouble.

After an arduous journey fraught with uncertainty about the weather, the wind appeared once again at our back and carried us swiftly to our destination. The crew was elated. When Egill first called out that he had spotted his reference point, I rushed to the prow to catch a glimpse of where we had sailed. The coastline was jagged and rocky, with nowhere to moor. More concerning were the massive, sharp rocks that thrust from the water like pikes from the bottom of a trap.

"What is this place?" I asked.

"The locals call it Armorica," Egill said, "home to a proud people called the Celts. We call it Bretland."

"We are no longer in Frankland?" I asked.

Egill laughed. "No, boy. Armorica is something else entirely."

I marveled at the richness of the land both above and below the cliffs. I called Asa to the prow—I thought of us as friends now—to see what I saw. The ocean around Armorica flourished with wildlife both in and out of the water. Flocks of seabirds circled us overhead, and the bravest among them swooped down below the mast to investigate our ship. Seals lounged on the larger rocks closer to the cliffs. They robed themselves in seaweed and basked in the little sun that shone through the clouded sky. Dolphins joined us on our journey and swam before and beside the ship as if to guide us through the rocks. They jumped high above the waves, flapping their flippers as if to amuse us. Asa, Bjorn, and I lit up with excitement at the sight of them, and our enthusiasm even inspired a few smiles and laughs from the rest of the crew. We had not yet landed, and already Armorica had me under her spell. That was when Eilif joined us at the prow.

"Go on," he said. "Climb."

At first I did not know what he meant, but I soon understood when Asa dug her nails into the wood along the prow's neck and climbed over the gunwale.

"You too," Eilif said.

Carefully, I climbed and joined Asa, my hands clasped to the dragonhead above me. I had never been so close to the beast, and only then did I truly see it. It was a serpent's head, carved with the markings of the gods and painted white and gold so it could be seen from far away. Its brow, adorned with vivid colors, gave the beast life. As I held on to keep my balance, its dark, soulless eyes stared through me into the distance.

At first I felt fear, but my courage held and excitement swelled in my heart. I stood ever taller above the ocean as a conquering hero upon his mighty steed. The passing of the wind through my hair and the splash of the water below invigorated my senses. Asa screamed with excitement, and she grew even louder when the dolphins skipped through the water below us. We were birds soaring in the wind as lords of the wind and sea.

"This is as close as any man will ever come to flying," Eilif said. "With a favorable wind, our ships are the fastest in the world. Remember that, boy. We are a proud people because we have much to be proud of."

Not long before nightfall, our ship ran aground on a pristine white-sand beach nestled in a cove beneath cliffs. Asa, Bjorn, and I were tasked with carrying supplies and finding a flat place to make camp out of the wind. We loaded our backs with all we could hold and marched together in high spirits, spurred by the excitement we had felt at sea. Even the coarse grass along the path from the beach to the countryside, with its sharp thorns and edges, did not deter our bare feet.

Not far off from where we had landed, we spotted a clearing that appeared to have been scorched and flattened by other men. We approached the grounds and deemed them appropriate for our camp. We dropped our loads and sat hip to hip on the sandy ground with great relief.

We rested while we waited for the others to join us, and Asa gave me a quick, playful poke in the rib. I retaliated, but she swatted my hand away before my finger ever touched her. We giggled. She looked down at her feet and swept the ground with her eyes, then shot me a glance from the side. Bjorn sat beside us all the while with his arms crossed and a furrowed brow.

"Ha! It is our camp from last year, is it not?" Egill said with a booming voice that interrupted our laughter. "And you said it would be covered over by now."

"A man is sometimes wrong," Eilif said.

"What now?" I asked.

"We are short on supplies, and the men are hungry. There is a farmer who lives not far from here. Take some silver and fetch us bread and eggs. He will remember us from last year. And take Asa with you. Strength in numbers."

"How will I speak with him?" I asked. "Does he speak our language?"

"Improvise," Egill said.

His response irritated me. It was neither helpful nor encouraging. Asa tugged on my arm as if to say I should ignore him. Bjorn stayed behind to help with the tents, while Asa and I left together along a beaten path through coarse beach grass until we arrived at a fence that enclosed a well-kept pasture.

Not far along, we encountered a wicket, which opened with ease. The ground was soft and cold, a welcome relief to my weather-beaten feet that had suffered the sharp slivers of the ship's deck for many weeks. Asa twirled and danced as we followed the beaten path across the pasture.

"I feel free!" she said as she skipped along beside me, out of breath. "I love this place!"

"Armorica is a beautiful land," I agreed.

"Let's play a game." She tapped me on the shoulder and skipped backward. "Now you catch me!"

It was a challenge I could not refuse. I charged at her with my hand outstretched, but she evaded me. She giggled and taunted me again. I lunged a second time. I nearly caught her, but my foot caught something on the ground, and I stumbled. Asa had a lightness in her feet that allowed her to float gracefully through the air.

"Too slow!" she teased.

I smirked at her, then bolted with all the quickness I could muster. She dodged my first dash with ease and ran along the path. I gave chase and followed her into a small wood where, in an attempt to evade me, she tripped and fell down a slight slope. Not able to stop myself in time, I fell with her, and we rolled together through leaves and mud to the bank of a small creek. I cannot recall how it happened, but I found myself pinned to the ground with Asa on top of me. She smiled. Before I knew it, her lips pressed against mine.

"I am sorry," she said as she pulled away.

"Why?" I asked.

"I shouldn't... we can't." She blushed, took a deep breath to collect herself, and said, "I like you. You have been kind to me. No one has been kind to me in a long time."

I smiled and wiped some of the mud off her face. "The others are waiting."

Asa grew quiet on the journey to the farm. She seemed withdrawn and guarded, almost as if we had never met. Her silence unnerved me. I did not understand women—I still do not presume to—and I frowned in frustration. My frustration grew to anger, and my mind wandered with all manner of thoughts and ideas, working to make sense of what had happened. As I thought about the kiss and where it might have gone wrong, Asa took my hand.

"The farm... it's there." Asa pointed at a farmhouse on the edge of a quiet woodland.

The farm was a small square building with wicket and daub walls and a tall thatched roof covered in green and grey moss. Along the side were stacks of chopped wood, bailed hay, and a handcart with a missing wheel.

We approached the farm from the path and knocked at the door. From within the building, I heard the clinking and clunking of iron, and the door opened. An older man with a thick grey beard peered through the gap. When he saw we were children, he smiled. He spoke to us in a language I did not understand. My first instinct was to pull the silver pieces from my pocket, but Asa surprised me once again by responding to him in his language.

"Give me your silver," she said to me mid-conversation with the farmer.

I obliged her. My mouth was agape with awe. Asa snatched the silver from my hand as soon as it glinted in the late afternoon sunlight, and she handed it to the farmer. When she reached out to hand over the silver, the sleeve of her tunic pulled back, and I saw a purple birthmark on her arm. The farmer's eyes lit up at the sight of the coins, and he disappeared into his farmhouse for a moment. When he returned, he handed over a basket filled with eggs and another three filled with bread, grains, and dried vegetables. He babbled some more, gave us a small wave, and slammed the door. I stared at the food in my hands, dumbstruck at what had just happened.

"We should be getting back. It will be dark soon," Asa said.

I nodded and said, "Where did you learn their language?"

"Celtic? I don't know it all that well. I learned it when... well, one day, perhaps, I will tell you all there is to know about me, but not yet," she whispered.

I looked upon her with admiration. She blushed, glanced at the ground, and shot brief, sweeping looks at me. We were young, and we were starting to fall in love.

"Hasting!" we heard a voice call out from across the pasture. It was Egill. "Hasting, are you all right?"

"We're coming!" I yelled.

We had completely lost track of time. What should have been a short errand had taken us long enough to raise suspicion at camp. Asa took my hand to begin walking back, but for fear of showing affection in front of Egill, I shrugged it off. I had not meant to hurt her feelings, but her demeanor changed in an instant to one of disbelief and resentment.

"Where have you been? We're hungry!" Egill said.

"We took a wrong turn by the creek," I said.

Egill took one look at Asa and said, "Is she all right?"

"I am fine," she growled.

We hurried back to the beach by following the path, joined the whole way by Egill. None of us spoke a word.

When we arrived, I was astounded by the quick work the men had made of setting up camp. They had erected pikes around the perimeter, and they had pitched three large tents around a central fire pit. There were no chairs, so the men sat in the sand, some with their legs crossed, and others in a lounging position with their worn feet close to the fire. Eilif emerged from the middle tent in his battle garments—a thick leather jerkin, bracers, and greaves—fitted and ready for combat.

"Ah! The explorers have returned," he said.

"Sorry," I uttered.

"We were more worried than anything," Eilif said. "Come, we are expecting guests before nightfall. Wash up and eat."

"Guests?" I asked.

"A king," Egill said with a grin ear to ear.

"His name is Nominoë. He is one of the three kings of Armorica," Eilif said. "His father was an important trade partner of ours. It was from him we bought our salt."

"Was?" I asked.

Eilif sat in the sand beside his men close to the fire and said, "Nominoë's father is dead."

As they spoke, three horsemen appeared at the edge of our camp. I had never seen horses before. On Hagar's farm we had raised pigs, goats, and asses, but no horses. They are too expensive to feed, stubborn to train, and make tough meat, Hagar used to say. They are majestic beasts and gallant in their stride. These horses were kings of the animal world, and they carried themselves as such, or so it seemed. The Celts had braided their golden manes and kept their coats brushed and shining. All the horses described to me by the Northmen were small but hearty; these were tall, graceful creatures with beautifully sculpted muscles and a smooth light-brown coat.

The horsemen wore brown woolen cloaks that covered them to their instep, and the rider at the forefront wore a tight-fitting velvet cap. The two horsemen behind him carried their leader's sigil, a white fox tail on a long burgundy banner that fluttered in the ocean's breeze.

Their leader was young, perhaps a few years older than I, and he carried himself with his chest held high. He exuded confidence. As they approached, several of Eilif's men moved to meet them at the camp's entrance. The Celtic leader raised his hand in a sign of peace. Eilif stepped forward to greet the Celts with caution in his eyes.

He gripped the hilt of his sword, which remained sheathed upon his girdle. The Celts' leader began to speak and, for a moment, I believed Eilif would reply to him as he had done with the Franks in Nantes. Here, he remained silent. The air grew thick with tension as the two groups stared at each other. From behind me, Asa's voice broke the silence as she spoke in the Celtic language, to the surprise of everyone present.

"You speak their language?" Eilif asked her.

Asa nodded.

"Thank the Norns! Come, tell them what I say. Ask him if he is Nominoë."

Asa put the question to the young leader of the horsemen. He answered in a manner everyone understood to be *yes*.

"Tell him I knew his father. We were partners in trade. I hope to continue that trade."

The two exchanged words amicably, and Eilif looked at me wide-eyed and filled with excitement. He had quite evidently expected the meeting to turn sour.

"Nominoë says he knows about the trade," Asa said. "He says he no longer has access to the salt his father traded with you because the Franks have occupied the marshes in Guérande, where the salt is from."

Eilif's excitement turned to enmity. "What does he mean?"

"He has an offer for us," Asa translated.

"Out with it!" Eilif exclaimed.

Asa rubbed her face and said, "He says he needs someone to draw the Franks away from Guérande long enough to retake the marshes with his army."

"Is he asking us to fight for him?" Eilif asked.

Nominoë again answered in a manner everyone understood to mean *yes*, to which Eilif said, "Ask him what he has in mind."

"He asks us to attack the coast south of the Loire, and to be sure they see us sailing that way," Asa said.

"He will pay us?" Eilif asked.

"In silver," Asa said.

"How much silver?" Eilif asked.

Nominoë glanced back at his companions, and one of them whispered words to him that none of us could hear. He readjusted himself in his saddle and gave his reply to Eilif.

"Will five hundred pounds suffice?" Asa asked.

Eilif tilted his head back and laughed. Until then he had merely peddled a few dozen pounds of silver each summer. Five hundred pounds would change his life.

Where had the Celts come up with this number? They seemed to understand we Vikings sought wealth above all else, but so much? It felt as though we had won a game of luck.

"Agreed," Eilif said. "Deliver the silver at sunrise, and we will raid somewhere south of the river."

"Nominoë says he will pay you after the deed is done," Asa said.

"I want to see the silver first," Eilif insisted.

Nominoë leaned in to whisper with one of his companions. They discussed the matter back and forth for a moment, then sat up straight on their horses once again.

"He invites you to his city to see the silver. But only you... and me to translate," Asa said.

"May I come?" I asked out of turn.

Eilif glared at me. Before he could say anything, Asa turned to Nominoë and asked him. The question risked upsetting the entire balance of the negotiation, and Eilif cringed when it was proposed. To our surprise, Nominoë again answered in that manner which everyone understood to mean *yes*.

Egill began to laugh so hard he bent over and fell to one knee."The gods have a twisted sense of humor,"

"Just... make sure the camp doesn't burn down while I am away," Eilif said.

Egill's laughter ceased. "You mean to follow them?" he asked. "But it could be a trap, to kill you."

"It is not," Eilif said. "If they kill me, you will avenge me. They will not risk it. And I have a feeling the girl knows more than she has let on."

We arrived at Nominoë's city the following afternoon, though one might have convinced me it was evening since the low-hanging clouds and light drizzle made the countryside a somber sight.

We met Nominoë and his two bannermen on the outskirts of the city where we passed through a wooden palisade in grave need of repairs. It stood the height of a tall man, but many of the wooden planks had rotted and fallen, leaving holes large enough for a smaller man to slip through.

On the other side, we passed along two rows of small, square houses, built in the same style as the farm we had visited the previous day. They were built side by side, with enough room between them to store tools and other household supplies.

Within the city, the muddy road gave way to a raised plank walkway. It connected all the main buildings and allowed those living there to travel from one place to another without soiling their feet. Nominoë led us to a small stone church built with white lime and mortar walls that had greyed from the rain.

"Nominoë invites us to pray with him in his church," Asa said.

Eilif and I refused. Nominoë did not appear vexed in the least. He entered the church, followed by his bannermen and Asa.

"Where are you going?" I asked.

"To pray," she replied.

My eyes opened wide with surprise once again, and I asked, "You are Christian?"

Asa nodded and, sensing my discomfort with the revelation, turned her back to me and entered the church behind the others. I crossed my arms and glowered in dismay. Eilif leaned against the church wall as if relaxed. He reached into his pocket and withdrew some sunflower seeds to chew. I looked back at him with anger in my eyes. This did not seem to bother Eilif, and he extended his hand to offer me some seeds. I refused.

"Full of surprises, isn't she?" Eilif said.

"Too many," I said.

"Women!" he scoffed.

We stood in uncomfortable silence for a moment, both deep in thought about what next to say. I felt Eilif had some wisdom he wanted to share with me but that he knew I might not like. All the while, I wrestled with my feelings for a girl about whom I knew nothing.

"Hasting, I like to think we have grown close, you and I, in the short time we have sailed together," Eilif said. His words drew my full attention.

"As do I," I said.

He gave me a half smile and said, "Do you understand what Nominoë wants?"

"To make us rich?" I proposed.

Eilif laughed. "Yes, but for a price. For four summers, we have sailed from the Northlands to Ireland, and to here. We have traded in furs, salt, and silver, and each summer our wealth has grown. But now… now the wars of the Franks and the Celts will draw us in. We will become woven into the politics of the South."

"For five hundred pounds of silver, is it not a fair price?" I asked.

"You are new to us and young, and so you do not yet know. You will be a strong leader one day, I think, and so this you should learn: when I was your age, I sailed on a ship that roved these shores. We plundered churches, farms, and towns, and our wealth grew. But soon the Christians learned when we would arrive and so abandoned their lands in the summer. Each raid grew more meager. When the wealth dried up, the men killed our chieftain and returned north. I learned that day to be cautious. I devoted my time to summer trade instead of plunder, and each summer I made silver, and my men made silver. I do not wish to raid, and I do not wish to make war. But to keep my trade, I must make peace with Nominoë. Tomorrow, that peace will require me—us—to raid, and to fight." He lifted himself from the church's wall and spat shells on the ground.

"It is what Vikings are supposed to do," I said. I did not mean to cut him off, but the words flew from my mouth before I could consider them well. "Does this mean you will take and trade in slaves again?"

Eilif scowled. "It is likely," he said. "You heard Váli as clearly as I—we will double our silver with slaves."

His answer bothered me at first. I had been a slave, and I knew that hardship well. Yet, I understood Eilif's motivations. He did not wish to lose command of Sail Horse, or the loyalty of his crew. It dawned on me at that moment the power wealth holds over men. Though we are the creators of our wealth, we soon become slaves to it.

With a disruption in his trade, Eilif had to work with what he had, even if it betrayed his principles. I found his predicament a cruel sort: he was a slave to his wealth and had to take slaves to make and keep his wealth. Like Hagar, his primary duty was to his followers. For the first time, I saw the same duality in Eilif that I had seen in Hagar, and I understood that perhaps Hagar, for as much as I hated him, was beholden to the same shackles of principle and honor that forced Eilif to return to the slave trade. The gods have a twisted sense of humor, indeed.

"What of next summer?" I asked. "Will you not need to earn five hundred more pounds?"

Eilif smiled at my words and said, "Most of my crew joined for a single summer, as is the case with most men who choose to rove. Next year's recruits will know little of what happened this year, except Egill and, hopefully, you."

As we spoke, Asa stepped out of the church to join us. She kept her head bowed low, as if embarrassed, and said nothing. Eilif looked at me as if to urge me to say something, but I had no words. A tense and quiet moment followed, broken only by the cacophony of Nominoë and his entourage stepping out onto the boardwalk from the church. They laughed as if the priest had told the most side-splitting joke they had ever heard.

"Are they ready to show us the silver?" Eilif asked.

"Follow me," Asa said.

Nominoë led us along the main thoroughfare of the city to a wooden two-story building with four thick pillars supporting the roof above the entrance. A soldier stood guard at the door and nodded to his lord as he passed. The bobbing of his head continued as the rest of us followed, which made the hair on the back of my neck stand up. My heart began to race and a dryness gripped the back of my throat. Something was amiss.

"Eilif," I muttered.

He stopped and turned to me, two steps from the doorway. "What is it?"

I shook my head to alert him to my intuition. His eyes filled with concern. He looked above and around for signs of trouble. From within the building, Nominoë urged us to enter. The more we waited, the louder his voice grew. Eilif shrugged me off and entered the building while I remained frozen in place outside. Asa took my hand ever so gently and, with a calm and reassuring smile, led me through the door.

Inside, the walls around us felt close and cramped. The low ceiling and smoke from the hearth on the far wall made it hard to breathe. My heart continued to pound in my chest and even skipped a few beats here and there, which made my angst worse. Every man who looked down at me on our way through the rooms gave me a shrinking feeling, one of despair and emptiness. I wanted to run or scream. We arrived at a small room in the back of the building where Eilif kneeled beside four wooden chests, each decorated with serpentine carvings and golden handles, and each overflowing with silver.

"Your five hundred pounds of silver," Asa said on behalf of Nominoë.

Eilif and our host continued to speak, but their voices faded into the background. My mind raced with thoughts of doom, and the walls closed in around me. My desire to escape overwhelmed me, and I darted from that room through the others and out the front doorway into the street. I panted and could not catch my breath. A knot formed in the pit of my stomach, and I felt as though I might die then and there, for no other reason than fear.

After what seemed like a long moment, the feeling of panic subsided. The fresh air and light rain outside helped to cool my head. Finally, I was able to stop the trembling of my fingers.

I later learned that the Northmen call what I experienced *Loki's Delirium*, for they believe that the great trickster himself enjoys tormenting the minds of mortal men to cause a panic for no reason at all. He strikes when men least expect it, and often when they need their wits about them most. Here he tricked me to believe danger lurked behind the gaze of every Celt around me, even though the threat was far from real.

As I waited outside in the rain, Eilif left the building alone to find me. When he saw me kneeling on the boardwalk, he called for me with anger in his voice.

"What has possessed you, boy?" He gripped my shoulder so tightly that my fingers tingled.

"I needed fresh air," I answered.

"You frightened me," he scolded. "They're all wondering about you."

I felt shame for what had happened. "I meant no disrespect," I said. "You saw all five hundred pounds?"

Eilif took a deep breath of relief and said, "Packed and ready for us, as soon as we fulfill our end of the bargain." He wiped his nose with his hand, then wiped his hand on his breeches. "There's something else."

"What?" I asked.

"Asa has asked to stay here," he said hesitantly.

His words were a hunter's spear thrust through my heart. "Why?"

"Hasting, my ship is no place for a girl her age. I know the two of you have forged a close bond... but look at this place. It could be a home for her. They promised her a fresh bed, a roof over her head, and food for the day," Eilif said.

"Are we finished here?" I spat.

Eilif nodded. We left without saying farewell and took to the road. I brooded the whole way back. When we arrived at camp, we were greeted by Egill, whose cheeks glowed from all the wine he had drunk during our absence. All the men had drunk their fill, and they all cheered when Eilif announced that Nominoë indeed had five hundred pounds of silver to give. It was to be a festive night to celebrate the most valuable enterprise any of these Vikings had ever embarked upon in their lives. As they celebrated, Egill sat beside me in the sand. I stared at the campfire.

"Why are you glowering? It is making my wine taste bad," Egill said with a heavy slur. "Is it the girl?"

I nodded.

"Bah! You're a Viking now; there will be plenty of women in your life soon enough, especially when we have that five hundred pounds of silver in our hands."

Egill understood the meaning of my silence and left me where I sat, alone. That night, the crew drank themselves into oblivion, for they knew what lay ahead. Raids were an ugly and dangerous business. Little did we know then that most of the men on the beach that night would not live to see the silver spent.

4

First Raid

The sun had barely broken over the horizon when we set sail toward the south. A fair wind carried the ship at a gallop along the coast of Frankland, allowing time for the crew to relax and eat their first meal of the day. Some of the men continued to drink wine to abate the pain from the previous night's intemperance, while others drank fresh water and napped on deck. Eilif sat at the steering paddle, while Egill and two others worked the ropes of the sail. There was no chatter among the crew that morning, and the atmosphere aboard was taut and uneasy. I went about my regular duties, and when I finished, I joined Eilif at the aft of the ship.

"Where did Nominoë tell us to raid?" I asked him.

"He called it Bouin. It is the second island after the mouth of the river," Eilif explained. "I'm not sure of the reasoning for targeting it, but it makes no difference to us."

"How will we prove we raided it?" I asked.

"A few severed heads will do," he said.

I laughed uncomfortably, thinking he had made an ill-natured joke, but Egill's disapproving scowl told me differently. When I understood they intended to return to Armorica with the heads of Franks we had not yet met, butterflies fluttered in the pit of my stomach. I had thought during our travels that Eilif and his crew were different, that they did not partake in the same kind of brutality I had witnessed in Hagar's lands. I was wrong.

Near midday, with the wind still at our back, we sailed a perilous strait between the coast of Frankland and a long and seemingly uninhabited island. Rocks protruded from the water and posed a real danger to us as we glided closer to the island, and although the tide was high, two of Eilif's men kept careful watch of the waters ahead of the prow.

As we traversed the strait, a small island came into view. Smokestacks reached for the sky from behind a light grove of trees that overlooked the dune. Several fishing boats floated on the water no more than a stone's throw from shore. These were small, rectangular craft powered by a single pair of oars, with enough room aboard for one or two men. When they saw our sails, they pulled in their nets and set their oars to water. I could tell they feared us, even from a distance. We were not the first Vikings they had ever seen.

"Reef the sail," Eilif commanded. "Oars to water!"

The men took their positions on the rowing benches and obeyed their chieftain's commands. Egill reached underneath one of the benches and pulled out a leather-bound drum along with two drumsticks tipped with wrapped cloth. He placed the drum on the deck and, with a grin on his face, he called me over. He sat at the aft of the ship with his legs wrapped around the drum and began to beat the sticks upon it one strike at a time. He kept a steady rhythm that matched the pulling and easing of the oars. When I stood over him, I saw he had a crazed look in his eye.

"Do you see how I strike the drum?" he asked.

I nodded.

"You will sit, and you will play. Strike hard, boy. We want them to hear us!" He stood, handed me the drumsticks, and plopped me down in front of the drum. "Play!" he said.

I beat the drum, but this did not please him.

"Louder!" he screamed. "I want to fill the air with fear—let them know the Northmen are here! Play! Louder! Bom, bom, bom!"

With each strike of the drum, I forced my arm downward with all the strength I had. In a short time, I mastered the rhythm. Egill led the men in a thunderous chant that both frightened and invigorated me.

The men repeated each phrase after Egill in unison: "Odin our Allfather, we shed blood at your altar; man's blood is our offer, Odin our Allfather!"

Eilif steered Sail Horse straight onto the beach where the locals had moored their ships. We crashed into the ground with a mighty thud, which sent me flying forward into a rower's lap. He laughed and helped me to my feet.

"Shields on deck!" Eilif commanded, and the men repeated the command.

Each man reached beneath his bench and pulled from below a rounded wooden shield painted with unique colors and designs and rimmed with rawhide. Some of the men pulled more than just shields from the hold; they also had armor and weapons stowed below. They donned leather bracers and shin guards, and some wore simple iron helmets. I wondered if the nose bridge on their helmets ever obstructed their sight during battle. Egill donned his own, a much more expensive-looking iron helmet with a visor that covered his eyes in the way dark markings encircle the eyes of an owl. Runic symbols covered all the edges of the mask, giving him an otherworldly and frightening appearance. As I marveled at him, I felt a hand touch my shoulder.

"I have an important mission for you," Eilif said.

When I turned to look at him, he too had donned fine arms and armor. He wore a full maille shirt, which was something I had never seen before. It had a black tint, apart from some rust, and it chinked like a sack of silver coins whenever he moved. Over the maille he wore a light surcoat that made his shoulders appear as wide as a bear's, and at his waist he girded a silver-hilted sword and a simple wood-hilted seax.

"Are you listening?" he barked. The question snapped me back into the moment. "Stay with the ship."

"What?" I said, confused.

"Stay with the ship," Eilif said again. "You and Bjorn must protect the ship while we are gone. If you see another ship, especially other Danes, find me in the village. I do not want anyone to catch us off guard!"

Panicked, I nodded my head in agreement. The crew jumped over the gunwale into the shallow water below and assembled on the beach. I rushed to the prow below the dragon's head to watch them. Eilif and Egill led their warriors in a chant, and they howled together like wolves under a full moon.

The small force of thirty men charged up a narrow path that cut through the dune from the beach to the village, shouting and growling as they ran. When the last man vanished from sight, I looked back at Bjorn and the empty ship with a sense of angst. On one hand, I felt enlivened by the crew's vigor; on the other, I knew their purpose, and it seemed wrong. For the first time in my life, my hand trembled for no reason, a tendency I have had ever since in the moments before battle.

"You look frightened," Bjorn said. "What troubles you?"

"I am not keen on slaughter," I said.

Bjorn chuckled and said, "It will not be a slaughter. We played the drum so they would hear us. Those who would have been slaughtered will have run."

"And those who stayed behind?" I asked.

"They stayed to fight—a fair challenge," Bjorn said.

I nodded and did not say more. A blazing afternoon sun battered the ship's deck while we waited for the crew to return. My tunic was soaked in sweat within a short time. An eerie quiet set in on the beach. I focused my ears for any sound from the raid, but I could hear nothing other than the rolling of the waves upon the shore. A voice broke the tranquility. I looked up to find a Frankish man approaching our ship from the dune with his hands raised above his head and fear written in his eyes. He spoke to me in his language. Unable to understand him, I talked back to him in mine.

"Go away!" I shouted.

I flicked my wrists as if to shoo away a pig, but the man didn't move. Gripped with fear, for I was still a young boy with far less strength than him in my arms, I searched for anything sharp within arm's reach. To my relief, I spotted a filleting knife planted in one of the ship's rowing benches nearest me.

Before I could reach it, the man saw the blade. He looked at me, then at the knife, and at me again with increasing panic. Both of us remained frozen, locked in a standoff of fear and confusion. Bjorn, who had not yet seen the man, walked toward me from the aft of the ship. He froze at the sight of the Frank.

When I reached for the knife, I heard the cheerful laughter of men approaching the ship from beyond the dune. The Frank heard them as well, and I shooed him away again to give him one last chance to escape. I wished he had.

The moment my fellow Danes crossed over the dune, they spotted the man and called for his capture. Though I do not know who threw the blade, he hit his mark. A throwing knife thudded into the Frankish man's back as he attempted to flee. He fell on the sand and struggled to crawl forward. Egill was first among the men to approach him.

"Have you ever killed a man before?" Egill asked me.

"No," I said with a quiver in my voice.

He put on a crooked smile and said, "He will be your first."

My legs turned to mush. Not wanting to disappoint Egill, I crawled over the gunwale and trudged through the receding water. He placed an ax in my hand and pulled the man up to his knees by his hair. The man looked at me with pleading eyes, and he clasped his hands together to pray. His tongue was a twitchy snake, thrashing about in his mouth as he begged for his life.

"Remember, he would not hesitate to kill you if given the chance," Egill said. "Go on, kill him."

As I raised the ax above my head, my breathing grew shallow, and my chest tightened.

"Kill him!" Egill urged. His voice boomed across the beach.

A few more men from the crew joined him to encourage me. I looked around for Eilif, hoping for him to put a stop to it, but he was nowhere in sight. "Kill him," they shouted. Their voices drowned out all other sounds. I looked again into the man's eyes. The color of his skin had turned pale from the loss of blood. *He is dead already*, I told myself.

With one last deep breath, I bore down with all my strength. The blade missed its mark. I had meant to drive it into the man's skull, but my swing fell to the right. As it landed, it sliced through an ear and lodged itself where the neck meets the shoulder. Blood oozed from the wound, but it did not spatter as I thought it might.

"Good! Again!" Egill said. "Kill him this time!"

Before I could raise the ax again, I heard a chinking of armor approach and the ax's shaft was seized from my hand. It was Eilif. He took the man by the hair and, while jerking upward, chopped at the sides of his neck. After four or five chops, the head lifted from the body, which fell with a muffled thump on the wet sand.

"That is how it is done, Hasting," Eilif said.

"The boy has turned green," Egill said with a thick, raspy laugh.

The others laughed with him. Even the sea, for all her effort, had not made me sick to the point of vomiting. The sight of the severed head sent me into an unstoppable spiral that culminated in the purging of my stomach. I felt my morning meal rise in my chest, and I stumbled toward the ship to lean against its strakes. There, I expelled all that my stomach held. When I looked back up, the crew had returned to their duties as if nothing had happened. By now, most of the men had crossed over the dune. They carried crates of goods—cheese, bread, and wine, as well as some livestock. Not far behind them, the first captured villagers appeared with rope tied around their wrists, led by one of Eilif's men.

"I expect you to scrub that off later," Egill said as he and Eilif boarded the ship.

"Will you put a bag over it or something?" I asked at the sight of the severed head.

Everyone laughed, including Eilif who said, "No, boy. You need to learn to tolerate blood. You say you want to be a Viking? Here you are!"

As the last words left his lips, he tossed the head in my direction. It landed at my feet, then rolled forward toward the shallow waves of the rising tide.

I fainted.

I awoke again to the lap and plash of the oars. It was a soothing sound, and one I had grown to enjoy. The raid seemed a fading dream in my mind, but I knew it had been real. As I opened my eyes, I heard Egill talking in the background with some of the crew. They spoke of all the things they would do with their share of the silver, since it now seemed a near guarantee. The raid had met little resistance, and from the sounds of it, they had razed the village to the ground. I tilted my head to see where I had landed and saw Eilif behind me at the steering paddle.

"Feeling better?" he asked. "You hit your head when you fell. Let Egill take a look at you before you stand."

His concern for my wellbeing surprised me. The man I had witnessed at Bouin was a calloused monster. Here, he acted as a father concerned for his son. When Egill knelt at my side, he felt underneath my neck and lifted my head from the deck.

"Any pain?" he asked.

"No," I said.

Egill nodded and helped me up. "You are all right," he said.

"How can you care so much for me, yet so little for the man whose head you took?" I asked.

The question gave Eilif and Egill pause. Looking back, I wonder what they must have thought of me at that moment. It seemed as if no one had ever posed such a question to them before, as if they had lived a life of acting without thought or care of the effect of their deeds. Egill scratched his head, dumbfounded. Eilif, on the other hand, had an answer I will never forget.

"You are one of us now," he said. "The world is a cruel, unforgiving place. If they had been in our position, those people we killed would not have hesitated to do the same. The best any man can hope to do is look after his own and fight those who would seek to do them harm."

"Besides, we gave them fair warning," Egill said. "The women and children fled, and the men accepted our challenge. It was an honorable fight, and we won."

I sat in silence for the rest of the afternoon to contemplate what I had witnessed and what Eilif and Egill had said. When I'd first met Eilif, he had shown himself to be a peaceful man with trade and wealth on his mind.

Now I knew him as a rover, a Viking, and on that first raid I had not appreciated what it meant.

Within myself I saw two choices: let the shock of it all defeat me, or rise to the occasion and travel the path the gods had chosen for me. After all, I had faced the Great Wolf and lived to tell about it. At least, that was what Egill had said. Courage filled my heart, and I got to my feet. I approached the severed head, which Eilif had placed in a basket two arms' lengths away from him, and stared at it a long while. Eilif watched me with great intrigue.

"Your heart will harden to it," he said.

"It is not the worst sight I have ever seen," I said.

I spoke true. When I examined the head, it seemed a far less horrible fate than that of Eanáir. The sight of her corpse chained to the rock, pecked away by birds and consumed by worms, returned to remind me of where I had been and the horrors I had already witnessed. With a heavy sigh, I reached into the basket, grabbed the blood-soaked head, and raised it up.

"My heart will harden to it," I uttered so only those nearest could hear my words. After a taut moment of silence, I lowered the head, placed a cloth over the basket, and then reached over the gunwale to rinse my hands in the sea.

"I hope to be as brave as you one day," Bjorn said to me while I washed my hands.

His words gave me pause. During the raid, Bjorn had seemed far more confident than I, as if his heart had dulled to the hardships of a Viking's life, but not so. No man is born desiring to fight and kill; such deeds are learned through tribulation and necessity. The first kill is the hardest and the one that marks a man the most. I will never forget the Frank's eyes, nor the pallor in his face, nor the grimace of pain when I severed his ear and split apart his neck and shoulder.

By nightfall, we had not yet reached our camp along the Armorican coast where we were to meet with Nominoë. Instead, we made camp along a sandy beach that curved inward away from the ocean, protected to the north by an outcropping of rock.

We moored the ship and made our tents, but we lit no fires to avoid unwanted attention from the surrounding plains. No one complained of this since it was summer, and the air remained warm throughout the night.

The following day, we left again at the break of dawn and journeyed for half the morning before arriving at our destination. Rather than beaching the ship, Eilif steered close to land and sent men to drive pikes into the ground and rope us in. It was high tide, and the ocean would later recede; if not carefully planned, it could trap the ship on the beach.

"Close enough to load and unload, and far enough to escape," Egill explained. His quips of wisdom never ceased to fascinate me.

We disembarked to make camp again and, most importantly, to build the fire that would alert Nominoë to our return. By midafternoon, the grounds appeared as if we had never left. All that stood apart from our last visit was the one person I hoped I would see again upon our return: Asa. Fewer than two days had passed, and yet my heart yearned to see her, to touch her skin and feel her warmth, and to lock her lips with mine. In a way, I found solace in thinking of her. It helped to ease my mind.

As fate would have it, we indeed met again that day. Not long after our fire roared and spewed a column of smoke toward the other realms, Nominoë arrived at our camp on horseback with Asa on his lap. When she saw me standing by the fire, she leapt from the horse, ran between the pikes, and jumped into my arms for a warm embrace.

"Are you all right? How was the raid?" She patted my shoulders as if to make sure I still had both arms.

"Fine... fine," I said. At first, I remembered that I had been angry with her when we left. But the events of the past two days now made those feelings seem trivial.

"It went well?" she asked.

"We did what we had to do," I said.

"Did you... kill anyone?" she whispered.

"He took a man's head," Bjorn interjected. "Not cleanly, but he did it."

I guessed that Asa would think less of me for what I had done, but to my surprise she smiled and stroked my face. As we spoke, Nominoë stood at the edge of the camp, waiting for someone to invite him in. His men stood close watch behind him with their hands clasped around their spears. Eilif approached the Celts and whistled to get Asa's attention. Nominoë immediately took to talking.

"He asks about the raid," Asa said.

"There were no surprises," Eilif replied.

"He asks you to show proof," she continued.

Egill brought over the basket containing the severed head. Eilif reached in and pulled it out for all to see. Nominoë covered his mouth and nose, as did his soldiers.

"Tell him we also have slaves, and he may speak with them if he so wishes," Eilif stated. Two slaves were brought forward for Nominoë to examine. "Tell him I have already spoken with them, and they are indeed from the island of Bouin."

Nominoë spoke again, but his words were so mumblingly quick that Asa could not translate all of them.

"Nominoë is not accustomed to the sight of blood," she said.

"Did you hear that, Eilif? He can't stand the sight of blood. Poor baby!" Egill exclaimed with his thick, rumbling laugh.

"Tell him I want my silver. I have earned it," Eilif demanded.

When she translated the words, Nominoë nodded. "You will have your silver in the morning," she said.

Nominoë and his men left the camp, but Asa stayed behind for the night. She and I watched the sunset together from the dune. There wasn't a cloud in the sky. It was as if the gods had made the world perfect for us at that moment so our growing affection might blossom into a thriving flower. It was an innocent affection—one we were not yet old enough to take to its full extent. What we felt for each other rivaled the love stories of legendary kings and queens, and even the gods. Our love was destiny, or so we thought.

After we spent the night in each other's arms, Nominoë arrived with a cart containing all the chests of silver he had promised. The men rejoiced at his arrival. Asa and I, however, remained solemn. When the commotion settled and Eilif had what he wanted, the crew set about dismantling the camp. Nominoë called for Asa as he went, and she walked away from me, her hand still holding mine. When our fingers drifted apart, the longing in my heart set in. Halfway through camp, she turned back, ran to me, and held me in one last embrace.

"Promise you will visit me," she whispered. "Promise me you will come back."

"Every summer," I said.

She leaned back to look at me. Her eyes were whirlpools, drawing me in whether I desired it or not. "You will? Every summer?"

I knew I could not promise I would return. Life at sea is hard and dangerous, and often deadly. Yet somehow I knew I would see her again. Nothing in this world or the next would have the power to stop me, I thought. I nodded yes, I would return. She smiled and sauntered backward, then turned away and rejoined Nominoë. She climbed upon his horse, and they rode off into the distance. As I watched them leave, I felt Eilif's presence behind me.

"I can teach you to sail, to trade, and to make war. But to love? That is something you will have to learn on your own," he said. "And whatever you do, don't go looking for advice from Egill. He's clueless."

Our ship left the Armorican coast loaded down with men, silver, and supplies. The atmosphere aboard felt festive. We were conquering heroes returning home from a hard-fought war. Eilif set our course for Jutland, the land of my birth, and the land where he and his men wintered.

It was not my destiny, however, to return to Jutland on that voyage. No, as we sailed from the safety of the land, we soon took sight of sails on the horizon. Ships so far from shore could not be Franks or Celts, and we knew the instant we saw them that they were Northmen.

"How many do you see?" Eilif asked with his hand raised above his eyes to block the sun.

Egill focused his gaze. "I count six."

His words sent a shudder of fear across the deck. The crew knew other Northmen would pose a challenge, and with five hundred pounds of silver in the hold, we risked much. Egill grasped my shoulder and pulled me in front of him. "You have young eyes. How many do you count?"

I stared as hard as I could. The sun made the water glitter like a sea of colorful jewels. It was beautiful, but it also made the ships harder to see. Still, I saw their shadows dancing about in the light and counted them. "Six," I said. "I see six ships."

Eilif's concern showed on his face. He kept his gaze fixed in the distance and ignored the nervous chatter that had gripped the ship. Egill reached below the gunwale and tore off a hunk of bread from one of the loaves the Celts had given us. He sunk his teeth into the crust with a loud crunch and began to chew with loud lip-smacks. Soon the ship fell into a tense silence broken only by the mash and thrash of Egill's chewing.

"Can we outrun them?" I asked.

Egill laughed. "Loaded down as we are? Not a chance," he said half-muffled with a mouthful of bread. As he spoke, a small piece flew from his mouth and landed on my tunic. He reached out with his meaty paw and swatted at my chest to wipe it off.

"Shields on deck!" Eilif commanded. The order surprised the crew. "Mount shields."

Each man drew his shield from below and placed it over the gunwale above his rowing bench where he locked it into place between two wedges nailed to the outboard. The shields covered the ship like dragon scales. Eilif pulled the steering paddle hard to change course for the fleet on the horizon, which he knew would give chase if we tried to outrun them.

A southerly wind helped pull the ship in their direction and toward the setting sun. As Sail Horse glided over the crest and into the trough of each wave, our shields rattled against the strakes. The rattling sounded to me like the low growl of a cornered beast preparing to defend itself.

"When a ship mounts its shields, it is a sign that we will not attack," Egill said. "Mounted shields cannot be used in a fight."

The thought made me squirm. Before us sailed six ships filled with warriors, and our leader had chosen not only to face them but also not to attack. The crew sprang into action, preparing all parts of the ship, and themselves, for a confrontation. We did not know who these men were, yet by virtue of their being Northmen so far from their homeland, their intentions were clear.

Eilif placed me on the steering paddle with the simple instruction to stay true, while he and the others donned their battle garments. Eilif chose to wear his leathers rather than the maille. When I asked him about his choice, he replied, "Maille sinks." At the front of the ship, several of the men had their trousers around their knees and their rumps hanging over the gunwale in the space between the shields and the prow.

"Shit sinks too," Egill laughed. All the others scowled with anxious eyes.

The men cut the throats of the slaves we had taken in Bouin and threw their corpses into the sea. Egill explained to me that their deaths served the dual purpose of sacrificing to the gods and lightening the ship to give us more speed.

"I need your young eyes," Eilif said. He took the steering paddle and pushed me toward the gunwale. "Do you see their sails?"

I nodded yes.

"Which is the biggest?"

Each ship appeared more massive than the last. With our sail and shields in full sight, they had begun to reef their own sails and set their oars to water. We had the wind at our back, and so we had the advantage of speed. They sailed in two formations of three ships. The three at the forefront were about the same length. The three in the rear were different. They were slenderer, longer, and the one in the center was the largest I had ever seen. I did not have time to count, but there must have been at least thirty rowing benches on each side of it. I pointed to the largest among them for Eilif to see.

"That's him," Eilif said.

"Who?" I asked.

"Their leader," Egill replied. "Our only chance to survive this meeting is to bargain with him. Then, at least, his followers may spare us."

Eilif steered us toward the gap between the first three ships. We passed close to one of them, perhaps an arm's reach, and its captain stood tall on the prow. He wore a dull green surcoat over a simple brown tunic, and his long dark hair was tied in a single knot behind his head. The look on his face was one of utter surprise, exacerbated by Eilif who gave him a friendly wave with a grin.

"I know that man," Egill said when he caught sight of the other ship's captain. "Yes, that is my cousin Bjarni! By the gods, this must be Jarl Thorgísl's fleet!"

"Friend or foe?" Eilif asked.

"Depends. Thorgísl is a complicated man," Egill said.

"Will he hear us out?" Eilif asked, and Egill nodded. "Reef the sail!" he barked. Three men sprang from their rowing benches to undo the knots and pull down the sail. They worked with precision and speed, and as the sail lumbered down the mast, the ship slowed. Eilif shouted again, "Dismount shields! Lock oars!"

I heard the booming scuffle of wood grinding on wood as the men drew out the oars and slid them through the oarlocks. They locked them in place, hovering above the water to be plunged in at Eilif's command. They sat in silence, awaiting the next order from their chieftain.

The enemy ships circled like a hungry pack of wolves. On the prow of their largest vessel stood a man with long black hair that flowed from underneath an iron helmet. He had a long, sharp nose and a maille skirt around his nape. His beard sat on his chest in a single braid held together by two silver rings. Above him stood a magnificent dragonhead with carved scales and a gaping mouth with sharp white fangs and a bright red tongue. The ship rowed to meet ours, and once they were upon us, the man on the prow spoke.

"Greetings, friends," he declared.

Eilif passed the steering paddle to me once more and ambled to the gunwale to reply. "I am Eilif, son of Harald."

"I am Thorgísl, son of Bíldr." He adjusted his footing to stand a little taller as his ship maneuvered to place him in our line of sight. His crew threw hooks over our gunwale and pulled our ship up against theirs. The waves increased in depth and number, which made the ships rock violently back and forth. "Tell me Eilif, son of Harald, where have you come from?"

"We raided some islands on the coast," Eilif explained.

"Find anything of value?" Thorgísl asked.

"Nothing. The coast here has been raided many times by our kin. We have nothing to show for our raids, if you intended to challenge us for our plunder."

"That was my intention," Thorgísl stated. "Do you expect me to believe you have set sail for the North empty-handed?"

"Thorgísl—" Eilif began before he was interrupted.

"Please, call me Thor."

"Very well, Thor," Eilif said, choosing each of his words with great care. "My second in command, Egill, says he knows you by reputation, and that you are an honorable and ambitious man."

The compliment pleased Thor. He smiled with yellow, crooked teeth and said, "I am."

"If you are a fair man, as Egill has said, then you will see no reason to keep us, and you will allow us to return to our homes in Jutland," Eilif said.

"Do you think me a fool?" Thor asked. He signaled to his men who approached the gunwale and prepared to board us. "I can clearly see your ship is weighed down in the water. What are you hiding from me, Eilif, son of Harald?"

Eilif looked down at the water below him and sighed.

"That is what I thought," Thor said. "And I challenge you for it."

"Wait… wait!" Eilif said. "You have six ships, and many men. We do not have enough silver to share among all of them. Surely you will want to know where we found our wealth to fill your own ships."

"I am listening," Thor said.

I looked to Eilif and shook my head. I did not want him to tell Thor about Nominoë. Asa lived among the Celts, and if Thor raided Vannes, it would put her in danger. Eilif whispered to Egill, who whispered back.

"We will take you there," Eilif said to Thor. "It is a city called Nantes."

Thor laughed. "Nantes? Our people have never raided a city of that size. You are lying."

"We are not," Egill said. "On my honor I swear, we came by our wealth through trade in Nantes. That is what we are—traders, not raiders."

Thor thought for a moment and disappeared behind his men. When he climbed up onto the gunwale at the prow again, he pointed to the sky and said, "My seer cast the runes and says you speak the truth."

Eilif's confidence found him again. "We have traded for many years in the city. We know it well," he said.

"You know a way in, then?" Thor asked.

Eilif nodded and said, "We do."

Thor stroked his beard in thought. He looked around at his fleet and considered Eilif's proposition. He had evidently not planned out where he would take his fleet to raid. I could see the greed in his eyes as he imagined the riches that awaited him in a city as large as Nantes, but I also saw trepidation and uncertainty.

He looked to his men and said, "Do we try it?" The deck of his ship erupted in excited chatter. Once the chatter ceased, he spoke again. "How will we split the plunder?"

"Nantes is so full of riches that we will not need to think of how to split the wealth," Eilif said. "And it is enough for me to keep what I have on my own ship."

Thor looked to the clear sky above and took in a deep breath. He raised his hands as if to thank the gods and laughed. "You know the way?" he asked.

Eilif replied, "I do—and I know how to pass the fortified bridge."

5

Into the Fire

Thor commanded Eilif to turn about and sail for the Frankland coast to lead his fleet to Nantes. Although we had made a good bargain with him, the crusty old jarl from Ireland made it no secret that he distrusted us in every way. For now, at least, we were alive. The journey gave us time to think and to prepare. Most of the men kept quiet, as they always did, waiting to hear of the plan that might let them live and keep their silver too—it was their only concern. Eilif stood motionless at the aft of his ship, his gaze distant and contemplative, and he said nothing until the white beaches of Frankland appeared on the eastern horizon.

"I do not like this arrangement," Egill said with exasperation. "Nantes is impregnable. Their walls are too tall and too well defended. We will die if we try to take it." He took a sloppy bite out of a slice of herring and smacked his lips as he chewed and talked.

"I have no intention of attacking Nantes," Eilif said. "But, without a bargain, Thor would have killed us and taken our wealth."

"Bah!" Egill voiced in frustration.

"We should not make an enemy of Thor," Eilif cautioned. "He's a powerful man in Ireland, even more than Hagar."

"I do not wish to be his ally, either," Egill said. "I will not swear to him."

"Perhaps we should swear," Eilif proposed.

Their talk of swearing intrigued me. This was my first voyage at sea, and my first crew, and I did not yet grasp Eilif and Egill's meaning. In time, I learned the importance of oath-taking in the fabric of our culture, especially among warriors. An oath binds a man to his lord, whether he is a jarl, a ship's captain, or a friend, and a man who upholds his oaths earns wealth and reputation. Oath-breakers face the wrath of the gods, whose judgment befalls them however the oath-keeper sees fit, but usually by the sword or ax. The Aesir, our gods, swore oaths to one another, and it formed the fabric of their laws; so too do the oaths of men make the fabric of our laws. An oath, I have since learned, is the most divine gift a man can give to another.

"No," Egill snapped back. "I did not come here to become someone else's chattel! I own land in Jutland... and have a title."

"We are not in Jutland, and Thor's noose is tight around our necks," Eilif lamented.

"What do we do? We have promised him Nantes. How will we deliver it to him?" Egill asked.

"Thor's fleet cannot pass the fortified bridges," Eilif said. "One ship with a generous bribe, yes, but seven? No amount of silver could pay for it. We will need to find another way."

"What if we don't take them to Nantes?" I proposed.

"You mean take them to another city?" Egill asked.

"No. Eilif said a ship can pass the bridge with a bribe. What if we were that ship?" I proposed.

"And Thor's fleet would be trapped downriver," Eilif mused.

"Precisely," I said.

Both Eilif and Egill raised their weary heads to look at me, their faces filled with intrigue. I was a ship's boy, and it was my duty to be quiet, to scrub the decks, and to cook for the crew. At least, that is what most ship captains would have expected of me, but Eilif was no ordinary captain. He had seen something in me, something unique, something I could not see, and whatever it was, it allowed me to move about the ship freely, to speak openly, and to join in the discussions between Eilif and Egill. Perhaps it was the wolf. They feared the wolf, and on occasion I sensed they feared me.

"He's right," Egill chuckled. "The damned kid is right! Eilif, if you tell the Franks to sink Thor's fleet, will they do it?"

"I am not certain," Eilif grumbled. "Although I have met the captain of the guard, Landry. He and I know each other through Váli."

"If you tell him what's happened and fill his pockets with silver, he may let us through," Egill said. "It could work!"

"All right," Eilif said.

He pulled the steering paddle toward his breast to direct the ship on a more southerly course. Thor's fleet steered to match us. When we reached the mouth of the river, the men set their oars to water and rowed. Thor's ship, with more men and more oars, rowed hard to close the gap between us.

Eilif ordered our men to ease their pace to allow him to catch us, for he sensed the man wished to have words before entering Frankland. When our ships glided upriver, the sound of the ocean wind and waves fell behind, replaced by a cacophony of chirping crickets, singing birds, and croaking frogs. The riverbanks were alive.

"These look like good farming lands," Thor said, his ship now parallel with ours. His voice boomed across the river and, for a moment, the riverbank fell silent.

"The farmers trade upriver from here," Eilif told him.

"You have a plan to breach the city?" Thor's eyes grew suspicious. He rolled his lower lip and bit at the dry skin. I had seen Hagar do this as well, and I knew it meant he felt uneasy.

"I do," Eilif said.

"Tell me," Thor said.

"My ship will take the lead and tie off on the riverbank. I will attempt to bribe the captain of the guard, and if he takes it, I will call for you," Eilif explained.

"And if he does not take it?" Thor asked.

"We will retreat and meet with you to discuss a new plan," Eilif said.

We remained silent from that moment forward, for our voices carried far on the river. It was evident from his questions that Thor did not trust us, and he even seemed to suspect our plan. We saw no other boats or barges as we rowed, not until we reached the fortified bridge.

On our first visit to Nantes, Egill had told me about the Frankish bridges. He had been raiding since the early days when Northmen first set about roving the lands in the West. He recalled a time when the bridges were impenetrable, designed to repel foreign raiders from the ocean who sought to plunder the principal cities of the empire. The bridges still stood, but strife among the Franks meant there were fewer soldiers to man and maintain them, and most had fallen into disrepair.

This one was no different. It was a bulwark of wooden planks and earth, flanked by a stone watchtower on each riverbank, and built upon five linking wooden arches. Any ship that wished to pass had to pay a toll, or else the guards would place timbers along the span to block passage. From the ramparts, the soldiers could hurl fiery arrows, oil, and rocks at the ships below.

As we approached, it was apparent that the Franks had already spotted our fleet and set timbers across the span of archways. We saw the Franks' polished iron helmets glittering in the afternoon sunlight as they stood watch over the river from their protected perch upon the bridge. Eilif had never seen the Franks so weary, and it made him nervous.

He signaled to Thor to keep his distance while he steered our ship to the shore below the bridge. Fifteen soldiers formed a defensive wall along the riverbank with round iron shields that covered them from throat to knee. They wore full maille shirts with thick blue cloaks tied at the shoulder of their dominant arm. One of them shouted down to us in their language.

Eilif raised his hands and replied to them. I surmised he explained our plan, who we were, and what the men who accompanied us hoped to accomplish. They listened, and when he approached them alone, they dropped their shields to the ground. A few pieces of silver later, and they were laughing together. Eilif evidently had kept his wit and charm even in their language, a skill that made me envious at the time.

When he descended the small slope of the riverbank, he jumped over the gunwale and ordered the men to row the ship toward the central archway. Using heavy iron winches on the bridge, the Franks lifted the timber to let us pass. Thor's fleet rowed to follow, but stopped when the timber fell back into place behind us.

"Eilif!" Thor called out, but we ignored him and rowed on.

I watched as the six ships under Thor's command maneuvered to turn around, and I heard the screams of his men as arrows filled their decks. The boat closest to the bridge stalled in the water, their oars motionless as the men aboard raised their shields to block the next Frankish volley. The Franks poured boiling oil over the bulwark onto the ship's deck, and a flaming arrow ignited a hellish blaze.

Screams of pain and horror followed. Just when we thought we were safe, fifty horsemen—ironclad from head to toe in maille and long blue surcoats checked with black —galloped in from the countryside. When they caught sight of us drifting in the river on the wrong side of the bridge, they assumed we had snuck past the defenses. They turned hard on their steeds and ran with us along the edge of the riverbank. Half of them wore crossbows on their backs, strapped over their shoulders with leather harnesses.

When they dismounted and stared us down through their arrow shafts, I saw they aimed to kill us. The arrows that struck our ship did not float like an arrow fired from a bow. These flew straight and cut through the men like a bear's claw through flesh. From the aft of the ship, it appeared as though a strong gust of wind had blown over the deck. Men crawled on the floor, reaching for their shields and weapons. Sail Horse's deck was stained red as if we had sunk into a river of blood. We all dropped to our stomachs, wounded or not, to stay clear of the next volley.

"At least we are rid of Thor," Egill chuckled. He always joked when he felt afraid.

Another volley soon struck the strakes and parts of the deck. The arrows sounded like a thousand woodpeckers working all at once to extract their next meal from the same tree. After the volley—silence.

"We need to get clear of here," Eilif whispered.

As soon as the words left his lips, hooks clunked over the gunwale and, pulled back by thick ropes, locked into place. The Franks dragged the ship to shore and aimed their crossbows at us. This time, they did not fire. They screamed at us, and at that moment, I wished for the river to swallow our ship and drown us all.

Eilif replied to them, his hands held over his head. He pleaded with them, but the men who had arrived on horseback did not seem keen to negotiate. When I looked back at our ship, all but half a dozen men still lived. Panic gripped me at that moment, and I felt a powerful urge to run. My leg twitched as if it had decided to start running without me. Before I could stop myself, I bolted over the gunwale and ran as hard as I could away from our captors.

As I ran, I felt a sting, then a warm dribble running down my leg. At first, I thought I had pissed in my trousers. When I looked down, I saw a crossbow bolt protruding from my leg a finger's width away from my groin.

"They shot me in the ass!" I managed to say before fainting and hitting the ground.

I awoke to a woman with long black hair dabbing at my wound with a wet cloth. Still dazed, I thought for an instant that I had died, and Eanáir had sought me out in the afterlife. Instinctively, I squirmed. The woman spoke softly to calm me down. She looked at me with soft brown eyes that creased at the edges when she smiled. Her gentle touch put me at ease, if for a moment.

It was then I looked at the ceiling and the four walls around me and saw that I lay on my side in a stone dungeon on a small cot made of hay and which stunk of horse droppings. The woman caressed my head and left the room. When the door closed, I reached for my wound and felt it with my fingers. Someone had stitched both where the bolt had entered my flesh and where it had come out again, and covered both ends with a sticky ointment.

No sooner had I leaned back to relax when the door swung open again, and through it walked three men. Two wore the attire of Frankish soldiers, with iron maille glittering beneath blue and black surcoats. Another wore a

black habit with a golden rope tied at his waist. The few
rays of sunlight that passed through the small barred
window opposite the door gleamed off his bald head. He
knelt at my side and took my hand in his. He spoke to me,
and though I did not know his language, I gathered from
his tone and expression that he had ill news to deliver. It
dawned on me that I was in a foreign land where I did not
speak the language, and I was alone.

An intense wave of fear gripped me, and I
squirmed backward against the stone wall of my cell, my
heart pounding and my fingers digging into the straw
mattress. The Franks sensed my fear, and the man in the
black habit whispered words of comfort in a tone that did,
for a moment at least, help to calm my nerves. I still feared
him and what he had planned for me.

When they left the room and shut the door, I
scurried to my feet as best I could and made for the
window. I gripped its stony ledge and pulled myself high
enough to look outside. The window overlooked an
enclosed courtyard, flanked on all sides by lime and
mortar walls. In the center of the yard was a large log with
a wood-cutting ax's blade planted in it. Men in iron
shackles sat in a line across the far wall, and among them I
saw Bjorn, Eilif, and Egill.

"Psst!" I whispered to them. Their heads remained
lowered over their chests. "Psst!" I whispered a little
louder.

Egill raised his eyes and scanned the courtyard. He
waved to say that he had heard me, but he also did not
want to draw attention to himself. I fell back into my cell.
The landing sent a sharp pain through my leg, and I
hobbled back to my cot. The air in the chamber was stale,
and they had left me no water to drink or food to eat. It
could have been worse—it was the end of summer, and the
stifling heat outside was made tolerable by the cell's cold
stone walls. I waited a long time for someone to visit, to

bring me food, or to help me escape. The gods answered my wishes.

A young servant girl, perhaps a few years older than me, entered the chamber at dusk. Her hazel hair fell to her mid-back, and the light blue gown she wore hugged her waist. In her hands, she carried a wooden platter with pewter plates, and on the plates were thin slices of chicken and steamed carrots and leeks. A hunk of fresh bread filled the room with its sweet smell, and my stomach felt as though it would leap from my throat to devour the meal.

When the girl saw me for what I was, she hesitated. With steady hands and a graceful bow, she lowered the platter to the ground and walked back through the door with her eyes fixed on me the entire time.

When the door closed, I hobbled to the plate and dug into the food. The herbs they had used on the chicken were like none I had ever tasted—basil, marjoram, tarragon, and a touch of lavender—a mixture I later learned the Franks use often. To wash it all down, they had given me a small saucer of watered-down cider. The taste was bitter, but it was better than nothing.

For days, this ritual continued. The man in the black habit visited me and spoke to me in his language, and each time it seemed he had more anguish in his eyes. After his visit, the servant girl delivered my meal, and each time she left the room in the same way, with vigilant eyes and far too much caution. It was as if they had captured a wounded stray dog in the city, but no one had the heart to put it down.

Outside, the men who had survived the bridge crossing rotted in their irons under a boiling sun during the day and in biting cold at night. Each day, they seemed to wither more and sink into the dirt.

Our misery continued until, on a day after I had lost count, I heard a commotion in the courtyard. I gripped the edge of the window, pulled myself up to look, and saw

Nominoë in his burgundy cloak and beautiful silks standing over the men in irons. Two of his own men stood at his back wearing padded gambesons with light burgundy and dark green surcoats, and they carried oblong shields at their sides that covered them from neck to ankle. We were saved, I thought. I could not have been more wrong.

A tall, square-jawed man with a thick black brow and straight black hair just long enough to cover his ears approached and screamed at Nominoë. He wore a long purple cape that glided above the ground as he walked, and underneath it he wore a shirt of light iron scales girded by a thick leather belt. Around his neck hung a silver pendant of the same cross Egill had made me wear in Nantes.

As he turned red in the face from shouting, two soldiers marched up from behind him, each carrying a massive wooden chest. When they cracked the chests open, silver coins spilled into the dirt. The Frankish man knelt and picked up one of the coins, and he pointed at it with even angrier shouts. Something told me that the Franks had found our silver, and the silver led back to Nominoë.

Shouts turned into fists, and a brawl broke out. The Celtic soldiers encircled their leader with their shields, and they pointed their spears at every man who approached them. During the standoff, I heard footsteps scuttling above my cell, and I saw several men on the battlements of the far wall with crossbows aimed down at the courtyard. As soon as they took aim, one of them fell from his perch and thudded on the ground with an arrow protruding from his back.

I lost my grip and fell back into my cell. Although I could not see, I heard the sounds of steel hitting steel, the scuffling of men struggling to kill one another, and the cries of agony of the men who lost the struggle. I gripped the ledge to look again, but a stray arrow glanced off the iron bars and nearly took off my head, so I retreated to my cot to wait in silence.

More shouts filled the courtyard, and the sounds of battle raged. Someone banged at my door, which sent me into a fit of terror, and with nothing to defend myself, I huddled in the far corner of the cell where the shadows were darkest. After several more bangs, the door swung open, and its iron lock flew across the chamber. A large man leapt inside. I took one look at him and realized it was Eilif. He had bloodied marks on his wrists and ankles, and he smelled like a cesspit.

"Can you walk?" he asked.

I nodded.

"Come!"

I stood as quickly as I could, but my wound still ached and made me limp. Eilif took my hand and dragged me into the corridor. We fled through a thick wooden door into the surrounding countryside. I looked back at the building that had kept me prisoner—it was nothing more than an old, dilapidated fort, too ancient to have been built by the Franks or the Celts, with stone walls crumbling at the sides and moss growing in every crack and crevice. It leaned over the edge of the river and looked as if it needed no more than a small push from a giant of Jotunheim to fall into the water.

We met a few of the other survivors in the woods beyond the clearing around the fort. Egill had escaped with some of the crew—how, I cannot say. They were fierce old Vikings, and it would take more than a few days in chains to break them. To my relief, Bjorn stood among them, shaken but alive.

Together we ran deeper into the thick forest of oak, beech, and pine north of the river where we hoped to find our way to Celtic lands. We trudged through thick underbrush of thorns and sharp leaves that cut and scraped our flesh with every step. After half a day's march, we found a clearing to rest. Near the clearing was an old cobbled road made of dark grey stones covered in white and green mosses. It looked ancient, and it crumbled at the edges where the ground had risen up to swallow parts of it.

"The Roman road," Eilif said. "It leads to Vannes. But we must be cautious. Troops use these roads."

"Roman?" I asked.

Eilif explained to me what he knew of the Romans. He said they were an ancient people, perhaps as old as the Aesir, our gods, and they had ruled Midgard from the frozen lands in the North to the burning deserts of the South. They had built roads to connect all of their provinces—for trade, for war, and for travel.

We Northmen have little memory of the Romans, but the Franks know them well enough. Charlemagne, the Frankish emperor's father, was a man obsessed with emulating their greatness, and he had employed men to uncover the mysteries of their past. They came from a shining city called Rome, where they had built towers that reached for the sky and palaces that spanned the stars. Men, Eilif said, had never been so wealthy and powerful, not before, and not since.

As we walked the road toward Vannes, I dreamed of these majestic Romans. I imagined their towers and palaces glittering with gold under the shadow of Asgard, and their roads stretching across our world from Rome like strands of hair from a woman's head, all leading back to the center. My dreams helped me escape the aching in my leg and feet. That night we did not build a fire, for it would have drawn too much attention. Even if we had wanted a fire, we had nothing but the rags on our backs with which to make one.

At the break of dawn, a light frost covered the trees and underbrush. Even the animals still slept, and the land was eerily silent. Not until the sun had fully risen above the horizon did we hear the crow of a rooster on a nearby farm.

With no weapons, we dared not follow his call to kill and eat him. Instead, we took to the road and walked in single file. We walked and walked, and I remember how badly my feet hurt, and how my arms and legs itched, and how the wound in my leg began to swell. With each step, my thighs rubbed together against the stitches. At first, it was no bother, but after two days of walking, I could not bear it.

By the afternoon of the second day, I had a strong fever and no strength to continue. The pain grew so intense that I lost consciousness in the middle of the road. I remember nothing of the journey from there, but Egill told me later that Eilif carried me over his shoulder all the way to Vannes. I remember the torch fires at night, the swarm of soldiers who greeted us, and the brief image of Nominoë's face as he leaned in to feel my breath, to see if I was still alive.

I was alive, but barely.

6

The Land of the Celts

I awoke to the sound of a knife chiseling a plank of wood with smooth strokes and sharp knocks. When I opened my eyes, I found Eilif sitting by my side on a short wooden stool that creaked when he shifted his body. He held a knife and a thick hunk of wood. The wood had no particular shape. He carved it forcefully, his eyes inextricably focused on his task. His tunic was covered in dust and wood shavings. The whittling kept him busy—so busy that he did not immediately notice that my eyes had opened.

I examined where I was before speaking, and saw that I had been placed in a bed with fresh straw and linens in a large room with other such beds, though the rest were empty. The walls and ceiling were made of dark wood, and there were no windows. Next to my bed stood a silver oil lamp that kept the room lit just enough for me to see.

"The boy lives!" Eilif said when he saw me scanning the room. He placed the knife and wood on the table beside the lamp and reached to grab me by the shoulders. "I knew it would take more than that to kill you."

"How long have I—" I began to ask.

"Two days," he said. "Egill will be pleased to see you. He sat here with you last night until your fever broke."

"Is it day or night?"

"There is daylight left for us to enjoy. Do you feel strong enough to walk?" he asked.

I nodded. My first instinct was to feel my leg, which I did, and the swelling and puss and stink had all gone. Someone had washed me, cleaned out my wound, and clothed me in baggy brown trousers and a simple tunic. My thigh felt stronger, and the stitches had begun to meld into my skin. I sat up slowly and moved my legs over the edge of the bed. My feet met with a cold stone floor.

"I almost forgot," Eilif said. He reached down and slipped my feet into simple leather shoes. "The Celts are excellent leatherworkers. See?" He lifted his foot onto the bed to display a clean leather shoe with green laces. The grin on his face was infectious.

"Where are we?" I asked.

"Far from the Franks, and safe from other Northmen... for now. Come, there are others who wish to see you," he said.

I walked with the gait of an old man. The rubbing of my thighs still stung, so I lifted my trousers high to wedge the fabric between my leg and my groin. It looked odd, but it was comfortable. Eilif opened a door on the far end of the room which let in a flood of daylight.

The brightness blinded me at first, but my eyes adjusted. I stepped out onto the wooden boardwalk of the city and found that the building where I had slept stood next to the small stone church where we had waited for the Celts to pray during our last visit.

The infirmary had a large wooden cross on the front, which to me meant it must have belonged to the church. We walked to Nominoë's hall and stood before the front entrance. The guards seemed to know Eilif and waved us through. The way I remember it, the lower level was a maze of small, low-ceilinged rooms, one after the other. This time, we took a stairway to the second level. It

THE LORDS OF THE WIND

had vaulted ceilings propped up by massive wooden beams and a deep hearth on the far wall. Three long, wooden tables squared off with the fireplace—two faced each other, and the third linked them together across from the hearth.

At the center table sat a man, alone, with his nose buried in a pile of thin, cloth-like sheets with mysterious inscriptions etched upon them.

"Greetings," the man said in the language of the Danes without looking up. It was Nominoë. "Sit, please."

"He speaks our language now?" I whispered to Eilif.

"Only a little," he said. "But he learns quickly."

We sat beside Nominoë at the table across from the hearthstone. Two men entered the hall behind us with wood in their arms, and they set about building a fire. The room was cold, and I welcomed their efforts to keep us warm. We sat in silence at first—it seemed Nominoë had run out of things to say in our language. He turned to face us, his demeanor light and welcoming. A few more servants placed carafes and platters of bread and cheese on the table, and as soon as Eilif gave me an approving nod, I ate like a starved wolf pup.

"Don't forget to breathe," Eilif said with a chuckle.

As I ate, several more people entered the hall, though I must admit I ignored them in favor of eating—until two soft hands perfumed with lavender covered my eyes, and a sweet voice said, "You have one guess, and you had better get it right."

"Asa!" I said with more excitement than I had felt in days.

She sat beside me, her arm still around my shoulder, and she gave me a smile that made my heart skip a beat. She wore a thin black habit with a hood stitched into the collar that hung down her back. Her hair was tied in a single braid, and she had washed since we had last met, which revealed her soft, pale skin. She took one look at me and laughed.

"What?" I said with a mouthful of cheese and bread.

Before we could spend any time together, Nominoë called for her. He spoke to her in his language, and she translated his words. "How are you feeling?" she asked.

"I feel all right," I said. Curious about what lay before him on the table, I looked at Nominoë and asked, "What are those?"

"They are parchments," he said. "Have you never seen parchments before?"

"No."

"You do not write to each other in the Far North?" Nominoë asked. He appeared dumbfounded.

"We have runes," Eilif said. "But they are not writing as you know it."

"And books? Have you seen any of those?" Nominoë asked.

I scratched my head and said, "No."

Nominoë tugged on Asa's habit, and she scurried from the hall, leaving us in utter silence. Soon she returned with a sizable leather-bound box filled with these parchments. She placed it on the table in front of me and opened it to reveal hundreds of parchments covered edge to edge with interlocked symbols.

"This is a book," she said. "You know how skalds sing of men's deeds?"

I nodded.

"Here, they write them down in books, and they preserve the deeds so that others may read them and learn of their ancestors."

I marveled at the book. Skalds may have recited the deeds of men, but they died, and the stories that passed onto other skalds changed. Books, I realized, do not forget, and do not die, and can hold the deeds of men forever. I thought back to my father's words that a reputation does not die. Here, I saw for the first time how that could be true. "Can you write?" I asked Asa.

"I am learning," she said.

Nominoë cut into the conversation and said, "Now that the boy appears to have recovered, when will you leave? A boat is ready at the docks. She does not have the speed of one of yours, but she'll get you home. We Vennetes are a proud seafaring people too."

"Tell him *thank you*," Eilif said. He then turned to me and glowered. "What happens next will not be easy. Egill and I will sail home to Jutland. You must stay here. Nominoë wants a hostage to guarantee we will return. The Franks have uncovered our alliance, and he fears they may also seek an alliance with other Northmen... with Thor."

I gulped. "A hostage?"

"They will take good care of you. It is to give the Celts a guarantee. We like you, boy; we will not leave you here forever. I look upon you as I would look upon my own son." He reached out and presented me with the misshapen piece of wood I had seen him whittle earlier. "It is a wolf. At least, that is what I wanted to make. It is to remind you of who you are."

"A Viking?" I asked.

Eilif smiled and said, "Not just any Viking; you faced the great wolf Fenrir and lived to tell the tale. Your destiny is entwined with that of the gods—of that, I am sure."

Nominoë cleared his throat in an apparent attempt to draw our attention and asked, "When will you begin your journey home?"

"Tell him we will leave at first light," Eilif said.

Nominoë nodded. He and Asa remained while Eilif and I left the table for the docks. The journey there was slow, but Eilif showed great patience with me. The piers of the city extended out from a flat, sandy beach that reached into the ocean alongside a sandbar at the mouth of the River Marle. Numerous boats, most of them weighed down with long fishing nets, floated over calm waters.

Vannes' coastline was part of a wide gulf called the Morbihan, with several nearby islands that shielded the city from violent storms known to strike the coast of Armorica. The Morbihan's narrow entrance and the islands within it made it a maze to navigate, which explained why, of all the coastal settlements in the region, Vannes had never been raided by Northmen.

As we approached the docks, I caught sight of Egill sitting along the edge of the nearest pier. His feet dangled above a small sailboat with room for no more than a half-dozen men. When he saw us approach, he hopped to his feet.

"There he is!" he said with open arms. He leaned in to embrace me and squeezed me against his chest. His beard smelled of sardines. "The gods almost gave me a reason to doubt them. The healer said you flirted with death more than once during the night."

"I am happy to see you," I said. I meant it. Egill may have been a fearsome-looking warrior, but he was a friend to me, and a kind one with a soft heart.

"He knows?" Egill asked Eilif.

"He does. He will stay," Eilif said.

"Do not worry, Hasting. When we reach Jutland and tell them of the wealth there is to be earned here, warriors will jump at the opportunity to follow us," Egill said.

"We will return," Eilif emphasized. "Do your best to learn all you can about the Celts and the Franks while you are here."

"I will," I said. "What about Bjorn?"

Eilif ran his hand across his nose and wiped it on his tunic. "Bjorn is my nephew," he said. "If I do not take him home, my sister will have my head on a spike."

Bjorn, who had listened from behind, inched toward me and said, "I owe you my life. One day, I hope, we will meet again."

"One last thing," Eilif said with a grin. "I told the Celts you are my son. It makes you more valuable to them as a hostage. You should not tell Asa, as trustworthy as she may seem, that you are not."

His words gave me pause. "You are the closest I have ever had to a father," I told him.

"Be wary of who you trust," he said. "You are in a strange land, among strange people. They will always call you an outsider, no matter how close they may feel to you."

"I understand. Do you have another ship in Jutland?" I asked.

"I have some friends who can help me build a new one, but it will take time... a year at least, if we have the silver to pay the shipbuilders. My wife has silver from last summer, and I think it will be enough... if she hasn't spent it all on clothes and perfume."

Eilif had never mentioned his wife before. If he had a wife, perhaps he had children, so I asked him, "Do you have a family in Jutland?"

"Only my wife. I had a son..." he said. For the first time, I saw a tear stream down his cheek. He cleared his throat and continued, "He is in Valhalla."

Egill put a hand on Eilif's shoulder to comfort him. He looked at me broodingly and said, "Stay alive."

"I will," I said.

Though I spoke with a confident tone, I had a sinking feeling in the pit of my stomach. Staying meant more time with Asa, but it also meant living far away from my people. I would indeed be an outcast, a wanderer in a foreign land with no home and no one to support me in times of need. For all I knew, Nominoë might lock me away as Hagar had done, and the thought made me restless. Eilif may have given me a carving of a wolf to remind me of who I was, but I began to question whether I had ever known.

When Eilif, Egill, and the few remaining crewmen left for the open sea, I expected Nominoë's demeanor toward me to change, but it did not. To my surprise, he welcomed me into his home, gave me a room with a hearth, fed me three meals a day, and allowed me to explore the city on my own, or with Asa. For the first few days, I followed Asa like a stray pup, always trailing at her heels wherever she went. I relied on her to communicate with the Celts for all my needs. She did not mind; in fact, she seemed to enjoy having me around, for I suspect she too felt out of place among the Celts.

She was still a mystery to me, and I had little knowledge of her past or how she had come to thieve in the streets of Nantes, but during those first few days, I did not dare ask her about it for fear of angering her. I could not afford to be abandoned yet, not until I learned the Celtic tongue. Asa taught me some words and phrases, but it was Nominoë who plunged me into their language and culture. He assigned me to work with the servants who cleaned and organized his house. They had no patience for me, and I had to learn their language, at least enough to know what they wanted me to do, as quickly as possible. His methods worked.

Within less than a fortnight, I had learned to listen and to speak comfortably. The more I learned, the more Nominoë involved me in his activities. He invited me to read with him and talk about the North, and I appreciated that he learned from me as much as I learned from him. When he taught me a Celtic word, he asked me to speak it back to him in my language. On occasion, we mixed the languages when talking to each other to be more precise, and it made us laugh.

The more I saw of Nominoë, the less I saw of Asa. She lived in what they called a convent. They described it to me as a place for women with no family and no prospect for a husband—a haven from the wiles of men who might otherwise have preyed on a young woman such as Asa. Christians, I learned, are particular in regard to the relations between men and women. With Asa occupied elsewhere, I spent more of my time with the Celts, which allowed me to master their language and culture.

Nominoë was a creature of habit. He awoke at the same time each day, read parchments in the morning while eating his first meal—often an apple and a few boiled eggs —and prayed at Mass before noon. He spent his afternoons reading parchments sent to him from other parts of Armorica and issuing orders through couriers who spent their lives on horseback. In the late afternoon, he trained with his fighting men to keep his blade skills sharp and to prepare for a Frankish attack.

"An invasion looms," he said every day, and he believed it. He included me more and more in these exercises, but his soldiers regarded me with suspicion, so I tended to watch. In the evenings, he conducted more of the business of governing his kingdom and retired to bed after his last meal of the day. In some of these things, he invited me to observe and to learn. He encouraged me to learn to read. When he conducted the most important business of the kingdom, he sent me to the church to help the head priest, a man named Conwoïon, to clean and organize for the next Mass. The most important task, according to the priest, was to make candles.

Winters in Armorica were dark and harsh, but writing still had to be done. I spent many days dipping wicks into wax. The first few candles I made were either too thin or too fat, but I soon had a rhythm and made candles that were more or less the same size. I saw my candles everywhere—in the church, in the infirmary, on Nominoë's table, and even in the taverns. At least I knew the work I did had a purpose, and I felt a certain satisfaction in that.

My first winter in Vannes, I spent at least half of my days learning to read. In the cold, the dark, and the rain, almost everyone stays indoors, except for those who tend the fields and gather firewood. I was not asked to toil with the peasants because, as Conwoïon said more than once, "Nominoë wants to gain your favor so that when you inherit your father's kingdom, you will look kindly upon Armorica."

Reading required that I study yet another language, called Latin, which I learned was the language of the Romans, the ancient people Eilif had told me about who had built the roads. If I wished to know more about them, I needed to read in their language.

Reading gave me access to some of the books in Nominoë's private collection, which he kept in a room called a library. He had an extensive collection of one hundred books, some short and others impossibly long. Some of the books in his library he had brought home from his travels, and others were copies of tomes written by monks on the history of Armorica. Conwoïon also had a small library; he said the largest he had ever seen was in Rome, where a man called the Pope lived. Conwoïon pleaded with me to read his favorite book, the Bible. I struggled with it; even when I understood Latin reasonably well, it made less sense to me than the other books.

There were other children, high-born sons and daughters of the lords of the Vannetais, but they shunned me. Their parents forbade me from studying with them, so Conwoïon had to teach me in private.

He took a liking to me, and he often told me that I had an unsurpassed thirst for knowledge, particularly for the past. He had never seen a boy my age learn Latin so fast. The other boys he taught preferred to play rather than learn. Conwoïon lamented that their high-born status made them challenging pupils. My curiosity, he found, was refreshing. I enjoyed our discussions, for I could learn only so much from reading. My language skills were not yet at the level needed to entirely grasp what some of the histories contained, so Conwoïon filled in the missing parts for me. It was through him that I learned the most profound truths about Armorica and the people who lived there. Many were not from Armorica initially.

Centuries before my birth, the Romans had ruled the world, but their empire crumbled from years of sin and decay. Their strongholds in Britain fell to Saxon invaders, and the survivors of the conquest abandoned their homes and fled across the sea to Armorica. Those who had escaped Britain were called the Britons, and they settled in the North and West of the land and renamed it Bretland. It was this name the Northmen took to calling the whole peninsula. Vannes, to the south, was inhabited by an ancient Celtic tribe called the Vanneti. When the Romans had conquered all of Gaul, they made the Vanneti governors of the peninsula. Nominoë and his people, who referred to themselves as the Vennetes, believed they were the rightful rulers of Armorica, but the Britons thought differently.

Armorica was not a united land. The fiercely independent spirit of the Celtic tribes made them brutal adversaries for the Franks and for themselves. For centuries, the Vennetes and the Britons fought one another endlessly until one leader, named Morvan Lez-Breizh, unified the land into a single kingdom. The peace he established lasted only until his death. He left behind no heir apparent, so the land fractured into nine provinces, and the ruler of each declared himself king.

Years of war followed, until Nominoë's father united the provinces of the Vannetais, Rennais, and St. Malo. A Briton chieftain named Tristan united the other provinces of Cornouaille and Léon, while the chieftain Conomor brought together St. Brieuc and Trégor and called himself the king of Domnonia. The ninth region, the Nantais, fell under Frankish occupation. Collectively, Tristan, Conomor, and Nominoë were known as the three Celtic kings.

The Vennetes' deep cultural ties to the ancient Romans made them all the more fascinating to me. Vestiges of the Roman past manifested in everything, from the way they groomed and dressed themselves to the way they fought. Nominoë and his closest advisors, as well as his warriors, shaved their faces and cut their hair short. Many of the lords of the Vannetais who visited Vannes from other parts of the province wore fine silk tunics and capes clasped at the shoulder by golden brooches, which resembled the images of high-born Romans whose likenesses were represented in the colored tiles on the floor of Nominoë's library.

The library, Nominoë explained, had once been the home of a powerful Roman politician; it was decorated from floor to ceiling with images of their conquests and triumphs. It had not weathered the fall of Rome well. The Vennetes had built a thatched roof over the arches where the ceiling had collapsed, and they had erected a network of wooden beams to support what still stood.

"This villa has lasted for hundreds of years," Nominoë said. "But it will not last another fifty."

While their affinity for Ancient Rome influenced much of their society, they were still, after all, Celts. Their language bore no resemblance to the Latin I learned to read, nor did it sound anything like the Frankish tongue.

Their Celtic past also manifested in how the peasants dressed and groomed themselves. The men who toiled in the fields and drank in the taverns wore long mustaches that dangled over their mouths like loose ropes, and their dress was not dissimilar to that of the Irish who toiled in the fields of Ireland. The men wore simple, single-colored tunics, often brown, and the women wore linen shifts under a woolen apron dress. Some days, when I gazed at the fields beyond the city, I could have sworn I looked out over Hagar's fields in Ireland's drizzling rain.

Though I spent my days in the company of men, I sought to make time when I could to visit Asa. The flame in my heart that had been kindled with our first kiss did not fade; the more time we spent apart, the hotter it burned. The nuns eventually grew suspicious of me. I made no illusions about my feelings, and neither did Asa. They capitulated to our schemes and allowed us to spend the afternoon together a few days each week, with Nominoë and Conwoïon's blessing as well.

During the winter months, we stayed indoors in Conwoïon's church, and we played a game Asa called chess. "It's like *hnefatafl*," she said, but the comparison was lost on me. I did not have the privilege of playing games in Hagar's hall, though I would later learn how to play *hnefatafl* as well as I could play chess—not well. We used a checkered marble board with ivory pieces that Conwoïon had brought back from one of his trips to Paris—a gift from another cleric. Each piece had its role, from the horseman to the bishop, and when we played, I felt the excitement of war surge in my heart. As much as I enjoyed the game, I found myself on the losing side more often than I would have liked. Asa was a ruthless opponent.

When the first spring flowers sprouted, Asa and I spent more time outdoors. A garden behind Nominoë's hall, once a Roman pool and a central part of the villa, allowed us to sit, talk, and play. It was that spring that Nominoë invited me to train with a sword, and Asa pleaded for me to teach her everything I learned.

She hatched a plan to borrow two wooden swords from the armory so that she could practice what I had learned from Nominoë's fighting men. Her indomitable spirit cast me under a deepening spell, one that grew even stronger when her bosom popped from her chest seemingly overnight. She was developing into a woman, and I into a man, and the tension between us, the youthful pull of lust, drew us closer together week after week.

We could not act on our impulses because Asa had joined the convent, and though she had not yet taken her eternal vows, the nuns urged her to remain pure until she was of the age to be married. They did not want her to mother a child outside of marriage. I know she had lived a hard life, and the sisterhood of the convent gave her comfort, but she did not want to stay among them forever. She told me she wanted to leave as soon as that first summer, and she wanted to leave with me.

If you had asked me that summer, I would have told you we were destined to be together forever and it was all part of the gods' plan. As a token of my adoration for Asa, I spent an entire day looking for a gift that she could wear, something that would show she was mine. I remembered the arm rings some of the Northmen wore in Ireland, and I looked for something similar. Nominoë gave me some money to spend around the city, and as luck would have it, the blacksmith had a small bracelet made of bronze for sale. It had a little ornament in the shape of a crescent moon dangling from one side. The bracelet was not much, but when I offered it to Asa, she cried with joy.

"No one has ever given me a gift like this before," she said. She hugged me tightly for a long moment, then kissed me on the lips. I was in love.

Our afternoons together continued through the first summer with no sign of my fellow Danes. I spent many days on the pier in the hot sun waiting, hoping for their return—some days with Asa at my side, and some days alone.

It was the summer I turned from a boy into a young man. I grew suddenly as tall as Nominoë, and my voice deepened nearly to that of Egill's, though it cracked almost any time I spoke. A scrabble of blond whiskers grew on my face, the first signs of a beard, and while Conwoïon recommended I shave, I declared my right as a Dane to keep it. Only when Asa found the whiskers unsightly did I cut them. I was fiercely independent unless Asa said otherwise.

When autumn's colors appeared on all the trees and across the countryside, I lost hope of Eilif's return that year. Nominoë did not seem displeased, however, and with my newfound size, he doubled my training as a fighter. I continued to read by candlelight at night and to train with sword, spear, shield, and bow from dawn to dusk.

I never learned how to fight as a Dane, so all I knew about combat was what I learned from the Vennetes. Their fighting style pleased me. Organized, methodical, and most importantly, focused on group effort—each man counted on his brothers-in-arms to shield him from harm. Yann, the master-of-arms, was an older soldier with a greying mustache, a short, broad nose, and thick, powerful legs. He evoked the heroes of Ancient Rome to warn us of the dangers of vanity in battle. He told us of Achilles, Ajax, and Heracles, and how they all had the same fatal flaw.

"They did not work well with others," he said to us one breezy afternoon. "How are we, mere men, to fight alone if even these heroes could not? Rome was not built on the shoulders of one man but on the shoulders of many. Men who fight together find victory together."

Late in the winter of my second year in Vannes, when the westerly winds blew over the Armorican coast, Nominoë called me to his hall in private. He sat across from his hearth, his eyes flickering in the firelight and his chin resting upon his clasped hands. Before him lay parchments of every kind, but one stood out to me before I had even reached the table. It had a red wax seal, the mark of a high-born Frankish lord. As I approached, he caught sight of me in the dull light and invited me to sit in the chair next to him. I sat and said nothing. There was a tension I had not felt before in Nominoë's presence. He placed a finger on the parchment and began to read.

"We have made inquiries among the Danes as to the identity of the man named Jarl Eilif. King Harald asserts he has never heard of a jarl by that name, nor of any such jarl who may have set to sea from Jutland in the past five years. God be with you." Nominoë sat back in his chair with a scowl on his face. "Does any of this sound right to you?"

"No," I said.

"Look at me," he snarled. He gazed into my eyes. "Never take me for a fool, Hasting. You know I will see through you. You are not here in my city by chance. You are here by my invitation." He leaned against the table and reached for a silver pitcher to pour himself a goblet of wine. "I sent a letter to a friend in Aachen who deals in the empire's relations with the Danes. They frequently speak, you know, the Franks and the Danes. I told him your story. It seems you lied about who you are."

"I did not lie," I said. My heart thumped like a hammer on an anvil.

"Eilif is not a powerful warlord, as I had hoped. Nor are you likely his true-born son—though I already guessed as much. Tell me, Hasting, how well did you know your companions?"

My voice trembled when I said, "I was a slave in Ireland, and Eilif bought my freedom so I could serve on his ship the same spring we came here. I knew him a few months, at most."

"Were you born a slave?" he asked.

"My father was a chieftain but was killed in a blood feud." I hoped he would believe me.

Nominoë crossed his arms and leaned toward me. "Do you have proof of this?"

"No. The only proof I have hangs at the waist of the man who kept me as a slave."

"What is it?"

"My father's sword."

Nominoë fell silent. He returned to reading his parchments while I sat and bit my fingernails. I could feel Loki's Delirium tugging at my mind. Finally, Nominoë broke his silence and said, "Your friend Eilif is not who he claimed to be. It is disappointing but not surprising. And it is not a total loss. You will be useful to me as an interpreter when the Northmen return to my shores."

"I would like to think of us as friends," I said.

Nominoë smirked and said, "You are bold, I'll give you that. And you are quickly becoming one of my best fighters. I am not pleased by your deception, even if it was not yours from the start. You will need to prove your loyalty and honesty to me. Here, in Armorica, that is what counts."

A messenger barged into the room from the stairway as we spoke. He was soaked from the rain and breathing hard. His tunic dripped onto the wooden floor and left a trail of puddles behind him. Without asking permission, he approached the table and handed Nominoë a scroll.

"News from the Britons, my lord," he said.

"I presume you've read it?" Nominoë said. "Out with it!"

"It's Tristan and Conomor, my lord," the messenger said anxiously. "They have made an alliance against you."

7

Pax Armoricana

On the eve of the Saint John festival, a messenger reported that Kings Tristan and Conomor had mustered an army near the town of Pontivy. They aimed to force Nominoë to abdicate and give up the lands of his father to older, more experienced men. Nominoë was young, and he had not yet tested his courage in battle. Though the military training he had received from Yann made him a formidable swordsman, training with wooden swords and fighting with cold, sharpened steel are two different things entirely.

I could tell he was anxious. In his first act, he mustered the lords of the Vannetais, and over the following days his closest allies arrived and camped on the outskirts of the city. Nominoë's army grew each day, but not quickly enough. Yann, who advised Nominoë on military matters, sent scouts into the countryside to track the army of the Britons, and each report he received gave them a more significant number of warriors. First, we heard they had five hundred cavalrymen and two thousand warriors with spear and shield. The following day a scout returned to say he had counted one thousand cavalrymen and five thousand men on foot. Nominoë's scribes scrambled together letters for his allies, the lords of the Rennais and St. Malo, but none replied. He feared they had begun to conspire with the Britons, perhaps because of his weakened relations with the Franks; or maybe they refused the call for fear the Franks might invade their lands in their absence.

During this time, Nominoë kept me close. I do not know why he wanted me at his side. Perhaps he felt he could confide in me since I was not a Celt and had no reason to betray his secrets. Perhaps he wanted someone younger than himself nearby so that he would not be the youngest man at his war council. Whatever his motivation, he asked me to join him for every meeting and every scout report.

My enthusiasm wavered, however, when Yann caught one of the scouts with a pocketful of silver he had not earned. We suspected he had been captured and bribed to return with false information. With little confidence in the ordinary soldier, Yann, on Nominoë's recommendation, tasked me with the next scouting mission. He assigned two of his soldiers to accompany me on horseback and sent us off with little more than a general direction to follow.

For two days we rode through the lush green countryside of Armorica, following the Roman road until we reached Pontivy. From there, we took the advice of a local farmer who said he had seen a column of soldiers traversing his lands toward the east three or four days earlier. My companions, who were far more astute than I at reading tracks, found a trail that led us into a nearby forest dense with moss-covered trees and thick, leafy foliage.

As we entered the forest, our surroundings grew eerily silent except for the sound of our horses' hooves on the leaf-covered ground. We passed a small creek that fed a crystalline pond overshadowed by a large, flat rock. On the rock sat a peasant with a simple fishing pole and a small basket. He recognized the colors my companions wore and, without a word, he pointed in the direction of the trail with a nod of his head.

The path continued deeper into the forest and led us to a clearing of long grass that was visibly trampled. Ash-covered holes in the ground told us men had camped there, and across the clearing we found a half-buried cesspit. Another trail meandered farther into the forest, but we stopped for the night since darkness had nearly overtaken us. I drew first watch. A crepuscular shroud draped over the land as the other fell fast asleep. My ears twitched at the merest click and crack in the forest, and my heart pounded in my chest at the merest glimpse of movement. When my watch ended, I found it hard to sleep.

The following morning, we resumed our quest to find our enemy. We followed the trail and emerged on the other side of the forest within half a day, and as the trees thinned, the land opened up into rolling green pasture. A thick blanket of dark grey clouds hung over us and dumped a deluge of rain that made it hard to see far into the distance. My companions managed to spot smoke through the rain, and we followed the trail toward it. At the end of the trail, we found a farm with its thatched roof smoldering from a recent fire. It appeared the Britons had moved farther into the Vannetais than we had thought, and they had begun to raid farms for supplies.

My companions spotted another column of smoke behind a grove of trees to the north of the farm; we left our horses in the trees and approached it. At last we had found them. The Britons had made camp at the crest of the adjacent hill, which made counting their numbers difficult because half their army was out of sight. I snuck around the edge of the wood to find a vantage point from which to count, while my companions stayed behind to warn me of any danger.

A large oak tree with thick, low branches proved easy to climb and served as the perfect lookout. As I began to count their numbers, the entire camp appeared to muster all at once. I froze in place. Many horsemen rode in the direction of my companions, and I feared they would be discovered. I counted the troops as they passed, and I waited until I could no longer hear them before I returned to my horse. To my relief, my companions were there waiting for me, and we mounted and rode at full gallop back to Vannes. Nominoë convened a war council the moment we set foot in the city.

"How many?" he asked in front of the other lords.

"Five hundred horsemen," I said. "And one thousand soldiers on foot, at least."

"God save us!" Yann said. "Where did they find so many?"

"They have not had to fight the Franks," Nominoë said more calmly.

"Nearly two-to-one!" one of the lords said.

"Good odds, where I am from," I added with a smirk.

Nominoë laughed. He turned to one of my companions and asked, "How well equipped are they?"

"Nothing out of the ordinary," the scout said. "Most of the horsemen rode bareback, and fewer than half the men on foot had shields."

"Did you see the same?" Nominoë asked me.

I nodded.

"So, they outnumber us two-to-one, but we are better equipped."

"They will be confident," Yann said. "We can use that to our advantage."

"I agree," Nominoë said.

"It could be a ruse," one of the lords said. "They may have more men elsewhere that the Dane did not see. And what about the Franks? What if they attack?"

"The Franks have no idea the Britons have rallied against us. Best we put them down before word reaches

Ricwin. We will march at first light to settle this matter quickly and quietly," Nominoë said.

"But, my lord, we are outnumbered! And we have no plan!" another lord said, his confidence in Nominoë clearly shaken.

"Where did you see them last?" Yann asked my companions.

"East of Pontivy, and heading south," one of them said.

"My lord, there is an old Roman fort in that area. It no longer has walls, but the trench is still deep. If we take a defensive position there, it could give us an advantage," Yann suggested.

"Agreed," Nominoë said. "Tomorrow we will march to the fort. From there, we will decide how to lure the Britons in."

At first light, we assembled the men who had answered Nominoë's call and marched along the Roman road toward Pontivy. Every man knew our odds, but morale was high. The Celts believed in their new leader, for he had proven himself an astute tactician and governor since his father's death. Conwoïon joined us for the journey and recited benedictions and hymns. He gave confession to the men who asked for it, and he recited their last rites in case they died in battle.

No more than half a day from Vannes, a messenger rode up from behind our line and delivered a message to Nominoë. The Lord Ratvili of the Rennais had arrived in Vannes and asked that we wait for him to join our army. His arrival made us rejoice, although we did not know how many men he had brought with him. He caught up with us by midafternoon with two hundred armored horsemen at his back.

"You are late," Nominoë said with a smirk as Ratvili approached.

"Am I the only lord from the Rennais to answer your call?" he asked.

"Indeed," Nominoë replied.

Ratvili grinned through his thick black beard. As the only lord to show his support, he stood to receive high praise and a better standing than the others. He shook his head and said, "They are busy sowing their fields. I am sure if given more time, others would have come."

"Time is a luxury I do not possess," Nominoë said. "If the Franks find out we are at war, they may send troops across the March. I had to act quickly."

"It would be wise, then, to leave word with your garrison in Vannes that any others who arrive to support you should help to secure the Vannetais to the east, in case the Franks do act, as you say," Ratvili suggested.

Nominoë took Ratvili's advice and sent his messenger back to Vannes with the instructions. We marched along the Roman road in utter silence for the remainder of the day. At nightfall, the troops made camp along the path. Though I had not drawn a watch, I spent a sleepless night. Now that the army had mustered and set out to confront the other Celtic kings, the prospect of battle was immediate.

That night I paced nervously through the camp. I eventually settled upon a grassy hill that overlooked the countryside. There was a new moon, so the land was dark except for a few flickers of light from farmsteads in the distance. The stars shone like jewels, and they had not changed; they looked as they had when I'd first sailed with Eilif. I closed my eyes and remembered the salty smell of the sea and the cold embrace of the ocean's breeze.

Before I knew it, Nominoë was kicking me awake. Without realizing it, I had fallen asleep in the grass under the starry sky. Nominoë stood over me in battle attire, replete with a golden conical helmet decorated with feathers, as well as a bronze breastplate. He looked majestic.

"Go fetch some food," Nominoë said. "Tristan and Conomor are on the move. We need to hurry if we hope to reach the Roman fort. You will need your strength, so eat well." He reached down to help me to my feet. When I stood on my own, he kept his grip on my arm and said, "Will you fight for me, when the time comes?"

"Of course," I said.

"You are not one of us. I do not expect you to fight. I ask you not as Nominoë, the king, but as your friend. Will you fight with me today? Will you be my brother-in-arms?"

I brought up my hand and interlocked my arm with his. "Yes," I said.

"Find me when you have eaten. We will ride together."

When the column of soldiers with their red-painted shields and glimmering bronze helmets began to march, Nominoë and I rode to the front to lead them. Ratvili led his cavalrymen to the rear in case of ambush. Midmorning, we left the Roman road and headed down a beaten path into the countryside. Along the way, scouts departed and returned to inform us of the enemy's position, which changed throughout the day. By early afternoon, the first bloodied scout returned. He reported a skirmish on the outskirts of a small wood not far from us. Our armies had found one another.

"The fort is there," Yann said. He pointed to a small hill with a grove of trees in the center and a rocky ridge-line along its backside.

"About damned time!" Nominoë said. "Bring the men up and prepare the defenses."

His warriors did as commanded. They brought the supply carts up the path and into the field, where they found what Yann had promised: a deep ditch and post holes where a Roman fort had once stood. They brought up pikes they had made in Vannes and planted them along the inner line of the ditch. Once the pikes were in place along the perimeter, the men set about erecting their tents and digging fire pits.

Not long after we had dug in, Tristan and Conomor's forces emerged from the woodlands in front of us. Their banners flapped majestically in the wind. My heart sank when I saw the number of men they had brought with them. Evidently, what I had seen in the countryside was only part of their army. Five horsemen rode ahead of the others into the field below us. Our archers took aim as a precaution, but the horsemen raised a white banner—a banner of truce—to signal they wished to talk.

"With me," Nominoë said, and we took to our horses to meet them.

Ratvili and Conwoïon joined us, while all the others stayed at camp to oversee the finishing touches of the defenses. We took half a dozen horsemen with us in case the meeting turned into a skirmish. When we met the Britons up close, I was surprised by how different they appeared in both dress and gesture. Contrary to the Vennetes, the Britons had full beards and long mustaches. Their arms and armor were made of thick leathers and furs, whereas Nominoë and his men wore iron and bronze.

Nominoë pointed out which man was Tristan and which was Conomor when we approached them. Tristan appeared the younger of the two and had long black hair tied behind his head. His men carried a green banner with white circles meant to represent the wind. Conomor wore a thick iron helm that resembled those I had seen worn by the Irish, and his men carried dark blue banners with white cormorants.

"May God watch over us," Conwoïon said first with his hand raised over his right shoulder.

"God willing," Conomor answered. "Thank you, Father."

"Rumor has it the two of you are quite good friends now, eh?" Nominoë said.

Tristan answered, "You heard correctly."

"So, which one of you is the bottom?" Nominoë asked with a smirk.

"Why, you—" Conomor snarled. He took a deep breath to collect himself. "Juvenile insults... I expected as much from you."

"Enough with the pissing contest," Ratvili blurted. "There are souls at stake here today, so state your demands."

Conomor nodded to acknowledge Ratvili. "I received a letter from the Franks that said Louis intends to declare you duke of all Bretland," he said. "That is a problem for me."

"The Vennetes have governed these lands for a thousand years," Ratvili said. "The Franks appointing Nominoë as duke changes nothing."

"Tristan has sworn an oath of fealty to me. He remains Lord of Cornouaille, but I am now the king of the Britons. I have come here today to ask that Nominoë swear the same oath to me. You will remain lord of the Vannetais, but I will be king of all of Bretland."

"Ha!" Ratvili laughed. "You? King?"

Nominoë reached out and tugged Ratvili's jerkin to silence him. "We are all Celts here," he said. "I have great admiration for the Britons. Our forefathers fought and bled together to repel the first Frankish invasion."

"They did," Conomor said. "But now the empire stands at our doorstep, ready to subjugate our people once more, and what have the Vennetes done? Kneel and kiss the emperor's feet!"

"What would you have me do?" Nominoë asked.

"Fight them!" Tristan said.

"A war with the Franks is a war we will surely lose," Nominoë said. "The only path forward is through diplomacy, but Louis will never take us seriously so long as we stand divided."

"Then swear to me," Conomor said. "I will lead the new rebellion. We've fought them back before. I fought for Wihomarc; I know our people can win."

"Wihomarc lost. The rebellion failed," Nominoë said. He paused for a moment and looked at the ground. I could see that he felt frustrated by Conomor's thick-headedness and struggled to keep his polite smile. "I agree with you. The Franks pose a danger to Armorica. But I do not believe you are the man to lead us through this crisis. I've met Louis, we have broken bread together, and we understand one another. I can ensure peace between the Franks and the Celts."

"There is no other man in Armorica better suited to it," Ratvili said.

"See?" Tristan said. "I told you he was conspiring with the Franks!"

"I will give you one last chance to redeem yourself," Conomor said. "Swear to me, and declare me the rightful king of Bretland."

"I will not," Nominoë snarled.

Conomor leaned to the side to look around us and at our army. "You have brought so few men with you. Did the lords of St. Malo and the Rennais not answer your call to arms?"

Nominoë appeared dumbfounded. "How do you know I called them?"

Conomor laughed. "Ah, to be young and naive again. My boy, this is war. Your messengers never reached St. Malo or Rennes."

"Now I will give you my demands. Leave the Vannetais, or we will make you leave," Nominoë said, undaunted.

Both Tristan and Conomor laughed. "You are in no position to make demands, boy. Did you think to send scouts behind your army?" Conomor said. Nominoë and I looked at each other with a terrible realization when he said, "You are surrounded!"

"My lord, we should take our leave," Ratvili insisted.

"And if I were you, Ratvili, I would take my men and ride back to the Rennais!" Tristan shouted as we left.

Nominoë turned about and kicked his horse forward with all his strength. We galloped toward camp, and when we arrived at the fort, we saw a second army contouring the backside of the hilltop.

"What's happened?" Yann asked as he joined us at Nominoë's tent.

"We've been lured into a trap," Ratvili said.

Yann's eyes opened wide with fear as he asked, "Did they offer terms of surrender?"

"No," Nominoë said. "They came here to kill me."

"With their superior numbers, they will attack us, and soon," Ratvili said. "We will be able to use their confidence to our advantage."

"Tell me what you are thinking," Nominoë said.

Ratvili wiped off the table in a fell swoop and took three chess pieces to represent the armies. "We are on the hill here. Their main army is across the farm there, and their smaller army sent to flank us is behind the ridge, here." He set the pieces on the table to show what he meant. He took a fourth piece and placed it next to the piece that represented Nominoë's army. "This is my army. I suggest I take my cavalrymen and flee west, and make sure they see me flee."

Nominoë snatched the chess piece away from him and said, "No, you will not use this as an excuse to abandon me!"

"Listen to me," Ratvili said. "It is the only way we can win. If I leave, they will attack with everything they have. While they are climbing the hill and fighting, my men will have a chance to flank and route them."

Nominoë stood silent for a moment, scowling with his arms crossed. "All right," he said.

Ratvili patted him on the shoulder and said, "Stand your ground. I'll be back. And I will kill Conomor the first chance I have."

"No," Nominoë said. "Your strategy is sound, but I want Conomor alive. He will declare me king of the Celts before the day is out."

The lords agreed to the plan. Yann ordered Nominoë's warriors to form ranks behind the pikes and to dig in their iron shields. They formed two lines, each consisting of two rows of men, and each facing a separate army. Ratvili did as he said he would and led his cavalry out of camp with their banners flying high for all to see. As he left, I could see the worry in both Nominoë and Yann. They did not trust that he would return, but they had no choice. If Ratvili wanted to take his cavalry away, it was his right to do so.

Ratvili's ruse seemed to have worked. After he left camp, the enemy began to move. Nominoë and I took our place in the second line of the foremost rank. We stood shield to shield with the other warriors, and our presence among them lifted their spirits. Conwoïon scurried along the backside of our line to recite prayers for the men, and he said a special prayer for Nominoë when he saw him.

"We fight as one! We will hold the line together!" Nominoë shouted. "Let us make our ancestors proud!"

In the histories, battles seem to unfold quickly and decisively. Real fighting, I learned that day, does not progress in such an idyllic manner. Armies move as fast as their slowest man, and commanders live and die at the speed by which their orders reach all parts of their army.

In a way, I felt privileged to watch Tristan and Conomor guide their warriors toward our line. They paused often to call warriors back who had marched too far ahead or to chastise those who had slowed and fallen behind. With great effort, they formed a line across the field to face us.

Once they took the position they wanted, they began a slow march up the slope toward us. Their archers sent a volley of arrows in our direction, but most landed in the ditch. Still, we raised our heavy iron shields overhead, and a few arrows met their mark. As they moved closer, we readied our javelins. Our archers sent a volley of arrows of their own hurtling toward the enemy. We knew they had met their mark when we heard the sound of their knocks against the Britons' shields. Their shields were smaller, round, and made of wood, and many of them splintered in the first volley.

I feared their cavalry the most. At each moment, I expected the Britons' horsemen to charge at us with their lances, but they did not. Our pikes must have appeared strong enough to dissuade them. Even without their cavalry, their warriors outnumbered us. Despite our better equipment and weapons, I feared they would overrun us. I was not alone in such thoughts. Many of the men around me trembled, and some let their bowels and bladders loose before the fight. We had not yet begun the battle, and already our ranks stunk of piss and shit.

No sooner had the Britons marched within a javelin's throw of our line when Nominoë shouted, "On my mark!" We raised our javelins overhead. The men began to breathe more heavily. Their knuckles turned white as they clenched the shafts and waited for the order to throw.

"Throw!"

A swarm of javelins whooshed through the air and struck hard against the enemy's shields and flesh. An entire row of Briton warriors fell in an instant. When we had thrown our javelins, we took up our spears and pointed them downhill. A volley of arrows fell suddenly upon us, and several of our men had not raised their shields high enough to stop them. We then heard a deafening war cry, and the Britons charged. They jumped the ditch and attempted to knock aside our pikes. We struck them down with swift thrusts of our spears.

As more of them died and fell into the ditch, their bodies piled higher and higher until they no longer needed to jump to cross over to us. Their numbers swarmed the line, and before we knew it, they pushed up against our shields. In such close quarters, we dropped our spears and drew our short swords, as Yann had taught us to do. The men on the back line kept thrusting with their spears while the men on the front line stabbed at the enemy with short, swift strokes. Block, stab, block, and stab again—the defense of our line tired our arms. It took no time at all for me to become out of breath and for my heart to feel as if it might leap from my chest onto the enemy.

"Hold the line!" Nominoë screamed, but his words could hardly be heard over the screams of dying men.

The first wave of the attack broke upon our shields, and their men retreated. We took a moment to catch our breath, but the day was not won. Their warriors had taken down our pikes, and their dead had filled our ditch. We were exposed.

As we regrouped and filled the holes in our line, the ground trembled beneath our feet. A wall of horses charged up the hill, over our ditch, and smashed into our ranks. Our spears found their way into the flesh of a few horses, but their speed and number were too much for us to halt. They pushed, kicked, bit, and trampled our men, and I was kicked clear off my feet and nearly stomped to death.

I managed to roll out from under a beast's hooves before they struck the ground; other men were not so lucky. A fierce struggle ensued where men on horseback turned their steeds to and fro to strike down our warriors, and we threw our spears and javelins at them to take them down. In the thick of the battle, I heard Nominoë scream, "Tristan! He is there!"

Indeed, Tristan had charged into battle with his cavalry and now found himself surrounded by our spears. The gods helped me that day by leaving a spare javelin planted in the ground an arm's length away from me. I was not the best javelin thrower Yann had ever taught, but I was skilled enough.

For a moment, the world around me seemed to slow, and in a swift, smooth motion, I took the javelin, aimed, and launched it with all my strength. It struck Tristan in the shoulder and knocked him off his horse. As he fell, his cavalrymen broke and fled. Behind them, Conomor's warriors attempted a second charge. Scattered and exhausted, we could barely form another line to repel them. We were lambs for the slaughter.

"God be praised! He has returned to us!" I heard Nominoë say.

Ratvili and his cavalry glimmered in the late evening sun as they galloped across the field and through Conomor's lines. His cavalry had the momentum of the high ground, and the enemy's footmen stood little chance to repel them. Their spirit broke, as Ratvili had said it would, and they ran. We shifted our attention to the other line that Yann defended, but when we arrived to help them, the enemy had already fallen back.

We had won the day, but at a high cost. Yann was mortally wounded. A sword had cut him open from groin to navel, and he bled out before the end of the battle. His dying words were that it had been an honor to serve such a remarkable young man as Nominoë. When told of this,

Nominoë's eyes watered, but he held his tears for his men. He turned to face the rest of us, raised his sword, and said, "*Vennetes victor!*" He was met with praise and cheers.

In the moments after the battle, I looked around and felt terrible guilt for what I saw. The survivors were bloodied and muddied, and the battleground stunk of guts, blood, and death. Mangled bodies covered the ground and wriggled like a bed of cockroaches as men with some life left in them crawled or reached for help. The worst were the men whose skulls had been trampled and crushed by the horses. It all felt familiar to me, and I remembered the face of the first man I killed. My morning meal attempted to rise through my chest, but so many hours after I had eaten, nothing came out.

Nominoë sought me out after the battle and put a hand on my shoulder. "You fought well today," he said. "Thank you, my friend."

"I promised I would fight for you," I said.

As we looked to the aftermath of the battle, Ratvili rode up to meet us. He smiled from ear to ear and held his chin high. "We have Conomor!" he said.

"We have Tristan," Nominoë said. "It is time to settle this matter."

We took the prisoners to Nominoë's tent and forced them to their knees. Both were wounded, and both appeared near death. Tristan looked the worse. He was pale, and the cloth our men had fastened at his shoulder was already soaked in blood. Conwoïon recited yet another quiet benediction, made the sign of the cross, and gave the floor to his lord.

"So many dead," Nominoë said. "It did not have to be this way."

"If you are going to kill me, do it. I have made my peace with God," Conomor said.

"No. You will live," Nominoë said. His statement surprised his captives. "Are you familiar with the Pax Romana?"

Both Conomor and Tristan shook their heads.

"When the Romans ruled this land, our people knew peace for more than three hundred years. Can you imagine? So many generations who never experienced the horrors of war. What a blessing!"

As Nominoë spoke, Ratvili leaned in and whispered, "I think he's been reading too many books."

Nominoë shot him an annoyed look and continued. "How did the Romans achieve such peace? It was simple. All young men of fighting age had to serve in the Roman army. Without warriors, the tribes could not muster a rebellion."

"You want us to give you all of our warriors? You could never afford it" Conomor said.

"You assume I will be paying for it," Nominoë said. "I will let you live. I will let you remain lords of your provinces. In return, you will remit a yearly tax to me to pay for my army, and all men of fighting age will join it, permanently. We will unify Armorica under one leader and be prepared to fight whoever might seek to invade us."

The other lords in the tent clapped enthusiastically. They had never heard this plan before, and I am quite sure Nominoë made it up on the spot. That was his way. He was smart and quick on his feet. Whatever the true source of his inspiration for the terms of surrender, the Britons accepted. Conwoïon drafted the terms on paper, made copies, and each party signed them.

Nominoë was from that moment, for all intents, king of the Celts.

8

The Meeting at Redon

As much as we want to believe we can survive on our own, all men crave the camaraderie of other men. The years I spent in Armorica could have been the loneliest of my life, but they were not. In Nominoë I found a leader who inspired me, one whom I could follow to the ends of the world if he required it. He earned my loyalty by showing loyalty to me, a lesson I have not forgotten. Rather than expel me from his kingdom—or worse, put me to death—after he discovered the lie behind my heritage, he kept me at his side. It helped that I had allies among the Celts, including Conwoïon, in whom Nominoë often confided. Conwoïon saw potential in me, and it was he, I would later learn, who in part convinced Nominoë to treat me as a Celt, and to keep me close.

In Conwoïon I found a close friend. Like Nominoë, he was young and ambitious, though not as young and energetic as I. We shared a passion for the past, the old world of the Romans, and we spent many afternoons and evenings reading about it and discussing it. His fascination with the Romans started with his family who had raised him to believe they had descended from Roman senators, a kind of nobility in Ancient Rome. Though the Romans had disappeared many generations ago, his family still benefited from the bloodline with land and wealth.

Our conversations eventually broke the rigid bounds of history to encompass everything, from my training with Nominoë and my affair with Asa to his desires to build a new abbey near a village called Redon. It was he who helped guide me through my most trying times, mainly when Nominoë and I did not see eye to eye. I confided in him my fears, and he, in turn, guided me with questions that forced me to think through whatever it was that troubled me. Sometimes he challenged my way of thinking, which upset me, but I always understood in the end the intent behind his words. Our conversations made me a better man, and for that I was grateful and thanked him for it. All he ever asked in return was that I do the same for him.

There was the issue of my age, which I did not care about, but others did. Conwoïon taught me to read and write in Latin, and in so doing taught me the Julian calendar which was used to track days, weeks, and months of a year. It is during this time that I began to remember dates and events—where and when they unfolded. From my time among the Northmen, I remembered little of how they tracked days, though I knew they counted them and had names for them. Conwoïon estimated by my size and maturity that I must have been sixteen or seventeen years old during my third winter in Vannes. But without a birthday, I could not know, and I could not keep track of my age.

"No matter," Conwoïon said to me. "We will baptize you, and you will be reborn. That will be your birthday."

Indeed, on April 3, of the year 832, Conwoïon, accompanied by Nominoë, Asa, two nuns, and a handful of warriors, walked me down to the shore of the River Marle. He ceremoniously led me into the water, leaned me back gently, and plunked me beneath the water's surface. When I reemerged, with water in my ears and nose, I heard the cheers of the men and women who watched from the shore.

"Today you are reborn," Conwoïon said as he leaned in to kiss me once on each cheek.

It could be said that my Christianization was something of a miracle for the Celts. For me, it was less so, since I had never participated in the religious ceremonies of the Northmen. I was a young man without a god; at least, that is what I thought at the time. Welcoming Christ into my life, as the Celts described it, seemed natural and the right thing to do to remain in their good graces.

The more they brought me into the fold, however, the more I felt my heart yearn for the old ways. I knew little of the gods, perhaps, but I had been touched by one of them, or so I had been told, and I still felt his presence within me. I felt his raw power, his rage, and his thirst for adventure. Not even the baptism washed away the wolf's mark. Though his enduring presence never left me, I played along with the Celts. I attended Mass, and I prayed to God. Some might even say I was a good Christian.

After my baptism, Nominoë set a date for an assembly at the site of the new abbey in Redon. He wanted to support his friend and advisor Conwoïon by pressing the issue with the bishop of Vannes and the Franks.

It was a messy game of politics. Conwoïon wanted the abbey built as a Frankish-style center of worship on Celtic land as a means to ease tension between the Celts and the Franks. "Two peoples, united under the one true God," he said of his project.

The Bishop of Vannes, a sultry old man by the name of Rainier, opposed the abbey, for he believed a Frankish-style center of worship, sanctioned by the Franks, would enrage the Celts and incite more bloodshed. Ricwin, the count of Nantes, supported him.

Despite the bishop's claims, however, both Nominoë and Ratvili, who owned the lands around

Redon, endorsed the building of the abbey. Violence, it seemed, was not the bishop's primary fear. No, abbeys and monasteries attracted pilgrims, so they invited wealth. On the eve of our journey to Redon, Conwoïon confided in me that he believed Rainier feared losing pilgrims to the new site, which was a two-day journey on foot from Vannes. The man had garnered Ricwin's support with little effort, since the count of Nantes sought to oppose Nominoë wherever he could.

For my part, I heeded Conwoïon, but I often struggled to understand the nuances of who wanted what and why. All I needed to know was that the abbey served as a means to an end. Though Nominoë had forced the other kings' submission, he knew the peace would not last. It was only a matter of time before the Britons would again rise up against him.

Nominoë dreamed of a day when Armorica would unite as a single, independent kingdom with one king. To do this, he would need the support of the Frankish emperor, Louis. After all, part of the conflict among the Celtic kings stemmed from the divisions created by the Franks. If that element vanished, Nominoë thought, and if he could gain favor with the emperor, the other kings would unite behind his banner. It all sounded logical, but politics seldom transpires without some measure of chaos.

We left for Redon on June 25, after the festival of St. John, and it took us a single day from dawn until dusk to reach it. Nominoë had not brought many men with him, for he wished to travel quickly and discreetly. Franks from Nantes had increased their raids along the southern border of the Breton March, emboldened by the return of their principal garrison of soldiers who had left to fight in the war between Emperor Louis and his sons. To capture a Celtic king such as Nominoë would have yielded a hefty ransom for poorly paid soldiers.

We traveled cautiously to avoid meeting anyone on the road. To my relief, we reached the site for the abbey without incident, and there we felt all the more secure by the arrival of fifty Celtic warriors—sent to greet us by our friend Ratvili. Ratvili himself had not yet arrived.

We crossed the River Oust on a wooden bridge that creaked and crackled as we passed. It was close to sundown, and peasant workers with rags on their backs and spades over their shoulders were walking back to their village on the shore of the River Vilaine. They had begun digging the foundation of the abbey at the top of a small hill that overlooked the confluence of the Vilaine and the Oust rivers to the south. Nominoë rode ahead to survey the grounds before dark, and I followed.

"The River Oust protects this hill from the east, and the Vilaine protects it from the west. Passing armies will prefer to cross south of the confluence to avoid crossing two rivers. So, the abbey will not be a target for looting," Nominoë explained.

Conwoïon joined us on his horse and said, "Quite a view!"

Indeed, the hill on which we stood overlooked all the land around us to the horizon. It was a beautiful sight of dense forests of oak, birch, beech, and chestnut trees, broken by patches of green pasture and farmland close to the rivers. As the sun sank over the skyline, the forests grew dark and quiet except for the sound of Ratvili's warriors making camp near the construction site. They erected a large tent for Nominoë where we had unloaded our supplies, and we helped gather wood for a fire.

Exhausted from the day's journey, Nominoë drank some wine and bit into a bread roll before he retired to his tent for the night. Conwoïon and I preferred the open air to a shelter and set our cots by the fire to watch the stars as we drifted off to sleep.

I awoke to Nominoë standing over me with one of his hands gripped around the hilt of his sword. He nudged me with his foot. "Are you awake?" he asked.

"Yes," I grumbled.

"Good. There is bread and dried fruit in my tent. Eat up; you will need your strength and wits today," he said.

"Will I be doing the talking?" I asked with a smirk.

"Some," Nominoë said.

His response sent a shiver down my back. I had not expected to participate in the talks at Redon, and I hoped he was not serious. He stepped over to Conwoïon and nudged him with his foot as well. The cleric made a sign of the cross as he awoke and sat up as if he had been stung by a bee. I gathered my things and did as Nominoë asked. The bread was chewy but washed down with a sip of water. It was not the best breakfast I had ever eaten, but it filled my stomach well enough.

Across the construction site, the Celts had erected a large tent with Nominoë's banner flying over it. Peasants from the nearby village joined in the work and brought carafes of wine and platters of food, including my favorite, cheese, along with a large banquet table carried up the hill by cart, and dozens of simple wooden chairs. As men and women bustled here and there to prepare for the meeting, Nominoë called to me from the edge of the tree line, a stone's throw from the construction site.

"Hasting, over here!" He sat on the thick trunk of a downed tree and invited me to join him."Ricwin will be here today," he said. "Do you know who he is?"

I nodded. "The count of Nantes?"

"Yes," Nominoë said with a smile. "You've been talking to Conwoïon about this, haven't you?"

"I have."

"Good, then I do not need to explain to you what is at stake here. Ricwin hates me, and he will do whatever he can to discredit me in front of the emperor. I have a plan to preempt him, but I will need your help."

"What can I do?"

"Remember the raid I sent you on when we first met?" he asked.

I nodded.

"Well, we were caught with our britches down when the Franks fished our silver out of the Northman ships they captured in the Loire. They used it to convince Louis we had hired Northmen to raid for us. Ricwin will almost certainly bring it up at the meeting to prove we are traitors to the empire. And that is where you will help me."

"What must I do?" I asked.

"Louis is a pious man. He values faith in God above all other things. I want to show him that we have made a good Christian of you. If I can prove that I have brought you to our faith, all may be forgiven. And the silver can be explained away as a failed attempt to convert your kin."

"How will you prove that I have become Christian?" I asked.

"You will read the Sermon on the Mount from the Bible. Can you do it?" he asked.

Conwoïon had taught me well, and I had read that passage several times, but I feared failing him in front of the emperor. I had never met an emperor before, and the thought of it turned my stomach. "Of course," I said with a forced smile.

In the distance, a horn blew twice, announcing the arrival of someone important. Nominoë and I hurried back to the construction site and stood before the large meeting tent. Two columns of maille-clad soldiers in blue overcoats painted with white fleurs-de-lis and carrying spears as tall as two men marched over the construction site and formed ranks before us.

A large, golden carriage drawn by four horses rolled thunderously over the ground in a semi-circle until the side of the cart faced us. Inside the carriage were four men, all well-dressed, but whose faces were shadowed. Two servants rushed to the side of the cart, one with a rolled-up carpet and the other with a stepping stool. When the carpet covered the ground, one of the servants bowed to us and opened the cart door.

The first man to exit the cart wore a simple golden band on his head and a silky, dark blue gown with golden embroidery. He wore several jeweled rings on his hands, and when he stepped down from the cart to the carpet, he looked to the sky and made the sign of the cross. "May God watch over us," he said.

"God is with you, my Lord Louis," Nominoë said.

Louis gave him a kind smile. "Forgive the military display. Dark have been my days of late." He stepped forward and held out his hand. Nominoë knelt and kissed it. I knelt as well, but no hand was offered to me. "Please, stand. I trust you are well?"

"I am. Shall we?" Nominoë said with an inviting gesture toward the tent.

The emperor was not so old, but he was frail. He had long, greying black hair, and a well-shaved, gaunt face. His thin figure was engulfed by his robe, and when he walked toward the table inside the tent, he took hold of Nominoë's arm for support. They seemed to know each other intimately, which surprised me considering the nature of the meeting. I would have thought them bitter enemies, but from what I observed that day, it was not the case. Two more men stepped out from the cart behind the emperor.

The first man looked Louis' age. He wore a light gold tunic underneath a burgundy cape. His hair was dark, as were his eyes, and he had a pallor about him that told me he had recently recovered from illness. When he looked at me, I recognized his square jaw and imposing regard. He was the man I had seen confront Nominoë at the river fort.

"You don't look like a Celt," he said.

I smiled and said, "I'm not."

As the man opened his mouth to ask another question, I heard the shouts of a familiar voice.

"Let me through!" Conwoïon said. Two Frankish soldiers had stopped him from approaching the tent. "I called for these talks. This is my meeting," he pleaded with them.

"Let him through!" Louis shouted from inside the tent.

"Oh, for pity's sake," Conwoïon lamented as the soldiers stood aside. "Finally, thank you. Ah, Ricwin, so good to see you."

"God is with you, Father," said the man closest to me.

"And Renaud d'Herbauges, thank you for coming," Conwoïon said to the man behind him. He had bright blue eyes, a hooked nose, and hair that he kept cut short above his ears.

"Where is Rainier?" Renaud asked.

Conwoïon approached us and said, "He is unable to attend, unfortunately. No matter; he gave me a letter to read at the meeting." He looked at me and smiled uncomfortably.

"Who's the boy?" Renaud asked.

"I am Hasting," I said.

"A strange name. Where is it from? Saxony?" Ricwin asked.

"My friends, we have much to discuss," Conwoïon said nervously. He extended his arms to usher us into the tent. "Come, we will answer all your questions."

We sat along opposite sides of the table with Celtic warriors at our backs and Frankish warriors at theirs.

Servants filled our goblets with wine and covered the table with cheeses, bread, and dried fruit, including pears, apricots, and raisins. No one spoke until Louis began.

"I have made a long journey to meet you here, in this desolate place," Louis said with a mouthful of raisins. "I would first like to begin by saying the empire is bankrupt. Our wars have cost us much, and I have nothing with which to support you financially. The most I can offer today, should I choose to do so, is an edict of land from the empire and the church."

"Thank you, my lord," Nominoë said. "Before we move further into the discussions, I have a gift for you."

Louis appeared pleased.

"It is not a physical gift, but a gift of the soul."

"Careful, Celt," Renaud said. "We want nothing of your cheap tricks."

"Come, my dear Renaud. You treat him as though he were your enemy. We are all brothers in the eyes of God," Louis said.

"Exactly," Nominoë blurted out. He was nervous, but only I could tell. "My gift to you is one of hope and piety. This boy sitting at my side is not a Celt, but rather a Dane. Yet you mistook him for a civilized man of faith."

Conwoïon jumped in and said, "Even you, Ricwin, did not guess that he is a Northman."

Ricwin nodded in agreement.

Nominoë placed a Bible before me and said, "I will show you something you have never seen or heard before. Northmen may seem uncivilized, but given the right encouragement, they can see the light of Christ as have we all."

"What's he supposed to do, eat it?" Renaud asked.

I opened the book, placed my finger at the beginning of the passage, and began to read from the text in Latin. Louis' eyes opened wide with intrigue. He leaned toward me with his elbows pressed on the table to listen to my recital. At parts, he even smiled, and his whole demeanor changed as if something had grabbed hold of him and lifted his spirit out of despair. When I finished reading, he clapped his hands together with delight.

"And he is a Dane, you say?" he asked.

Nominoë nodded.

"You know, we have had many Danes come to our faith, but none have ever learned to read with such eloquence. I am thrilled."

"I am delighted you are pleased, my lord," Nominoë said.

"Oh, how I wish Anskar were here to witness this," Louis said.

Renaud stood up and slammed his fist on the table. "Lies!" His outburst gave us all pause. "This is a ruse to win you over. Can't you see? Have you forgotten what they've done? Do you not remember Bouin?"

"Please, calm down," Ricwin urged him.

"We found your silver, Nominoë!" Renaud growled. "We know you paid them. It was an act of war. Had our army been at full strength, I swear we would have burned your city to the ground."

"You wound me," Nominoë said. "The silver may have come from Armorica, but we did not give it willingly."

Louis raised his hand. "If we hold onto old trespasses, we will never come to an accord," he declared. "We are here in good faith to renew the friendship between our people. The Celts have erred, certainly, but so have we. It is the nature of men to sin."

"Let he who is without sin cast the first stone," I said.

All their eyes were upon me. Louis, especially, marveled at me, as if he had seen a vision of Christ himself.

"Outstanding," he said.

Disgusted, Renaud stormed out of the tent.

"You will have to forgive my vassal—he has a terrible temper," Ricwin said. "As for me, I am impressed by this young man. Perhaps the Northmen can be civilized after all."

Louis shifted his gaze to Conwoïon and asked, "Where is Rainier?"

"Apologies, my lord, but he is too ill to travel," Conwoïon said. "He did, however, send this letter." He held out a sealed parchment, which Ricwin took and gave to Louis.

Louis broke the seal and unrolled the parchment. He read through it without making a sound, with everyone watching him, and rolled it back up when he finished. "My God, that man is longwinded." We all chuckled. "But... no surprises. He offers the same worn argument as always."

"Is his argument convincing to you?" Nominoë asked.

"I cannot believe a new place of worship would cause bloodshed. What do you think, Ricwin?" Louis asked.

"The Breton March is an unstable place. The merest suggestion of an abbey under an imperial edict could spark a fire that burns for years."

"Then again," Nominoë argued, "we Bretons are Christians, and an abbey on the Breton March might serve as a buffer to prevent would-be raiders from crossing over into your lands."

When they spoke of the Breton March, I remembered a book I had read in Nominoë's library on the subject. After the Franks had invaded the former Roman province of Gaul, they had failed to subdue the Celts of Armorica. The border between Armorica and Frankland became known to the Franks as the Breton March, named for the Britons who had settled there. Although the Britons

146

and Vennetes were sometimes enemies, the Franks saw no difference between them. Where the Vennetes called the land Armorica, and the Britons called it Bretland, the Franks called it Britanniam, and they called all the Celts Bretons.

"What about the other Breton leaders?" Louis asked. "What do they think?"

"What do they think of Nominoë, is the better question, I think," Ricwin said. "A young man with little to no experience, and none in battle as I can recall. The other Bretons must look down upon you."

"Nominoë is well respected among the other leaders of Bretland," Conwoïon said. "They will follow him, whatever his decision."

Nominoë and Conwoïon were careful to say nothing of the battle we had fought against the Britons. Revealing such strife would have encouraged Ricwin.

"What's in it for you, then?" Ricwin continued.

"Peace," Nominoë said.

Ricwin scoffed at his answer and said, "Unite the provinces, you mean."

"Could you explain what you mean by that?" Louis asked.

"If there is peace on the Breton March, and he becomes your favorite of the Breton chieftains, it gives him leverage for submitting the others to his rule."

"A united Britanniam with a loyal subject of mine as its leader is precisely what I have sought for thirty years," Louis said.

"And a united Britanniam means a strong Britanniam, which is a threat to the Frankish lands around the March," Ricwin said. "Including Nantes."

As the two bickered back and forth, Nominoë raised his hand to garner their attention. "If I may," he said, "there is one more thing Count Ricwin has not thought to consider."

"Which is?" Ricwin snarled.

"The Northmen. Remember that many Celts of Armorica are cousins of the Britons of Cornwall, and we write to each other from time to time. From them, I have heard of Northman invasions in Ireland, and many raids in the land they call England. They fear an invasion is imminent, and we could be next. Already we have seen fleets of ships willing to sail to our shores for our wine, our salt, and our silver. More will come."

"I lived in Ireland," I said.

Louis turned his attention to me. "Is it true? That Northmen are invading Ireland?"

"It is," I said.

"So, we must risk a united Britanniam to protect against a Northman invasion," Louis said while stroking his chin. "And here I thought this meeting was about an abbey."

"Can we count on your support?" Conwoïon asked.

Louis sat back in his chair and crossed his arms. "I will need to pray. God will grant me the wisdom to give you an answer."

"My lord, if I may," Ricwin said unexpectedly. "The Northmen pose no threat to our cities. It is absurd to think that—"

"I will pray!" Louis said with a raised voice, the first sign of anger he had shown the entire meeting. He settled back into his chair and continued, "I will return to Aix-la-Chapelle and ask God for his guidance in my personal chapel. You will have my answer within the fortnight."

With those words, the emperor returned to his cart with his soldiers, and they left with the same booming ruckus with which they had arrived. Nominoë sighed with relief when they were gone, and he poured himself a few celebratory goblets of wine.

"It's not won yet," Conwoïon said.

"No, but our friend Hasting here certainly helped our cause," Nominoë said with a grin. "Louis was impressed; he even said so."

"Do you know Louis from before?" I asked.

"I do," Nominoë said. "When I was a boy, I spent three years as a page to the emperor in Aix-la-Chapelle. That is where I learned how to deal with Frankish lords, and how I came to be considered a favorite of Louis."

As I reflected on the meeting, a messenger burst through the entrance of the tent, winded and panicked. "A message from Vannes, my Lord!" he said as he handed over a rolled-up parchment. Nominoë unrolled it and read quickly through the lines. His hand began to tremble.

"What is it?" I asked. He handed me the message.

My Lord Nominoë,

Vannes burns. There is no doubt in my mind that this was the work of savage Northmen, propelled by God for our sins against Him. The church and convent are burned, our brothers and sisters of the cloth murdered, and I only escaped by the quick thinking of your cousin who whisked me away from the carnage on horseback. I write to you from Nantes, where I have taken refuge until our city is secured.

God be with you,
Rainier

I, too, began to tremble. The first thought was for Asa. I felt my innards twist with fear, and there was weakness in my limbs from despair. Conwoïon took the letter and read it. He gasped aloud after each sentence. As we sat together in silence, Ratvili entered the tent. He had drunk wine for lunch, which gave his plump cheeks a rosy glow. When he saw our faces, he knew something had happened.

"What troubles you, my friends?" he asked.

"Vannes has been sacked," Conwoïon said when Nominoë could not find the words. "Northmen."

"I will muster my men; we will march immediately!" Ratvili said.

"Thank you," Nominoë said sourly. His voice was faint from the dryness in his throat. "Our horses," he then said to his warriors behind us. They too appeared distraught—their families lived in Vannes.

We set out in the early afternoon with a small army at our back. Ratvili's support, while crucial to our return to Vannes, did not comfort us. We knew we would arrive days too late to make a difference. All we could do was pray that some people had survived. We hoped that by some miracle a few had either escaped or hidden away. I wished, most of all, that Asa had found a way to stay alive.

We marched until dark and made camp along the road to Vannes. It was eerily silent, for no one knew what we might find the following day. I stayed awake, pacing anxiously through the camp. I find it hard to describe those moments now, though I feel as if it all happened yesterday. In the night, I found myself caught between hope and despair. Was she alive? Was she dead? Looking back, it seems the impatience of youth had gripped me, yet if the same were to happen to me today, I might do the same, or worse.

The following morning, we marched for Vannes and, as Ratvili had predicted, we caught sight of the city by early afternoon. We saw no smoke, and we heard no sounds of conflict. Ratvili's warriors stormed the city looking for any lingering Northmen. They found none. Strangely, most of the buildings had been spared from the fires—except the church and convent. The streets were devoid of people, and we searched all the houses, but the entire city had been abandoned.

Ratvili called for us. He had taken to investigate the burnt remnants of the convent, which had been made of wood, and he found jewelry in the ashes: a half-melted necklace here, a warped ring there, and burnt pieces of cloth.

"I believe they were burned," he said with a tremble in his voice. "All of them."

"It can't be," Nominoë said. He dug through the ashes and found a charred piece of decorated hem that once belonged to a woman's dress.

More of us joined him in sifting through the ashes. We searched through pile after pile and found many more trinkets and burnt garments. It became clear that the Northmen had rounded up all the people of the city and burned them in the convent. When I helped Ratvili move one of the fallen beams, we found two bodies half burned, and the sight of them made me vomit. I dropped to my knees and cried, and that is when, with my hands in the ash on the ground, I felt something small and solid. I pulled it up to see—it was a bronze bracelet with a melted crescent moon that dangled from it.

9

Treasonous and Oath-Breaking

In the days that followed the raid, Celts who had fled into the countryside now trickled home in small groups. They joined in the effort to repair damaged buildings and take an inventory of who had perished in the convent fire. Many of them had witnessed the attack, and Conwoïon interrogated the survivors.

Something about what had happened did not sit well with him, so he spent his days scouring for evidence of who had carried out the raid and why. Nominoë and Ratvili seemed content with Rainier's report—that they were Northmen, and that the attack was retribution from God for their sins. Which sins, they did not know for sure, but God, in their estimate, had found reason enough to punish them.

I retreated to Nominoë's garden with a carafe of wine to myself and no desire to speak with anyone. The others let me be, for they knew the pain I felt, and none stopped me when I returned to Nominoë's cellar for more. My heart ached without respite.

I spent my days and nights in agony, numbed by the sweet taste of wine. The Celts frowned on drunkenness, so I kept to myself, alone in my misery. Those days are a blur in my memory, though the pain I felt still stings when I think of it. Conwoïon eventually sought me out. Shocked by the sight of my drunkenness, he spent a day as my chaperone and kept me away from the cellars.

He waited at my side until the haze of intemperance passed.

The following day, when my head pounded and my throat felt dry as sand on a summer day, Conwoïon greeted me with a goblet of water and hot soup. It did not take long for me to cry and lament over my sorrow. When I looked in my friend's eyes, I saw understanding. He may not have lost someone close to him in the raid, but he had lived such pain in his past. I took the water and gulped it down.

"The loss of a loved one is like the sting of a bee," he said. "The more we are stung, the better we handle the pain, but a sting is still a sting. In time, the pain passes, and we are left with nothing but its memory."

"Is that supposed to make me feel better?" I grumbled.

"It is what the abbot said to me when they took me into the brotherhood. My father drank himself to death after my mother died, and I was orphaned, alone, in pain."

"I was an orphan too," I said. "But I was sold into slavery, not an abbey."

"Perhaps our stories are not so different, you and I," he said with a smile. "Look, I understand your pain, but we need you. I need you to get well and to recover your strength so you can help me find who did this and bring them before God's justice."

I sat up on the side of the bed and slurped the soup he had brought me. My stomach swirled, and I had no appetite, but I forced it down to make him happy. After I swallowed the last drop, I said, "Will you accompany me to the beach?"

"Whatever for?" Conwoïon said with surprise.

"When I was in Ireland, the men jumped into the cold ocean after a night of heavy drinking. It made them feel better."

Conwoïon smiled. He had grown used to my odd ideas. "Lead the way," he said.

We walked together to the beach below the city in silence. The docks where the River Marle fed into the Morbihan had been burned, and all the boats had vanished. I stripped naked and faced the waves, took a few deep breaths, and ran into the water, splashing and thrashing until I dove head first beneath the surface. The sea's cold embrace made my skin cling tighter to my body and made my nipples shrivel like raisins.

As I had hoped, the swim eased the throbbing in my head. For as long as I could hold my breath, I floated beneath the surface to enjoy the tranquility of the silent underwater world. Only when my body ached for breath did I return to the air above. As I broke the water's surface, I heard men murmuring on the beach. Two monks in black habits had approached Conwoïon, and the three of them talked while I swam.

"Hasting, come! I want you to meet someone," Conwoïon said.

I slipped out of the water and into a large wool blanket Conwoïon had brought for me. A light west wind blew over us and gave me a chill while I still dripped with water. The men who had joined Conwoïon on the beach had arrived by boat along the eastern shore where the dock had stood before the raiders burned it.

"This is Brother Arnulf, and Brother Bertrand," Conwoïon said. "They came here from the monastery of Landévennec to help with my investigation."

"Investigation?" I asked, puzzled.

"Yes. I am not certain that what we believe to have happened, happened. Brother Arnulf was kind enough to offer his help," Conwoïon explained.

"So, you are the Northman we have heard so much about," Arnulf said with a soft smile. He had the look of a Briton, with dark brown eyes, a strong chin, and an impeccably straight nose. The wrinkles along his eyes and down his cheeks when he smiled told me he was not a young man, but not particularly old, either. Neither he nor Bertrand had any hair on their heads, but Bertrand did have thick, grey eyebrows that curled at the edges.

"I am," I replied.

"You are familiar with their customs, are you not?"

"I am."

"Good," he chirped. "I will have need of your insights during our investigation."

"Why?" I asked.

Conwoïon cringed, for my bluntness might have offended Arnulf.

Arnulf paused, looked me in the eye, and said, "We are here to investigate whether the Northmen raided the city, or whether it was someone else who wants the Vannetais to believe the Northmen raided it. War brings out the foulest behavior in men."

Back in the city, I slipped away to find fresh water to rinse the salt from my body, as well as clean clothes for the day. When I rejoined the monks in the early afternoon at the convent, they had already combed most of the grounds. Their fastidiousness impressed me. On the edge of the convent, they had collected the remnants of personal items in loosely woven straw baskets, and each was cataloged in a massive ledger. Conwoïon helped by pointing out areas he had already examined, and they swept through the ashes and under the collapsed wooden beams for evidence. Under one of the poles, Arnulf found charred bones.

"This is indeed strange," Arnulf said. "Until now, we assumed the fire burned so hot it turned the bones of the victims to ash. Yet here, where the fire should have burned hottest, we find bones."

"Such a fire should have also melted jewelry, should it not?" Conwoïon asked.

"Indeed," Arnulf said. He scratched his scalp, and the ash in his fingernails left dark marks across his head. "The military men did not find this suspicious at all?"

"They hardly took the time to look," Conwoïon said. "Nominoë has a kingdom to govern. He left the investigation to me."

Arnulf called me over. He took my hand and guided me to a place where I could see the entire convent floor. "Tell me, Northman, what do you see?"

"Ash, burnt wood," I said.

"Yes," he continued, "but look closer."

I surveyed the grounds a moment longer. In the ash, I saw the footprints left by the monks and myself and noticed they tended to all lead to the same place in the center of the structure. Bertrand wiped off another brooch and placed it in one of the baskets. They had hardly filled a single basket when there should have been much, much more.

"All the personal items are in the same place," I said.

"Aha!" Arnulf said. "And that is not all. Convents have silver—candles, chalices, platters—and yet there is not a single piece of silver, melted or otherwise, in the whole place. And now we have these bones that, if the fire had burned as hot as we first thought, should not be here."

"Are you implying that those are the remains of the only victim of the fire?" Conwoïon asked.

"Yes," Arnulf said.

I mulled Arnulf's words for a moment while attempting to piece everything together. My heart swelled with hope, and I almost expected the monk to tell me that Asa had not perished in the fire. Arnulf reached down and pulled one of the bones from the ash. He turned it lengthwise and examined the joints.

"This bone still has marrow," he said.

I felt out of breath. Arnulf took his time to say anything more, and the anticipation became too much to bear. "What are you thinking?" I asked.

Arnulf must have seen the discomfort in my stance. He stepped back a few paces and handed the bone to Bertrand. "There is a fire in this one, isn't there?" he said.

"A poor choice of words given where we are, but yes, you will not find a more willful young man," Conwoïon said.

"Tell me, Northman, what might cause your people to fake the deaths of others?" Arnulf asked.

His insistence on calling me Northman, rather than by my name, irritated me. Were he not a monk, I might have thought to strike him. I clenched my fists and said, "I do not know."

"You think it was Northmen, after all?" Conwoïon asked.

"Oh yes, I do. One of them left something behind, and it appears to have been unintentional. Bertrand, the pendant, please," Arnulf said.

Bertrand dug through the artifacts in the basket and pulled a small wooden trinket from it. He walked it over to Arnulf who held it up high in the afternoon sunlight.

I recognized it immediately. "That is Thor's hammer, Mjolnir," I said. "It is made of wood. How did it survive the fire?"

"It didn't. I found this along the path from the beach," Arnulf said.

"It could have been left there intentionally if the attack was carried out by someone who wanted us to believe they were Northmen," Conwoïon suggested.

"No," Arnulf replied. "Someone with such a motive would have made it more obvious, I should think. I found this piece by pure chance. It was hidden away where it might never have been found if not for our arrival."

"And the bishop's testimony should count for something," Bertrand said, breaking his silence. His voice was smooth and not at all what I expected.

Arnulf cleared his throat and said, "Indeed. He said he clearly saw their ships, and that it was unmistakable. No one in Armorica or Frankland could build such ships, as a forgery or otherwise."

"So, Northmen came, sacked the city, and faked a massacre. But why?" Conwoïon asked.

"Because they were paid to do it." I had worked out what had happened while the others deliberated.

Arnulf appeared intrigued. "Tell us what you are thinking, Northman," he said.

"It is a guess, but perhaps the Northmen were paid in silver by someone who wanted to hurt Nominoë," I said.

"That doesn't explain why they faked a massacre," Conwoïon said.

His words gave me pause. I thought back to my days as a ship's boy and remembered what the shopkeeper in Nantes, Váli, had said.

"It does," I said. "Whoever paid the Northmen probably told them to slaughter everyone. But Northmen are not in the business of slaughter. There is much wealth to be gained from slaves."

My words sparked a sudden excitement in Arnulf. "Of course! I see it clearly, now. The jewelry, the missing silver, the bones—it all makes sense." He stepped over the collapsed beam and walked to the place where they had collected the most artifacts. "They took everything with little value to them and put it here. They must have known we would search the ash after the fire." He proceeded to walk to the basket, grasped a handful of the items and held them up for us to see. "Bronze, copper, and some iron— these are peasants' personal items."

"I can't believe I missed all these clues," Conwoïon said. "We must tell Nominoë this instant what we have found."

We all rushed from the convent to Nominoë's hall and barged in like raiding barbarians. Nominoë was buried in his afternoon writing, and when we entered the building, he jumped back in his chair with surprise. We crowded around him, still breathing hard from our march.

"Who are these people?" Nominoë asked.

Conwoïon spoke clearly and carefully: "They are Brothers Arnulf and Bertrand from Landévennec. They are here to help me investigate the raid."

"Ah, good. And what did you find?" Nominoë asked.

"The convent fire," Conwoïon said through heavy breathing, "was a fake. The men and women and children were taken as slaves."

Nominoë appeared perplexed. I could see the next question he wanted to ask in his eyes, and before he could speak, I said, "They were probably hired to slaughter everyone, but they took slaves because of the wealth they can gain from selling them in the North."

Nominoë motioned with his hands for us to calm down and sit at his table. He snapped his fingers, and one of his servants approached him. The servant leaned in, and Nominoë whispered in his ear. Soon, the table was full of goblets of wine, platters of cheese, and husks of bread. As we settled in, Nominoë relaxed. He took a quick drink of his wine and began asking more questions.

"Arnulf, you are the abbot at Landévennec?"

"No, lord," Arnulf replied. "Brother Bertrand and I are beekeepers."

"Beekeepers?" Nominoë said with surprise, and he turned his head slowly and deliberately toward Conwoïon.

"My apologies. Arnulf and I have known each other for many years. I asked for his help in this matter because, before he joined the monastery, he served as reeve to the lord of Quimper, and he investigated many crimes. Since taking the habit, he has helped the church investigate oddities, false claims of miracles, and the like. I believed his keen eye would help my investigation," Conwoïon explained.

"All right. What did you find?" Nominoë asked. "From the beginning."

Arnulf carefully laid out his evidence. He explained how the bones found in the nave should not have survived if no others had, and he presented the artifacts he had collected to show that none were made of silver or gold. Lastly, he put forward my speculation that the Northmen had been paid by someone to carry out a massacre but took the victims as slaves instead. Nominoë listened to all of it.

"Let us say you are right," he said at the end of Arnulf's presentation. "What am I to do?"

The monks stared at each other. "Lord, we merely uncover the truth. We are not in a position to say how to use it," Arnulf explained.

Nominoë sat in silence for a long time. He put his elbow on the table, rested his chin on a clenched fist, and gazed at the far wall. All the while, Arnulf, Bertrand, and Conwoïon ate and drank their fill. I had no appetite and sat and waited for Nominoë to say something. Eventually, he did.

"If I had to guess who paid the Northmen to attack my city, it would have to be the Franks," Nominoë said. "But who among them would dare? Louis seeks peace. He would not risk it with such an act."

"There is one way to find out," I said. It was the first time I had spoken, and Nominoë delighted at the sound of my voice.

"What do you suggest?" he asked.

"Someone will need to find the Northmen who did this and ask who paid them," I proposed. I knew what I wanted, and I was leading Nominoë to it.

"You believe she is still alive, don't you?" Nominoë asked with a softer tone.

I nodded.

"There is no force more powerful in this world than love. I almost envy you."

Conwoïon spat out his wine. "You want to go after them? But... you can't, not alone. How foolish! Besides, you have become one of us. We have fought together and bled together; you cannot abandon us now!"

"I am afraid Conwoïon is right," Nominoë said. "We will find out who did this through other means."

Anger swelled in my chest and sent my innards into a fury. I gritted my teeth and said nothing more. Nominoë saw through me but said nothing to press the issue.

"I have more work to do, but I thank you, Arnulf and Bertrand, for making the journey to Vannes. Conwoïon will see that you are comfortable and well fed. If you should find anything else at all in regard to the raid, please do not hesitate to tell me."

After the meeting, I stormed off to my bedchamber. I kicked my bed and tore my beddings to pieces. When I sat down on the floor against the wall, I held my head in despair. I considered ending my life, but it was a fleeting feeling that passed when I came to my senses. The wine's bitter bite still clouded my judgment. I gazed out the window at the evening sky and thought about Asa.

The sky had turned an awe-inspiring mixture of red and purple, and I wondered if she saw it too. I glanced back at my bed and noticed I had knocked Eilif's woodcarving onto the floor. I picked it up and chuckled at how little it resembled a wolf. As I fiddled with it between my fingers, I remembered what he had said to me before he left. I was a Northman, not a Celt, and I should not forget who I was. A Viking would not mope around in a small room. He would do what he desired. What I wished was to rescue Asa and make whoever had taken her pay for what they had done. To find her, I would need a ship and a loyal crew, but who would follow me? I would need to prove my noble blood, but I hadn't the slightest idea how.

At nightfall, when most of the townspeople had settled in to sleep, I dressed in my battle attire and threw on a thick, dark cloak. I took my sword but not my shield, for it would have proven too heavy and cumbersome for the journey. When the city fell silent, I snuck out of my room and hurried off toward the countryside.

I planned to take the road to Nantes and hoped Váli still tended his shop. I expected he would know where I might start looking for the men who had raided Vannes. As I scurried in the dark from building to building, I happened upon a small group of men with torches patrolling the streets. I tiptoed around them and darted off in the opposite direction. On the edge of the city, where the boardwalk turned to mud, I heard a voice call out to me.

"I had a feeling you might try to leave tonight," Nominoë said. He stood alone, and I could only make out his shadowy figure by faint torchlight.

"I must find her," I said.

"I know." Nominoë stepped closer and put his hand on my shoulder. "We will miss you, you know."

"I will return," I said.

"Of that I am sure," Nominoë said. "Have you heard the story of the crab and the seagull?"

"I haven't," I whispered.

"There was once a crab trapped on a sandbar. The crab wanted to cross the lagoon to shore, but in the water were hungry fish who would surely eat him. So, he asked a passing seagull to give him a ride. The seagull laughed and said the crab would pinch his neck if he let him onto his back, and they would both drown. But the crab pleaded and pleaded, and finally, the seagull, convinced that the crab would keep his word, agreed to take him to shore. The crab climbed on the seagull's back and, halfway across the lagoon, he pinched the bird. As they fell, the seagull asked why the crab had pinched him, since the two of them would now surely die. The crab replied that he could not help it... pinching was in his nature."

"I would never betray you," I said, believing he thought of me as the crab in his story.

"That is not what I meant," he said. He smiled and squeezed my shoulder. "You have been a loyal friend. I have enjoyed our time together, but I knew that I could never contain your desire to leave one day. Adventure is in your nature—you made that fact abundantly clear when you described your people—and I cannot change it."

Nominoë reached around his belt and untied a small purse. He placed the bag in my hand and patted me once more on the shoulder. I took the purse, tied it to my own belt, and covered it with my cloak. We stood in silence, neither with the right words for our parting.

"I will find out who did this," I said. "I promise."

"If the Franks ordered the raid on Vannes, they have broken their oath to us at Redon. It will mean war," Nominoë lamented.

"And I will return to fight at your side," I said.

"Your path may lead you elsewhere, and if so, I will understand. All I ask of you now is to remember us. Remember us when you have your ship and crew, and look to the shores of Frankland for wealth."

Rather than say goodbye, I nodded and ran off into the night. I followed the old Roman road through the fields and forests of Armorica until I reached a quiet village near a large, open clearing. Not a single fire flickered, and I thought at first that no one lived there, until I found some dim, smoldering coals left in a kiln in what I assumed was a blacksmith's workshop.

By the pale light of the moon, I found my way to a barn where I burrowed into a pile of hay and wrapped myself with my cloak. I slept lightly and awoke at first light when the villagers began to open their houses. It was a Celtic village whose houses had the same thatched roofs and mud-caked walls as Vannes, but much smaller. My stomach growled with hunger, so I stood conspicuously in the open and waited for a villager to notice me.

A short, barrel-chested man in a tan apron, with thick, hairy arms, passed me on his way to the blacksmith workshop. His eyes were sunken and tired as if he had left his soul in bed to sleep, but his body had arisen to start his daily work.

"Is there a trader in this village?" I asked him.

The man paused and looked at me with a blank stare. "Who are you?" he asked.

"I am a traveler, and I need food," I said.

He looked me over from head to toe and motioned to me to follow him. We walked to his house a few paces away, and he knocked on the door and said, "Nolwenn, a traveler here to see you."

The man left me at the door and returned to his workshop. A woman with a healthy girth and brown braided hair met me. She smiled and pushed me away from the door, closing it behind her so I could not see inside.

"Travelers are supposed to stay at the tavern," she said. She took my hand and walked with me toward the other side of the village near the Roman road. "Have you never traveled before?"

"Not along the road, no," I said.

"It's quite all right. You must have come from Vannes?"

I nodded to say yes.

"Someone should have told you. There are villages all along the road, spaced apart about the distance a man can walk in a day. Each has a tavern where travelers can eat and sleep, but it will cost you. Do you have money?"

"I do," I said.

She pulled her hand back for an instant and said, "You're not a runaway, are you? No lord is going to come looking for you?"

"No. Why do you think that?" I asked.

She paused and smirked. "You are dressed like a lord's son, and you are alone. And that sword of yours is sticking out from under your cloak."

We entered a more substantial structure with two stories and a staircase along the outside wall that led to several doors on the upper level. We entered through the door on the lower level where Nolwenn sat me down on an uneven wooden bench at one of six tables. The place was empty except for a drunken man who slept near the far wall.

"I'll find the tavern keeper for you," Nolwenn said.

When she returned, she brought over a slender man with simple farm clothes, long black hair, and a thick mustache.

"If you want food, you pay first," he said.

I reached into the purse, pulled out one silver coin, and placed it on the table. Nolwenn and the man both looked at the coin as if they had never seen one in their lives. "Is it enough?" I asked the keeper.

"Yes," the keeper said.

"How many more of those do you have?" Nolwenn asked. Her demeanor had changed, and it made me nervous.

"I would rather not say," I said. "Please, I just need some food and drink, and I will be on my way."

The keeper brought me a hearty meal of eggs, bread, soup, and a large goblet of watered-down ale. I was a starving wolf and devoured the meal as soon as the keeper had brought it. Once finished, I stood up, thanked the keeper and Nolwenn, and left for the road. At the next village, I knew to visit the tavern and was more careful not to show my silver.

It took several days and nights to reach Nantes, but the journey was not unpleasant. I had not realized how busy the road was for trade and saw many people traveling with ox-drawn carts loaded with goods. The taverns at night filled with locals and travelers who talked and drank together. Many seemed to know each other from previous journeys. Although I did not join them, I learned what life was like for the common people. I had not understood that I had held such a privileged place in Vannes, and my journey offered me a sobering insight into life outside Nominoë's court.

On the northern bank of the Loire River, I found a deserted village of charred buildings with dilapidated foundations. The Roman road cut through the town to a stone tower that defended the river. It was as I remembered. The tower connected to a bridge that crossed the Loire into Nantes. The walls did not seem quite as tall as I remembered them, but they were impressive to say the least, particularly when compared to the woodworks that defended Vannes.

Two Frankish soldiers stood guard at the entrance and inspected those who arrived and departed by the bridge. Although the settlement around the entrance appeared abandoned, the flow of men and women and carts and oxen passing through the tower made for a crowded affair.

To avoid attracting the guards' attention, I offered my assistance to one of the tradesmen who was struggling with his cart. I helped push the cart from the rear and kept my head down, and we passed without incident. Once in the city, I searched for the market Eilif and I had visited, and where I had first encountered Asa. I walked street after street until I found the church that had overlooked the market, but I found only an empty courtyard in its shadow. Frustrated, I sat on the stone steps in front of the church and sank my head into my hands.

"Spare a coin for an old pauper?" I heard a man say nearby.

A man with blond hair and a greying beard moved closer to me, holding a small wooden cup. He had longing eyes, and when he held out his cup, I saw the bone of his wrist through his skin. What's more, he smelled of death. Yet, rather than tell him to leave, I examined him. Blond hair in Nantes was not typical, nor did the Franks wear beards.

"Váli?" I asked.

The man lowered his cup. "How do you know my name?"

It was Váli after all. He was unrecognizable.

"I am Hasting. We met many years ago when I was a boy. I sailed with Eilif," I said.

"I... I do not remember you," he said.

I stood to my feet. "Please, try to remember. A girl stole his purse, and I chased after her. We sold you white furs from the North." Váli said nothing. "Come, I will buy you food and drink."

Váli seemed dazed, unable to remember where he stood. When we walked to the nearest tavern, they turned us away for the smell of him. The tavern keeper was kind enough to point us in the direction of the bathhouses across the bridge on the southern bank of the river.

The bathhouses were a collection of small conical tents with large wooden barrels filled with fresh water. Bath maids helped patrons wash their clothes, but Váli's smelled so rotten we decided to throw them into the cesspit. Thankfully, they had some spare clothes to sell to us. It took a long while of scrubbing to finally rid Váli of his stench. I paid the bath maids double what they had asked, so they did not complain.

When they finished with him, Váli smelled of fresh lavender and appeared a whole new man. I, too, took the opportunity to bathe and change my undergarments. The bath maids even freshened my leathers. Cleaned and content, we walked back to the tavern and took a seat at one of the tables where we ate and drank our fill. The more he ate, the more Váli seemed to regain his wits. We retired early in the night, took a room on the upper floor, and each slept on our own cot until morning.

As the sun's rays shone through the cracks in the shutters, I felt around for my things. Váli had already left, and I could not feel my purse around my belt. I panicked. Had he stolen my money and fled? Without a moment to lose, I sprang from my cot and descended the staircase to the tavern. To my relief, I found Váli at one of the tables eating. He smiled when he saw me.

"My savior!" he rejoiced. "Come, join me. The food is excellent."

"Where's my purse?" I snarled.

"Oh, my apologies." He reached into his pocket, pulled out my purse, and tossed it to me. "It slipped off your belt last night, so I took it for safekeeping."

"You could have robbed me," I said.

Váli scowled at the suggestion. "I am not that kind of man."

I sat at the table with him and ate another hearty breakfast of eggs and bread. The keeper even had a few apples for us to eat.

"What has happened since I last saw you?" I asked him.

"The Franks outlawed trade with Northmen. They seized all my wares and shut down my stand. I should have left when I had the chance. I was a fool for thinking I could stay," he said. He then turned the conversation around and asked, "Why did you seek me out?"

He listened attentively as I told the tale of how I had risen in the ranks of Nominoë's court and fought to unify all of Armorica under one king. From time to time, he seemed to disbelieve my story. When I reached the part about Asa, the raid, and my flight from Vannes in the dark of night, he crossed his arms and leaned on the table in thought.

"I can't decide if you are brave or stupid," he said. "I mean no offense. But if you are who you say you are, you should have stayed among the Celts. From what you describe, you had a home there, and men who considered you their kin."

"I must find Asa," I said. It was all I cared about, and all I could think about.

"If she was taken as a slave, you will have a hard time finding her," Váli said. "The Northmen trade slaves across the known world. She could be anywhere."

"I was hoping you could help me find where to start," I said. "You are the only other Dane I know. I thought perhaps you might still have contact with them."

"Alas, no. I have been trapped within these walls all this time," he muttered. "However, I do know of a place where we might find Northmen. I would be willing to tell you where to find them under one condition."

"Which is?" I asked.

"Take me with you," he pleaded.

His demand surprised me. "You wish to follow me?"

"I cannot live here any longer; I will surely die. Take me with you, and I will follow you to the edge of Midgard," he said.

"Yes," I replied. "I would be honored."

Váli embraced me and rejoiced at my decision. He was my first follower—the first man who pledged his life into my service. He made a spectacle of the moment and knelt before me to swear his oath. I had not asked for it, but I did not refuse it, either.

When he calmed down, he leaned in and whispered, "Not far from where the Loire meets the ocean, there is an island. On the far side of this island, out of sight of the Franks and Celts, lies a hidden Northman base from where they launch raids and trade with the North."

"Does it have a name?" I asked.

Váli nodded. "Herio."

10

Mystic in the Woods

Using the coin I had left, Váli and I bought supplies
for the journey ahead. We filled hunting packs
with dried fruits and meat, and some bread,
hoping to ration what we had as long as possible. I bought
Váli a long hunting knife in the event we might need to
defend ourselves, and he thanked me for it. Still fragile
from his starvation as a pauper, he tired quickly. I hoped
he could at least endure until we reached the island, but I
had my doubts.

Once we had fitted ourselves with what we
thought we needed, we paid a ferryman to take us to the
mouth of the Loire. His barge was simple and flat, hardly a
ship in my mind, and not one that could navigate more
turbulent waters. He promised to take us as far as a town
called Indre, home to a well-known monastery. He
remained wary of us for the better part of the journey and
ignored some of the questions we asked him. His silence
and frequent glares unnerved us at times.

"Do you plan to travel farther?" he asked rather
unexpectedly as we arrived at the port.

"Yes, we are traveling to the island of Herio. Do
you know of it?" I asked.

"I know of it," the ferryman said. "It's a dangerous
place this time of year, I hear."

"What makes you say that?" I asked.

THE LORDS OF THE WIND

"The Northmen, of course," the ferryman said. "They raid the monastery every spring and summer, or so I've heard."

"Do you know how we might find safe passage to the island?" I asked. I did not expect him to know the answer.

He looked at me sideways and said, "If I were you, I'd take that question to the monastery. They sail to and from Herio weekly to take pilgrims to see the relics of Saint Philibert."

I thanked him, and when we arrived at Indre, we disembarked as fast as our legs could carry us toward the village. We had barely enough daylight left to find a tavern for a meal and a place to sleep. The tavern keeper, I found out, was sympathetic to Nominoë and, seeing my attire, he welcomed us warmly. While we had not crossed the March back into Celtic land, the people in Indre, I soon learned, were Celts. Váli and I slept well that night, and at daybreak we walked to the monastery to find a monk who might help us.

In Vannes, the holy men of the church started their prayers and labor before sun up, so I guessed the monks in Indre likely did the same. As I predicted, a small group of them emerged from the monastery after their morning prayers and headed toward the gardens to begin their day's work. Váli and I approached them, cautious not to frighten them. Before I could ask anything, a dark-haired monk intercepted us.

"What is your business in Indre?" he asked. He was a young man, not much older than me, and he had a soft, round, featureless face.

"We're looking for a monk who can help us," I said.

"Help with what?" the monk asked, keeping his hands clasped together and covered by the sleeves of his habit.

"We seek passage to Herio," I replied. I kept a reasonable distance, for something about his demeanor made me uncomfortable.

"What business do you have there?" he asked.

"Can't you tell?" Váli said with a chuckle. I heard mockery in his voice, and I feared he might upset the monk. "We're pilgrims."

"Where from?" the monk asked.

His unbroken line of questioning unnerved me. I paused for a moment and looked at Váli. He shrugged as if to say perhaps I should tell the monk the truth. "Vannes," I said.

The monk darted off into the monastery without another word. We were left standing there, quite confused. After a taut moment of silence, Váli said, "We should visit the port. Surely someone there can help us."

I agreed. Together, we started to walk away when we heard the shriek of a high-voiced man. The young man who had questioned us had returned with an elderly monk at his side, and he called for us to stop. They walked over as quickly as the old man could manage with his walking stick. Not only was he aged but also fat, which made walking all the harder for him. He kept his grey hair longer than other monks I had seen, and he had a clean-shaven face that showed a myriad of wrinkles trickling from his cheeks to his chins.

"My name is Léon," he said. "I hear you are looking for passage to Herio."

"You heard correctly," I said.

Léon looked at me inquisitively. He moved closer and said, "My colleague tells me you are from Vannes. But you are not a Celt, are you?"

"No, I—"

"Enough with the questions," Váli interjected. "Can you take us there or not?"

"Isn't your friend feisty. With hair and beard such as his, I might even venture to say he is a Northman," Léon said.

"Does it matter?" I asked.

"Indeed, it does." Léon stood a little taller. "Northmen do not make good pilgrims. Tell me, truthfully, what is your business in Herio?"

"We're looking for someone," I said.

"Forget him," Váli said. "Let's go to the port; someone there will take us."

"Wait," Léon pleaded. "I apologize. I am a curious man and tend to ask too many questions. We can offer you passage if you have the coin."

I laughed and said, "An old friend told me once it is a good thing to ask questions; it means you are not dimwitted. But you must also know when to be silent."

"A wise friend, indeed," Léon said with a smirk. "God smiles upon you, young man. You arrived just in time—one of our ships leaves for the island today. It will cost you three deniers each to board it."

I reached into my purse and dug around. We had spent nearly all of the money Nominoë had given me. At the bottom of the bag, I found a large coin, thicker than the others and softer. When I pulled it out, I saw that it was a single gold coin. Léon admired it as I held it in front of him.

"Will this suffice?" I asked.

Léon nodded. His eyes filled with greed, and for a moment I saw him as a desperate rat pining for food.

"Come," he said. "I will show you to the ship."

The monks led us to the port where they spoke briefly with the ship's captain. Léon paid him in silver, and he welcomed us aboard.

"The coin!" Léon pleaded.

I tossed him the coin with a flick of my thumb. The old man scurried to catch it and managed to snatch it out of the air before it hit the ground. He smiled and waved to us in thanks. Váli and I settled in for the voyage between several large crates of supplies destined for the monastery on Herio.

"Do you have any idea what that coin you gave him was worth?" Váli asked.

I shook my head.

"Well, it was worth more than six deniers."

I shrugged. It was the one coin I had left. From that moment forward, we would need to rely on our packed supplies to survive.

The ship did not depart immediately—they waited to see if any others might pay their way to the island. None showed. It was not a large ship. It had a square aft, a wide birth, and it lacked speed compared with Sail Horse. Despite its shortcomings, it was sturdy and sailed well.

We launched from the port and rode the current of the river to the sea, and there the crew lowered the sail. A strong wind blew from the south, which slowed our journey. As we traversed the open water, the captain, a broad-chested man with a fat nose, a wrinkled brow, and thick, grainy stubble on his face, sat with us to rest and eat.

"Léon said you are pilgrims," he said with a deep, raspy voice. "I haven't had pilgrims on my ship in many months. They are too afraid of Northman raids."

Váli started to turn green as we spoke. He had not sailed in many years, and the motion of the waves made him ill. He rushed to the gunwale and expelled his breakfast into the ocean. A colony of seagulls dove from above to claim a portion.

"You don't have the look of pilgrims, but your friend vomits like one, sure enough," the captain said with a chuckle.

"Are you from the island?" I asked him.

"No. My family is from Ampam. The monastery pays me to ferry supplies from Indre to Herio, and monks when the spring comes. A few years ago, we ferried supplies from Ampam, but ever since the Northmen burned it, we've made Indre our home."

"Why in spring?" I asked.

"You don't know?" he retorted, flabbergasted. "Every year the monks leave the island in spring to avoid the Northman raids and return in winter when the Northmen have sailed home. They have been doing it for nearly twenty years."

"If the monks left, who are the supplies for, then?" I asked.

"Some stayed this year with a garrison of soldiers from Nantes," he said. "They've built a castrum to defend the island and hope to repel the raids this summer."

"Do you think they will?" Váli asked.

The captain snorted as he laughed and said, "No."

It took three days at sea to reach Herio. The island was a curved fishhook, and the harbor, village and monastery stood where the hook curved in on itself toward the mainland. We arrived in the afternoon and were greeted by a sweltering summer heat. On the hill above, we saw the wooden palisade of the castrum and the moat below it. The wall stood the height of two men and reminded me of Hagar's fort. It looked sturdy, but not impregnable.

We headed for the village to the west to find the local tavern, as well as someone who would know the location of the Northman base. The town was nearly empty, with few locals walking about in the midday sun. The tavern keeper was napping in a chair outside, beneath the cover of a light cloth canopy. When he saw us arrive, he crossed his arms over his thick belly but did not bother to stand.

"I'm not open," he said brusquely.

"We are looking for something," I said. "Do you know of any other settlements on the island?"

"There are several." He took on a haunting tone and said, "Go back to where you came from. Leave this place before it's too late."

"Jovial fellow, isn't he?" Váli scoffed. "Where to?"

I looked around the village for clues. The houses were built in the same style as those in Armorica, with wicket and daub walls and thick thatched roofs. They were laid out in a semi-circle around the town's well, which faced the monastery up the hill. Closer to the monastery, there were a few two-story houses built with lime and mortar walls, and I surmised they either belonged to the wealthiest villagers or the monastery.

The ground was soft and sandy, and although a suffocating heat had gripped the island, a strong ocean breeze occasionally gusted through to cool us off. Beyond the houses stood a crumbling wall, and beyond that, farmland and salt marsh as far as the eye could see. I put my hand up to blot out the sun, and ahead I saw what appeared to be a road.

"Over there," I said to Váli.

We walked to the edge of the village and found a cobbled road in far worse shape than the one between Vannes and Nantes. Grasses and moss and sand had swallowed most of it into the earth. I knelt to feel the stones and to see where it led.

"Do we follow?" Váli asked.

"I do not have a better idea," I said.

Váli took in deep breaths while we followed the road through the marshes. He had spent so much time confined to the city, with putrid, stale air, that he relished every moment of our journey. The island was long and flat, and it seemed for a time that we had not made any progress. I looked behind us every so often to gauge how far we had walked. The monastery's white limestone walls glinted in the distance and reminded us of where we had begun.

As the day passed, we began to run low on water. Beside the road on both sides were salt marshes, but none of it was potable. The farther we moved away from the monastery, the stronger the wind blew. We welcomed it, for it helped to cool us as we walked in the sun.

At sunset, the wind and heat both subsided, and we arrived at the edge of a small forest with thin maritime pines. By the time we found the forest, we had lost track of the road; it had vanished beneath the sandy soil along the way. At the woodland's edge, we could see a column of smoke rising above the canopy. Someone lived nearby.

We followed a beaten path deep into the trees and trod lightly in case of trouble. The surrounding foliage was alive with creatures we could not see, and I did not doubt that a wild boar or two called the forest home. Wild boars are foul creatures, and dangerous. Many a man died hunting them in the countryside around Vannes, and I knew if we encountered one it would spell trouble for the both of us.

Enough light remained to guide our way, and it did not take long before we happened upon a deep ditch covered in pine needles and sand. A sickening smell filled the air around it. Váli knelt down, dug into the soft soil, and uncovered a few bones. When he dug deeper, he found a human skull with hair still attached to the scalp and a golden brocaded band tied to the bone.

"What have we found?" I asked. My mouth was agape, and I felt the tremor in my fingers return. I had seen death before, but not like this. In battle, the dead are honored and buried with their last rites. Here, the bodies of the slain had been tossed into the ditch like diseased chattel. Who could have done this, I thought? What men could show so little regard for the dead? Though I did not know these people, I felt anguish for them.

"The base we were looking for, I think," Váli answered. He pulled back his hand and covered his mouth with his elbow. His eyes watered, and he turned away to hide his tears. He collected himself and said, "I knew these people. I had heard a rumor this had happened, but I did not want to believe it was true."

"You knew about this?" I clenched my fists at the thought that Váli had deceived me. He had promised to lead me to a hidden base of Northmen, not a mass grave.

"No," he declared. "I heard whispers. I thought for sure they were mere rumors and nothing more. I am sorry, my friend, but I think we have reached a dead end."

"We should find a campsite. I saw smoke when we entered the woodlands; someone still lives here," I said.

"Over there," Váli said. He walked to where we could cross the ditch. "The encampment is that way."

Váli led on, and we continued carefully in the direction of the smoke. Not far from where the dead lay, we happened upon a clearing in the woods with a stone well at its center. The trees around the clearing had scorch marks on their trunks, and many of their needles had turned the color of rust. If there had once been a village, it had been so utterly demolished that not a trace of the houses or other structures remained.

"As good a place as any to make camp," I said of the clearing.

"I don't want to make camp here," Váli said with a tremble in his voice. "This place… it is for the dead."

The clearing led to another beaten path that guided us to the backside of a dune, and from there we climbed to its crest and arrived at a tranquil beach with not a soul in sight. A westerly wind blew over us; we basked in its cool reprieve and watched the sun sink behind the skyline. When I looked back at the forest, I could no longer see the smoke we had spotted from the other side of the wood. The hair on the back of my neck stood up at the thought that someone was out there, watching, and they had perhaps extinguished their fire when we had crossed into their land.

"We should make camp in the clearing," I suggested again.

Váli looked up at me with a sudden pallor and said, "Why can't we make camp here? Or there? Or anywhere else?"

"We are looking for whoever made the fire. We should make ourselves known, and they will find us... if they are still here."

Reluctantly, Váli followed me as I collected twigs and branches on the way back. We dug a hole near the well and built a fire using the flint I had brought from Vannes, and we unpacked our hunting sacks and unrolled our blankets to settle in for the night. In the firelight, we searched the surroundings for larger branches and foliage and erected a small barrier about knee-height around camp. It would not stop a man, but it would dissuade a wild boar should one find us of interest. Once finished, we sat beside the fire and ate what little rations we had—some dried fruit and salted pork—and cracked open our gourd of wine to calm our nerves. With some wine to warm his belly, Váli stood up and examined the well.

"Do you think there is fresh water down there?" he asked.

He had sparked my curiosity. I, too, stood and took a closer look. We had ignored it in the daylight, but now that the salted pork had dried our throats, we both felt the urge for fresh water. Váli felt around the edges for anything that might help us, to no avail.

"We will have to find a way to reach down there tomorrow," I said. "If it's water you want, I have a little left in my pack, I—"

When I turned back toward the campfire, I paused mid-sentence. A man in a dark cloak was sitting across from us, eating our salted pork and drinking our wine.

Saying nothing, I nudged Váli who turned to look and froze. We stared at him as we leaned against the well, unable to move at first. I reached across my body and grasped the hilt of my sword.

"You won't need that," the figure said in the language of the Northmen. It wasn't a man at all, but a woman. She kept eating without giving us a single glance.

I let go of my sword. My heart was a bucking horse, thumping and thumping until I worked up the courage to move closer. After all, I had seen battle and lived, and she was just an old woman. Why I felt more fear from her than an army of Britons is a curious question. Perhaps it was the haunted locale, the ditch of bodies we had found, or that we were alone in the wilderness, or her sudden appearance from the darkness. My fear subsided, and when I caught my breath, I sat beside the fire.

"Careful, Hasting," Váli said. Although he did not say it, his tone suggested he had every Northern superstition running through his mind at once.

I stared at the woman a moment and said, "We are looking for a Northman base. Do you know of it?"

"I did," the woman sneered with a mouthful of salted pork.

I had to choose my questions carefully. "Where can we find it?"

"You already did," she said.

I laughed. "Stop these games."

"I am not playing any games," she said with a booming voice, and her sudden outburst sent a jolt through my body. She pulled back the hood of her cloak to reveal an aged face with thick burn scars on one side, from her cheek to her ear, and blue tattoos that resembled the branches of a tree on the other. Her hair was black as night, tied tightly behind her head, and her braids were adorned with silver rings.

"Who are you?" I asked.

She smiled and said, "A wanderer."

Her head swayed back and forth when she spoke, and when she reached for more food, she patted the ground in a sweeping motion until her hand touched what she sought. When I looked more closely at her in the flickering of the light, I saw clouds drifting across her irises.

"Are you blind?" I asked.

I reached over and waved my hand in front of her face. With dazzling speed, she contorted my arm, and I found myself with a knife at my throat. Váli drew his weapon and stepped forward, but stopped when I gestured for him to stand back.

Our guest laughed. "You are brave but reckless," she said. She released me from her grip, and we returned to our places.

My cheeks flushed as I brushed myself off and asked, "If you cannot see, how did you know to speak to us in our language?"

"Magic." She laughed again. "I heard you speaking to each other in the woods."

"What is your name, wanderer?" Váli asked. He looked more at ease now that the woman had not slit my throat.

"Names... they always ask for a name. My name is not important," she muttered. "I am Oddlaug. Tell me, what brought you to this hidden place?"

"We are searching for Northmen," I said.

"I know, but why?" Oddlaug said.

"I... I hope to journey north to find someone."

Oddlaug scratched her head and said, "Who?" I hesitated, and before I could speak she said, "A girl? Interesting."

"How did you know?" I said aghast.

"A feeling," she said. "I think it would be helpful if you told me everything from the beginning, and slowly."

I obliged her and shared my life's tale from my time in Hagar's hall, to my voyages with Eilif, to my life at Nominoë's court. I gave as much detail as I could remember, though already I had lost some of my earliest memories. My first encounter with Asa I remembered clearly, and I took our guest through every detail about her.

Oddlaug listened and even smiled at certain points of interest. She allowed me to speak uninterrupted and showed great patience for my scattered storytelling. When I finished, there was a long, quiet pause.

"How's your skill with a blade?" Oddlaug asked.

"Good," I said.

"Thank the gods, because you would make a dreadful skald." She and Váli laughed harder than I would have liked. She repositioned herself and continued. "I have three questions."

"Ask them," I said.

"How old is Asa?"

"My age... sixteen, perhaps seventeen years old."

"Did she tell you where she came from?" she asked.

"She never did. She said one day she would, but she never got the chance."

"Did she have any markings on her body?"

When she asked the question, my mind flooded with the memories of our kiss in the woods in Armorica and our brief encounter with the farmer. I remembered when her sleeve pulled back as she handed the farmer some silver. I said, "Yes, she had a purple mark on her arm. How did you know?"

"My boy, to me she is royalty, and it warms my heart to know she is alive," she uttered.

"Who said anything about her being alive?" I asked.

Oddlaug took one last swig of wine and leaned into the dirt to sleep. I had many more questions for her, but she began to snore, and I took it to mean she had finished speaking with us for the night. Váli and I slipped into our blankets and slept, although uneasily. Neither of us trusted the old woman, but we took it as a good sign that she did not kill me when she had the chance.

At daybreak, while Váli still slept, Oddlaug woke me with a pat on the shoulder. She led me to the beach, and while we walked, she held my arm for support. The ocean was tranquil, the wind had not yet picked up, and the sky was cloudless and shone a brilliant blue. I could not think of a more beautiful place to live in the summer. What a waste that Oddlaug had lived there without her sight. We stood in silence and listened to the birds chirping in the trees behind us, the seagulls squawking in the distance, and the waves breaking white on the sand.

"To find Asa, you will need a ship, and men to follow you," she said. "From here, it is an impossible task."

"What happened to this place, Oddlaug?" I asked.

"The same as has happened countless times among our people. One man coveted the wealth of another, and he took it by force."

Her words resonated in my heart. "My father was killed for his wealth, too," I said.

"Your father was a chieftain?" she asked.

I nodded.

Though she could not see, she nodded back. She reached into her cloak and pulled from it a curved knife with a jewel-encrusted golden hilt. She took my hand in hers, and before I could react, she drew blood. I pulled back my hand and watched in disgust as she licked the blood from the blade. "You do have noble blood," she said with a smile.

"Are you a Sami?" I asked her, dumbfounded.

Oddlaug laughed. "No, but I am familiar with the magical arts. I am a *völva*. At least, I was."

I stared at her for a moment, fascinated by the little I had seen. She gazed into the distance as if to admire the ocean and horizon. As beautiful as it was, my mind fixated on the task before me.

"I will need more than your word to convince other Northmen of my noble blood," I stated.

"You will. Do you have anything of his? Your father, I mean. A ring? A jewel?"

"A sword," I said.

Oddlaug rejoiced and said, "Let me see it."

"I don't have it," I said. "A chieftain in Ireland took it when he bought me as a slave."

"I see," Oddlaug said. "At least you know where it is. Come, I want to show you something."

She tugged at my tunic and led me back toward our camp. We walked from the beach to the well and passed by Váli who had awoken and was building a fire. When he saw us walking together, he gave me a quizzical look, and I nodded back at him that all was well.

Oddlaug and I continued along the beaten path into the woodlands. How she knew her way through the trees escaped me. It was as if she could see, except for the few times she reached her hand out to feel what lay in front of us. I knew where she wanted to take me. The thought sent my heart into a flutter and my stomach twirling. Once at the ditch, she pointed to the dense layer of pine needles, dirt, and sand that covered the bodies.

"Stay here," she said.

She released my arm and stepped down the edge of the ditch. Her feet slipped, so she squatted down to sit in the dirt. Her hands felt around, and when she pushed farther into the soft ground, part of it caved underneath her. A plume of dust wafted into the air and released an indescribable stench that burned my eyes and nostrils.

Oddlaug appeared undaunted. She felt around some more until her hands grasped a long cloth sack that she pulled from the horrific scene. Bones now protruded from the dirt in every direction, some with bits of cartilage still clinging to the joints.

"Can you help me up?" Oddlaug asked.

I reached down with one hand while covering my nose and mouth with the other. In a quick succession of jerks, I helped Oddlaug crawl out of the ditch onto solid ground. She began untying the knot of the rope that kept the sack shut, although several holes had formed within it. Dark stains covered the cloth. I dared not guess what had spilled onto that sack. Once she worked through the knot, she reached in and pulled out another bag, this one with fewer stains and fewer holes. Once through the last knot, she removed both sacks to reveal a large leather satchel. The satchel had many ties along its side to keep it closed, but rather than untie each one, she took a knife and cut through them. Inside the satchel, she revealed a small fortune of gold coins.

"It is my former lord's wealth, or at least what is left of it," she said.

"You could buy a ship with this," I said.

"A small one, yes." She held out the satchel and pressed it against my chest. "I want you to have it."

"What?" I asked with utter astonishment. "Why?"

"Do you think I would survive a journey at sea to Ireland?" she scoffed. "All I ask in return is that you find Asa, and give her a good life. This was her home, and like you, it was taken from her. She has lost everything. Perhaps you can give her something back."

I accepted the satchel and closed it to keep the coins from spilling out. "Where will I find Northmen to take me to Ireland?" I asked.

Oddlaug laughed and said, "The monastery attracts Northmen as honey does a bear. I suggest you start there."

We walked back to our camp without another word. Upon arriving at the tree line, Váli bustled about to serve us with the little food we had left. Oddlaug seemed off. A dark cloud drifted overhead, casting us in shadow. A chilled wind followed, as well as a stampeding wall of rain that roared as it rushed through the woodlands. Váli covered himself in his cloak and met me at the tree line to take cover.

He glanced around and asked, "Where's your friend?"

I turned to where the old woman had stood before the rain. All I saw was an empty woodland obscured by the deluge. "She was here, just now," I said over the storm's rumble.

Váli was haunted. He looked back to the well, then into the woods. "She was?" he asked.

"You did not see her with me before the rain?" I asked.

Váli shook his head. "You were alone." His eyes wandered to the satchel in my hands. "What is it?" he asked.

I gave him a smile and said, "hope."

11

Bears and Honey

Thoughts of Oddlaug and what she had revealed to me weighed on my mind, and I wondered about her sudden disappearance. Though I now had wealth, I felt dismayed that we had not made much progress in finding a Northman ship to take us to Ireland. Váli seemed not to mind any of it. He was satisfied that he had left Nantes and had another Dane to converse with in his native tongue.

On the long walk across the island, he spoke at length about all manner of subjects, and I enjoyed it, for it helped to pass the time. He knew a great deal about the gods, so I asked about them and their great deeds. I had not heard these stories since my time in Hagar's hall. At the village, it seemed the tavern keeper had not moved since we had seen him last. He grumbled as we approached, and he leaned toward the side, snorted, and spat on the ground.

"We could use a place to sleep," I said to him.

"You're still here... damned fools," he muttered.

I took a slow look around the village, and it appeared even emptier than the last time we had walked through. Váli glared at the man. He had little patience for men with no sense of commerce. I pressed the tavern keeper and said, "Please, we need food and a place to sleep."

"Do you have coin?" the man asked.

THE LORDS OF THE WIND

I had nothing but gold coins, and I did not want to spend them. "No, but we can work," I proposed.

"Does it look like I have any work for you?" He paused and took a look around the village. With a great sigh, he said, "It doesn't matter, come in. We'll all be dead soon, anyway."

He grimaced in pain as he stood and waddled to the tavern entrance. We followed him in to find an empty chamber with a low ceiling and several long tables along the walls. He urged us to sit as he made his way into a back room to fetch some food and drink. When he returned, he brought three carafes of wine and a basket of stale, dark bread. He sat with us at the table and handed each of us our own carafe. We stared at them, waiting for him to bring some goblets, but when he took a large gulp from his carafe, we understood that we were meant to drink without them.

"You never found the Northmen, did you?" he said with wine dripping down his mustache.

"You knew about them?" I asked.

"Of course I knew about them." He leaned in to whisper and said, "The next supply ship will arrive in a few days. Since you haven't found what you were looking for, you should return to the mainland before *they* return."

"They?" I asked.

"The Northmen! Are you dimwitted?" he shouted with trepidation in his voice. "The Franks' new fortifications pushed back two ships earlier this summer, but they'll be back... and with many more ships, I am sure."

"That is what we were hoping," I said.

My words gave the tavern keeper cause to plunk down in his chair and pull back his wine. He gazed at us with squinty eyes and said, "Who are you?"

"I am Hasting, sworn to King Nominoë of the Vannetais. We are on a mission to seek out the Northmen who raided the city of Vannes. We have reason to believe they acted on behalf of someone else," I explained.

"They raided Vannes? They grow bolder each summer," the tavern keeper said. He made the sign of the cross and took a large drink from his carafe. "You should have told me you were a Celt from the beginning. These are Celtic lands, and my family is a proud Celtic people."

"Why have you not left for the mainland?" I asked.

He groaned and said, "I am too old and in too much pain for the journey. Besides, the Northmen have no interest in a fat old man such as I. Five years I have stayed in my tavern in the summer, and they haven't bothered to kill me yet." He took another hefty drink from his carafe and pressed his hands against the table to help himself to his feet. "You are welcome to stay here tonight, but if you wish to stay longer, you will need to pay. The monks will have work for you. They harvest salt from the marshes all summer, but since most of them have left for the mainland, they are always in need of more hands to help."

Váli and I sat a while longer until the setting sun robbed the tavern of its light. The tavern keeper showed us a room on the second floor where we could sleep—a small space with a single cot with fresh straw—and he retired to his own bedchamber.

The following morning, we did as he had suggested and walked the path to the monastery. We left our belongings in the room, expecting to return to them in the evening with coin to pay for our stay. Once at the monastery, we encountered a ditch that surrounded the entire property, and on top of it stood a wooden palisade with pikes facing outward from underneath. The one entrance was a small wooden gate with a wooden bridge across the ditch. When we approached the gate, I noticed it was cracked open. No one had locked it shut. We inched into the courtyard to find the monks but saw no one.

"Hello in there!" I shouted, in the hopes of attracting someone's attention.

The monastery was smaller than the others I had seen on the mainland, but it stood tall above the rest of the island so that it could be seen from far away. Low stone archways formed the entire outer wall of the lower level, and from the shadows, a monk emerged in a black habit with a golden rope tied at his waist. He had long black hair and a youthful vigor about him.

"Who are you?" he snarled.

"Pilgrims looking for work. The tavern keeper said you may need help in the marshes," I said.

"Pilgrims? In summer?" the monk asked. "Who allowed you to make the journey?"

"Léon, in Indre," I replied.

"Of course he did," the monk mumbled to himself. He looked us up and down and said, "You don't have the look of pilgrims."

I made the sign of the cross and said, "We wish nothing more than to pray before the holy relics of Saint Philibert."

"To pray before the relics, you will need coin," the monk said. "Which I assume you do not have?"

"We can work," I said.

The monk crossed his arms and said, "All right, we do need help with the salt harvest. Have you ever harvested salt from a marsh?"

Váli and I shook our heads.

"Brother Bertric will show you. Go down to the marshes and meet with him. Tell him Brother Hincmar sent you. For every ten sacks of salt you collect, I will pay you one denier. Sound fair?"

I had never worked for money before, but in my experience monks were trustworthy people, and I took his word for it that he would pay us fairly for our work. Váli did not complain either, so I knew the monk had not offered us a rotten wage.

We did as he asked and left the monastery for the west of the village. When we reached the marshes, we found four monks toiling with the sleeves of their habits rolled up and their feet ankle-deep in mud. They used long wooden rakes to skim the surface of the silt, and with each stroke, they collected thick piles of sea salt which they made into large mounds on the edges of the marsh. Another monk bagged the salt in cloth sacks and carried it over to a wooden shed with a wood-planked roof for storage.

"We are looking for Bertric," I said.

The monk bagging the salt replied, "Come here, lads. Are you here to help?"

"Hincmar sent us," I said.

"God be praised! We are desperately shorthanded," Bertric said. He wiped his sweaty face with his sleeve and ran a hand through his curling brown hair. Light scruff covered his face, and he had youthful brown eyes with a strong brow. The other monks also looked quite young, perhaps a few years older than me. "Take a sack and start filling. I'll teach you more as we go."

For the next two weeks, we labored with the monks to collect and store salt. Váli and I kept to ourselves and spoke to the monks when we had a question about our work. We had no interest in learning about them, and they appeared to mirror that sentiment. The days were long and hot, and fresh water was scarce. It was hard work, but the coin we earned allowed us to pay for our room at the tavern along with plenty of food and wine.

Salt farming is a simple existence. At high tide, water from the ocean fills the marshes. At low tide, the water is trapped in the square evaporation ponds by small wooden levies, and it dries for several days until it reveals a thick layer of white salt crystals that flicker in sunlight.

To keep the work moving, we alternated marshes so that some dried while we collected salt from others. Once the salt was loaded into sacks, we led a mule-drawn wagon to the monastery and stacked the salt in a cold stone cellar.

Each week, a ship arrived from the mainland with fresh supplies for the monastery and the town and left with a cargo hold full of our salt. I remembered how valuable salt of this kind was to the Northmen and surmised it held as much if not more value for the Franks. A monastery such as this one, I thought, could stand to make great wealth from farming salt.

As summer slipped away, I began to lose hope that the Northmen would come. Our tedious toil wore on me, as did the heat, and I felt the urge to abandon the island and find some other way to travel north. When my frustration reached its peak, the gods saw fit to send me that which I desired.

Váli and I returned to work midmorning, as we had done each day during our stay, to find an empty marsh without a monk in sight. They had always arrived before us at dawn, and their absence told us something had happened. Something kept them from their labor. From the marsh, we could see the monastery standing silently in the morning light, as it always did. Birds chirped and twittered, broken by the insufferable crowing of the monastery's lone rooster.

"Should we check on them?" Váli asked.

I climbed atop one of the salt mounds for a better view, and once I had the harbor in my sights, I saw several longships rowing toward the shore and one already tied off at the dock.

"They're here!" I exclaimed.

Indeed, the Northmen had arrived, as did my chance to join them to find Asa. We hurried back to the tavern to gather our things and, most importantly, the wealth Oddlaug had given me, and made our way up the path to the monastery. Our host, the tavern keeper, saw us off with a look of dread on his face. The palisade gate was open without a mark on it, as if the Northmen had entered the monastery grounds without the slightest struggle. I poked my head through and called out in my native tongue, "Who goes there?"

I heard an instant reply: "Ulfr? Is that you?"

"Tell him your name and your father's name," Váli said.

"I am Hasting, son of Ragnar," I said.

A single Northman emerged from the monastery to greet us. He wore a blue wool tunic adorned with gold braid along the neckline and snug cuffs on his wrists, and a full skirt over loose trousers. He had a clean-shaven face and long blond hair tied behind his head with a silver brooch.

"You're not one of mine," he said with a gentle, almost womanly voice.

"I am not," I said. "We were shipwrecked some weeks ago, and most of my men drowned. We have been marooned here ever since, waiting for another ship to take us home."

Váli nodded in agreement. We had discussed what I should tell the Northmen if they ever appeared, to lessen the chance they might kill us. Váli suggested we tell them we were shipwrecked, though I did not relish the idea of lying. I took his advice, however, since he knew the Northmen better than I.

The Northman examined me and said, "What did you say your name was?"

"I am Hasting, son of Ragnar," I repeated.

"Ragnar? That could be anybody. My cousin's name is Ragnar," he said.

I looked at Váli with no idea what to say. He sprang to my defense. "Hasting's father is a wealthy chieftain in Jutland."

"You're the son of a chieftain?" the man asked. He crossed his arms and smirked. "Prove it."

Váli nudged me with his elbow and glanced at my satchel. I understood his meaning. I reached under my cloak and drew out a gold coin. It glittered in the sun's light, and the Northman gazed at it with curious eyes.

"Pretty," he said.

"I have plenty of wealth to pay for the journey," I said.

"Do you have a name?" Váli asked.

"Halldóra," the Northman replied.

"You're a woman," Váli said with surprise.

"What... you couldn't tell?" she snapped.

She raised her arms and looked down at her tunic. I, too, felt surprised. She had a masculine face with a thick brow and square jaw. Except for her hair tied with a brooch, nothing about her seemed womanly.

"You are the captain of your vessel?" I asked her as I put the gold coin back in the satchel.

"Of my ship, yes. Of the fleet, no," she said.

"How many ships?" Váli asked.

"Twenty," she said.

"The monks must have fled when they saw you approaching," Váli said. "They have a lookout, up there." He pointed to a third story tower on the far side of the monastery.

"There wasn't a man here when I arrived," Halldóra said. She was distracted, and she gazed past us as she spoke.

"Are you expecting someone?" I asked.

"Yes, him," she said, pointing toward the bridge.

I turned to find a dozen men led by a warrior who was clad in iron maille with leather guards on his arms and shins. His long black hair flowed past his shoulders and melded with his beard over his chest. He looked at me with icy blue eyes, and as he drew closer, his massive stature became more apparent. I shrank at the sight of him, as did Váli.

"Anything of value?" he asked.

"They took everything, Lord Hakon," Halldóra said with a slight bow of her head.

"Who are these two?" Hakon asked.

"Danes," Halldóra said.

"Danes? In these parts?"

"The son of a jarl... shipwrecked, so he says," she added. From her tone, I surmised she did not believe me.

"I am Hasting, son of Ragna—"

"I don't care who your father was, boy," Hakon interjected. "Frankly, I don't care who you are. What I care about is silver... wealth. Now you can either help me find what I want or disappear before I pull your heart out through your throat."

"I would take the second option if I were you. This place is empty," Halldóra said.

"No," I stated. Váli looked at me wide-eyed, but I kept my eyes fixed on Hakon, who remained stolid. "You won't find silver if the monks fled; they would have taken everything of value. What you do not yet realize is that this island is a treasure trove of wealth, if you know where to look."

Hakon crossed his arms and said, "I'm listening."

"Beyond the village are marshes that produce the best sea salt you will ever taste. It is worth its weight in silver, if you know where to sell it," I explained.

"Salt?" Hakon asked. I had piqued his interest. Even the dimmest of the Northmen knew the value of quality salt. "Show me."

I led Hakon and his men along the path to the village and out into the salt marshes. Once at the shack where we stored the sacks, I stood in front of a pile of salt the height of two men. Hakon surveyed the marsh and, when he saw four other mounds of the same height, he smiled for the first time since we had met him. I swiped a small handful of salt from the pile and brought it to Hakon to taste. He pinched the crystals between his fingers and pressed them against his tongue.

"How did you know about this?" he asked.

"We've been here a while," I said.

"Hasting, son of Ragnar, you say?" Hakon said more cheerfully.

I nodded.

"I will remember the name. I presume you also know where we will fetch a good price for this salt?"

"I do," I said.

Hakon leaned back, pulled one of his men toward him, and said, "Bring up the men and have them bag and load the salt onto our ships." He released his man and turned back to us. "Hasting, son of Ragnar, it appears I owe you an apology. Without you, we might have left this place empty-handed."

"I am honored to have helped," I said.

Hakon put a hand on my shoulder and said, "Shipwrecked, hmm?" He looked down at my wrists. "You have no arm rings."

"No," I said.

"And what is this?" He reached for the satchel containing my wealth.

I blocked his hand with a swift jerking motion and pushed him with all my might. One of my hands struck him in the sternum, and he staggered backward to catch his breath. He growled as he heaved from the blow, but when his men reached for their weapons, he waved his hand to tell them to stand down.

"Full of surprises, this one," he said between heavy breaths. He collected himself for a moment before speaking again. "Hasting, son of Ragnar." Hakon felt underneath his arm guard and pulled from it a silver arm ring with two serpent heads facing each other on the ends.

He tossed it to me and said, "Your first… of many, I am sure."

"You honor me," I said. His gift surprised me, and it calmed my nerves for a moment, for I had thought he would try to kill me. My racing heart slowed, and the flush in my cheeks lessened.

"The salt will fill at most four of my ships," Hakon said. "You will sail with Halldóra and take her to where she can sell it. From there, she will take you home, if that is what you desire. Though I presume your father will not appreciate that you return empty-handed, without ship or crew. If it is wealth you are after, come back and see me."

"And you?" I asked. "What will you do?"

"I have many more ships to fill, and Christians make fine slaves," he said.

From the sound of it, Hakon and his fleet had just arrived in Frankland. But I had to rule him out as the man who had attacked Vannes, so I asked him, "Have you raided anywhere else in the area?"

"Not this year," he said. "Why do you ask?"

"Curious," I said.

He shot me a sidelong look, then turned to Halldóra and said, "May the gods favor you and see to your safe return in Lade with your coffers filled with silver."

Halldóra bowed to him, and with those words, he returned to his fleet. Váli and I followed Halldóra to the monastery. Her men awaited her there empty-handed, and she barked at them for their laziness. She had them join the others who worked to bag and load the salt on the ships. She said few words to us as we followed her, though she did not seem displeased by Hakon's orders. Once her men had all left the monastery, she led us behind the fortifications and down a steep bank to the ocean. Her longship, a modest vessel with fifteen oars on each side, sat on a narrow beach surrounded by jagged rocks and thick-rooted trees. The other ships had docked in the harbor below the monastery, but Halldóra had wanted to surprise the monks from behind, had they kept their courage and defended the grounds.

More men trickled in from all around and, once all of them had returned, they worked the ship back out to sea and rowed through the rocks to the harbor. Váli and I sat at the aft of the ship, astonished that our ploy had worked. When the last sack of salt made its way onto Halldóra's deck, we set sail for the horizon.

"Where to?" Halldóra asked as she took her place at the steering paddle.

"To Ireland," I said. "To Hagar."

"You're taking us to Veisafjǫrðr?" Halldóra asked.

"You know it?" I said.

"Hagar is well known to the people of Lade," she said. "We stay at his longphort often to have our ships fixed for the long journey home."

"You know he is a trustworthy trade partner, then," I said.

Halldóra nodded and said, "And I know the way."

Our first days at sea were quiet. Halldóra's crew did not trust us, and we did not trust them. On the third night, when the wind was calm and the crew took some much-needed rest in the open ocean, we drank and talked. As the mead flowed and the conversation remained lighthearted, Halldóra pressed me on the story I had told her. She sat close to me while Váli chattered on with the others.

"How did you come to be on that island?" she asked. "The truth this time."

I looked to Váli for guidance, but he was in the middle of his story. Rather than carry forward the lie, I told her about how I had sailed to Frankland with Eilif, how we had earned great wealth fighting for the Celts, and how we had lost our ship in the Loire. She followed my words closely, particularly when I spoke of my time among the Celts.

"So the shipwreck was not entirely a lie," Halldóra said with a slight slur to her words. "Though it was not the whole truth."

"Did you think I was lying?" I asked.

"I did. And I could have killed you for it. But the two of you looked as harmless as sheep," she said with a laugh. "Tell me, then, why did you leave the Celts after so long?"

"I fell in love with a girl… a Dane. She was taken from me," I said.

"Taken by Northmen?" Halldóra asked.

I nodded and said, "I will stop at nothing to find her."

I told her about Asa and the affection that had grown between us, and the raid that had changed everything. Halldóra placed a hand over her heart and sighed. She stepped over me and muddled through a crate on the far side of the ship, and when she returned she placed a small wooden totem in my hand. It was a woodcarving of a woman with long hair and plump breasts.

"Do you know who that is?" Halldóra asked.

I shook my head.

"She is Freya, the goddess of love. Too often she is ignored by our people. Take me, for example. My parents married me to Hakon when I was not yet eleven. There is no love in such arrangements."

"You seem to respect each other," I said. Truthfully, had she not mentioned it, I would have never guessed she and Hakon were husband and wife. They had acted as if they barely knew each other, let alone ever shared a bed.

"Oh, yes, but respect is not love," she lamented. She paused for a moment and stared longingly toward the horizon. "We are a people who thrive on our stories, but seldom do we live them. You are an interesting person, Hasting; more interesting than I have met in a long time."

"Thank you," I said. I held out the totem to give it back to her.

"Keep it. May she watch over you and help you find your love," she said with a kind smile.

For weeks we sailed a tempestuous ocean with little food or fresh water to sustain us. Summer's tranquil seas had changed, and the winds of winter had begun to journey down from the North, which made for rough sailing. I thought at times Váli might die, but he pulled through. Journeying to Hagar's longphort was a gamble, but if I remembered correctly, he traded in all manner of things, including salt and slaves. I thought perhaps those who had taken Asa might have sold their slaves in Ireland, and Hagar's longphort seemed an excellent place to start my search. And I needed my father's sword.

Halldóra took an interest in me during the voyage, though her combative nature made conversations difficult. She enjoyed challenging anything I said, and when she spoke, she made it clear she believed she held authority on every subject. As much as I wanted to like her, she annoyed me to no end. Váli did not mind her, and he had many conversations with her where I remained quiet. Those conversations often spilled over into the crew, who had all learned to tolerate some of the more questionable things Halldóra said. In the time we spent on her ship, I learned to appreciate her methods and saw why so many men had chosen to follow her.

We arrived in Veisafjǫrðr during a brief spell of good weather and tied off the ships on Hagar's pier at high tide. Memories of my time there flooded my mind. My heart raced at the thought of seeing Hagar again, though I doubted he would recognize me. A few men greeted us and took our names, and we followed them to the village. Hagar's men asked that we leave our weapons on the ships, and they checked underneath my cloak for anything larger than a fishing knife.

Hagar's hall seemed smaller than when I had left, but it remained almost unchanged. We sat on the mead-benches along the walls and waited for our host, and two of Halldóra's men placed sacks of salt near his dais. When Hagar entered the hall, he appeared old and crippled, and he walked with a curved back that made his left shoulder slope below the other.

"Welcome, honored guests," he said. "Odin smiles on me this day. I thought the raiding season was over."

"Greetings, Hagar, I am Halldóra, wife to Jarl Hakon of Lade."

"Northmen!" Hagar rejoiced. "Praise the gods. Too few of your kin visit my hall. All summer, I am visited by Danes, and I grow tired of them." He examined each one of us, and when he looked upon me, he paused. His gaze intensified a moment and, satisfied, he continued on to the others. "So, what have you brought me?"

Halldóra pointed to the sacks at his feet and said, "Salt. Four ships full."

"Salt?" Hagar said. "No slaves?"

Halldóra looked at me with glaring eyes and said, "Lord Hakon collects slaves as we speak. My ships carry salt, and we were assured you would take it."

"It depends on the quality," Hagar said. "We make our own here, you know, but it is silty and wet."

I stood up and stepped toward Halldóra and said, "Taste it, Hagar. I assure you this salt has no equal."

Hagar leaned down and fiddled with the string that tied the sack shut. He pinched a few crystals and rubbed them between his fingers, and tasted it. When he stood again, he looked at me searchingly and said, "Where did you get this?"

"Frankland," Halldóra said.

Hagar's gaze intensified once again. "I have tasted this salt once before, and the man who gave it to me..."

As he mumbled to himself, a group of servants entered the hall with food and drink, and I recognized one of them as Gyda. She directed the others to serve us and helped Hagar sit in his chair. Although she had aged a little, she appeared healthy. When she turned to look at Halldóra and me, she dropped the carafe in her hand.

"What have you done, woman?" Hagar howled. He looked up at her and saw that her eyes were fixed on me. He grasped her wrist and said, "You see it, too. It's that foolish slave boy who tried to kill me! Have you come back to finish the job?"

"Slave boy?" Halldóra snapped.

Tears streamed down Gyda's face. Yet, though I should have feared for my life, I felt the pull of my destiny. Here, in Hagar's hall, I had a chance to learn about my past, about who my father was, and to prove to my new allies that my father had indeed been a chieftain. Hagar had alluded to my father's title and reputation a few times, and in my heart I needed to know what he knew. I stepped closer to the dais with clenched fists.

"No," I said to Halldóra. I turned to Hagar and saw his husmän, Karl, at his side with a dagger and ax in his hands. "Tell them who I really am," I growled.

Hagar grumbled in his chair. "You are a pest," he said.

"Hasting, you're going to get us all killed," Halldóra whispered through gritted teeth.

Hagar's deep, rumbling laugh filled the hall. He laughed and laughed until it turned to a harsh, dry cough. With his hands pressed on the arms of his chair, he stood up and stepped toward me until the tip of his nose nearly touched mine. His breath reeked of stale mead. "I should kill you where you stand, boy. You are a fool for coming back here," he said.

I took a deep, deliberate breath and said, "Tell them who my father was." With each word and each breath, Hagar and I moved menacingly closer to one another. When he opened his mouth to answer, I felt a blade press against my throat, and an arm reach around my chest to hold me back.

"Slowly now, with me," Halldóra said as she guided me a few paces back. Váli stepped forward to help me, but I put out my hand to tell him to step back.

"Smart girl," Hagar said with a smirk. He turned his back to us and returned to his chair. "The salt you have brought me is quite valuable, indeed. Danes will pay a high price for it when they come here to resupply."

Halldóra kept her knife at my throat and said, "I look to you to make an offer."

Hagar's predatory eyes fixed upon me again, and he smiled. "Kill the boy, and I will offer you a price you cannot refuse," he said.

"And if I do not kill him?" Halldóra asked. The blade at my neck began to tremble.

"Either way," Hagar said, "I will have your salt."

12

A Holmgang Mess

Halldóra's blade broke the skin on my neck. I felt the warm trickle of my own blood run down my skin and seep into my tunic's braided collar. Hagar's desire to see me dead did not surprise me, but that Halldóra might act upon it did. I was young and naive and thought our time aboard her ship and her admiration for my cause counted for something; but she desired wealth, the same as her husband, ,and cared little for anything or anyone else.

The tremble in her hand told me she did not wish to kill me, but I knew she would if pressed. She tightened her grip around the knife handle, and I closed my eyes and waited for the rusted iron to cut deeper into my throat.

"Wait!" Gyda cried out. Halldóra froze. "Hagar, please, I—"

Gyda's words had distracted Halldóra. I remembered my military training and used a technique Yann had taught me to break free of such a hold. Before Halldóra could slice into my flesh, I stomped on her toes and thrust my hands upward and between her arms. I grasped her knife-bearing hand and twisted it around until her elbow faced inward toward her breast. She released the knife, which I caught before it hit the ground. Halldóra stepped back, wide-eyed and holding her arm.

"Karl, kill him," Hagar said. Karl did not move. "Karl! Kill him!"

I stood before Hagar with a knife in my hand and not a warrior between us. Karl sheathed his blade and slipped his ax back into his belt. He crossed his arms and gave me a nod. Hagar's most loyal warrior had turned on him, and in a fit of rage, the old man stood clumsily and reached down the side of his chair to draw a sword.

When he held it in front of him, I saw that it was my father's sword. He charged at me, wild-eyed and screaming like a madman in a spine-chilling war cry.

For the first time, I was not afraid. I knew him, I knew his tricks, and I knew he was little more than a crippled old man. As he swung my father's sword at me, I ducked out of the way and slipped Halldóra's knife between his ribs. He thudded behind me on the ashen ground.

Halldóra knelt beside his body and said, "He's dead." She looked up at me, her eyes filled with wonder. "Where did you learn to fight like that?"

Karl approached his master's body and peeled back his eyelids to peer into his eyes. He then looked to the ceiling and cried, "Odin!"

A moment of silence followed, and all I could hear was the sound of my own panting. I should have felt some relief to have killed the man who had tortured me during my childhood, but I felt anger and sadness in my heart instead. With Hagar dead, I also feared I had killed my chance at learning about my past, about my father, and about my heritage.

Gyda joined Karl to mourn Hagar, and she cried. I struggled to understand her tears, for he had abused her for many years. It angered me that in his death, the people he most abused mourned him. To the astonishment of Karl and Gyda, I reached down and pried my father's sword from Hagar's lifeless hand. I admired the fine craftsmanship of its golden guard and pommel and the beautiful leather of the handle. Never before had I held my father's sword, and that first time filled my heart with awe and pride.

"The elders will gather and elect a new chieftain," Karl said. "And we will bury Hagar with what he needs for the afterlife. That sword was his favorite possession."

"It was my father's sword," I said. "If you want it, you will have to take it."

Karl nodded in agreement. "It is yours, then."

"My men are at your service," Halldóra said.

"No need," Karl said. "He will be buried with the others. A simple grave will do."

"And the boy?" Halldóra asked. "Is he to pay a *weregeld*?"

"No," Karl said. "He defended himself, which he is allowed to do by our laws." He turned to the rest of the men in the hall and said, "Hasting is under my protection. No one will harm him."

Hagar was buried that same evening in a cemetery north of the village. Karl and his warriors dressed Hagar in his most elegant clothes and his favorite bearskin overcoat, and they carried him to the graveyard together. I refused to witness the ceremony and stayed in the great hall with Váli and Halldóra and her men. I did not care to see him laid to rest, and I did not believe he deserved in death the respect shown to him by his warriors and his slaves. Gyda stayed behind to visit with me, although she remained wary of me after what she had seen.

"I am happy to see you alive," Gyda uttered.

"As am I," I said with a smirk. "And I am happy to see you, too."

"Why did you come back?" she asked.

"Someone dear to me was taken as a slave by Northmen, and I thought they might have brought her here," I explained. "And I wanted my father's sword back."

"What does she look like?" Gyda asked.

"She is about Halldóra's height, light blond hair, green eyes. You would remember her if you saw her," I explained.

Gyda shook her head. "So many slaves have passed through here, I cannot say if I have. If Hagar had kept her for himself, I would remember, but he took no new slaves this summer."

Halldóra sat across from us scowling. She had her hands clasped around her goblet of mead but did not drink. I ignored her for as long as I could, but her gaze wore on me.

"Do you have something to say?" I asked her.

"You have made a terrible mistake. Now Hagar is dead, and I have four ships full of salt I can't sell," she said.

"You will sell it," I said. "The elders will elect Karl, I am sure, and he knows what it's worth as much as Hagar."

"You're a fool if you think they won't kill you," she spat.

"Kill a jarl's son? I doubt it," I said.

"You're no jarl's son," she growled.

Gyda leapt to my defense and said, "He is. I remember when Hagar bought him from the Danes."

Halldóra looked daggers at her and stuck out her tongue. "A slave's word means nothing," she said.

"That's enough," I said. I was brimming with confidence after having killed Hagar, and Halldóra did not appreciate my tone. Her scowl deepened. "Do you remember what they said about my father?" I asked Gyda.

Gyda looked around the room, as if searching for the right words to say. "Only that he was a jarl, and he died in the war between Harald and Horic."

Gyda's words gave me little more than what I already knew, and no proof of my claim. I sulked for a moment in silence. Halldóra took a long drink from her goblet and said, "Wealth makes kings, not bloodlines. Since I have met you, you have been obsessed with proving you are a jarl's son, but no one cares."

"I care," I said.

"The stubbornness of men will never cease to amaze me," Halldóra said with a sigh.

We returned to the ships before sunset. Halldóra chose to stay aboard with her men for the night, while I collected my things and returned to Hagar's hall with Váli. Váli and I sat alone in the main chamber, and I made a fire since no slaves had come to do so. With their chieftain dead, I expected some of them might try to escape into the countryside, though the Irish had always helped round them up on Hagar's behalf.

We settled in on makeshift cots along the side of the hall where guests slept, and we tried our best to rest. Outside, I could hear the various conversations among the warriors who discussed plans to support one man or another to succeed Hagar. Their whispers made me anxious at first, but when I tried to focus on their voices, I fell asleep. I slept until midmorning, when Karl entered the great hall and woke me. He sat me at one of the tables and offered me food and drink. Váli joined us and listened.

"My sons remember you fondly," Karl said.

"They do?"

He nodded. "They would have loved to see you."

"Where are they?" I asked.

"They've gone a-Viking this year," he said. "As you did."

"It is a hard life," I said.

"I know. I did it too, when I was their age. That's how I met Hagar," Karl explained. He paused and took a bite of some salted fish.

"Why did you let me kill him?" I asked.

He smiled and said, "I didn't. By law, you made a fair challenge. Hagar always killed challengers easily. I did not expect you to win."

"What will happen now?" I asked.

"You will most certainly be banished from here," Karl said. "But I do not think you had planned to stay."

"No," I said. "I will leave with Halldóra."

Karl laughed and said, "She left in the night, before dawn."

My heart sank. I realized that I had offended Halldóra in more ways than one, and I was marooned in Ireland with no ship. The tremble in my hand returned, and I took a drink of the mead Karl had brought to me. "I will find another way," I said.

Karl leaned in and whispered, "I must be careful in what I say before the elders choose our next chieftain. But I will tell you that I owe you a debt for killing Hagar. When I am elected, I will do what I can to help you."

As these words rolled off his tongue, the village elders, chattering amongst themselves, entered the hall and sat on chairs near the dais. A few warriors trickled in as well, but they said nothing. Free men and women then filled the chamber as on the day Hagar had punished Eanáir. Last among them to enter was Hake, the skald, whose eyes appeared swollen and who languished at the loss of his master. I remembered him fondly from my childhood but did not know what to make of him now. I slid to the far end of the bench, away from all the others, and listened to the elders speak, led in their conversation by Hake.

"Hagar is dead. His body lies in the ground, and his spirit travels to the next life," Hake said. "The task falls upon the elders who have gathered for this *thing*, to decide who will take his place as chieftain. He had no sons or daughters, and his wealth and his lands and the loyalty of his people will pass to one who is not his blood. I call to you: who should take his place among us?"

The elders, six of them in all, whispered to each other. They said nothing aloud in response to Hake who waited in front of the growing crowd. After a short while, the elders ceased their whispering and sat in silence.

"Two men have presented themselves to me this morning to take his place," Hake continued. "Karl, son of Ulfr, Hagar's husmän, seeks to take his lord's place. Ole, son of Grjotgar, also Hagar's husmän, seeks to take his lord's place. Are there any others?"

One of the elders stood and said, "These are the names we have discussed."

"And have you chosen your man?" Hake asked.

The elder nodded and said, "Karl, son of Ulfr."

There was little suspense, not even for me. Karl had served as Hagar's husmän for more years than any other and deserved to rule in his stead. He moved to the front of the crowd and stood next to Hake who passed him a horn filled with mead. "When you drink from the *sjaund*," he said, "you become our chieftain. May you lead us with honor."

As Karl raised the horn to his lips, Ole, a broad-chested man with dark hair and an unkempt beard, who stood at least a head taller than Karl, stepped forward and said, "How can you let this traitor take Hagar's place? He let Hagar die when he should have defended him. He has no honor!"

Karl spat at Ole. Ole, in turn, spat at Karl. Hake intervened. He stood between them with his arms extended and said, "Ole, do you challenge Karl to a *holmgang* for your right to take his place?"

"I do," Ole declared.

"He can't!" Karl cried out.

"By our laws, it must be so," Hake said. "It is a fair challenge."

The hall erupted with screams and shouts among the people who all disagreed on what should happen next. Hake struggled to maintain order, and warriors rushed to the front to separate Ole and Karl who had stalked closer to one another, itching for a fight.

"Hear me!" Hake said. He said it again and again until the hall quieted enough for him to speak. "Karl, do you accept the challenge?"

Karl nodded.

"Then we must establish the rules."

"Fight me with shield and ax if you dare," Karl said.

"One shield, one ax," Ole said.

"According to our laws, there must be at least one day for the warriors to prepare," Hake said.

"I am ready now," Ole snarled.

Karl stepped closer until the two stood nose to nose and said, "As am I."

Hake had panic written on his face. He had lost all control of the ceremony of succession. The combatants left the hall for the courtyard outside, followed by all the free men and women of the village. They formed a circle as wide as the length of a small longship and cheered in support of the man they wanted to succeed Hagar. Warriors brought up an ax and shield for each man. Karl and Ole approached each other at the center of the circle. Hake met them there and stood an arm's length between them. Váli and I watched from outside the circle with our arms crossed.

"If Ole wins, he will blame us for Hagar's death," Váli whispered in my ear. "We should be prepared to run."

"Karl is a good fighter," I said. "He will win."

"The winner will draw first blood or knock the other out of the circle," Hake said for all to hear.

"No, to the death!" Ole said.

"It's about time this happened, Ole. I have dreamed of killing you for years," Karl said.

Hake took in a deep breath and sighed. He knew he could not stop the two of them, so he backed away. The crowd fell silent for a moment before Hake gave the word to fight. I watched him with the same anticipation as everyone else. He raised his hand for all to see, and with a swift motion, he lowered it to his knee. Karl charged at Ole with two fast strokes of his ax. Each stroke knocked thunderously against Ole's shield. On the second blow, Ole curled his shield around and forced Karl's ax to the ground. He jabbed at Karl's face with the tip of his shaft, locked the curvature of his blade against the rawhide of Karl's shield, and tore it from his hand. In one swift move, Ole had disarmed his opponent. Karl staggered back and took a defensive stance.

"I yield," Karl pleaded.

Ole did not listen. He approached Karl, raised his ax, and swung. Karl raised his hands to shield himself, and the sharp edge cut through him like an oar through water. Blood spattered across the courtyard. Ole hacked at Karl a few more times to finish him off and turned to the crowd with his hands raised to the sky to celebrate his victory. At that moment, Váli tugged on my shoulder.

"We need to leave—now!" he said as quietly as he could.

I stepped backward and turned to follow him into Hagar's hall to collect our packs and weapons. Váli swiped food from the table, including bread, apples, and salted meat, and filled his bag to the brim. We hurried toward the longphort, hoping to attract as little attention as possible. Ole continued to celebrate with the other warriors, and they had not seemed to notice us leave. Once at the dock, we found a small trade vessel with ten oars on each side. It bobbed in the shallow water of a receding tide. Four men were aboard cleaning and arranging the equipment. I hopped from the dock to the deck and drew my sword.

"We are taking this ship. Either help us get it moving, or die," I said.

All of them scurried to the dock and ran for the village. Váli untied the ropes and shouted, "I'll row, you figure out the sail."

He jumped down, sat at a rowing bench near the prow of the ship, and put an oar to water on each side. Meanwhile, I examined the reefed sail and rigging. It took time for me to remember how it all worked, and the tremble in my hand did not help. Váli managed to row us out to where the Northmen would need a ship of their own to reach us, and that gave me more time to work the ropes and loosen the sail. As I worked, I heard shouting from shore and saw Ole and dozens of his followers rushing toward the dock.

"Hurry, Hasting!" Váli said.

He continued to row as hard as he could, but it was not enough to keep us away from the others for long. They pushed several ships into the water and, with a full crew, set out their oars to give chase. They moved far faster than us, and I feared they would catch us before long. I worked the ropes as best as I could, raised the sail, and tied off the main rigging to hooks on the gunwale. At last, I took hold of the final two ropes tied to the bottom corners of the sail and pulled back to tighten them. The sail filled and jolted the ship forward.

"Take the steering paddle!" I screamed, and Váli pulled in his oars and jumped to the stern.

He looked back and watched as we put more distance between us and our pursuers. Not long after, they abandoned their pursuit of us. I am sure they could have caught us if they had tried, but they must not have known it. We both breathed a heavy sigh of relief.

"There are other longphorts in Ireland," I said as I moved from rope to rope, ensuring the sail remained full. "We should see what we find at the others."

"Do me a favor, Hasting; next time, don't kill their chieftain," Váli sneered.

Sailing a ship alone, even a small one, is hard work. I taught Váli everything I could, but it still took a few days for him to become useful, and he never learned the knots. We contoured Ireland toward the north and did not dare venture too far from the coast. At night, we lowered the sail and drifted further from shore to avoid beaching. We took turns at the steering paddle while the other slept, in case the current tried to pull us into the rocks. The jagged, cliff-laden coastline broke and gave way to a large bay with sandy beaches and smoother waters.

As we entered the bay, we saw other longships approaching from the north and heading toward a settlement on the far side. We decided to follow in hopes that they would sail for a longphort. Lucky for us, they did, and what we found there was a bustling city many times larger than Hagar's village.

"You are a lucky bastard," Váli said. "One more day and we would have run out of food."

The port followed the curvature of the bay, with a wooden boardwalk and thatch-roofed houses all along the water's edge. Piers stretched out from the boardwalk into the ocean, and some had thatched coverings while others had none. Each pier had dozens of ships tied off to it with men loading and unloading goods.

Váli and I reefed the sail and rowed to the best of our ability toward the farthest pier on the edge of the city where there appeared to be room for our ship. We bumped into the pier a little harder than we should have, but Váli did well to leap from the prow with a rope and tie us off. With a few more strokes of my oar, I managed to move the aft of the ship closer to the pier, and I threw him a second rope to secure the stern.

A man approached with a fancy green cap and gold-braided tunic, his hands clasped in front of him. He exchanged a few words with Váli, who pointed to me.

"I am Gríma, and I manage this pier on behalf of our Lord Thorgísl," he said.

"Thor?" I asked.

Gríma nodded. "There are only two of you?" he asked. "Where is your crew?"

"Somewhere in there." I pointed to the city.

Gríma frowned and said, "Do you have coin to pay for your ship? You can't keep it here for free, you know."

To my astonishment, Váli handed him a denier.

Gríma bit into it and smiled. "You have come from Frankland? I am impressed. It is not easy to sail a ship this size with only two men, though I have seen it done before."

"Can you show us to Thor's hall? We wish to meet with him," I said.

Gríma laughed. "You want an audience with Thorgísl? Are you mad?"

"I don't know, why?" I asked.

Gríma stuttered. "You… who are you?"

"I am Hasting," I said.

Váli interjected and said, "We are looking for someone, and we had hoped your lord could help us."

Gríma scratched his head. "Go to the mead hall and find a man named Kormak. He is Thorgísl's husmän. If he sees fit to present you to the jarl, he will do so. Good luck."

We left the pier and entered the city. As we walked, I asked Váli, "Where did you find the denier?"

Váli shrank and said, "I kept a few that we earned working the marshes in case we would need them later. I was afraid you might spend them all. I hope you will forgive me."

I did not like that he had kept it from me, and I cracked my knuckles as we walked. "No matter," I said. "Do you have any more?"

Váli nodded.

"Good, we may need them. You keep them for now. Did you take any of the gold?"

Váli shook his head to say no. He remained quiet until we reached the main thoroughfare of the city—a bustling street with carts and shacks filled with all manner of goods, including shoes, pottery, leather-works, and vegetables and grains from the fields.

My shoulder ached from carrying my pack around, but I did not trust Gríma, so I had brought my wealth with me. We passed a merchant who sold meat displayed on racks in front of his shop, and the smell of it made me sick. He had a rabbit, pheasants, chicken, and some cuts of salted cod. Váli bought us some roasted chicken legs for a snack as we made our way up the street. Farther along the thoroughfare, we arrived at a clearing with a well in the center and a majestic hall on the far side with a massive double door made of oak. We looked around for someone to guide us, and we found a young man sitting under the overhang of the hall's roof, sharpening axes on a whetstone.

"We are looking for Kormak," I said.

"What for?" the young man asked.

"We wish to speak with Thor," I explained.

"You cannot wander in off the street to see Thor," the young man asserted.

"How do we get an audience, then?" I asked.

The young man paused in his work. He took a quick look at us and said, "Who is your master?"

"I am my own," I said. I pulled back my cloak and rested my hand on the hilt of my sword.

"And him?" the man asked.

"Váli is sworn to me," I said.

"I am," Váli said with a quick nod.

While we spoke with the young man, a large procession of warriors walked toward the hall. When they reached the double doors, servants opened them to let them in. As they passed, I spotted a familiar face.

"Halldóra!" I called out. She peered through the crowd, and when she saw my face, she turned away as if she had not seen me. "Halldóra!" I said again.

After my second attempt at calling her name, she could no longer deny that I was there. Her men nudged her and pointed in our direction, and with a fair amount of brooding, she clenched her fists and marched over to us.

"Hasting," she said through gritted teeth. "It's good to see you alive."

"It is a shame you did not stay to see the *holmgang*. You would have enjoyed it," I said.

"I knew that place would implode after you killed Hagar. You must understand, I could not risk the lives of my crew," Halldóra said. "I should have told you. I shouldn't have left you for dead."

"You were right; they did try to kill me," I said.

Halldóra's cheeks reddened. "Please understand —"

"It's as you've said," I interrupted. "All you care about is wealth. I am not offended."

"All right!" Halldóra barked. It made us all jump. "I feel terrible. Please accept my help to find the girl you are looking for as my apology. But, only here. If you need to travel elsewhere, you will need to find your own ship."

"I have one," I said with a grin.

She rolled her eyes and said, "Of course you do."

"How do you plan to help?" I asked.

"We will... speak with the jarl; he's an old family friend. Come, he has invited us to his hall with the leaders of two other fleets to discuss trade."

Váli and I followed Halldóra and her men through the double doors. It was not much larger than Hagar's hall, except the entirety of it had benches and tables where Hagar's had bedchambers. Dozens of men from all over the North sat at the tables while servants bustled about with carafes and goblets to serve them drink. After the first pour, a tall man wrapped in a massive bearskin entered the hall with a host of warriors at his back. He held a long drinking horn in one hand and patted men on the back with the other as he walked between the tables. I recognized him. It was Thor.

"Welcome one and welcome all!" he cheered. "Welcome to my hall. Drink up and eat heartily. My generosity knows no bounds. You are guests at my table, and each of you will eat and drink his fill."

The look in my eyes alerted Halldóra to my discomfort. I felt a powerful hand take my shoulder. Thor bent forward over the table to gaze at us at eye level, and he hovered so close to me that I could smell his breath. He gave Halldóra a broad smile.

"Cousin!" he said with glee. "Where is Hakon?"

"Still in Frankland," she said.

"And you?" he asked.

"I have brought salt to trade."

"Excellent," Thor said. "The salt here in Ireland is rubbish. It rains too much, even in summer. It will be good for us to have something we can use to salt our fish." He laughed and spilled mead all over the table. "Good, good. Drink, and we will discuss trade later. Drink!"

He stood upright again and walked to the other tables, greeting them with equal cheer. The man I had met did not have an ounce of charisma, yet in his hall there was an aura about him. Even I, as frightened as I was that he might recognize me, felt drawn to him.

We did as he asked and drank the mead. I had not drunk true Northman mead in many years, and I could not tell if it tasted as it should. I prefer the taste of wine to mead, but I consumed what they gave me without any objection. When my goblet ran dry, a servant filled it again, and the other men at the table drank at an astounding pace. They raised their cups and shouted, "Skal!" and drank it all down in an instant. Váli drank at his own pace and watched as the others pulled me into their festivities.

As the night drew on and we drank and ate, I grew drowsy and drunk. At one point, I could not string words together to make a sentence, and the men around me laughed. Váli sat at my side the whole night and helped me outside when I needed to vomit. If not for him, I might have made a complete fool of myself. I remember nothing of what happened after Váli sat me back down at the table, except that the festivities continued after I fell asleep.

At dawn, a bucket of water splashed across my face. I awoke in terror, and it took me a moment to settle down. I was still at the table, and the others had gone to sleep along the walls of the hall. Across from me sat Thor. He wore a simple brown tunic with a brown braid on the collar, and he ate slices of apple with a long hunting knife. I watched him eat for a moment and felt his men hovering over me. My hair fell over my face and water dripped on the table. I ran my hand through it to pull it back. Water ran down my spine, which gave me a chill. The hall was silent except for the sound of Thor crunching his apple. When I gathered my wits, I noticed his men had taken my sword from my belt and laid it out on the table.

"Tell me," Thor said after a long silence. "Where did you find this sword?"

13

My First Crew

Thor had my sword laid out on the table in front of him. He marveled at it, and he ran his hand along the blade. I remained silent. While he had not recognized me, he seemed to recognize the sword, and I feared I may not have the answers he would want. Halldóra woke up to find us sitting across from each other, and, with a stern countenance, she took a seat beside Thor. Servants entered the hall and delivered platters of meat and fruit, as well as clean water. Thor urged me to eat and I reached straightaway for a piece of bread and some water.

"This is a fine, fine blade," Thor said.

"It was my father's sword," I said.

"Was your father a king?"

"He was a chieftain," I said.

"Was?"

"He was slain for his wealth. The sword is all I have left to prove my bloodline," I said.

"Noble blood matters little here. In Jutland, perhaps, you might convince a jarl or two to take up your cause, but here you are judged by your deeds." Thor took another bite of his apple. "Halldóra tells me she found you in Frankland, shipwrecked."

I nodded and searched her eyes for what she might have already told Thor. She knew I had been a slave, and she had questioned whether the sword was my father's. If she had told him all she knew, he might kill me. My heart quickened, and I felt my face redden. My reddened face always betrayed me.

"I hear you are the man responsible for killing Hagar," Thor said.

Again, I nodded.

"I am impressed."

"Did you know him?" I asked.

"I never met a bigger turd," he said. "What you did took courage. Hagar had never been beaten in a fight. He even bested me, once." Thor pulled down the collar on his tunic to show me a thick red scar across his chest. "Valhalla will greet him warmly."

Thor's words and relaxed demeanor put me at ease. I almost felt as if he treated me as an equal. The man I had first met on the open ocean with Eilif had presented himself as fearsome and ruthless, yet across from me at the table he appeared far less imposing. Had he known where we had first met, I do not think he would have spoken as kindly to me. He sheathed my sword and passed it to me across the table.

"You should have seen him move," Halldóra said. "I've never seen a man move like that."

Thor laughed. "By the gods, you have never said anything so kind to me."

"You don't move like him," she said.

Thor turned to me and said, "It takes quite a man to impress my cousin. Tell me your name."

"Hasting."

My response was dry and quick, and Thor appeared put off by my abruptness. "I will remember it," he said. "Halldóra tells me the salt was your idea. Brilliant, I must say. It will fetch a high price with the Danes and Northmen who trade with us."

"I am honored by your praise," I said.

Halldóra put a hand on Thor's shoulder and raised her eyebrows at him as if to say something. "Of course," he said to her. He looked at me and continued, "You are looking for a girl. She was taken by Northmen?"

I nodded.

"From where did they take her?"

"A city called Vannes," I said. "Do you know it?"

"Alas, no," he said. "I have not ventured as far as Frankland in many years. My last expedition ended in failure. The Franks are a tough breed."

"Have you traded in slaves with Northmen who raided in Frankland this year?" I asked him.

Thor puckered his lips and raised one of his eyebrows in thought. "Not that I can remember."

"Perhaps you would allow Hasting and me to search among your slaves," Halldóra suggested.

"Because it's you, I will allow it," Thor said.

Halldóra pulled me from the table and led me out of the hall into the courtyard outside. Thor remained at the table eating and drinking, and when we left, some of his other guests who had slept in the chamber joined him at the table. Váli followed behind us with a squint in his eye. I could tell he had drunk his fill of mead and the bright sunlight made him uncomfortable.

Halldóra took us behind the hall to an area filled with tents. Whereas Hagar had devoted one of his longhouses to his slaves, Thor's lived in tents made of linen and insulated with hides. Warriors carrying whips patrolled the grounds, keeping a close eye on the slaves who wore simple tunics and trousers, some with iron collars and others without. I asked Halldóra why there were no fences or other enclosures to keep the slaves from escaping, and she explained that they had nowhere to go—if they escaped, the Irish would kill them in the countryside, or they would drown in the sea. When we reached the center of the slave camp, Halldóra patted me on the back.

"Have a look around," she said. "Good luck."

I shouted to all the slaves around us in the Celtic language, "Anyone from Armorica?" No one answered. I called out again. Still, no one answered. I shrugged and said to Halldóra, "I don't think she is here."

We turned to return to Thor's hall when a woman cried out from behind us, "I am!" When she reached us, she collapsed at my feet and held me at my knees. "Hasting!" she said, out of breath. I did not know her, but she knew me.

"What is your name?" I asked her. I reached down and pulled her up to her feet.

"Awena," she replied.

Her arms were thin as bones, and her skin was dark and covered in lacerations. She wore a scarf over her head, tied into the knots in her hair, and her clothes were old and unwashed. Around her neck, she wore a handmade wooden pendant of a cross that she must have made herself since she had arrived in Ireland.

"Where are the others?" I asked her.

"Did Nominoë send you to find us?" she asked.

"Yes," I said, but she had not answered my question. "Where are the others?" I asked again.

Awena shook her head. "They put us for sale in markets… here, and in other places. A farmer here bought me, but I was the only one. The others they took away."

There was one question left for me to ask. "Where did they take Asa?"

Awena stood back, anger written on her face. "You did not come to save the rest of us?"

We heard a call from across the encampment. Awena turned and said, "That's my owner. He's taking me back to his farm tonight."

I reached into my cloak and drew out a gold coin to hand to Váli. He understood what I wanted him to do, and he walked over to meet the farmer. The coin was worth far more than what the farmer would have paid for her. I knew I could not afford to hand over a piece of my wealth for every person taken from Vannes, but Awena knew something, and buying her freedom was a cost I had to endure.

"You're mine, now," I said. She looked at me in fear, as if unsure whether to hug me or to cry. "I bought you, and I will take you home. But first, I need you to tell me where they took Asa."

"They sold her, and only her, to some men in Frankland," she said.

The revelation gave me pause. "Frankland? The Franks don't buy slaves, especially Christians."

"Please," Awena pleaded. She could see my anger and probably feared I would focus it on her. Her trembling legs gave away once again, and she fell to her knees and wrapped her arms around my shins.

"It's all right," I said as I held up her chin. She sobbed inconsolably. "I am here to help you."

Halldóra looked at Awena with disgust. "This woman is weak. She won't survive a day at sea."

"If I could only find the men who raided Vannes," I said.

Váli sauntered back from speaking with the farmer with a whimsical glee about him. "I know who raided Vannes," he said. "And you are not going to believe me when I tell you."

"Out with it, man!" Halldóra said.

"A pair of sea captains by the name of Eilif and Egill," he said.

"What?" In that first instant of hearing their names, my mind refused to believe it. My heart could not accept it.

"Are you all right?" Halldóra asked. "You look pale."

The world around me started to spin. Loki's Delirium set in, and I felt the hands of the trickster god tightening his grip on my soul. It felt as if he had tied a noose around my neck and pulled it up to hang me. My chest tightened, my breathing quickened, and I wanted to scream.

"The farmer said they set sail for Ribe, in Jutland. That is where we must go if we hope to find them," Váli said.

Just as Loki's grip felt strongest, another feeling within me rose to the surface. My fear and panic subsided, and in their wake, I felt anger and rage. I clenched my fists and my jaw, and my vision sharpened like a starving wolf that had spotted its prey. The call of the wolf ensnared me, and my heart filled with bloodlust.

"It's time to go hunting," I said.

Thor proved an excellent host during our stay. He believed that my father had been a chieftain, and he believed in me as well. It helped that I had the support of Halldóra. Before she left, she urged her cousin to help me where he could. Thor never asked me to swear to him. Though he admired my youthful vigor, my skill with a blade, and my most recent deeds, Halldóra said he had no interest in recruiting a Dane, at least not one with a claim to a title. Such men, he said, made poor followers. I did not mind—I wanted to avoid the constraints of Norse hierarchy until I found Asa.

On the morning of Halldóra's departure, as I watched her ships sail east toward sunrise on a calm, breezeless day, I felt the weight of the task before me. She had helped to prepare my ship for my long voyage to Jutland, stocked it with food, drink, live chickens, fishing equipment, and a cat to hunt vermin, and she had paid for it to thank me for the wealth she had made from the salt.

The ship we had stolen from Hagar's village—or as Thor put it, earned as a war trophy—was barely large enough to make an ocean voyage. I thought about trading it with some of my gold for a larger one, but I would have needed more crew and supplies, all of which would have strained my wealth. It was no Sail Horse, but it would make the journey across the sea.

While searching for men to join my crew, Váli suggested I use some of my gold to buy silver arm rings. Arm rings, he said, would serve as both payment and a symbol of the men's loyalty to me. Though I had begun my life as a Dane, I still had much to learn about acting like one. We bought a small chest to hold the arm rings and my wealth, and we took the better part of an afternoon building a secret compartment under the ship's planks to stow it.

Váli had become more than a follower of mine—he was an advisor and a confidant, and he knew all of my secrets. Had he decided to take my wealth and leave me behind, he could have, but he felt a deep sense of loyalty toward me, and helping me ascend as a chieftain in my own right was, for him, a matter of honor. I wanted to name him my husmän, but he refused, saying he lacked the traits of a warrior required for such a title. He had gained weight since we had arrived in Dublin. I could no longer see the bones in his arms, and his gaunt face had plumped up, which made him look years younger.

We received permission from Thor to recruit warriors from his city. Except for his husmän, he said any free man who wished to go a-Viking with us could. He expressed his desire to join us, but business at home, including overseeing a new peace with the Irish, prevented him from leaving. Norse farmers, he said, had a bad habit of starting fights with the Irish.

I made no illusions that our first task would be to find and fight Danes. Fighting did not frighten the men with whom we spoke, and they were intrigued by my future plan to trade salt from the monastery at Herio. They had seen what Thor had paid Halldóra for it, so they knew if they fought for me and lived to see it, they could make tremendous wealth. The men with whom we spoke had also learned of my deeds, of how I had killed Hagar, and talk of a young Viking with exceptional skill spread like wildfire in the city. By the time I heard what was being said, the man about whom everyone spoke did not resemble me much; at least, I did not think so. Despite some of the fabrications, my growing reputation bolstered our recruitment efforts. Reputation, as my father had said, is everything.

Most men, unfortunately for us, had a duty to their farms and families. The men most eager to join us were young, unattached, and landless. None, however, relished the prospect of sailing long distances in winter. Raiding was done in spring and summer when the seas and winds were favorable. Winter posed a more significant challenge for sailors, with more frequent storms and bone-chilling winds. In all, we recruited twenty young men, paying each with a silver arm ring.

Váli saw that each swore fealty upon their arm ring, and he guided the ritual since I had never before asked a man to swear to me. Each man repeated the same ceremony of placing a hand on the arm ring and reciting an oath in witness of Odin. The oath changed a little from man to man, but the core message remained the same: they pledged their lives to me, willing to die if needed. It was their chance to earn fame and wealth, which every young man desired above all other things, or to die trying. They were my first crew, and I felt pride at what I had accomplished. Váli called it luck.

"In a good way," he specified. "All the heroes of the skald's songs were lucky."

We left Dublin the day after a storm had wrecked most of the ships along the docks. The wind and rain had arrived onshore during high tide, and it pushed the water higher than any of the Dubliners had ever seen. It even flooded parts of the city. My ship survived unscathed. The crew saw it as a sign of good fortune for our voyage.

At dawn, under a red sky, we set sail for the East in search of Eilif and Egill. The farmer who had sold Awena to us said they had set out for Ribe, a town on the coast of Jutland. The oldest among my recruits, a thirty-year-old warrior named Fafnir, served as our navigator. He had learned to read the sun and stars from his father. Thor had recommended him, since he had sailed to Ribe before and knew the way. It had taken more silver to convince him to join the crew, but we were desperate for someone who could guide us.

Awena remained aft under the gunwale with a large woolen blanket wrapped around her. She acted like a captured dog, and she growled at anyone who tried to approach her. Váli attempted to give her food once or twice the first day, but she kicked at him to fend him off. On the morning of the second day, her skin had taken on an ominous pallor. At one point, she leaned over the gunwale to vomit, and when she sat back down, she collapsed. When she rolled out of her wool blanket, I noticed she was more starved than we had first thought.

"I've seen this before," Fafnir said. "Happens to slaves often. They refuse to eat, and so starve."

It was a hard lesson in the harshness of life at sea. As much as I wanted to take Awena home, she would not survive the journey. By day's end, she was curled into a ball on the deck, while her fingers clutched her blanket so hard that her knuckles turned limestone white. Váli felt her neck and shook his head. She had stopped breathing.

He and Fafnir rolled her in her cloak, lifted her from the deck, and tossed her into the water. I was heartbroken, but I did not show it. Her corpse drifted and bobbed in our wake.

A man always remembers his first crew. My men were brave, bold, daring, and most of all, loyal. I wish I could have kept all of them at my side forever, but that is not how going a-Viking works. The sea is a merciless mistress, and she claims any who falter. Awena was the first to die on my ship, but not the last.

Our journey lasted many weeks, though I found it hard to keep track. Among my crew, several showed themselves more valuable than the others. There was Sten, a farmer's boy with broad shoulders and a thick skull. His hands were massive, and his grip unmatched when handling the ropes. There was Gørm, son of a blacksmith, who had short brown hair and a slender build. Rumor among the others was that his birth mother was Irish. There was Torsten, a less vocal but talented sailor. He worked hard and listened to orders. He and Sten worked well together and manned the sail with the skill of a whole crew. And there was Ulf, and Trygve, and Frode, and Arne, and Erik, and Troels. Finally, there was Rune. Among all the men, Rune was the most special to me. He carried himself with grace, and he knew how to tell a good tale. His father had been a skald, and Rune had taken after him. He kept his hair long in a horsetail and his light beard trimmed. Even his eyebrows had been carefully plucked when we left Dublin. Each man had his qualities, and each contributed something unique. On Váli's suggestion, I fraternized with them when I could.

At long last, we rejoiced when Torsten shouted from the top of the mast that he had spotted a town in the distance with boats coming and going. Fafnir watched from the prow and looked back to me with a smile. He recognized the coastline and confirmed his waypoints. We were tired and weather-beaten, but alive and happy to have arrived. Two of the men, I cannot remember their names, suffered from terrible stomach pains, and one of them died before we landed. The other died later that night on shore. What they ate I cannot say, but when food spoils at sea it makes for perilous eating.

Ribe's docks were full, so we ran our ship aground on a nearby beach with wicket fences that marked out plots where visitors could land and camp. A horseman wearing long, silky robes and carrying a flailing banner of a stag's horns rode out to meet us on the narrow dirt path that led to town through shallow, grassy dunes.

"Jarl Magnus welcomes you to Ribe," he said. His horse neighed and bucked with discomfort. He was a large man, and the horse was small. "Who is your leader?"

"I am the leader," I said.

"What is your name?" he asked.

"I am Hasting, son of Ragnar," I said.

"What business do you have in Ribe?" the horseman asked.

"I am looking for someone," I said. "Men by the name of Eilif and Egill."

"Magnus would know," the man said. He paused and looked me over. "I can take you to the great hall, but you will need to pay to keep your ship here."

We paid him what he asked, a few pieces of silver, and the men started to make camp on the beach. The horseman asked that I bring no more than two of my men with me. Magnus, he explained, did not trust Vikings. A fleet from Vestfold had tried to raid Ribe the summer before last, and ever since, the jarl had grown weary of those who rove.

For a few extra pieces of silver, we had supplies, including mead, delivered to the ship. My men were overjoyed. I chose Váli and Fafnir to accompany me to the great hall. Fafnir had met Magnus and knew his temperament, and Váli knew mine.

Ribe was a large town about twice the size of Dublin and constructed in a similar way. Closer to the water were boardwalks and wooden houses with thatched roofs, and further inland the homes were larger and built with a variety of techniques and materials, including a few houses made from turf. In the center, we found the great hall, and when we arrived, we found the double doors open, with slaves cleaning the tables.

The hall reminded me of my father's, with totems of the gods hanging over the entryway and carvings of stags and wolves and boars on the pillars that held up the roof. An engraving of two serpents facing each other looked over the entrance, with their slithering bodies decorated in Norse knots. The horseman led us to a man sitting on a small wooden stool at the door. He had his arms crossed and he leaned against the pillar behind him. When we approached, he rocked forward, stood, and adjusted his clean white tunic.

"A bit late in the year for Vikings, no?" the man asked.

The horseman patted me on the back and stomped off to see to the delivery of food and drink for my ship. We waited for the man in the white tunic to speak again. "I was speaking to you," he said to me.

"We... we haven't gone a-Viking yet. I am looking for someone," I said.

"You have found someone," the man said.

"Is Jarl Magnus nearby?" I asked.

Fafnir leaned into my ear and whispered, "That's him."

Magnus grinned and said, "Who is asking?"

I felt shame that I had not asked him for his name first. "Hasting," I replied.

"What makes you think you have a right to visit me in my hall?" he pressed.

Sensing Magnus' frustration, Váli interjected, "He is our chieftain."

"To whom are you sworn?" the jarl asked.

"To no one," I said. "I am my own man."

He rubbed the beads in the braids of his beard as he thought. "Who is it you are looking for?"

"Vikings by the name of Eilif and Egill," I said.

The jarl frowned. "What do you want with them?"

"They've stolen something from me," I said.

Magnus grinned. He inched toward me, put his hands on my shoulders, and said, "You and I have that in common."

He welcomed us into his hall, and we sat at his table. Dozens of his warriors appeared behind us, and I wondered if we had walked into an ambush. Váli and Fafnir noticed too, and their eyes betrayed their apprehension. Magnus sat at the head of the table with a goblet of mead. When he did not offer us any, I understood he did not trust us.

"How do you know Eilif?" he asked.

"I sailed with him," I said.

"Recently?"

"No," I replied.

He relaxed a little and took another sip of his mead. "What did he steal from you?"

"A girl," I said.

"A slave?" he asked.

"No, a lover," I stated.

"Strange." He fiddled with his beard again. "He had several slaves when he was here."

I ignored Magnus' rebuff at my assertion that Asa was not a slave. "So he was here?" I blurted. I regretted cutting him off, but I had to know.

Magnus broke into laughter, which confused the three of us. "He always comes back here," he said. "It's his home."

I gazed at Magnus' face and saw the same hair, the same brow, the same eyes, and the same straight nose as Eilif.

"Are you—" I began.

Magnus cut me off. "His brother? I am. Did he mention me?"

"He mentioned his brother was a landowner, but he never said your name," I said.

"A landowner? That's it?" Magnus scoffed. "Not *the largest landowner in Jutland*, other than the king? Bah! I don't speak well of him, either. He has humiliated our family too many times."

Váli put his hand on my shoulder to let me know he wished to speak. "If I may, what did he do?" he asked.

Magnus twirled the hairs of his mustache. He licked his lips and said, "He stole my best ship. There is no finer vessel in all of Midgard."

"Do you know where he went?" I asked.

"I do. And I would have chased after him, but I cannot leave Ribe. There is too much for me to do here before winter," Magnus said.

"I think we can help each other," I said. Magnus perked up as I spoke. "You want your ship back, and I need Eilif to tell me where he sold the girl. If you tell me where to find him, I promise to bring back your ship."

Magnus crossed his arms and said, "Even if I thought you could bring him in, why would I trust that you won't take my ship off to whatever hole you came from?"

"On my honor, I promise to return it," I said. "And you do not have much of a choice. Trust me to return it, or let Eilif sail it to the ends of the world to be captured by someone else."

Magnus chuckled and wagged his finger at me. "I like him," he said to his warriors who stood over us. "You have a quick tongue, boy, but do you have what it takes to capture my brother?"

Váli touched my shoulder again and said, "He killed the chieftain, Hagar."

"I did not know him," Magnus said.

I pushed Váli's hand off my shoulder and said, "I know Eilif, and I know his tricks. I can capture him."

Magnus took a large drink from his goblet and said, "All right, I will tell you where to find my brother under one condition."

"Name it," I said.

"Kill him."

14

The Giant's Throne

Once we resupplied the ship, we set a northern course. Magnus had explained to Fafnir where to find Eilif, and he seemed certain he could get us there. He said we would need to navigate deep into the Northernmost fjords, which was both a long journey and a perilous one. If the northern winds didn't freeze us, the Northmen of the surrounding lands might sink us. We would need to sail with caution and avoid other ships along the way.

Eilif had taken refuge in a fjord on the edge of Midgard called the Giant's Throne, a place Magnus described as having a stone slab as tall as the masts of one hundred ships and with the shape of a throne's backrest. It was a land riddled with fairies and elves and monsters of all kinds, he said, which unsettled some among my crew. The Giant's Throne bordered Sami land and lay along the trails they used to herd reindeer.

My men did not protest aloud about the journey, but I gathered from their chatter they would have preferred to sail to Frankland. Some of them held deep beliefs in the gods and the old ways, and to them, the Far North was a strange and terrifying place—a land of myth, home to mystical forces that men could not hope to challenge. I kept an eye on a few whom I thought might foment fear and discord. Luckily, none did.

A few weeks of hard sailing took us to a frozen land of crystalline waters filled with floating chunks of ice. The farther north we sailed, the more the days shortened and the nights grew long. At first, I marveled at the beauty of the northern twilight reaching into the unfathomable vastness at the edge of Midgard, but I soon became weary of the short days and long nights.

We had stocked the hold with thick wool blankets from both Dublin and Ribe, and we used every last one of them. We pitched one of our tents from gunwale to gunwale and tied it with a rope to the mast. It shielded us from the wind, rain, and snow, and we huddled together for warmth when we took our turns resting. Persistent ice covered the deck, so we had to stack oars across the rowing benches and rest on top of them. It made for precarious sleeping, but at least we did not freeze to death in our sleep.

The coastline's jagged rocks, ice, and unforgiving wind made our journey hard, but what made it harder was that we often could not find a place along the fjords to stop and make camp. There were no beaches, only rocks and cliffs, so we had to sleep on the ship. One of my crew, a young man named Arvid whom I later regretted to have not known better, fell asleep against the gunwale near the prow while on watch one night. When we awoke the following day, we found him frozen through and through. His icy pallor and blueish-purple fingers and nose marked me, but at least he did not suffer. I could see in his face that he had fallen asleep before he died. Such is the cruelty of the cold: it waits for its victims to fall asleep and, in the darkness, it claims their lives.

One morning I awoke with Loki tugging at my heart. I gasped into the frigid morning air and my mouth dried in an instant from the cold. My head bumped against the tent, which had begun to slump from the weight of snow and ice. I gripped my blanket, covered my head and face, and stepped into the open. A fog had fallen over the sea, but this was no ordinary fog. Everything it touched was covered in ice. The ice had grown into thick slabs upon the deck and gunwale overnight, and the ship sat lower in the water. I woke the others, and we used our axes, spades, knives, and other tools to hack it to pieces and throw it overboard. It felt like a fruitless endeavor. The ice built up as fast as we could break it. We spent the morning in a panic, praying to our god of choice that we not sink into the frigid sea.

When the fog lifted, we all breathed a heavy sigh of relief. It was then that Fafnir spotted the waypoint Magnus had told him to find. There was a massive stone slab that had slipped from the fjord onto the rock below to form a platform reminiscent of the Dolmen I had seen in Bretland, but much, much bigger.

What a relief it was to find that damned waypoint. Our spirits were high as we rowed through the rocks into the fjord, and we glided along the smooth waters therein. On either side of us were sheer cliffs that reached for the sky, sprinkled white with snow. Night fell again, but within the fjord we were shielded from the wind of the open ocean.

No words can give justice to the Giant's Throne, and when we first took sight of it, we all stood a long while in silence and stared in awe. The stone that formed the throne's back was smooth and grey and rose from the fjord into the sky so high I could barely see the birds that circled its peak. Two smaller stone slabs jetted out from the cliff like armrests made for monstrously large arms. For a moment, I believed we had arrived in Jotunheim, the land of the giants.

Past the Giant's Throne, the waters narrowed into a rocky beach that was nestled between the towering cliffs. At the beach, we saw a small pier and boats, one of which was a majestic warship that I assumed belonged to

Magnus. The other ship was unmistakable—it looked like Sail Horse and must have been the ship Eilif had built to replace it. We rowed to the dock and tied off behind the warship and the new Sail Horse, and I disembarked with Váli. The fjord was silent. No crickets chirped, and no birds sang their songs. Few animals, it seemed, lived so far north.

"There's no one here," Váli said. His voice boomed across the fjord.

I shushed him and replied in a whisper, "See the path leading away?"

He saw it and nodded. We walked the path a short distance to see how far it would lead us away from the beach, and it climbed into the fjords and snaked along the sand, rocks, and snowdrifts. It was too dangerous to take my men up the path. I knew our best chance of finding Eilif in the vast Northern lands would be to make him come to us.

We made camp on the beach and used dried driftwood to build a fire. Its warmth boosted the morale of my men who had felt a chill in their bones since we had crossed into the fjords. Without trees to fell to erect pikes around camp, I told my crew to sleep on the ship again, much to their dismay. I had to ensure no one would ambush us in the night, and it seemed the sensible option. Váli stayed on the ship to watch over the men, and I took Fafnir, Rune, and Gørm to camp onshore with me. The men sleeping on the water, I was sure, slept better than us.

On the beach, we were exposed, and so kept a restless eye open for any men approaching along the path. By daybreak, no one had come to meet us. Our fire sent a column of smoke into the sky, visible far across the Northern lands, and I hoped Eilif would see it. We waited for another day, and still no one appeared. When I felt most discouraged, a man in a thick cloak descended the path to the beach alone. My crew grasped their arms in fear at first, but they relaxed when the man revealed himself, and they saw that I knew him.

"Egill!" I said.

He looked at me sideways and said, "Do we know each other?"

I approached him and pulled back my hair. "I have grown since you saw me last," I said.

"Hasting?" he said after gazing at me. "My boy, what in Hel's name are you doing here?"

"I'm looking for you," I said. "Well, you and Eilif."

Egill looked at his feet, chagrined. "Eilif, he, uh, he... he is dead."

"When?" I asked. "How?"

"A week ago, perhaps two. I have not kept track of the days," he said. He was grief-stricken and spoke with a slight tremble in the back of his throat. "A sickness came over us all, and a frost followed. Then the Sami attacked and... only I survived."

Váli pulled me back and leaned in to whisper, "Do you think this could be a trick?"

I shrugged. If it was a trick, Egill had proven an astute liar, which I had not known him to be when I sailed with him. "Where are the bodies?" I asked. "I wish to help you honor them."

"Our camp was half a day's journey from here," he said. "But I already sent Eilif to Valhalla on a burning pyre, and the others too. There is nothing left there but sickness and death." He wiped his eyes and nose with his cloak and looked up again. "Why are you here? How did you find this place?"

"Eilif's brother sent us," I said. "He wants his ship back."

Egill laughed through his tears. "That bastard, Magnus!" he exclaimed. "It doesn't matter. He can have it."

I invited Egill to sit by the fire, and he accepted. We sat in silence at first, and I waited for him to say more. My crew kept their distance in case he still carried the sickness, or in case the gods sought to punish him further and anyone who helped him. Váli gave him a bowl of stew and sat at his side.

"Egill, old friend," he said.

Egill glared at him. "Váli? What is happening here? You, the boy... is this a trick of my eyes? Have I died? Is this Niflheim?"

"No, old friend," Váli said. "You are alive."

Egill shook his head. He ate as if he had not tasted food in days. When he slurped down the last drop of the stew, he reached out to Váli and begged for more. Váli obliged him. As he filled the bowl with more stew from the iron pot on the fire, Egill said, "Something tells me you are not only here for Eilif's ship."

"No," I said.

Váli handed him his second bowl and said, "A farmer in Ireland told us you sold him a slave from Armorica."

Egill slurped down the stew and made us wait for him to speak. He was stalling.

"I remember you, boy," he said at last. "And I remember what you saw in the water."

His words provoked a sudden fear within me. Images of the great wolf Fenrir flashed before my eyes and, sitting in a Northern land where Midgard and myth so easily melded, I squirmed where I sat.

"You remember it too," Egill continued when he saw my discomfort. "He chose you."

Rune, who sat behind me with some of the others, blurted out, "What's he talking about?"

All eyes were on me. Egill laughed and said, "You mean to say you have not told anyone about what you saw? What you did?" He stood and leaned over the fire so that the flames flickered in his eyes. "Our ship was caught in a violent storm. I saw Thor throwing his thunderbolts into the sea, searching for something, or someone. The wind and rain and thunder sent our ship twirling, and our two ship boys, Hasting and Bjorn, fell overboard. A long time passed, but I managed to pull him from the water and breathe life into him once again."

"Surviving a storm is hardly a deed worthy of song," Rune said.

"It wasn't the storm or the water that frightened us," Egill continued. "It was what the boy said when he awoke. He'd seen a wolf in the water, hunting and preying. Fenrir could have taken his soul, but he didn't. He spared Hasting. When I prayed to Odin and looked to the runes to explain it, all they told me was that he had been marked. Every throw of the runes, I drew the wolf. Even now I sense it; he thirsts for blood."

At first, I thought Egill's story would sow distrust in my crew, and I stood to face them to calm their fears. But it had the opposite effect. Rune and the others had wonder in their eyes. They had never met a man touched by the other world, and it elevated my image to that of a god. Perhaps it was best they heard it from Egill. If they had heard it from me, they would not have believed it. Even Váli looked at me differently. I turned back to Egill, whose smile proved infectious. Flattered as I was, I realized Egill had dodged my question about the slave he had sold in Ireland. My smile faded.

"I know you raided Vannes," I growled. I did not want him to play any more games. "You know why I am here, whether by the gods or your own deduction. Where is she?"

Egill stood back and said, "I'll tell you, for a price." He had not changed at all.

"All right," I said.

Though I felt growing anger at his impetuousness, my memories of him kept me from lashing out. He looked around at my men and saw that I had done well for myself.

"First, I want you to swear that you will not harm me when I tell you," he pleaded.

Váli chuckled and said, "There's more than one demand?"

Egill ignored him. "The price is my life. Eilif is dead, and I am an outlaw. If I stay here, I will freeze or starve. You know me, Hasting. I can cast the runes for you, and I can sing songs of your deeds. I ask you to restore my status as a free man and take me into your charge."

"You want to join my crew?" I asked, surprised.

Egill nodded.

I looked at Váli who shook his head. I understood his meaning. "I will agree to the first. Tell me where I can find Asa, and I swear I will not kill you under any circumstance. For the second, I cannot agree until I hear what you've done with her."

I saw in Egill's eyes that he held a soft place in his heart for me, and perhaps it was why he so quickly gave up his only leverage. "Do you remember when we escaped from the dungeon in Frankland?" he asked.

"Of course," I replied.

"It was not by accident," he said. "Eilif struck a deal with the Franks to get our ship back."

"The ship sank, I thought," I said.

"That's what Nominoë was meant to think," he explained.

The revelation opened my eyes to a dark truth. Not only did Eilif lie to Nominoë, he lied to me. My anger swelled within my chest and I reached for my sword as I said, "I waited for you."

"I know," Egill said. "We did not expect Nominoë to take a hostage."

"And the raid? If you were meant to disappear, why did you raid?" I asked.

"Eilif still owed his brother hundreds of pounds of silver for the ship," he explained. "We tried to earn the silver through trade, but it took too long. The Franks were willing to pay us what we owed and more for a single raid. When Magnus learned of it, he gave us another ship and a crew. We were swords for hire, nothing more."

"Why did you fake a massacre?" I asked.

Egill looked at me with utter astonishment. He must not have expected me to work out that they had staged the fire.

"The Franks asked us to kill everyone. We did not feel comfortable with that." Egill paused. He looked at his hands as they trembled from the cold and said, "We took Asa too. I did not recognize her at first, but she knew us. She had the same fiery spirit from when we had first found her."

"What happened to her, Egill?" I asked.

"The Franks betrayed us," he muttered. "They ambushed us on the Loire and killed many of our men. Asa leaped into the water before I could catch her. Last I saw her, she was taken by the Franks."

I looked to my crew who squirmed at my rage. I knew I would need to produce wealth for them if I hoped to keep their loyalty, but I needed to find and rescue Asa. As much as I wanted to sail straight for Frankland, my one chance at saving her was to build up the strength of my fleet, and quickly. I would need all the help I could muster, from my men, from Magnus, and even from Nominoë. That the Franks had arranged the raid on Vannes gave me the leverage I needed to ask for his support.

"I am with you," Egill said. "The Franks broke their oath to us. We returned to Jutland with none of the silver we had promised Magnus. That's why he threatened to confiscate our ships and make us toil in the fields like thralls. So we fled."

"The Franks have no honor," I growled. "They are treasonous—oath-breakers. I will see them punished for what they have done."

"We are with you," Rune said as he stood. All my men stood with him. "We are all with you."

"What will you do with him?" Váli asked, pointing at Egill.

"Put him in irons," I said. "Egill, you are now my prisoner. I will take you back to Magnus so you can tell him of Eilif's death. But hear me: you are not part of my crew. You will need to earn my trust if you hope to regain your freedom."

"Hasting, what about the sickness?" Rune asked.

"If Egill still carries it, he could doom us all," Fafnir added.

Egill thought for a moment and looked at my men stolidly. "The fact that I am still alive should be proof enough that the sickness has passed, no?"

"I have an idea," Váli suggested. "We have three ships. The smallest will not need a crew. We can tow it by rope. Egill can ride on the ship in tow, and if the gods try to kill him, we will cut him loose."

I turned to my men and asked them, "Does anyone think it is a bad idea?" None of them protested. I turned to Egill and said, "If you survive the journey, we will know you are not cursed."

Egill did not smile, but he did not scowl either. We split the crew and supplies among the ships for our journey back to Jutland—Váli took Sail Horse with Ulf, Trygva, Frode, Arne, Erik, and Troels, while I took the warship with the rest of the men. We towed the ship we had stolen from Hagar with Egill aboard.

It took every man working at his fullest to row the warship into the fjord. On the ship were sixty oars, and we had men enough for ten of them. The sail was more massive too, but Fafnir had sailed on Thor's warship and knew how such vessels worked. I contented myself to sit at the steering paddle while he barked orders to work the ropes. A strong winter wind was at our backs most of the voyage, which was a welcome reprieve to the struggle we had faced sailing north.

All was not well aboard my ship, however, and whispers of overthrowing me as chieftain started to circulate among my men. The journey north had taken its toll and worn their patience thin, and they did not see the benefit to themselves. I could see in the eyes of a few the resentment they felt, and I did not feel surprised when Fafnir warned me of their plotting. Something needed to be done.

I remembered how Hagar had dealt with would-be traitors—he picked out their leader and killed him. Though I did not relish such a thing, I saw it was a necessity of life for a chieftain. Three days from Ribe, I decided to end the whispers. I asked Fafnir to show me the man who whispered the most. He pointed to a young man named Ole who, for most of the voyage, had kept to himself. He had hair black as the night sky and a thick overhanging brow that made him look angry even when he smiled.

"Ole," I said with a booming voice to call him over. He approached me with great caution. "I hear you have something to say about me to the others."

He looked at Fafnir with fury. "Says who?"

I kept my eyes fixed on Ole and said, "It is a small crew—secrets do not stay secrets for long." I stood to put us on even footing. "I do not like that my men are conspiring together. For us to be successful, I need absolute loyalty from every one of you."

"We are not conspiring," Ole said. "Only observing that you have not delivered what you promised."

"I told you in Dublin that we would not sail to Frankland to make wealth until after we had sailed north," I said.

"Yes, but you never said you would take us to the frozen wastelands beyond the fjords. We think it was reckless," Ole retorted.

"We?" I asked.

"Yes. I am not alone in thinking such things," he replied.

"What would you have me do?" I asked him.

Ole grinned and looked back at his friends. "That you must ask the question is proof you are not fit to lead us. You are not a Northman. You do not know our ways."

His suggestion that I did not act like a Northman enraged me. He had slandered me in front of my men, and I knew it gave me the right to kill him. I drew my sword, and Ole pulled a seax and hunting knife from his belt to defend himself. It was the first time I had held my father's sword in a fight. The blade felt light and balanced, crafted masterfully from the finest steel in the North.

I lifted the sword above my head in a stance the Celts called the *falcon*, and I waited for Ole to try and strike from below. He took the bait. When he lunged forward, I brought my blade down to meet with his seax. My sword swiped his to the side, and I thrust up across his chest and neck. I even nicked his ear. Ole's wool clothes had absorbed the slash, but he stumbled backward, stunned by the speed of my movement. He growled and leaped at me again in a wild charge. I used his momentum against him, parried to his left, and sent him into the gunwale. On his back, he had nowhere to run. As he squirmed to get away, I slid my blade into his heart.

"Are there any others who believe I am unfit to lead?" I cried out to the rest of the crew.

None answered. Fafnir approached Ole's lifeless body, pulled open his eyelids, and roared to the sky,

"Odin!" to warn the gods that a warrior had left Midgard to join them. We wrapped the corpse in a wool blanket and threw it into the water. As Ole's body drifted past the ship in tow, Egill called out to me.

"I see you are a man short," he said. "I can help you. I am a good sailor. And I think we have proven that I am not cursed. If the gods had wished to kill me, they would have done it days ago."

He was right. I needed every man, and the loss of Ole would make our approach to Ribe more difficult. "You would need to swear to me," I said.

"I will," Egill said. "I have seen what you do to those who don't."

I wanted to trust him, but my gut told me he had other plans. "All right," I said.

Egill swore his loyalty from across the water, and we pulled him in so he could climb aboard. Váli overtook us in Sail Horse as we did so, and they furled their sail to slow their pace. He looked at me and made questioning hand gestures.

Once Egill had climbed aboard, we set course for Ribe with haste. Three more days of sailing brought us to the beach where we had camped during our first visit. My men were cold and starving. Not until I stepped foot onto the beach and watched them unload the ships to make camp did I realize how much they had starved on the journey. All of them had slimmed and looked gaunt. While we prepared a tent on the beach, Magnus himself rode to us with his husmän at his side. He laughed when he saw the warship returned to his land.

"Where's my brother?" he asked from his horse.

"Dead," I replied.

He looked at me with a frown and said, "You killed him?"

"No," I said. "The North did."

Magnus saw Egill among those who had returned and said, "Why is he here?"

I put my hands on my hips and looked around at my men. "I needed him," I said. "We were shorthanded."

"He is an outlaw. You should have killed him," Magnus said, peeved.

"Kill him I may," I said. "But for now, he is my prisoner." I approached Magnus' horse and looked up at him with a scowl. "I brought back your ship, as promised."

"You have," he said. "You have proven your honesty and loyalty. I will honor you."

It was then I saw the power of a good deed. Magnus invited us to his hall, and we feasted for five days and five nights. His largesse showed no bounds, and my men welcomed it. We ate, we drank, we sang, and we fraternized with Horic's men and shared stories of great deeds, both of gods and men. I allowed my crew to do as they wished, even when they took servant girls to satisfy their desires.

Magnus and I kept our wits about us and sat together each night to observe the feasts. We laughed together, drank together, and formed a kinship I would not have expected before our journey to the Giant's Throne. He was like his brother in almost every way. Neither of us talked about sailing or raiding. We were warriors celebrating a victory, and we lived as if the following day would be our last. When the feasting ended, Magnus invited us to winter in Ribe to gather our strength before sailing for Frankland. I would have preferred to sail straight away. The merchants in Ribe were expensive, and my wealth was not limitless. Yet considering the near mutiny aboard my ship, I thought it best to stay a while longer to allow my men to fatten up and to recover from the arduous journey we had taken.

We were allowed to make camp in a clearing behind the town where we pitched our tents next to the stone totems that marked the plots of farmers' fields. Though Ribe offered ample distraction to my men, I emplaced a set of rules I had learned from my mentor Yann to maintain order. The last thing I needed was one of my warriors putting his hands up the wrong dress and embroiling us all in a fight.

During the day, the men trained with their weapons. I learned that none of them except Sten could fight with proper form. Rune showed promise with a blade, as did Gørm, but the others were heavy-footed and slow. If I hoped to find Asa, my men would need to know how to fight like professional soldiers. Franks, with their heavy shields and lances, would make quick work of this bunch.

There was also the problem of equipment. My crew had none. Fafnir had experience crafting shields, so he showed us how to make our own. Shield-making took practice and, for most, their first attempt splintered with a single blow. Ribe's blacksmith learned my name soon enough. I spent more gold there than anywhere else in town, and he praised me as his best customer. Thankfully, I had Váli who knew the art of commerce, and he negotiated a fair price for each blade.

Though I could not pay my men outright, the swords, axes, and shields, plus the gift of learning how to fight, were not unappreciated. The men who had whispered of overthrowing me now sang my praises where they went, and my reputation in Ribe grew. Soon the townspeople murmured when I passed, telling stories they had heard about me and my adventures. When I overheard them speaking of how a woman who may have been Odin in disguise had helped me on my way, I knew Váli had been out drinking and running his tongue. I did not care. The attention made it easier to ask for lower prices on goods. To this day, I do not know who told

Magnus' skald about me, but he sang the songs of my deeds, and he called me *Hasting the Wolf*.

Near the end of winter, when the weather warmed and the rains seemed endless, Magnus paid us a visit. He approached me with urgency in his step, took me by the shoulder, and said, "King Horic is near."

15

Bjorn Ironsides

I had earned enough respect from Magnus to receive an invitation to his hall when he welcomed King Horic. The king's men wore expensive clothes and equipment I could not hope to afford for my crew. They wore hauberks, bronze-plated belts, fur overcoats, and each sported several gold and silver arm rings on both wrists. Even their beards were decorated with silver rings and glass beads.

King Horic wore a simple circlet on his head and a blue silk robe trimmed in gold. On each finger he wore a jewel-encrusted ring, and on his wrists he wore more arm rings than I could count. The bronze brooches that held his fur overcoat were decorated in Norse knots. Seated side by side, Horic made Magnus look like a pauper. The king's men filled every seat at Magnus' many tables, and I sat beside Magnus opposite the king.

"To what do I owe the pleasure of hosting you, my king?" Magnus asked Horic as they ate and drank merrily.

"I am recruiting," Horic said. "It's raiding season."

"Heading to Frisia again?" Magnus asked.

Horic nodded as he took an oversized bite from a roasted chicken leg. "Nothing fancy. I hope to bleed the empire a little and keep them away from my lands."

For all the expensive clothes and ostentation in his demeanor, Horic was not an imposing man. He was short compared to Magnus, and he had a slender build and narrow shoulders. The women in the hall, who were the wives and daughters of the wealthiest townspeople, did not seem to mind. They gazed admiringly upon his fair face, his kind blue eyes, and his well-trimmed hair and beard. Or perhaps it was his wealth they admired.

"I have few men to spare," Magnus lamented.

"What about that brother of yours?" Horic asked.

Magnus lowered his head and said, "He is dead."

Horic paused to look at him. He tried to show empathy for his host. "Let us hope he is received well in Valhalla."

"Let us hope," Magnus said under his breath.

"Who else can you send with us?" Horic asked.

Magnus looked at me and grinned. "Hasting will go with you."

I raised my eyebrows and looked at him with my mouth agape. "Eh," I started.

"Hasting?" Horic said. We had not been introduced, even though I sat two seats away from him. "Where are you from, Hasting?"

"My father was a chieftain in Jutland," I said.

"A chieftain? Which one? They are all friends of mine," Horic said smiling.

"His name was Ragnar," I said. "He was killed in a blood feud."

"As is too common." Horic leaned in to hear me better. "How long ago was this?"

"Ten years, at least," I told him.

"Ten years…" Horic's eyes lit up all at once. He turned to look down the table and said, "Bjorn! Yes, Bjorn." He waved to one of his warriors near the other end of the table. "Bjorn, come here."

A tall young man with a thick chest and powerful arms approached the king. His blond hair was short and his beard even shorter, and from his right temple to the middle of his neck he had a long purple scar.

"Bjorn, wasn't your father a chieftain named Ragnar?"

"He was," Bjorn replied.

"This man here, Hasting, says his father was named Ragnar," Horic said.

Bjorn looked me up and down and asked, "How old are you?"

"I am not sure," I said.

Bjorn scoffed. "You don't know how old you are?"

"It has been hard to keep track," I said. "How old are you?"

"Seventeen," he said. He looked much older.

"I don't remember having any brothers so close in age to me," I said.

"Neither do I," Bjorn said. "But my father was known to have many concubines. You could be one of his bastards."

His words wounded me. I had remembered being treated as a legitimate son, and I knew my father—I had spent enough time with him before his death to remember him. Bjorn had angered me, and I stood to my feet. "You insult me," I growled.

Horic chuckled. "He's got some bite to him," he said to Magnus.

"It was merely a suggestion," Bjorn said. "I meant no offense."

I reached for the hilt of my sword, which alarmed Horic's men. When they all stood, I paused and said, "I only want to show it to Bjorn." I pulled it out a little further but did not unsheathe it all the way. "This is my father's sword."

Bjorn looked at it and laughed. "Your father is dead? Mine is still roving the seas and making bastards!"

We laughed together, and Horic and Magnus joined us. When the laughing stopped, I sat again, and Horic spoke. "It is hard to say if I knew your father, Hasting. If he was a chieftain in Jutland, I should have known him, but many farmers and landowners have called themselves chieftains these past years."

"It does not matter," I said. "I have no desire to claim land in Jutland."

My words must have intrigued Horic. "What do you desire?"

I felt the eyes of all the men at the table on me. Finding Asa was all I had on my mind, with no thought of what I would do after I found her. In thinking of how to answer Horic's question, I recalled my father's words. I remembered that he had said a man's reputation survives him beyond his death if he lives his life well. I recalled how I had felt when the skald sang his songs about me to the admiration of the townspeople. It was uplifting.

"I want to be remembered," I answered.

Horic ran his hand through his hair and smiled. "Remembered?" He chuckled and looked at Bjorn. "That," he declared, "is the answer of a true warrior."

"You honor me," I said.

"Come, come," Magnus said, "my nephew is among the most celebrated warriors in your service."

"Nephew?" I asked with surprise.

"Yes, Bjorn is my sister's first son by her first husband," Magnus explained.

"So Eilif was your uncle as well?" I asked Bjorn. He nodded. "And you sailed with him?"

"When I was a boy," Bjorn said.

"Bjorn, we know each other. I sailed with Eilif. I am the one they left in Armorica."

Bjorn's eyes opened wide when he remembered me. "You saved me from drowning!" he said as he stepped toward me and reached for my shoulders. "I owe you my life."

"You know each other?" Horic asked.

"Yes," Bjorn said. "Hasting was a ship boy for my uncle, Eilif. If not for him, I would have drowned in that storm. And... the wolf."

"The wolf?" Magnus asked.

Bjorn looked around at all the men at the table. He squirmed a little when he said, "Yes. We believed the wolf Fenrir had escaped, and Thor had given chase. In the water, Hasting saw the wolf and pulled me away from his jowls, or so I heard. I do not remember it. When my uncle's friend Egill cast the runes, he saw what Hasting had seen. It haunts my dreams to this day."

Everyone present remained silent. For such strong men, they all seemed unnerved by Bjorn's story. Horic gazed across the room into the shadows along the far wall and nodded.

A chilled draft blew across the tables and made the fire flicker, and a shadowy figure wearing a thick black cloak entered the hall through a side door and circled the tables. The figure removed her hood to reveal one of the fairest faces I had ever seen. She had crystalline eyes, hair the color of pure gold, and skin smoother than the finest eastern silk. Blue tattoos covered her neck up to her jaw line, and when she looked around the room, her gaze entranced the men. Horic stood and smiled.

"Hasting, this is my völva, Skírlaug. She has the vision," he said.

"The vision?" I asked.

"She can see the world beyond ours and interpret the will of the gods," Bjorn explained.

Horic continued, "If what you say is true, and you did see the great wolf, she will know it."

Skírlaug eclipsed the men around me as she approached my table. She pulled up my chin and gazed into my eyes. I felt as though my soul had begun to fall into the whirlpools of her irises. Her eyes, I realized, were as drawn to mine as mine were to hers. The confidence in her expression faded, and she tried to pull away from me in fear. I did not consciously take her hand; I realized I had when Horic shouted at me to release her. She withdrew her arm and held it in pain, her eyes still locked with mine. She held her hands out and raised them over her eyes to break our stare. Exhausted, she stepped back into Horic's arms.

"What happened?" Horic asked with haunted eyes.

"He did see the wolf," she said.

"I don't understand. Why are you frightened?" Horic asked.

Skírlaug shook her head and said, "I cannot explain it. I saw a glimpse of his destiny and... all I will say is you would do well to honor him. He will prove a formidable ally, or a ferocious enemy."

She stroked Horic's face and stood to her feet. As she left, she looked at me once more, her regard filled with awe and fear.

Horic nodded and sat back in his chair while stroking his beard. Bjorn shoved the man who sat beside me out of the way and took his seat. His movements were short and abrupt. Horic leaned back with his mead and gazed at me with inquisitive eyes. He wanted to recruit me, but I had no interest in sailing with him. In Ireland, I had avoided entering Thor's service, and I had no intention of joining the king of Jutland. Given my story and connection with Bjorn, and the odd encounter with his völva, I saw he would try to convince me to swear an oath to him.

"Hasting had planned to sail to Frankland," Magnus said to break the silence.

"Frankland?" Horic blurted out. Mead spilled from his mouth into his beard. He raised his goblet for a servant to fill. A slender young girl scurried to him in an instant. "It is a rich land, but too well defended."

Magnus took a large drink from his own goblet, wiped his face with his sleeve, and asked, "What do you say, Hasting? Is Frankland too hard a target?"

"Yes," I answered.

My answer surprised them all. Horic put a hand on his hip and turned to face me. "Why would you sail there, then?" he asked with a touch of exasperation in his voice.

I took a deep breath to gather my courage and explain to a quiet mead hall full of warriors why I desired to sail to Frankland. The king would see through a lie, so I told him about my enslavement in Ireland, how Eilif had seen something of value in me and bought my freedom, and how I had spent the past four years among the Celts learning to read, write, and fight. I told them about the raid, about Asa, and even about Oddlaug and the hidden base we had hoped to find.

Horic listened to all of it. His brow furrowed when I spoke of killing Hagar and of the help I had received from Thor, but I expected him to have a poor opinion of the Northmen. When I finished my telling, he sat back and crossed his arms. He looked around the room at all the blank faces of his men who sat in disbelief at my tale.

"You have proof of all of this?" Horic asked.

"Egill and Váli can attest to my honesty," I said. "About my father, all I have is his sword."

"That your father was a chieftain is the most believable part of it all," Horic declared. "I would speak with Egill and Váli."

"Egill is here?" Bjorn said. "I have not seen him in years."

Magnus cleared his throat. "Egill is not welcome in my hall," he exclaimed. "He is an outlaw."

"Egill is sworn to me," I said to Horic.

The king nodded his head. "We will go to him, then."

I led Horic, Magnus, and Bjorn to my camp in the dark. The rain had cleared, but the ground was still soft and damp. As we approached, my men stood and gathered at the far end of the fire. They seemed nervous, as was I.

Horic stopped before the fire pit and said, "I am looking for Egill and Váli."

Váli stepped forward and said, "I am Váli. Egill is at the cesspit."

"Your chieftain has told me a fantastical story that I am struggling to believe," Horic said. "Are you willing to swear that he has told me the truth?"

Váli answered him, "Whatever he has said to you, it is true. I know how mad it sounds, but I was there for much of it. When I think back on what we have done together, I do not believe it myself."

Egill stumbled back into camp smelling like an empty barrel of wine. He worked his way through the rest of the crew to the fire and shouted, "Where's the mead?"

Magnus clenched his fists. "Egill, you drunken fool!"

Egill heard his voice and froze. "What are you doing here?" He looked around and saw the king's finely crafted arms and armor flickering in the dim firelight. "What did I do this time?"

"You were named to swear to the truthfulness of your chieftain's story," Horic said.

"What did he tell you?" Egill asked with a sway in his shoulders.

"I told him about Hagar," I said. "And how Eilif took me from his hall; and how you left me among the Celts as a hostage."

Egill bowed. "It is true," he said. "And he faced the wolf Fenrir as no man has done before. Did he tell you about that?"

"I told them," Bjorn said. "I remember when you cast the runes. Skírlaug confirmed it. She has the sight, as you do."

Egill inched toward us. "The runes do not lie," he said. He reached into his pocket, pulled out a handful of small finger-length bones, and tossed them on the ground. "Pick one," he said to Horic.

Horic knelt in the mud and looked at the bones with curious eyes. In the dark, none of us could see the symbols carved into them, not even Egill. The king reached for one of the bones that had rolled closer to him. He held it up in the firelight for Egill to take. Egill laughed.

"Even now, the beast watches us," Egill said. "Look!"

Horic read the rune and, shaken, he looked back at me and said, "It is the wolf."

"A fine trick," Magnus said, unconvinced. "Are all your runes of the wolf?"

Egill reached down to pick up the other runes and handed them to Magnus. As the jarl read them, his coy smile turned to a deep frown.

"Your mother was Sami?" Horic asked.

Egill nodded.

"Eilif believed Egill had inherited his mother's powers," Bjorn said. "I swear I have seen that it is true."

"He cannot be trusted. Sami are not allowed in my hall, and for good reason. Thieves and liars, all of them. And worse, Egill is an *ergi*, unmanly and perverse, and he seduced my brother with his magic," Magnus insisted. He spat at Egill's feet.

"He is more in touch with the gods than you and I," Horic said. "Thank you for sharing what you know. You have given me much to contemplate."

Magnus turned and marched back to his hall. Horic put a hand on my shoulder; his grip was soft and comforting. I felt that he believed me, even if Magnus did not. Behind us, I heard my men chastise Egill, whispering harsh words until he agreed to stop drinking and slip into his tent to sleep.

"Best you stay here, tonight," Horic said.

"What is an *ergi*?" I asked before he left.

Horic paused to look at the ground. He considered his words before saying, "An *ergi* is a man who lies with other men."

He left me at my camp with a sinking feeling in my stomach. That Egill was an *ergi* worried me. It did not take long for me to realize that Magnus had accused Egill of being Eilif's lover. I had never heard of such a thing, two men lying together, nor did I understand it. The shock of it unsettled me. I returned to my tent in the dark while my men drank by the fire. My thoughts distracted me, and I set about arranging the blankets and furs of my cot. Before I could dive into them, I felt a presence behind me, and I found Skírlaug lurking in the shadows.

"Hasting the Wolf," she whispered.

"Is that what you call me?" I retorted.

"It is a good name," she said.

"What? The Wolf? It's not all that original," I said with a smirk.

Skírlaug stepped around me in a small circle with her hand brushing against my chest, back, and shoulders. "You are handsome," she said.

Her words jolted my heart to life. Her touch aroused me, and I noticed how beautiful she was. She pulled me into another deep stare and gripped my tunic to draw me toward my furs. Entranced, I was powerless to stop her. Without breaking her gaze, she pulled up her cloak and dress, sat back into the furs, and pulled my hips in between her legs. Her legs wrapped around me and made me her prisoner.

"Who are you, Hasting?" she asked.

I had no words to answer, and my silence endured far too long.

"I sense something else, or someone else—a part of you," she said. "Yes, I see him now."

"Who?" I asked, our eyes still locked together.

"*Him*," she voiced. "He has imprinted on you, given you his strength." Her lips touched mine. She took my hands and guided them to her hips, then reached up to pull me in by my neck. With her other hand, she undid my trousers and guided my shaft where she wanted it. "Bite me," she said as her legs gripped harder around my hips.

Without thinking, I leaned into her neck and sunk my fangs into her flesh.

"Harder." She pulled at my hips with her legs and forced me to thrust.

I felt the sting of her fingernails digging into my neck and back, and I grasped her hips with all my strength. The beast inside of me took control. Each thrust shook the tent, faster and faster, harder and harder, and her moans grew louder until they turned to screams. My men heard her cries and the shaking of my tent, and they cheered for me. When the deed was done, she adjusted her clothes and vanished into the shadows.

I slept with my sword clutched close to my chest that night. My heart ached with guilt at what I had done. It was the good Christian in me that protested what had happened with Skírlaug, not the Dane. A Dane would never have felt shame for it, but I had spent too much time among the Celts who preached chastity until marriage.

I thought of Asa and how angry she would have been with me, and I wept. I fell asleep, then jolted awake as if no time had passed at all, only to see the sun had risen. Outside my tent, my men had made food and begun their day's training. I sat by the fire pit next to Rune who ran a sharpening stone along the blade of his sword.

"Magnus' men were looking for you," Rune said.

"Why didn't you wake me?" I asked.

"They said to tell you to meet them at the mead hall when you are rested," he said. He continued to sharpen his blade as he spoke. "Do you think they will outlaw us?"

"Why would you think that?" I asked.

"Váli said *ergi* is a serious offence, and since Egill did not challenge the accusation, he bears the reputation," Rune said.

"I will sort it out."

Rune paused and said, "Magnus thinks you could be *ergi* as well."

My nervousness dried in my throat. "Who told you that?" I asked.

Rune nodded his head in Váli's direction. I stood up and marched over to him, interrupting his practice with an ax.

"Why are you telling the crew Magnus thinks I am *ergi*?" I asked.

Váli did not bother to stop swinging when he said, "It's obvious. And I think you were a fool to let Egill live. He has put all our lives at risk."

My faith in him was shaken. It was not the first time Váli had done or said something behind my back. I returned to my tent, washed out my mouth with fresh water, girded my sword, and marched for the mead hall. Magnus would apologize, I thought, because I would make him. When I crossed the hall and stepped into the courtyard, I found Horic and his men standing in a circle talking with Magnus. One of them saw me charging toward them and warned his king.

"Hasting!" Horic said. "Come, we have much to discuss."

I found his demeanor unsettling. "What about?" I asked.

"Where do I start?" he jeered.

"My men think Magnus believes I am *ergi*," I said. "I am here to—"

"Nonsense!" Horic interjected. "Magnus and I discussed you at length last night. We are impressed." He had his hand resting on the girded hilt of his sword when he stepped closer to me. "I admit, I am curious. You said you learned to fight with the Celts. I would like to see how it looks." He puckered his lips and put out a faint whistle, and Bjorn stepped forward to join him at his side. "Bjorn is my most skilled warrior. Let us see how the fighting styles of the Danes and the Celts compare."

I reached for my sword, but Bjorn stopped me by saying, "You won't need that, it's not a duel."

Another of Horic's men walked over to me and handed me a wooden sword with a shallow guard and a thick pommel. It was light and awkward in my hand, but it was not my first, so I adjusted my grip in the way I knew how. Horic and the others walked to the edge of the courtyard, leaving Bjorn and me to face each other.

Bjorn seemed relaxed, and he had an off-putting smirk on his face. I raised my weapon in the stance of the falcon and waited for him to attack. He glared at me, then glanced back at Horic who urged him to move forward. As he approached me, I asked him, "Where did you get that scar?"

"A bear," Bjorn said. "It is why they call me Ironsides. And yours?"

If he had indeed fought a bear, I was in trouble, I thought. "A good beating from Hagar," I said.

Bjorn lunged forward, and I parried his stab with ease, all while holding the Falcon pose.

"You are light on your feet," Bjorn said.

He lunged again. I bore down with my blade to deflect his, then brought it back up in a swift slash, but he dipped out of the way and hopped backward. He danced a little on his feet as he caught his breath.

"Get on with it!" Horic shouted.

I took small, quick steps toward Bjorn before he could reposition himself and swung my blade with three short strokes at his shoulders. He blocked all three, pushed my weapon aside, and drove his elbow into my ribs. I staggered backward.

"Do all Danes fight with such dirty tactics?" I said to taunt him.

My question enraged him. He charged at me and swung his sword with such speed I could not hope to block each stroke. I dove out of the way, rolled on the ground, and sprang back up to my feet. Bjorn charged again. As Yann had taught me, I used his momentum against him and swooped my blade over his, grasped his wrist, and twisted his hand until his grip loosened on his hilt. As the sword hit the ground, Bjorn's powerful arms broke free of my hold and he lifted me off my feet. I found myself slammed on my back and pinned

"Pretty move," Bjorn said.

I drove up with my arms and pushed Bjorn's hands into the dirt. He lost his hold of me, and I rolled to my side and reached for my sword. When I stood again, I said, "You rely too much on your strength."

Our swords clashed with echoing clunks and clanks, and neither of us was able to gain an advantage. In a final move, I used a trick I had learned from the Celts to disarm Bjorn a second time. He swung hard from below, and as I parried, I let my sword linger behind me and in front of him. His attention shifted to the sword, which allowed me to move my weight to his side and kick hard against his pommel. I lifted my sword against his chest and smiled, victorious.

"And you accuse me of dirty tactics?" he growled.

"Enough!" Horic roared. "I am impressed. He disarmed you, Bjorn... twice."

"He does not fight with honor," Bjorn said.

"It is certainly not a fighting style we are accustomed to seeing," Horic admitted.

I lowered my sword and gave Bjorn a coy smile. "I can teach you a few moves if you would like."

Bjorn scowled and grumbled to himself. Horic put his arm around my shoulders and walked with me to the mead hall. The double doors were open, and servants bustled about cleaning after the night's feast. He sat me at a table near the entrance where there was ample light from outside, and he called for Bjorn to join us.

"In the morning, we plan to sail for Frankland. Frisia is as barren as my first wife. We Danes are at war, you know, with the Obrodites and the Rus, and wars are expensive. I would like to raid where I can actually line my pockets with silver."

"And you think I can help you," I uttered.

"Precisely," Horic exclaimed. "I received a message from my man in Aachen that the emperor's eldest son has joined the rebellion against him. The empire is crumbling from within. A door has opened for us, Hasting. It is time to look to larger prizes."

The rebellion had begun before I left Vannes, and the garrison of Nantes had not shown signs of weakening. I feared Horic had mistaken an old report for a new opportunity; I knew he would walk into the same trap as Thor. In fact, I had the sense from what Egill had told me that the Franks had fortified their fleet and strengthened their river defenses in the Loire. The emperor's strife with his sons had not yet affected the regional lords of the empire, particularly along the border with the Celts.

"Frankland is still well defended," I suggested.

"Can you not think of a place—a wealthy place— where we can strike and make ourselves rich?" he asked.

I thought about his question while dodging his eager regard. Horic wanted to sail to Frankland, and I knew I would not change his mind. Asa remained my focus. I had planned to sail to Vannes to enlist the help of Nominoë in finding her, but with Horic's fleet at my back, I could not hope to go there without starting a fight. Looking around the courtyard for inspiration, I contemplated how to make Horic happy in a way that would allow me to continue on my own journey.

"How valuable is salt in Jutland?" I asked.

Horic chuckled at the question. "It's invaluable," he said. "The Franks control all the mines. Why?"

"I know of a place that produces the finest salt in Midgard," I said. "And it has farms enough to make all you would need, but..."

"But?" Horic urged me on.

"The island is abandoned. You would need to farm the salt yourself," I explained.

Horic gave me a quizzical look. "You want us to sail to Frankland to farm salt?"

When he said it out loud, it sounded ridiculous. Yet I had worked the marshes, and I knew how to farm the salt. "A raid could never hope to capture all the wealth the island can produce," I said. "If you controlled it, it would line your pockets with silver all summer, every summer."

"What about the Franks? Won't they march on the island to repel us?" Horic asked.

Truthfully, I did not know. I knew what Váli and I had seen—an abandoned monastery with working levies to the salt marshes, ripe for the taking. The ferryman, the ship captain, the monks, and the tavern keeper had all made it clear that the empire had little interest in occupying the island again. It was the monastery's salt, and the church existed separately from the tidings of the continent, or so it seemed. I explained all of this to Horic who glowed with excitement with each passing moment. To add to his enthusiasm, I told him the island could also serve as a base to launch raids across Frankland.

"It sounds too good to be true," Horic said. "There must be something… some threat we are not seeing."

"The problem I foresee is other Northmen. Hakon of Lade, Thor of Dublin—they know about the salt too."

Horic spat at the ground in disgust. "That's a big fucking problem," he snarled.

"I know, but none of them know how to farm the salt," I said. "I do."

Horic put his hands on his lap and took in a deep breath. "All right, Hasting, son of Ragnar, you will lead us to this island. At worst, it is an excuse to raid in Frankland."

From somewhere under his breath, I sensed his distrust. Perhaps that is how kings live their lives, never trusting others for fear of betrayal. Nevertheless, he ordered his men to prepare their ships and asked that my men and I join his fleet the following day.

Before parting, Horic looked at me with deep consternation and asked, "Do you have a given name?"

"I do not know what that is," I said.

"It is a name your followers give you," Bjorn explained. "A name you earn through your deeds… mine is Ironsides because they say my skin is hard as iron."

"The bear cut through it easily enough," I said with a chuckle.

"A bear's claws can cut through iron easily enough," Horic said. "So, what do your men call you?"

"They have not given me a name, but Magnus' skald has," I said.

"And?" Horic asked. Both he and Bjorn leaned in to hear me.

"Hasting the Wolf," I said.

Horic smiled and took in another deep breath. With inspiration in his voice, he said, "Tomorrow I sail to Frankland with Ironsides and the Wolf."

When I delivered news of our departure to my crew, they rejoiced. Sailing to Frankland with Horic was an honor far above and beyond what I had promised them. We loaded Sail Horse and Hagar's ship full of supplies from Magnus who, by Horic's command, had to help fund part of the fleet. I had hoped he would let us take his warship, but his generosity did not extend that far, and he had already allowed me to recruit forty men from his town.

At sunrise the following day, a horn blew out over the tranquil waters of the bay, signaling the start of the journey. Váli approached Sail Horse on the beach before we pushed her out to sea.

"Hagar's ship," he said, "she needs a name."

"She's your ship now. You should name her," I said.

Váli's cheeks turned red, and he swelled with pride. "She is small but sturdy, light and fast. I shall call her the Sea Fox."

I gave him my approval with a nod and a smile. Váli returned to the Sea Fox to set her to water with his crew. Though I did not show it, I had started to wonder about his loyalty. Twice he had undermined me, and I struggled to understand why. Perhaps he felt his age and experience gave him the right to do so. Whatever the cause, I feared I might soon need to redress him, and I did not take pleasure at the thought. He had proven invaluable to me as a follower and a close friend.

Horic's fleet numbered two dozen with Sail Horse and Sea Fox. They allowed us to take the lead and guide them from Jutland, along the coast to Armorica, and on to Frankland. Fafnir took the steering paddle while I stood at the prow, as chieftains and kings did, and signaled to the other ships our direction. The bronze weathervane atop our mast pointed south, and a favorable wind filled our sails. The gods, it seemed, had blessed our journey. Horic and his ships followed in an unbroken line. I stayed at the prow, gazing into the distance. Rune noticed that I was not acting like myself and approached me to speak.

"Forgive me if it is not my place, but is something the matter?" he asked.

I looked at him and smiled. "Your concern is well appreciated, Rune." I breathed a heavy sigh as the wind blew my hair in every direction.

"Is it Váli?" he asked. "You seemed angry with him yesterday morning."

"You are observant," I said.

Rune looked at his feet before he spoke again. "I've wanted to say for some time…Váli means well, but he is prideful. He has said things to the others that we all agree were… out of place."

"Thank you for telling me." His words evoked further frustration. "I will speak with him in Frankland."

Rune smiled and bowed. When I reached to shake his hand, he pulled me in for an embrace. "It is an honor to sail with you," he said.

I had not been embraced by another man since I left Armorica. It felt foreign to me. Rune must have taken notice of my self-isolation and my avoidance of physical touch, and he'd guessed I needed a friend I could trust.

I had grown more distant even in the short time since we had left Ireland. Part of me wanted to let loose and bond with the men, but another pulled me away for fear of showing weakness. Leaders had to show strength, I thought. I had created a prison for myself in my mind, and it made me feel alone. Rune's gesture awoke me to the fact that I had not forged close enough bonds with my men, and I would soon regret it.

I had been so focused on finding Asa that I had neglected my most important duty as their chieftain. We had spent months together, and still, I felt I did not know them well. That night, when Fafnir cracked open the mead, I joined my crew, and I learned each of their stories.

16

King of the Salt

Fafnir was the son of a wealthy farmer who lived in the Oslo Fjord. He had thirteen brothers and sisters, and the oldest of them, his brother Arn, had taken ownership of the farm when their father died. His sisters were married to other farmers, and his brothers had left to join the armies of the Northmen. At twelve years old, Fafnir had sailed as a ship's boy to England and Ireland, and he made Dublin his home. He was sworn to Thor and had sailed with him on many raids, including the one in Frankland.

I did not know until I asked him, but he had journeyed to Herio before and had almost died when Thor failed to overcome the Frankish defenses on the Loire. He showed me the scar on his leg from a crossbow bolt he had received on that day. He sat beside Egill as he told the story of how they had escaped, and he lamented Eilif's trickery.

"It would have been a brilliant move if the Franks hadn't captured us," Egill said with a chuckle.

Fafnir had put the calamity behind him and was able to laugh about it. The story gave them something in common, and their friendship blossomed during our journey. Their closeness in age helped. As navigator, Fafnir needed no reminder of the waypoints and landmarks—he knew them all. I saw that the rest of my crew looked up to him, and they obeyed him when he spoke. He was a calm man who laughed softly and smiled often.

With Egill, they told jokes back and forth until our sides ached from laughing. My crew's morale, which had faltered before, remained high with Fafnir's help. More and more, I relied on him for counsel concerning the other men.

Egill had the respect of Fafnir, but not of the crew. While he was the most seasoned man aboard, and his stories of far-off adventures roused the men's imaginations, they made his life aboard miserable. I never caught any of them tormenting him, but I heard their whispers.

One night, when the winds were calm and the moon shone overhead, I awoke to find him standing on the gunwale crying. I thought he might jump. The loss of all his friends, Eilif in particular, weighed on his spirit, and I did not know how to help him. In the morning I asked him how he felt. He looked at me with tired eyes and shrugged.

"The gods no longer speak to me," he said. "I have lost the sight." His abilities to commune with the world beyond ours had played a central role in his life, and to no longer possess them meant he had little left to live for. Fafnir, who noticed Egill's sadness, whispered into my ear that we should give him a more significant role on the ship. I had not yet given him much to do because I did not trust him. The ire he had provoked from Magnus and Horic, and the unchallenged accusation that he was an *ergi*, made me nervous.

A few weeks into our journey, we came upon a land with many rocks protruding from shallow water. I did not recognize it, but Fafnir assured me we had reached Northern Armorica. We passed between two large islands he called Jarð and Geirr, both named for the first Northmen who had landed there and raided.

A thick fog blanketed the land and sea, and we had a hard time seeing the rocks beneath us and between the islands. The fog did not lift the entire day. I heard renewed talk of a curse among the men, but they ceased their whispers when I approached them. Even I began to fear the gods had lured us into a trap. When night fell, we found ourselves immersed in blackness. Neither the moon nor the stars shone in the sky. All we could see were the faint flickers of the other ships' torches.

The water was calm, at least, and I fell asleep. I awoke with panic in the dark of night as waves and rain battered our hull. The sea tossed us around like a child's toy. We were at the gods' mercy. Behind us, I heard a booming crash and the howling of desperate men on the wind. One of our ships had wrecked against the rocks. I ordered my men to set their oars to water, to find the boat and save the men we could, but Fafnir grabbed me by the shoulder and roared, "We are blind in this darkness, and we will shipwreck if we go after them!"

I felt helpless. Their screams filled the night, and at dawn we heard them no more. When the sky brightened and the rain and waves subsided, we found ourselves in another fog.

"We are cursed," Sten declared.

This time, we all believed it. One by one, the ships would crash against the rocks, and we would all die. The fog did not lift for two days, and until it did, we could not sail away from it. Desperate for answers, I peered over the gunwale for a sign from the gods in the water. I saw nothing. Behind me, I heard a ruckus and turned to find Fafnir and Egill wrestling over a large, heavy sack. Rune joined in to help Fafnir, but Egill pulled it free. I saw he had tied himself to the sack, and I understood what he planned to do.

"Egill, wait!" I cried out.

"I am sorry, Hasting," he said with tears in his eyes. "It is my curse. I should have died with Eilif in the North."

He tossed the sack over the gunwale and was dragged into the water. Fafnir and I watched as his body sank out of sight. I never saw him again. We pulled back from the edge and sat on the rowing benches in disbelief.

Fafnir was beside himself with grief. I did not know it then, but he knew he had made a navigational mistake. We should have sailed around the islands, not through them. Sad as we were, not long after Egill's leap into the deep, the wind picked up and the fog lifted. It had been Egill's curse, after all. We had lost two days and had not yet passed through the channel between Jarð and Geirr. When we could see across the water to the skyline, we took sight of driftwood and supplies floating in the water between us and the rest of the fleet.

"Where is Sea Fox?" Rune asked.

None of us could see it.

"Take us around," I commanded.

"Go back? Toward the rocks?" Fafnir replied.

"Do it!" I barked.

The crew set their oars to water, and we rowed back into the channel. I steered us clear of the rocks, though we grazed a few, and each one sent a wave of fear across the deck. Bloated bodies bobbed near the spot where the ship had wrecked. None had survived. Rune, Fafnir, and I examined the wreckage from afar and agreed it was Sea Fox.

Taken with grief, I handed Rune the steering paddle and sat on the deck holding my head. Fafnir guided us out of the channel to rejoin the fleet. My men were silent. They, too, had lost friends. We met Horic's ship in open water, and he called over to me.

"I am sorry for the loss of your ship," he said. He had seen the wreckage too. "Your man Váli captained it?"

"He did," I said.

Horic pressed his fist against his chest and bowed to show his respects. Life at sea is hard and perilous, and every Dane present that day felt the loss of Sea Fox.

We sailed on, all of us feeling battered and beaten. I wrestled with the thought of whether men lost at sea could hope to enter the hall of Valhalla. Fighting the ocean seemed a brave enough deed, but Fafnir and Rune insisted the gods had other plans for Sea Fox and her men.

The loss of Váli wounded me the most. Sleepless nights followed sleepless days, and the long voyage wore me down. I confided more than I should have in Rune, but he proved a good listener and a trustworthy confidant, and Fafnir had also given him his trust. To cheer us up, he told stories he had learned from his father, and the crew appreciated the distraction.

When we took sight of Herio, I breathed a heavy sigh of relief. It had been a year since I had left, and what a long year it had been. During our approach, we spotted a Frankish ship sailing away from the island toward Indre. The monks must have seen us from their lookout and fled as they had done the preceding summer. I ordered Fafnir to reef the sail to allow Horic to catch us—I needed to speak with him.

"There's a dock near the monastery, but the inlet that leads to it drains out at low tide," I said to Horic as his ship drifted beside mine. "If we enter, we will not be able to leave until the next tide."

"Do you expect a fight?" Horic asked.

"No, but it would be prudent not to trap our ships," I said.

Horic examined the island's shoreline and said, "If we leave our ships here, they will be exposed to the weather, or worse. At least if we take them in, other ships will not be able to sail in until the next tide, either."

I agreed with his reasoning. That the low tide could work to our advantage had not crossed my mind. We rowed up the narrow channel to the docks where we tied off the first few ships, and the others tied off along the sandbar that jutted out to the ocean. Two dozen ships required a great deal of careful maneuvering, and they took up a lot of space onshore.

Horic met with me at the base of the slight hill to the monastery. He examined the wooden palisade constructed around it and grumbled that I had not mentioned it. To my relief, it was as I had remembered it— the monastery and village appeared deserted, and the palisade gate remained cracked open. After enough men had joined us, we marched to the palisade gate and passed over the bridge and through the archway. Horic sent his men to search the monastery for anything of value but found nothing.

"We could use this," Horic said, looking around at the fortifications. "In case we are attacked. Why did they build it?"

"To repel Northmen," I explained.

"Why aren't they using it?" Horic scoffed.

"I've never seen it used, so I don't know," I said.

I led the king back out of the fortifications and to the salt marshes. We had arrived early in the season, and the monks had not yet begun their harvest. We found a few bags from last year in their hut, which I used to give Horic a chance to taste the salt. I presented him an open bag, and he swiped the surface with his fingers.

"It's salt," he said with his fingers pressed against his tongue.

"Better than the salt you buy from the Franks in Saxony?" I asked.

"I am not a salt connoisseur, Hasting. I can't tell the difference," he said.

Bjorn approached and also tasted it. "It's good," he said.

Horic looked around at the long, flat island and smiled. "It looks like Frisia," he said. "But warmer."

Bjorn concurred. "And a bit windier," he added.

Our men unloaded the ships to make camp. Horic ordered his things taken to the monastery's largest bedchamber, and he posted two warriors in the lookout tower to watch for approaching ships. The Franks did not worry him; he feared other Northmen. His men set up a camp within the fortifications, and Bjorn made his own camp in the village.

This summer, not a soul had remained in the town, not even the tavern keeper. He had, however, left his cellar full of wine. I said nothing, hoping to keep it for my crew. If Horic or Bjorn had found it, their men would have guzzled it all down in an instant.

By the time all the camps were made, the fires and torches lit up the monastery and village, and the island appeared to be a bustling town. The first night, the camp remained quiet. We all rested from our long voyage, happy to have found firm land on which to sleep. In the morning, Horic found me at my tent, which we had set on the outskirts of the village beside Bjorn's camp.

He clapped his hands as he approached and said, "Let's get started."

He wanted me to show his men how to work the marshes. I obliged him and spent the morning showing group after group of Danes how to operate the levies, how long to wait for the salt crystals to form, and how to rake it into piles. Horic's men did the rest and engineered tools and materials to transport the salt to their ships. They made sacks from the grasses on the beach and in the fields, and constructed wheelbarrows from the oak trees in the forest behind the monastery. Their industriousness impressed me. All that slowed them down was the time it took for the sun to dry the marshes and form the crystals.

Within the first two weeks, they had loaded two of their ships to the brim. When I saw they could handle themselves, I made preparations to leave. I met with Horic in the lookout tower to tell him. He sensed my presence as I approached and spoke first.

"You're leaving me," he said with a scowl, gazing across the sea toward the mainland.

"Yes," I stated.

"How long?" he asked.

"I cannot say," I replied. "If you have left before I return, I will rejoin you in Jutland when I can."

"We won't be leaving," Horic declared. "I want to leave a garrison here to hold the monastery. This is my island now, and I want to name you chieftain."

"You honor me," I said. "But the island only produces salt during the summer."

"So we will only hold it in summer," Horic suggested. He crossed his arms and leaned against the cold stone wall behind him. "And the summer after that, and the one after that, and we will sell salt the world over, and Danes and Northmen will sail here to load their ships. What an enterprise!"

Horic had silver in his eyes; he was underestimating the dangers of staying too long in Frankish territory. I thought to tell him of the fate of the other Northman base that had attempted to take root on the island, but I feared I might upset him.

Eventually, the Franks would learn of our presence and send a fleet and army to destroy us—and I had no doubt they would kill us. I expressed my concerns to him, but he brushed them off. He believed the civil war would keep them occupied on the mainland and leave us to our business on the sea.

"I hope you are right," I said.

Horic turned to me and put his hand on my shoulder. I saw a hint of sadness in his eyes when he said,

"Come back in one piece, and let's hold this island together."

I bowed and left the monastery with urgency in my step. Vannes was a two- or three-day sail away, and I could not wait to see Nominoë again. The news I carried with me would shake the foundations of his rule over Armorica, but at least he would know the truth. He would know the Franks had plotted against him during a truce, and that Renaud had sought to undermine the peace between the Celts and the Franks.

We got underway on a pleasant spring morning with clear skies and a favorable wind. We saw no other ships across the entire ocean. All that lay before us was open, placid water. After three days of uneventful sailing, we reached the Morbihan. Celtic fishermen watched us sail by with fear written on their faces.

Sail Horse galloped across the water, and as we passed through the islands in the bay, my mind flooded with memories of Armorica. Nominoë had rebuilt the docks in Vannes, and all the hulls of their burned ships had been salvaged. The Celts saw us approaching and mustered several dozen cavalrymen on the beach to meet us. Had we desired to attack the city, the horsemen would have made quick work of us. I stood at the prow of my ship and waved, hoping they would see me and lower their guard at least a little.

Fafnir worked with Rune and Sten to reef the sail, and the others set their oars to water to guide us to the water's edge. I urged Fafnir to make sure we did not run aground in case we needed to make a quick escape. If for whatever reason Nominoë did not recognize me, I wanted to ensure we could flee.

"Greetings!" I projected toward the beach in the Celtic language.

One of the horsemen guided his steed forward to the water's edge and said, "Greetings, Northman."

His voice was unmistakable. "Nominoë, my friend, it is good to see you," I said.

He removed his bronze helmet and rested it on his saddle. "Dear God, what have they done with you?" He laughed.

"I have much to tell you," I said. "May we come ashore?"

"I am sorry, Hasting, but even now, Frankish spies watch us," he explained. "I cannot be seen consorting with Northmen, so I must ask you to leave. But, do you remember the campsite where we first met?"

"I do," I replied.

"Make your camp there, away from the city, and I will find you tonight," he said.

We turned the ship around and took it out of the Morbihan and along the southern coast of Armorica. By nightfall, we reached the beach and had little light left to set up our tents and gather wood for a fire.

I felt as though I had returned home. The ocean breeze and the fresh, crisp air of the pastures and woods reminded me of how much I loved this land. I waited around the campfire late in the night for Nominoë to arrive, but he never did. At sunrise, I awoke to Fafnir kicking me in the side.

"Are you sure this is the right place?" he asked.

"It is," I replied. "He will come."

My crew felt uneasy about how exposed we were, so I allowed them to erect pikes around the camp. The labor, at least, kept them busy. I feared Nominoë might see it as a sign of distrust, but better to explain to him why we had erected fortifications than to let my crew feel vulnerable and question my leadership.

By the afternoon, the pikes faced outward toward the countryside, and my men lounged around the campfire drinking mead and eating salted fish. Later in the day, I heard the distant galloping of hooves echo across the land.

The sound put my whole crew on edge, and they took up their arms. Finally, I thought, Nominoë had arrived.

To my utter astonishment, a corps of cavalrymen stampeded over the rolling hill with their lances pointed forward. We had just enough time to gather our weapons and shields, and no time at all to form ranks. I had been caught with my britches down.

At the last moment, the cavalry charge slowed and turned away from the pikes. They had not expected us to build defenses around our camp. Their horses could not hope to jump the ditch and two rows of sharp points. I examined them as they passed and saw they were not Celts. Their iron maille, blue overcoats, and heavy shields betrayed their true identity: they were Franks.

The question on my mind was: why had they been allowed so far into Armorica? Several of my men shot arrows at our attackers, but none of them met their mark. The cavalry circled around again as if they might try to jump our defenses, but they instead rode off from where they had come.

"We need to leave," Fafnir exclaimed.

"I agree," I said. "Take the men back to the ship and make sail for Vannes."

"What?" Fafnir said, surprised.

"There's something terribly amiss here, and I need to know what has happened," I said.

Half the men stood with their shields from hip to neck along the defenses while the other half packed the tents and supplies. They loaded the ship in short order, and long before the cavalrymen returned. We fled down the path along the cliffs to the beach and set sail. As we drifted toward open ocean, I saw the Franks standing tall atop the cliffs, watching us flee in the pale evening light.

We sailed for Vannes and landed Sail Horse on the far side of An Arzh, the island nearest the city, making camp within a small wood away from the Celtic village on the other side. As darkness fell over the land, I prepared to leave my men behind and find my way to the city unseen.

"If I do not return by tomorrow at midday, sail back to Horic," I said to Fafnir. He scowled at my words. I knew he thought what I planned to do was foolish.

By the light from the stars and moon, I snuck across the island's farms toward the village's port. The houses' shutters were closed and their fires dim. With my cloak pulled around me, I scurried to the dock and untied one of their fishing boats. It was a small rowboat with a makeshift sail, and it smelt of fish guts and rotten crab.

I rowed into open water and hoisted the sail to catch what wind I could. The wind in the Morbihan was not strong, and it seemed for a long time that I was not moving. At long last, I reached the beach below Vannes.

The main gates would be shut, so I made my way to a door along the side of the wooden wall near the church, which I knew how to open without a key. Luckily for me, Conwoïon had not changed the lock.

Few guards patrolled the boardwalk, and most of the torches had been extinguished. I tiptoed to Nominoë's hall, careful to avoid meeting anyone along the way. In the upper window, I saw a flicker of candlelight, and I knew Nominoë had stayed awake late to read.

At the entrance stood two warriors, both leaning against the wooden frame of the door. I had no chance of getting past them, and I could not let them know of my presence. Nominoë had said Frankish spies lurked everywhere.

Without a sound, I slipped along the side of the building to the wine cellar and hoped whoever had entered it last had forgotten to lock it. But when I pulled on the latch, it clanked and would not release. I looked around for another way in and saw one of the windows on the second floor had been left open. Climbing proved impossible. Desperate, I resorted to the one solution I could think of. I tossed pebbles through the window into Nominoë's living chamber.

The first pebble I threw struck the thatched roof and clattered when it hit the ground below. It echoed across the courtyard and silenced the crickets. When the crickets resumed their chirping, I threw my second pebble. I heard it clang inside, followed by the grinding of a chair on the wooden floors. A head popped out the window.

"Who's there?" Nominoë whispered.

"Hasting," I whispered back.

As soon as I spoke, torchlight danced on the ground toward me. The guards had heard something. I slipped around the side of the building, and when I emerged on the other end, I saw the soldiers had left the front door unguarded. I tiptoed along the wall and slipped into the building unseen. At the top of the stairs, I saw Nominoë still looking out his window and speaking to his guards.

"Some children are up to mischief, I think," Nominoë said. He turned and found me standing across from him, and he stepped away from the window. "I had a feeling you would come."

"You have much to explain," I snarled.

He invited me to sit beside him at his table in front of the hearth. It reminded me of the years I had spent with him learning to read and write. What a difference a year makes in the life of a young man. I kept my cloak wrapped around me when I sat, and I did not lean back into my chair.

"You never came," I said.

"No," Nominoë said. "But the Franks did, I presume?"

I nodded.

"Damn it all! They have spies even among my soldiers."

"My warriors think you sent them," I said. They had suggested no such thing, but I wanted to press Nominoë to reveal his betrayal if there was one.

"Never," he declared. "We have lived dark, dark days since you left, Hasting. My peace with Louis has opened the door for Ricwin and his war-hound Renaud to encroach on my kingdom. They support the emperor's sons, and they have met me with nothing but aggression for supporting their father."

"Send them away, then," I suggested.

Nominoë scoffed at me. "To push them away would mean war, and I do not have the men or the money to fight."

"They do?" I asked.

"Even now, their silver lines the pockets of my own people and turns them into spies," he said. "I cannot utter a word without Ricwin knowing what I've said. I am a prisoner in my own land. That is why I could not meet you. But, somehow, they knew where to find you."

"I have more ill news," I uttered. "The Northmen who raided Vannes were paid by the Franks to do it."

Nominoë sat forward, put his elbows on the table, and ran his hands through his hair. "If what you say is true, it was an act of war." He thought for a moment in silence. "It makes sense," he continued. "They knew I had allied with Northmen against them. A raid on Vannes would nullify any future alliances. Well played, Ricwin."

"We haven't lost yet," I said. "Now that you know the Franks are responsible, you can revisit an alliance with the Northmen."

Nominoë gazed at me with sorrowful eyes. "Did you find Asa?" he asked.

I bowed my head and said, "The Franks have her."

"How?" he asked. He crossed his arms and leaned forward over his knees. "The Franks are not the only ones with spies," he continued. "I will make inquiries. But… if she is a prisoner, I do not know how we will get her back."

"Take Nantes," I said. "That is how."

"With only the one ship?" he asked.

I grinned. "I've brought a king with me," I said. "We have two dozen ships, and perhaps one thousand warriors."

Nominoë shrank at the news. "Twenty ships?" he lamented.

"We've established a stronghold on Herio," I explained.

"Bold," Nominoë muttered under his breath, "and unprecedented. Renaud d'Herbauges will march against you." He leaned back in his chair and crossed his arms. "I do not wish for the Northmen to attempt an attack on Nantes."

"Do you have a better idea for me to find Asa?" I asked him.

"Perhaps we do not need to fight," Nominoë suggested. "We could use this to our advantage. If Horic draws Renaud's army to Herio, it will leave Nantes without men to defend it. My army can march on Nantes to force a negotiation to lessen Frankish raids and release Asa."

"You would seek to occupy Nantes?" I asked.

"No, my friend. We could never hold it. Besides, sacking the city might give the emperor and his sons reason to rally against us. No, the threat of sacking it should suffice, and then we will have them by the balls. It could help take the pressure off Vannes."

"I saw a ship leaving the island when we arrived," I mentioned.

"Renaud already knows, then. And knowing him, his army has already set out for the island," Nominoë said. "He will want to defeat the Northmen before I find out he has moved his army so far away. Perhaps that is why they found you so quickly at your camp—to prevent me from learning about your fleet. Let us hope they report to Renaud that they sent you running."

"What will we do?" I asked.

"Return to Horic and tell him what I plan to do. I will send spies of my own to find out if Renaud has left his stronghold in the Pays de Retz. If he has, the Celts will march on Nantes."

He reached for two goblets and a carafe of wine and placed them in front of us. "Drink with me. Let us toast to this mad plan!" We drank together in silence, and when we finished, I stood and made my way to the door.

"I promise you, whatever negotiations come of our plan, Asa will be a part. I will see that she is returned to us," Nominoë said.

I nodded and slipped out into the night.

17

The Hammer and the Wedge

We took sight of Herio in the early afternoon of our third day at sea, and as we approached, I saw the shadowy dance of sails in the distance. Though I could not see them, I knew the Franks had launched their fleet toward the southern tip of the island. I hoped Horic had seen them from the monastery's lookout.

We arrived at port after the midday meal, when most of the Danes had returned to their tents to nap. Many of their ships had sacks of salt stacked to the gunwale; it appeared their production had increased since I left. I searched for Horic in the monastery with Fafnir and Rune, expecting to find him in the lookout, but he was nowhere to be seen. None of the men in their tents seemed interested in speaking with me, and my patience wore thin. I left the monastery for the village to look for Bjorn, whom I hoped had not gone to nap. I found him sitting by the well sharpening his ax.

"Where is the king?" I asked.

"He should be in the lookout," Bjorn said.

"He's not there," I said.

"I do not know where he is, then," Bjorn stated.

"The Franks are coming," I said.

Bjorn looked up at me with wide eyes and asked, "How many?"

"I do not know," I said. "But they will outnumber us, I am sure."

"Hasting!" Horic called out. He had spotted us from the far side of the village. He marched over with long, powerful steps. "Did you find what you were looking for?"

"Not quite," I said.

"Tell me everything," he insisted.

I explained what Nominoë and I had discussed; I told him about the brewing war between the Franks and the Celts, and the plot by the Franks to frame Northmen for the Franks' aggression. Horic furrowed his brow as I spoke, and he crossed his arms in thought. Bjorn stood up and joined him at his side.

"A fleet approaches from the south as we speak," I said. "We saw their sails."

"It is true," Fafnir added.

"I saw them too," Rune declared.

"How many?" Horic asked, concerned.

"We could not see them clearly enough," I said.

Horic gazed out across the flat marshlands. "Do we flee? Or do way stay and fight."

"We fight," Bjorn said. "My king, you said yourself you wish to hold the island."

"I am blind," Horic said. "I do not know their numbers."

"Send me to scout," I said. "I have done it before, and I know the island."

Horic nodded, put his hand on my shoulder, and said, "Bjorn and I will prepare this ground for battle."

I took Fafnir and Rune back to the ship and asked them to prepare my men for a fight. For the scouting mission, I named Gørm and Torsten to join me.

We set out as soon as we had eaten enough to fill our bellies, and carried with us the weapons we would need to defend ourselves, and nothing that could slow us down. I led us along the Roman road toward the south and kept a quick pace through the marshlands to the southern sandbar. Most of the island interior was barren with sandy soil, and with no trees to take cover, I feared the Franks might see us from far away. Rather than walk toward the Franks, I led my men to the edge of the woods nestled behind the western dunes. It was where Váli and I had met Oddlaug, and I wondered if she had survived the winter.

We did not penetrate far into the woods, but far enough to hide from enemy scouts. Dusk approached, and we settled in to wait for dark. The Franks' campfires would tell us where they were. When darkness covered the land, I saw the campfires and torches we sought, but they were to the north of us. The Frankish army had marched far faster than I had expected. I sent Gørm to the east and Torsten to the west, while I approached the center, and I told each man to find his own way back to the monastery to report his counts. I tiptoed across the marshes near their camp, careful to keep my head low. When I had snuck in close enough to see the whites of their eyes reflect the firelight, I heard a loud snap and felt a powerful bite cling to my ankle. The pain made me howl into the night sky.

"Caught one!" I heard a man say in the Frankish language.

I grasped the iron jowls around my ankle and pulled hard to break free. I was a wolf caught in a hunter's trap. Frankish soldiers surrounded me with spears and torches. They took my sword, dragged me by the arms closer to the campfires, and threw me to the ground. Two of them worked the trap and took it off my leg, and though I should have felt some relief, the flow of blood sent me into a panic; I thought I might bleed to death.

Five men kept their spears pointed at my chest as if I might bite them, while innumerable others gathered to gawk at me. By the fire, I was able to sit up and scoot away from them, and I tore off a piece of my tunic and wrapped it around my wound. To stop the bleeding, I took off my belt and fastened it around my leg.

"Move!" I heard a voice shout. The men spread apart, and through them, a man dressed in maille and a thick, blue overcoat approached me. "A scout... they know we are here."

He disappeared back into the sea of soldiers. With all of their troops pushing and shoving each other to get a look at me, I took comfort in the fact that Gørm and Torsten would have an easy time counting them. When the man in the overcoat returned, he brought with him the leader of the army: Renaud.

"Good idea... those traps," he said to the man in the overcoat. "Take him to my interpreter."

Many hands picked me up and dragged me through their camp. Hundreds of tents lined a central pathway, and as we passed them, more and more men emerged to catch a glimpse of me. Word about my capture spread, and the soldiers did not hide their curiosity. Most of them had never seen a Dane before, but they had heard stories.

The men who carried me took me into a large tent by a central campfire and sat me on a small wooden stool. Renaud entered with them, took off his gloves, and placed them on a table set along the backside of the tent. He reached into a large wooden chest and withdrew several knives and other instruments of torture, as well as a long wooden stick.

"Bring me the interpreter!" Renaud shouted.

He held up the stick, swatted it down with a snapping motion, and whipped my leg under the belt. I howled in pain and fell off the stool. Renaud's men lifted me back up. I huffed and puffed and reached down to hold my leg. Renaud whipped at it again and hit my fingers, and when I pulled my hands back, he lashed at it again. The second time I almost fainted.

"He won't last long, this one," Renaud muttered. "Where is the interpreter? Bring her to me!"

The interpreter walked into the tent with a thick hood and a shadowed face. My wound ached, and I could not hold still. The room spun around me, and my vision narrowed to a thin tunnel. I fixed my eyes on Renaud, the focus of all my rage and hate, and gathered my strength to face him.

"Ask him how many men they have," Renaud said.

"Ask him yourself," the interpreter replied.

I knew her voice. "Asa?" I asked, astonished.

She pulled back her hood to reveal herself. My focus shifted, and I saw she was with child. "He speaks your language," she said. "Ask him yourself." Her tone was cold and calloused.

"Asa, I—" I began, but Renaud swatted my wound again.

"Who is he?" he asked her.

"He was a friend to Nominoë when I last saw him," she said.

Renaud scowled. "I thought we had driven a wedge between the Celts and the Northmen."

"I believe you have," she said. "He is here with the Danes, and not with the Celts."

I had many questions, but I did not speak for fear of having my wound whipped. Renaud examined me and said, "I know you. You were the Danish boy we met at Redon."

I nodded.

"By God, did they send you away after the raid?"

I nodded again.

Renaud smiled. "I could not have hoped for a better outcome."

Renaud raised his whip, but Asa reached out and grasped his wrist. She reached her hand around his soft shaven face and caressed it. My heart sank. The way she looked at him and touched him told me something I did not think possible: she was his. Renaud lowered the stick and took a deep breath.

"Do you need to torture him?" she asked.

"Yes," he said. "Yes, I do."

"How many men do you have, Hasting?" Asa asked me.

I felt compelled to tell her: "One thousand."

She stroked Renaud's face again and said, "There, now you know. Come to bed. It is late, and you have a battle to fight in the morning."

Renaud nodded with a crazed look in his eye. He handed the stick to the soldiers behind me and left with Asa, arm in arm. My stomach churned from the pain of the wound. Thoughts of Asa and how she had shown such affection for Renaud clouded my mind. She was not a prisoner at all, but an accomplice to the Franks.

I felt betrayed. At first, my heart filled with sadness, but the more I thought about it, the more my grief turned to rage. All this time I had sought to find her, to rescue her, and all the while she had cozied up to the man who had set everything into motion. Renaud's men clamped me in irons and tied me to the massive table in the tent. I felt my blood leaving my body, and I was helpless to stop it. In the night, when the campfires died out, and all the torches were extinguished, the tent fell into utter blackness. It reminded me of the blackness of the deep sea when I had faced the wolf.

When all the chatter between the Franks had ceased, I heard rustling at the entrance to the tent. The door flaps fluttered, and I saw a shadow approach me, illuminated by the moonlight shining through the opening. Delicate hands took mine and worked on the irons to release them. When my hands were free of their restraints, I grabbed the person by the neck and squeezed her throat.

"Hasting, stop!" Asa cried, her voice a mere whisper.

"You betrayed me," I growled.

"No, please, let me explain," she begged.

I thought about killing her. I almost did, but I released her before she lost consciousness. She held her neck and gasped for air.

"You have changed," she whispered.

"It has been a hard year," I said.

"A hard year... for you?" she spat.

"It seems as though it turned out well for you. You and Renaud—" I said.

"Do you think I want to be with him?" she snarled. "You pigheaded... dimwitted... fool!" Though I could not see them, I knew tears streamed down her face. "He put this damned child in my belly against my will. He beats me, whips me, burns me, forces me to do things to him you cannot imagine. I am his slave."

What she said struck deep at my heart. I could not imagine the horrors she had lived, and I felt overwhelmed with guilt for what I had said and done. "I am sorry," I said.

Asa took a heavy breath and said, "Now go. Leave."

"Come with me," I said.

"I can't."

"Why? What's keeping you here?" I asked.

"Hasting, you and I... we cannot be together," she said.

"But we can!" I said.

"It was not meant to be," she said with a quiver in her voice. "Renaud is a rich man, and his mother has taken a liking to me. She has promised me they will care for my child."

"Do you think Renaud wants you to have his bastard?" I asked. "Would he bring you to a battle if he did?"

"He needed an interpreter," she snapped.

"I doubt he would have done the same with his pregnant wife," I said.

"I am his wife!" she roared through a whisper. "We are bound by God now, and there's nothing to be done to change it," she said.

I had almost forgotten she was a Christian and believed in the bounds of marriage. Brokenhearted, I leaned forward and knelt before her. My hands trembled, and she took me in her arms. "I sailed to the edge of Midgard to find you," I said.

"I know," she whispered in my ear.

I knew then that I would not change her mind. We stayed together a moment longer in a tender embrace, and when it ended, she pulled her hood over her head and left the tent. My wound still ached, and when I attempted to stand, I could not put much weight on it. I had no idea how to escape the camp. It seemed an impossible task. How to find my father's sword had seemed just as unattainable, but the idea that I had prevailed against impossible odds before gave me hope.

To help myself stand, I leaned against the table and, to my surprise, my hand brushed up against something. It was my sword. Asa must have placed it on the table on her way out. Without a moment to lose, I took the sword and hobbled out of the tent and into the marshes. No one saw me escape.

I started in agony toward the monastery but knew I would bleed out before reaching it. Instead, I turned to the west toward the remnants of the Northman base.

After a long, painful journey, I entered the woods and called out, "Oddlaug!" I listened for a response but heard none. "Oddlaug, I need your help!" I shouted.

As I called for her, I ventured deeper into the woods one painful step at a time. I felt myself slipping out of consciousness. When I reached the clearing where I had first met Oddlaug, I slumped against the stone well and faded into blackness.

I awoke to the comforting warmth of a fire and a thick wool blanket over me. It was day, but low clouds and a heavy drizzle had covered the land and sea. Whoever had taken me in had raised a tarp overhead to keep out the rain. Ocean waves rumbled in the distance beyond the dune, and the forest canopy swayed in the occasional gust of wind.

When I sat up, I found my leg wrapped in cloth with a wooden stint on each side. Blood had soaked through the fabric, but at least the bleeding had stopped. I felt weak and hungry.

There was no one around. The trees hissed, creaked, and crackled as another gust of wind passed through them. I sat with my back against the well wall and stared a long while into the fire pit someone had dug into the ground. The tarp stretched over me enough to keep out the drizzle and rain but not hold in the smoke.

"Oddlaug?" I called out.

My call was met with silence. I needed to return to my crew to lead them in battle, though I did not know how I would reach them. Placing my hands on the wall, I attempted to stand. The instant I put pressure on my injured leg, it crumpled. My heart sank. I was a mauled wolf who could no longer chase prey.

"You won't make it far like that," a voice said from behind me.

I turned to find Asa. "What are you doing here?" I asked her.

"I'm saving your life," she said. "You would have bled to death if I had not sewed you up."

"You... you came back for me?" I asked.

She walked to the fire and lowered herself to the ground using the well's wall for support. Her belly had grown so large that it took great effort to sit so low. She took a deep breath before she continued.

"God knows, I love you, Hasting. When I saw how blood-soaked my gown was after our embrace, I knew you would not make it to your camp."

"You followed me here in the dark? How?"

She nodded and smiled. "You made a lot of noise. And I know these marshes and woods better than any."

I remembered what Oddlaug had said. "Your family lived here," I uttered. "What happened to them?"

Asa stared up at the canopy, her eyes welling with tears. "They were killed by a Northman named Thorgísl."

"Thor?" I blurted out with surprise.

"He and my father were bitter rivals," she explained.

"The battle," I blurted out.

"Relax," Asa said. "Renaud will not march today. He does not like to fight in the rain. Be happy I rescued you, and rest."

I laughed and said, "I'm supposed to be rescuing you."

Asa scowled and said, "Hasting, I never needed rescuing."

"But you were taken, and—"

"I was taken from here too, and sold into slavery, and I escaped. I can handle myself," she said.

"Handle yourself? But Renaud, and the child," I said.

She slapped me across the face and said, "I did the best I could in a difficult situation. That I am married to him is a triumph. He should have discarded me in a cesspit, but I charmed my way into his heart, and his mother's, and I will be a noblewoman with a noble son. I will never go hungry, and neither will my child."

I held my cheek and remained silent. She had a way with words, and I felt guilty for what I had said.

"I thought we belonged together," I said. "Even Oddlaug said—"

"What did you...?" she interrupted me. "Did you say Oddlaug?"

"Yes, I met her here on my first visit to the island. She gave me your father's wealth to help me find you," I explained.

Asa had a haunted look about her. "You met her?"

"Yes."

"It is not possible," she said. "She was slain alongside my father."

I felt my throat leap up with a gulp. Váli had suggested we had seen Odin. Had I met the king of Asgard disguised as an old völva in the woods? I leaned forward to brace my leg; I could feel my heart beating in the wound. Asa crossed her arms over her cloak and stared into the fire. Even she, a Christian, seemed unsettled.

"Let us say you did see her," she said after a long pause. "What she did, she did to help you, not me."

"What will you do now?" I asked.

"My place is with Renaud," she said. "There are worse ways to live than as the wife of a powerful lord. He will be count of Nantes one day."

She laughed, and it made me smile. For the first time, we laughed together. It was a tense moment, but a relief from the seriousness of our situation. I understood what she asked of me. Our conversation had given me cause to think about my place in the world, my desires, and what I planned to do next. In no way did I stop loving her, but what she said rang true. We could not be together.

"So, you will return to him," I said. "Will he not be suspicious of where you have been?"

"It is not the first time I have gone riding on my own in the morning," she said. "He will scold me, but I will find a way to turn it around on him."

Asa stayed with me a while longer, but she soon left for her horse. I stood as best I could, and we embraced one last time. She drifted away until her silhouette became obscured by the trees and drizzle, and then she vanished into the woods.

I stared at the tumultuous sky and wondered what the gods had planned next for me. Asa had served as my purpose, and now that purpose was gone. I had no land, no title, and no desire for such things—I refused to be bound by them.

The wolf Fenrir entered my mind, with his blood-soaked fangs and fiery red eyes, and I thought about his escape from Asgard. The gods feared his power, and they sought to tame him and bind him in chains. If he had marked me, perhaps he had seen in me the same potential. Kings and lords would seek to restrain me, whether in chains, by land, or by marriage, to limit my power. I would refuse them, to stay forever free to grow in strength, prowess, and reputation, and to roam the realm of men as a wolf on the hunt. I thought these things and more, but the gods seldom allow us to make our own decisions.

I hobbled into the woods and snapped a tree limb to fashion a walking stick. My wound ached with each step, but with the help of the stick I managed to walk. In the distance, I saw the Frankish camp unmoved. Asa had spoken true. I charged into the wind and rain with relentlessness, and before too long I reached Horic's camp.

Upon my arrival, several warriors ran out to help carry me. They led me through rows of pikes meant to prevent a cavalry charge into the village. Most of the warriors remained inside the houses or in their tents to stay dry. Streams of water trickled down the slope to the monastery and toward the inlet, forming pools of mud near the docks. When we entered the monastery, I saw that the Danes had turned it into a mead hall. The warriors who carried me sat me at one of the tables and brought me a silver chalice full of wine.

"We found this treasure buried in the crypt," Horic said, pointing at the wine. He grinned. "We thought you were dead. I am overjoyed to see you are not."

"I have been told I am lucky," I said.

"Your men Gørm and Torsten made it back," he said. "They counted two thousand soldiers."

I took a drink from the chalice, closed my eyes, and smiled. "Good wine," I said.

Horic's brow furrowed. "Hasting, I need your insights here. I have not fought the Franks so far from Jutland," he said with urgency in his voice.

I put my goblet on the table and said, "They may outnumber us, but we have the monastery as well as high ground."

"Are you proposing we dig in?" Horic asked. "Out of the question. We would be trapped, surrounded, and they could burn our ships."

"If you meet them on the field, their cavalry will cut you down like a sickle through wheat," I said.

As we spoke, a warrior entered the monastery and called for Horic. "Horsemen along the road. They want to speak with you." Horic stood. "They asked for Hasting too," he said.

I saw concern in Horic's eyes. Two warriors helped me up and walked with me so I could follow their king. We stepped down to the edge of the village and found Bjorn with several dozen of his warriors standing behind the pikes. They faced a dozen Frankish cavalrymen. Renaud led them. At his back, I recognized another figure. He wore long white robes and had a silver ring on each finger. It was the bishop, Rainier. I knew in that moment he had aided the Franks in their betrayal of Nominoë. He had known the Northmen would strike Vannes, and he had saved himself before they did.

"There he is," Renaud exclaimed.

"There he is, who?" Horic replied in the Frankish language, to my relief. *Of course he did*, I thought; he had fought with them often along Jutland's southern border.

"Hasting," Renaud said. "Last night he was my prisoner. This morning he was gone... with my wife."

Horic belched a hearty laugh. "Perhaps if you satisfied her better, she would not run off with my men!"

One of Horic's warriors translated what their king had said, and all of them laughed. Renaud's horse neighed and sidestepped, and he struggled to control it. He pulled hard on the harness and turned in a circle, and when he turned back to us, he revealed his teeth through a menacing grimace. As we laughed, he reached into a sack tied to his saddle and drew from it a severed head. It had long hair and blood spattered across the nose and mouth. Our laughs ceased in an instant.

"Three of my men witnessed her release Hasting," he said.

At first, my mind struggled to comprehend what I saw. My heart raced, my face lost its color, and I felt as if I could not breathe. Horic looked at me and said, "Did you know her?"

"Asa," I whispered.

"Asa?" Horic said aghast.

My hand gripped Horic's jerkin, and I stepped forward to say, "She was your wife! She carried your child! How could you?"

Renaud called out to me, "Hasting, whatever she told you was wrong."

"Disloyalty, lying, and adultery. These were her sins," Rainier added. "Renaud had every right to end her life. And you were the cause. The burden of guilt rests squarely on your shoulders, Northman."

Renaud led his horse forward a few steps and said, "King Horic, this is your last chance to flee. Tomorrow the rain will clear, and my army will destroy you."

Horic opened his mouth to speak, but Renaud kicked his horse, and he and his cavalrymen galloped away. They had left Asa's head in the mud. As they rode off, I cried to the sky and to the gods. Tears welled in my eyes, and I cursed into the distance, swinging my fists and kicking my feet.

Horic's men fought me back and held me down, and Horic did what he could to comfort me. Bjorn, who had grown to admire me, looked at me with sorrowful eyes. They carried me back to the monastery, everyone shaken by my guttural moans. I howled the entire night, pacing the monastery corridors and cursing the Franks for their treachery and malice. Asa's death changed everything. The Franks had to be punished. I had to make Renaud pay for what he had done.

The following morning, Horic sat beside me at the table where the men ate their first meal of the day. He seemed unnerved by my sudden calmness.

"Are you all right?" he asked.

I nodded.

"I know you may not think this will help, but I understand your pain. My wife was killed by the Franks. If you need to talk—"

"Thank you," I said.

"Look, we need your help," Horic said. "The Franks outnumber us, and we are short on ideas on how to counter them."

I leaned over the table and said, "I know what to do."

18

The Avenger

Renaud's army marched through the marshes in well-defended columns of soldiers with heavy iron shields and lances. Their cavalry followed close behind, their arms and armor glimmering in the afternoon sun. As he had said he would do, Renaud marched as soon as the rains had passed. Horic and I tracked their approach from the monastery's lookout, and we kept an eye on our fleet that had left the inlet and waited for the signal to sail from the beaches, nestled within the rocks on the northern coast of the island. Horic had all of his belongings taken to his ship, and when he saw the Franks approach, he prepared to leave.

"Are you sure it will work?" Horic asked me as he stood above the stairwell.

"I will not fail," I said.

Horic vanished into the cold dark of the monastery's stone corridors. I gestured to my men who stood on the battlements, prepared for a fight. They, in turn, signaled to the men in the courtyard below. For a while longer, I tracked the Franks' movements and committed their positions to memory. They prepared for a direct attack from the south, and I saw no sign they would try to surround us.

When they pushed through the pikes along the edge of the village, I hobbled down the stairs to the ground floor and joined my men. My leg had not healed, but

Fafnir had fashioned a wooden stint that allowed me to walk. Bjorn had volunteered himself and the men under his command to stay with me, and he met me with a firm handshake.

"Horic has left?" he asked.

"He has," I said. "Your man has the message ready?"

Bjorn looked to one of his men on the battlements and waved to him. His man drew an arrow with a parchment rolled around its shaft and shot it toward the Franks. We waited a moment until his man signaled what we had hoped to see. "They took it," Bjorn said. He put his hand on my shoulder and said, "Good luck."

I climbed up to the battlements while he ordered his men into formations to repel the attack. We had left the gate open, hoping the Franks would attempt to storm the monastery without trying to knock holes elsewhere in the palisade. Bjorn would meet them there and use the gate as a choke point.

The Franks brought up large wooden shields on wheels that took four men to maneuver. Their crossbowmen hid behind them, out of reach of our arrows. Before the battle began, Renaud rode forward on his horse, the blue banners of his house swaying behind him in the wind, and he held out a piece of parchment for us to see.

"You can write," he said. "Impressive... for a Dane."

Rune, who stood beside me on the battlements, asked, "What did it say?"

"I will avenge her," I said.

The Franks took aim with their crossbows and fired. Bolts whizzed past our heads and struck the palisade with booming knocks. As they reloaded, we replied with arrows of our own. Few of ours met their mark, but some found their way into enemy flesh. Columns of men with their shields raised over their heads snaked up the hill with ladders in tow and raised them against the wooden wall. We repelled a few of the ladders the instant they fell against the ramparts, but once men scaled them, they became too heavy to push. We fired arrows and threw rocks, but they climbed their way to the top, undeterred.

Meanwhile, two columns of soldiers charged the gate. When they entered the courtyard, they found themselves surrounded by shields locked edge to edge. As more soldiers poured in, they packed together and pressed against the shield wall.

I had never fought in a Danish army, and I marveled at the tactics they used. Early in the battle, the Franks were a school of sardines trapped in Bjorn's net. The slaughter did not last long. My men were overrun on the battlements more quickly than I had hoped. I limped from place to place, using my sword to block blows and dodge stabs.

One Frankish soldier nearly cleaved my head from my shoulders when he leaped over the palisade and swung at me with a broadsword. I met his blade with mine, and though I could not parry, I used his swing to guide him into a gap between the beams of the palisade. With both of our swords stuck, I drew a knife from my belt and ran it into his chest. As the color drained from his face, four more soldiers leaped over the ramparts to face me.

"Bjorn!" I cried out. "We are abandoning the wall!"

Bjorn nodded. Several of my crew were slain as we withdrew. In the fray of battle, I took notice of their bodies but did not take in who they were. Once the last man in the retreat hit the ground, we cut down the ladders to the platform. The Franks were trapped, lest they wanted to break their legs jumping down. We ran around the monastery to the far side of the palisade to a hole we had made to secure our retreat.

Bjorn and his men held their shield wall and walked backward at a steady pace, thrusting spears and swinging axes above their shields, and felling those who dared to approach them. His men did this on both sides of the monastery and prevented the Franks from advancing toward those of us who fled. When they arrived at the escape hole, they broke formation. Bjorn and his best warriors fought savagely as the rest of the men slithered away into the forest.

As I watched Bjorn fight, I marveled at his skill, his ruthlessness, and his utter brutality. He had dropped his shield and taken a second ax from a fallen warrior, and he wielded them with lethal precision. Frankish soldiers charged, surround him, and yet they could not come close to touching him. His axes swung around, swift and powerful, and as the last man passed through the escape hole, he stepped back, gave his opponents a bow, and slipped through the opening. My men pushed a cart filled with branches, twigs, and oil in front of the hole and set it ablaze. It stopped the Franks in their tracks.

We darted through the oak forest, careful not to fall between the giant slabs of stone overlooking the ocean.

"Hopefully that was not too easy," I said as we watched the ships glide away from shore. I hoped Renaud had not caught on to our ruse.

"I think it was," Bjorn said. "But only for us."

Bjorn and his men boarded their ships and set sail with haste to join Horic, while I stayed behind with my men. We hid among the rocks and trees to watch them depart.

No sooner had Bjorn's ship drifted off beyond our view than Rune pointed toward the south and cried out, "There!"

Within our line of sight, we saw the Frankish fleet had made a full turn and was trying to blockade the inlet to keep Horic's fleet from escaping. They had seen Bjorn's ship and sailed to chase him, but they could not hope to catch the Danes. The enemy fleet sailed close to shore, so my men and I slipped deeper into the forest.

We camped in the woods for two days before I sent scouts back to the monastery. If our ruse had worked, the Franks would have left to return to the mainland, believing they had defeated us. Nominoë, as far as I knew, was marching on Nantes, so Renaud and his army would have other places to be.

The first reports did not inspire confidence. My men reported that the entire Frankish army still camped below the monastery grounds. More concerning, ships from the mainland seemed to be delivering more troops and supplies. Renaud, I believed, had worked out our plan. Somehow he knew the moment he left, we would return to retake the island.

If Renaud had kept his army on the island, it could mean that Nominoë had not mustered his own against Nantes. Our plan, it seemed, had failed.

On the fifth day, as we prepared my ship to sail to find Horic, a massive fleet sailed into the waters off the northern shore of the island. At first, I panicked. I thought Horic had returned too soon. But Rune squinted at the ships' sails and said, "They are not Danes."

"Who are they?" I asked.

"Northmen," he replied.

"I count thirty ships," Fafnir said. "But the trees make it difficult to see."

"Thirty ships?" I said with a gasp.

As we watched, one of the ships broke from the group and steered toward a beach among the rocks. I remembered Halldóra had done the same when I first met her.

"It's Hakon," I said.

Fafnir gave me a quizzical look. "Hakon of Lade?" he asked.

"Yes."

"We should help them," Rune said.

"No," I said. "The gods have delivered us a gift. Renaud does not know the difference between Northmen and Danes. He will think it is our fleet. When he pushes them back, they will leave."

My men understood my shrewdness, but they did not like it. Most of them were Northmen and thought they should help their kin. Nevertheless, we remained hidden in the forest, watching as the ships sailed by and entered the inlet. Halldóra's ship landed in the same place as before, and she climbed the cliffs to the backside of the monastery.

In the distance, we heard the cries of dying men. When the sounds of battle ceased, I sent Gørm and Torsten to investigate. They returned far too quickly for my liking, and both said, "The Northmen won."

Astonished, I led my men out of the forest to the monastery. We entered through the hole in the back of the palisade and inched toward the courtyard. Corpses littered the ground. Blood flowed down the hill as the rain had done the day before the battle.

As I surveyed the grounds, Halldóra appeared in the castrum's gateway and said, "Shipwrecked again?"

Overcome with emotion, I reached out to embrace her, and she allowed it.

"Not exactly," I said.

Behind her, down the hill, the Northmen stabbed at the slain Franks to ensure none had faked their death. Few of the bodies I saw were Northmen.

"There were two thousand men here," I said.

Halldóra laughed. "Where did you come up with that number?"

"That is how many took the monastery from us," I said.

"We fought no more than one hundred," Halldóra said.

I put my hands on my hips and grinned. "He faked it," I said. "He sniffed us out and played our own trick on us."

"Who?" Halldóra asked.

"Renaud," I said.

I explained how Horic had wanted to hold the island and what we had begun to do with it. Our plan, to fake a retreat to mislead the Franks into returning to the mainland, intrigued her. When I told her my scouts had seen Renaud's army at full strength, we all laughed together. Renaud was far more cunning than I had thought. He had indeed left for the mainland, but he had stationed enough of a garrison to trick us into thinking he hadn't.

"That explains all the empty tents," Halldóra said.

While we spoke, I took a moment to look across the battlefield toward the marshes and saw, a stone's throw beyond the downed pikes, a round object lying in the mud. Rune saw where my gaze had landed. I wandered off mid-conversation toward it, and Fafnir explained to Halldóra what had happened to Asa. She clenched her chest and cried. The closer I drew to the object, the more certain I was that it was Asa's head. I knelt, heartbroken and trembling, and touched her hair. Her face was severely beaten; I could not have even recognized her.

"Her head will need to be rejoined with her body if she hopes to reach the afterlife," Rune said. He had followed me down the hill, and I had not heard him approach.

I looked to the village where the Franks had left a dozen horses near the tavern. "Can you ride?" I asked him.

Rune nodded, and we took two horses and rode out to the site of the Frankish camp. I could feel the gaze of my and Halldóra's men as we galloped into the marshlands. I did not care what they thought. I had to find Asa's body. The Franks had left behind a mess of broken tents, garbage, and feces, and it smelled foul—worse than Nantes on a hot summer day, and worse than any cesspit I had ever encountered.

We scoured the grounds looking for a headless body. On the far side of the camp, there was a large tent with decorated trim that was slumped over a pile of garbage. I dismounted and looked beneath. Rune saw I had spotted something and so joined me to toss the tent aside. Lying among the detritus, we found a woman's body wrapped in a cloak, her neck a fleshy mess of purple and red. Flies swarmed around her.

"Is that her?" Rune asked.

"I think so." I pulled back the cloak to reveal a flat stomach. "But she was with child."

Renaud was more insidious than I had thought. Had he torn the infant from her belly? The thought of it sent a chill down my spine. We carried her body and lifted her onto my horse. Neither of us said a word.

At the monastery, Halldóra and her crew met us and showed us to a pyre they had made for Asa during our absence. Tears streamed down my face. We joined the head and the body on the pyre and set it ablaze. Something did not feel right when the smoke and flames took hold. I doubted myself in the moments before the body burned.

Halldóra tried to hold me back when I leaped toward the fire and grabbed at the body's right arm. I pulled back the sleeve and looked for the birthmark that would confirm her identity. It was unmistakable.

Smoke enveloped me and, for a moment I am sure, everyone thought I would die in the fire. But Fafnir and Rune pulled me from the smoke, and I stepped back and rejoined Halldóra and the others. The wind-fueled fire carried the body's ashes upward and on to the next world. Jarl Hakon appeared at Halldóra's side to watch as the smoke reached for the sky. He shook my hand and patted my shoulder to try to comfort me.

"I will grieve for you," Hakon said, staring into the flames. "Ours is a hard way of life."

"You have my thanks," I said.

Hakon put his meaty paw on my shoulder and asked, "What will you do now?"

"Horic will be here the day after next," I said. "After everything, I would hate for there to be a fight."

"Why do you assume we will fight?" Hakon asked.

"In my experience, the Northmen and the Danes do not see eye to eye," I replied.

Halldóra chuckled and slapped me on the shoulder. "We will see."

The couple returned to their ships and left me to watch the pyre smolder. Sten worked up the courage to approach me, his steps slow and deliberate. He stood at my side in silence and we watched the fire burn. When I glanced up, he was gazing into the distance with a single tear in his eye. He held up his hands and looked into them.

"I do not know if this will help, but I wanted to tell you that I feel what you feel," he said. His single tear turned to a sob. "The Irish killed my mother and sister last year. I know—"

I reached around his thick chest and back to bring him in for an embrace. It lasted a mere moment before his sobbing stopped. My hand lingered on his shoulder. Behind him, the rest of my crew had gathered around, and Fafnir spoke for them. "Whatever you need," he said.

"Thank you," I said. "You have all served me well. I promised you wealth, and I will see to it that you all have it."

"What about the girl? Will you not avenge her?" Gørm asked.

"I will," I said.

My men looked at each other, wide-eyed and murmuring. Fafnir stepped forward and said, "We are with you. Not for wealth, but for honor."

Rune was last to speak with me. I could see the grief written on his face. He did not need to say anything. We both knew what the other felt. A long while passed, and the two of us remained to watch the burning pyre. When the others had gone, Rune said, "May the gods welcome her with open arms in Valhalla."

When the pyre had died out and all that remained of Asa were her ashes, I sent my men to bring around my ship while I helped the men of Lade decide on a place to make camp. Hakon had wanted to use the monastery as a base, but on my advice he instead erected a large tent in a field to the west of the village. I thought about Horic's return with apprehension. How would he greet Hakon and Halldóra? How would they receive him? It felt as though we had set a course for disaster, and no one seemed the wiser to it.

Hakon's fleet had brought mead, to the rejoicing of my men, and they shared it liberally. Few wild animals inhabited the island, and when Hakon's men set out to hunt, they returned with nothing. To fill their stomachs, they sent the smaller ships out with nets to fish, and they caught large sea bass I had not known swam near the coast.

On the day he said he would return, Horic and his fleet appeared. They rowed up the inlet, and I went to meet them. I thought if I met Horic and explained what had happened, his approach to Hakon might prove less hostile. When his ship arrived at the docks, his men leaped over the gunwale and tied it off.

"Hasting, my boy, what in Hel's name happened here?" Horic shouted.

"Some friends of mine arrived," I said.

Horic looked around at the fleet of ships and crossed his arms. "Friends of yours?"

"Hakon of Lade, and his wife Halldóra," I said. "They saved us. Renaud was one step ahead of us, and had they not arrived, we would have lost the island."

"This Jarl Hakon, is he friend or foe?" Horic asked.

"Whichever you choose," I said. "I've told them what we plan to do with the island, and they have no interest in challenging you for it."

"What do they want, then? Why are they here?" he pressed.

"Come, we can discuss it with them," I said.

Horic and his best warriors, including Bjorn, followed me from the dock to the Northman camp. There we met with some of Hakon's warriors who guarded the entrance. They had erected pikes and dug trenches in case they needed to defend themselves. Hakon and Halldóra walked hand in hand to meet us.

"Jarl Hakon," I said, "this is King Horic of Jutland." Hakon gave Horic a slight bow.

"You are far from home," Horic said.

"Indeed, we are." Hakon smiled. "We are honored to meet you, King Horic; your reputation precedes you."

The two leaders faced each other with their chests and chins held high, each attempting to appear taller than the other. Seeing the growing contest, I stepped between them and said, "Now that we have made introductions, we should discuss relations between the two of you."

"This is my island," Horic said. "We have worked hard all spring to farm salt and sail it home."

Hakon reached out to shake Horic's hand. "The island is yours." Horic looked at me with a surprised grin. With their hands clasped around each other's wrists, Hakon continued, "We've come for wealth, and we do not intend to leave empty-handed."

Horic looked around at the island's vast salt marshes and barren, sandy soil, and said, "We will need supplies. Food, drink, and slaves to work the fields."

"It sounds like you are asking us to raid," Hakon said. He looked at me with a piercing gaze and smiled. "That is what we came here to do."

"We would pay you in salt, of course," Horic said.

Halldóra stepped forward and spoke to Horic. "We'll take it. Jarl Thor of Dublin will pay handsomely for it."

"As will the Danes," Horic said. "And the Northmen of the Oslo Fjord."

"The question remains: where do we raid?" Hakon asked.

"I know where to find every monastery from here to Jutland," I declared. "Monks are hard workers and will make fine slaves for the marshes."

I could not believe the words that had come out of my mouth. What had happened to me? When did I become so ruthless and calloused to taking slaves? Indeed, it had been a long year.

The following day, Hakon's fleet fixed to leave, and I had my men prepare our ships to lead them. I already had in mind where we should raid, and if my memory served me, I knew Hakon's fleet would find plenty of supplies and slaves to bring back to the island.

We sailed several days in stormy weather and hugged the coastline until we reached the mouth of the Loire. We spotted Renaud's fleet north of the river mouth, and they hoisted their sails to intercept us. Frankish boats were wide and bulky with a tall gunwale and a raised platform at the stern. They moved at a crawl compared with our ships, and they had a hard time maneuvering in the shifting currents. I had my men reef our sail to allow Hakon to catch up to us so we could speak. His men threw grappling hooks over our gunwale to pull us in and keep our ships steady.

"The way is closed," Hakon said.

"It's Renaud's fleet," I explained. "They must have known we would try something."

"Is there somewhere else we can raid?" he asked.

"Yes," I said. "But with thirty ships, I think we can take them."

"You would have me attack?" Hakon asked.

I looked back at the Frankish fleet approaching us at full speed. "Yes," I replied.

"There's a good reason why Northmen have not fought a sea battle with the Franks. Their ships are sturdy and carry many men. I have been told they are nearly invincible," he insisted.

"Nonsense," I said. "The Celts have fought them successfully for years on the water."

Hakon gazed into the distance. He looked at his men and at his fleet, stood back from the gunwale, and shouted, "Prepare for battle!"

His men shouted together in support. He leaped to the aft of his ship and signaled to Halldóra to prepare for a fight. His men unhooked us, and they lowered their sail to pick up speed. All of his warriors, except the few who worked the sail, drew their arms and armor from below the rowing benches. With the wind at our back, our ships gained speed and cut through the waves which broke white upon our hulls. It was a beautiful sight to see the fleet bearing down on our enemy.

Like the seabirds over the cliffs near Hagar's village, we floated with the current of the wind. We charged like spears through the water, mastering the wind in all its fury and harnessing its power. We were untouchable predators bent on carrying out unspeakable terror on our prey.

The Franks had not expected us to sail at them. They turned their ships in an attempt to maneuver out of our way, but to no avail. Our first ships ran up against theirs, and our warriors leaped across the gunwales to strike and fight. More of our ships crashed against theirs, and they found themselves fighting off the warriors of several boats at a time.

When all the Franks aboard one ship were dead, Hakon's crew returned to theirs and sailed to the next. We picked them off one by one with ease. I had expected more of a fight, but then again, I had not before heard of any battles between the Franks and the Northmen at sea. The myth of the invincibility of the Frankish fleet melted away in the short time it took Hakon's warriors to devour them like birds of prey swallowing their catch.

I had hoped to find Renaud on one of the ships, but I had no such luck. The vessel we boarded had a light crew, all of them sailors except for a dozen or so armed soldiers. Franks proved hard to kill. Their thick shields and skill with a lance made them fearsome enemies, even when outnumbered and cornered.

My father's sword had dulled since I had taken it from Hagar, and I had not taken the time to sharpen it. When I parried one of the Franks and slashed at his arm, it did little. I had to stab him hard in the ribs instead, each stab breaking bone and spilling more blood. As I disemboweled my opponent, Fafnir fell backward and forced my arm further into him than I had intended. Gulls circled overhead, and as they do with fishermen who clean their fish at sea, they swooped down to take bites of the man's guts. One of them managed to snatch a Frankish soldier's intestine and unrolled it from his torso as it flew away.

I did not lose a single man in the attack, and by the time we had slain the last of their crew, Hakon's ships had already set sail toward the river.

Within sight of the battle was the monastery I had led Hakon to raid: Indre. It was far enough away for us to strike fast and leave before the Franks could muster a response, but close enough to strike fear into the region's capital, Nantes.

My ship landed first. We charged up the hill to the monastery to find that most of the monks had fled. Even the village below had fallen quiet. We entered the monastery through a low stone archway and stormed through the corridors. My men found more silver than they could carry. I led them to the chapel where I knew the monks kept their most valuable possessions. At the altar, I found one monk praying to a statue of Jesus on the cross, his hands clasped together. He felt my presence behind him and cowered with tears streaming down his face. I grasped him by the nape with my still-bloodied hand and looked in his eyes. He winced and tried his best to turn away.

"Don't kill me, please," he begged.

"I will not kill you," I said with my head tilted toward him. "What is your name?"

"B-b-bertric," he said.

"Bertric," I growled, "I need you to do something for me. Go to Nantes and tell Ricwin, Renaud, and the bishop Rainier that Hasting was here."

"Hasting?" the monk asked after a visible gulp.

"That is my name," I said.

"I could not have imagined a viler scourge on our land," he uttered through shallow breaths.

My smile unnerved him. He quivered as I held him by the nape and whispered into his ear. "Tell Renaud I am coming for him."

I released him and sent him running into the countryside. All the others we found, we dragged to Hakon's ships as slaves.

When Hakon landed with his wife, they ransacked the village and monastery and took everything of value—livestock, food stores, and wine, all of which Horic had asked us to bring back. Once we had filled our ships, we set out upriver to the next target. I led them to every settlement I had seen on my journey to Indre, and at each one, we took slaves, supplies, and we burned their villages.

For seven days and seven nights we feasted and drank to celebrate our victory over the Franks. With his fleet destroyed, Renaud could no longer move an army across the bay to challenge us. The island was ours. During the celebrations, Horic and Hakon struck an agreement over how to manage the export of the salt. Both men recognized the salt's tremendous value, particularly for the salted cod trade in the North, and both believed regular shipments from Herio would bolster their wealth.

Neither man accepted that the other should have a sole claim over it. Horic thought he should own the land since he had found it first, but Hakon disagreed in light of his victory over Renaud's garrison and fleet. He had earned a claim to the island too. Bjorn helped to broker an agreement between them, and to please both parties he suggested they choose me to govern the island as an independent jarl. What made the deal unusual was that they had me swear an oath to both of them. In the spring and summer, I had to treat them equally, and in the event of a war between them, I could not join either side. I was a young man, steadfast in my belief and understanding of the world, but still naive in many ways, and I saw the agreement they struck as favorable to me. Above all things, I wanted my independence and to swear to no one lord or king.

Loaded down with sacks of salt and supplies for the journey home, both Horic's and Hakon's fleets sailed for the North. Their departure left me with an empty feeling that lingered in my stomach for a few days. Bjorn stayed behind when the others went. He and his men were not farmers or blacksmiths. They were warriors, and they did not need to rush home. The silence gave me time to reflect on all that had happened, and I felt the weight of what I had witnessed and all I had done.

Though the winds of winter had not yet appeared, I fell ill. A fever gripped me and robbed me of my strength. I could hold down neither food nor drink. The wound in my leg had not healed well, and it had begun to fester and stink. The monastery's cold walls felt uninviting, but they at least kept out the wind. Fafnir ran cold, wet cloths across my forehead to cool me, and Rune recited poems about the gods and their deeds to comfort me. At times I believed the fever might take me, as did Fafnir and Rune. At other times, I thought the pain might stop my heart. Lying in my cot on the third day after Hakon and Horic had left, I heard a commotion outside. Bjorn entered the monastery and picked me up by the shoulders.

"There's a ship," he said.

"I am too ill," I protested.

"They asked for you by name," Bjorn explained.

He pulled my arm around his shoulders and walked with me to the docks. His men had mustered with all their weapons and armor, and they stood facing eight monks in black habits who had disembarked from a small ship built in the Frankish style. They each wore a large wooden cross around their necks, and they all had their hands hidden within their sleeves. Every one of them appeared terrified.

"They're suicidal," Bjorn said with a chuckle. A few of his men chuckled with him.

"I will speak with them," I said.

"How?" Bjorn asked.

"I know Latin."

"You know what?" Bjorn scoffed.

"It's a long story, and I hope to tell it to you one day. For now, I will speak with them," I said.

My legs began to find strength, and I limped toward the monks. As we drew closer, I heard them chattering among one another. They did not speak Latin, and not the Frankish language, either. They were Celts.

"I am Hasting. What, may I ask, is your business on my island?" I said in their language.

None of them seemed surprised that I knew it. They nodded to each other as if to decide on the spot who should speak.

"I am Brother Gael," a monk in the middle said. He was short and very thin. I almost mistook him for a child. He stepped forward with a slight tremble in his leg and continued, "I have come with assurances from Lord Nominoë that you will hear us out."

"All right," I muttered. My fever felt worse, and my shoulders ached as though the weight of an entire ship pressed down upon them.

"We beg for your mercy. The bones of our patron, Saint Philibert, remain hidden in the monastery. We do not wish to reclaim this land on behalf of the church, but we do wish to retrieve him. You have no idea how important he is to us," Gael pleaded.

Bjorn leaned in and whispered in my ear, "What do they want?"

"Bones," I said.

Bjorn glanced at me with a puzzled expression. He crossed his arms and glared at the monks as he said, "We should take them as slaves and make them work the marshes."

"Please," Gael reiterated.

As he spoke, my vision blurred and the world spun. I fell to my knees and struggled to catch my breath. The Northmen watched my struggle without moving. Gael bolted to my side. He felt my burning flesh and looked back to his brothers.

"He is ill," he said. "Bring me my medicines." He stroked my hair and ran his hand along my back to look for wounds. While he searched, he asked, "Why do they not help you?"

"They would have, given enough time," I explained. "I am a warrior, and helping me too soon might offend me."

"Do you have a wound? Something that could fester?" he asked.

"My leg," I groaned.

Gael pulled up on my pant leg and found where the iron clamps had bitten me. "It needs to be cleaned," he said. One of his brothers approached and gave him a leather satchel. "I can help you, but only if you allow us to recover the bones of Saint Philibert."

"What in Hel is he saying?" Bjorn spat.

"He says he can heal me, but for a price," I said.

"I don't trust him," Bjorn said.

"Neither do I," I said. "So, we will keep them prisoner in the monastery, and if I do not heal, you will kill them to avenge me."

I translated what I had told Bjorn for Gael, who squirmed at the thought that his life now depended on my recovery. Bjorn helped me to my feet and carried me to the monastery, and his men used the tips of their spears to encourage the monks to follow. Gael asked for wine from the cellar, clean water from the well, and salt from the marshes. Fafnir and Rune, accompanied by one of the monks, gathered all of it and brought it to my chamber.

"This will hurt at first," Gael said as he prepared his ingredients to mend my wound. He handed me the wine and said, "For you."

I took several deep sips of the wine while Gael worked to heal my wound. Bjorn stood over him with his arms crossed. Gael first cleaned the wound with water. He cut away the parts of my flesh that had turned purple and black, and when he was finished, I could almost see my bones. Next, he reached into his satchel and withdrew a variety of herbs, which he sprinkled into the gaping holes. Finally, he filled my wound with salt from the marshes.

I was delirious with pain and howled for all to hear. Even the gods, I suspect, heard my screams. Gael held my leg and let the salt work into my blood for a long while and, when he deemed I had had enough, he rinsed it out. He sewed the wound shut and covered it in a thick, clear ointment from his knapsack.

"I did not see any sign of spreading," Gael said as he finished his work. "You should heal in time."

"We will see," I said.

Bjorn dragged Gael from my chamber. Where he took the monks, I did not know, but while I still breathed, I knew they would not be harmed.

For days, the fever persisted, and each day Gael returned to examine my wound. Each day he said the injury appeared to be healing, but he did not understand why my fever had not yet broken. On the fifth day, I awoke at dawn feeling dry and warm, and the strength in my body had returned. I stood on my leg, and it did not ache too much.

Overjoyed, I left my chamber with the walking stick I had fashioned for myself and hobbled around the monastery while the others still slept. I found the monks confined to a cellar below the main hall, and I used the key hanging next to the door to enter and wake them.

"You're free to go," I said.

Gael was the first among them to wake. I saw that Bjorn and his men had not beaten them, but their habits were soiled and smelled of a cesspit. He stood to face me and said, "Thank you, but the relics?"

"Yes, take them and leave this place," I said. "I'll make sure no one stops you."

I hobbled away and left the door open to allow them to escape. They scurried out of the cellar like rats from a sinking ship, and they bolted for the chapel. Out of pure curiosity, I followed them and watched as they pulled apart loose stones in the floor to reveal a secret chamber from which they removed a large reliquary that took all six of them to carry. They ran out the main door and down the hill without waking any of my men or Bjorn's, and they took no time at all to reach their ship. I had never known monks to be sailors, but these monks indeed were, and I marveled at the skill with which they maneuvered their boat away from the dock and out to sea. As I watched them drift into the distance, I felt a hand rest upon my shoulder.

"You let them go," Bjorn said.

"I did," I replied. "They kept their end of the bargain. I am healed. And they came at the request of Nominoë. He will be an important ally if we hope to hold the island through winter."

"Fine... fine," Bjorn said.

"What will you do now?" I asked him.

"I should ask you the same. My men are warriors, and they will winter here if I ask them. Yours are not; they will want to sail home to see their families."

I had not thought about my men wanting to return to Ireland. Bjorn was right—they had agreed to one season of raiding, and we had already done so much more. If I did not honor my promise to them, they would kill me. Fafnir, Rune, Sten, Gørm, Torsten, Ulf, Trygva, Frode, Arne, Erik, and Troels were all the men I had left, and they had served me faithfully. I needed to stay to defend the island, but they did not.

"If they leave, I will have no sworn men to defend me if the Franks attack," I said.

Bjorn stepped in front of me, knelt upon one knee, and said, "I will swear to you."

"Don't be stupid," I said. "Why would you swear to me? You have men, ships, and the king's favor."

"I owe you my life, Hasting, and you are the only man I know who has faced a creature from another world and lived. I have admired you since we were young men, and now I admire you more for all we have seen and done together." He looked up at me with his brilliant blue eyes and said, "I believe in you."

On Bjorn's advice, I visited my men in the monastery and gathered them around the table.

"You served me far better than I could have asked when we left Ireland," I said, "but you have families and kin. I must stay here, but I want to give you the chance to sail home for the winter, and return here next summer."

"I will stay with you through the winter," Rune said first.

A silence followed his words. He was the only one who wanted to stay. "I understand," I said. "Fafnir, I will give you Sail Horse for the winter."

"Hasting," Fafnir said with a stutter of emotion. "I cannot accept such a gift."

"It is not a gift, Fafnir, it is a loan. And you will bring her back to me in the spring," I said.

"But…" Fafnir said.

"But what?" I asked him.

"I do not wish to return. If I do sail again, it will be with Thor," he said.

"I understand. Rune will accompany you to Ireland, and he will recruit a new crew to bring next spring." I patted Fafnir on the shoulder. "Do not feel ashamed; I understand your decision."

Rune opened his mouth as if to protest but stopped himself from speaking out. I could see in his eyes that he understood my decision. The others all tried to thank me at once for allowing them to sail home, and their voices melded together as one. We embraced around the table, and a few of them shed tears at our parting.

We prepared Sail Horse for the journey and loaded her with food, mead, and salt, and I saw them off the following morning at dawn. I walked the path through the forest of oak trees behind the monastery, along the coast, and kept pace with Sail Horse as they rowed her northward. Bjorn accompanied me and, when we reached the beach at the end of the woodland, we stood upon the crest of the dune and waved to them. Rune waved back as the others worked to bring in the oars and unfurl the sail.

"I hope to see her again," I said.

"You will," Bjorn said.

"We have a long journey ahead of us," I lamented. "I still do not know what the Franks will do, or the Celts. And I need to prepare the marshes to make salt for Horic and Hakon."

"And we need to raid for more slaves," Bjorn said.

"We have so much to do."

"And so many adventures to embark upon," Bjorn added.

I smiled at him and said, "You're excited about staying in Frankland for the winter, aren't you?"

He reached around with his thick, powerful arm and took me by the shoulder. The rising sun shimmered upon the sea, and a mild wind from the south had overtaken us.

As we both gazed toward the horizon, Bjorn took in a deep breath and said, "We're going to have a lot of fun, my friend."

The end of Book One.

HISTORICAL NOTE

There are many famed warriors from the Viking Age who successfully lived up to the reputation of their people, but perhaps none so much as Hasting. Referred to in the Gesta Normanorum as the scourge of the Somme and Loire, his life was lived for adventure. Although he did not carve out large swaths of territory for himself as many others had done, he built an enduring reputation as a man of great prowess, largesse, and cunning.

Hasting's story begins as many in the Viking Age did: ambiguously. We do not know for certain who his parents were, although it is suggested in the Anglo-Saxon Chronicle that he was a son of Ragnar Lodbrok. The Chronicle also suggests that he was a Dane, but that too is difficult to verify. His first raid of notoriety was that of the sack of Nantes in 843 A.D. in which he is named in the Annales D'Angoulême as being among the Vestfaldingi, or men of Vestfold. The sack of Nantes was a cataclysmic event that sent ripples throughout the Frankish Empire and marked the beginning of more aggressive Norse incursions in the region.

Hasting is thought to have spent a great deal of time in the Bay of Biscay during his early life, but mentions of him in the sources are sparse. The Chronicle of Nantes mentions he forged an alliance with the usurper Lambert to take Nantes, but the Chronicle is generally considered as having fabricated many of the details of the event. The Vie and Miracles de Saint Martin de Vertou suggests the Vikings were invited into the city for the festival of Saint John, which indicates that prior to the sack of Nantes there may have been semi-amicable relations between the locals and the Scandinavians.

With so much ambiguity in the sources, it is difficult to piece together Hasting's life, despite his notoriety in the Gesta Normanorum and the Anglo-Saxon Chronicle. My novel is an attempt to give life to a character who has seldom been the focus of the main narrative despite having been the living embodiment of what it was to be a Viking. I attempt to recreate his early life, follow his journey from slave to sea captain, and set the stage for the famous events he orchestrated in his later life, which I will cover in later novels.

Primary sources attesting to Hasting's life:

- Gesta Normanorum, by Dudo of St. Quentin
- Gesta Danorum, by Saxo Grammaticus
- Histoire des Normands, by William of Jumièges
- Annals of St. Bertin
- Chronicon, by Regino Prum
- Annales D'Angoulème
- The Anglo-Saxon Chronicle
- Chronique de Nantes
- Historiarum Libri Quinque, by Raoul Glaber

A Note on the word Viking

A curious error in nomenclature has led to disagreements over the precise definition of the word Viking. For many, the word describes Scandinavians who lived during the so-called Viking Age. Others contend the word should describe what it has described since its first use in Old Norse: those who left home to raid and to plunder. It is a contentious issue that has long plagued both the study of Vikings and the place of Vikings in popular culture. Language matters, and how a person uses language greatly affects their worldview and how they perceive people, objects, and concepts. It is no surprise, therefore, that there are a growing number of people who are dismayed by today's liberal use of the word Viking to describe a great number of things that it originally did not.

The word Viking is derived from Old Norse. While its origins are not well understood, we do know the word began not as a noun, but as a verb. The Saga of Egill Skallagrimsson offers us one of the most compelling examples of the word's original use, and his is the closest example to the usage of the word in its native form. In his opening passage, he describes a man named Ulfr as a man who, "*lá hann í víkingu og herjaði*," which translates roughly to, "He was roving and fought." In this context, the word Viking described an activity—roving—rather than the man. Later in his saga, we find the word used in a different context with a much different meaning:

> 'With bloody brand on-striding
> Me bird of bane hath followed:
> My hurtling spear hath sounded
> In the swift Vikings' charge.
> Raged wrathfully our battle,
> Ran fire o'er foemen's rooftrees;

Sound sleepeth many a warrior
Slain in the city gate.'

Here Egill uses the word to describe a group of people partaking in a certain action, which tells us the word Viking was also used to describe the men who partook in "roving and fighting." It is this dual usage that has led historians to say the word Viking described both an activity and a profession. Jugglers juggle. Traders trade. Vikings go a-Viking. When the Viking Age ended, so too did the profession of roving and fighting. Hence, usage of the word Viking declined. Old Norse spent the next several centuries morphing into the modern languages of Norwegian, Danish, Swedish, and Icelandic. Although Icelandic is the closest modern language to Old Norse, Old Norse itself is considered a dead language, like Latin. In this context, the original usage of Viking disappeared almost entirely for many centuries until it experienced a revival led by nineteenth century historians from Western Europe.

No one really knows where nineteenth century historians, and later, society, picked up the word for use in non-Scandinavian languages. It may have been borrowed directly from the Scandinavians of the day, or perhaps taken from the Sagas of the Icelanders. Historian Eleanor Rosamund Barraclough explains in her book, *Beyond the Northlands*, that the first modern use of the word Viking was recorded in 1807, three decades before Queen Victoria's coronation. The word was not reserved for the "men who roved," but instead referred to the entire Norse world. It is an unfortunate oversimplification and mischaracterization of a time and people we now know to have been far more complex than previously acknowledged. From 1807 forward, this usage dominated the histories and the arts of the nineteenth and twentieth centuries and is by and large how most people use the word today.

In this novel, the word Viking has been used by Hasting as a descriptor of his chosen profession. The word was not likely used during his time in the way it is used in this novel, but my decision to employ the word was the result of my desire to communicate Hasting's willful choice to embody the traits of those who roved, and to become the best among them.

ABOUT THE AUTHOR

C.J. Adrien is a bestselling author of Viking historical fiction novels and has a passion for Viking history. His Kindred of the Sea series was inspired by research conducted in preparation for a doctoral program in early medieval history, as well as his admiration for historical fiction writers such as Bernard Cornwell and Ken Follett. He is also a published historian on the subject of Vikings, with articles featured in historical journals such as *L'Association des Amis de Noirmoutier*, in France. His novels and expertise have earned him invitations to speak at several international events including the International Medieval Congress at the University of Leeds, the Oregon Museum of Science and Industry (OMSI), and conferences on Viking history in France, among others. C.J. Adrien earned a bachelor's degree in history from the University of Oregon, a master's degree from Oregon State University, and is currently searching for the right university to complete his doctoral thesis.

To learn more about the author, visit www.cjadrien.com

Did you enjoy Hasting's story? Leave it a review: https://www.amazon.com/product-reviews/B07TWSLWG6/

Made in United States
North Haven, CT
29 March 2024

50681781R00203